You're the one for me

COLETTE INTERNATIONAL
· BOOK 2 ·

ZELDA FRENCH

Nerds and Otakus will always be welcome here.

Part One

—

'**I**'

—

1

LOVE STARTS WITH AN "A"

Alberto, Alberto, Alberto.

At the beginning, there was Alberto.

Impossibly tall, with slender limbs; always moving in slow and gracious motions. An elegant neck supporting a gorgeous head of soft, dark hair. Sharp cheekbones, cat-like blue eyes. Everything about him was feline, including his aloofness. Like the truly divine-looking people, he treated his beauty with an air of contempt, brushed it aside, going as far as concealing himself under layers of fashionable but thick clothing.

To him, his beauty was just an afterthought.

But to me...

Alberto was haunting every dream of mine, and after a while, every passing thought.

When Alberto smiled, the stars faded back to the shadows in disgrace. Renaissance painters and sculptors, vain poets, every artist worth their name would have torn their hair at the sight of him. My own artist's soul he ravaged daily, every time he passed me in the corridors at school without noticing me.

Every day, to repeat the mantra *Alberto, Alberto, Alberto*.

Longing for him and begging for him to be *my* Alberto.

Alberto's full lips didn't part very often. He had not much to say, and if the rest of the world was not hanging onto his every word, I personally was itching to hear the sound of his voice. I was his, faithfully, and had been for ten months now, ever since the day I entered the stuffy classroom which hosted the newly created drama club and saw his tall figure hunched over a chair. Intrigued, I tiptoed toward him. His head tilted; his cool gaze swept over me.

I was immediately and hopelessly smitten.

Alberto was my God. I loved him and feared him and ached for him. Gradually, I learned to love him more than I loved my studies, my hobbies, my books, my films… All my endeavours, artistic or otherwise, now bore the name Alberto.

I was only sixteen then. An age when disregard for your own ignorance was commonplace.

A fearless age, which forces you to rush madly into the fray, chasing passion and heartbreak with a feverish ardour, until they find you first, crash into you headlong, and flatten you to the ground.

The age when first love comes as brutally as a summer storm, leaving you shaken, frightened, exhilarated.

Everyone wanted Alberto. Everyone with eyes and taste, I mean. And I wanted him most of all. After all, we shared the same love for *the arts*, the same interests. We were both born in cold and dreary January. We both liked to wear dark colours in winter time. We also both came from Mediterranean countries. He was Italian, my parents were Tunisians. And, of course, we were both gay.

But many wouldn't agree with that statement.

Ladies from the classes above or below, haunting the corridors, their claw-like fingers clutching their bags, loved to trail after Alberto in a single line, hoping for a fleeting glance or more. He never showed them any interest, which was how I first began to believe he might be just like me, and that I had all my chances. Then I observed at length and noticed he didn't show much interest toward any boy either. I took it as a sign that, like me, he was unbearably picky.

It would take much to move a deity like Alberto; it would take true artistry. And the cogs in my head were working hard at it. One day, he would be mine, I swore by it. For a moment in his god-like arms, there was nothing I wouldn't do.

That's why I was relieved, when, during our weekly drama club session, Alberto didn't see me trip over my own bag as I was called to the stage. I even double-checked. He wasn't looking.

That day, I wanted, once again, to muster the courage to speak to Alberto. We had exchanged a few words here and there since we first met, of course, but it didn't count. Our longest conversation outside the Drama Club had to be that time I asked him to pick up the pen I may have purposefully dropped, and he said, "Hm?" My heart leapt at the same time as my throat constricted, so a really unfortunate sound escaped my lips, and I had to shuffle away in shame.

Summer was approaching with its promises of exceedingly uncomfortable weather and idle days spent in the empty, sun-bleached streets of Paris. Soon I would be torn from him for three months, and I couldn't bear it. I had to speak up. All I had to do was walk up to him when the bell rang and ask him his plans for the summer. It wouldn't be easy. Alberto stuck to his best friend, the Danish mountain Sander, like gum to a desk, and I didn't intend for him to eavesdrop on our conversation. For months, I waited for Duvauchel, our drama teacher, to seriously pair us together on stage, but he'd always failed to do it.

My life aspiration was to become an actor. I was practising daily, and I was pretty good at delivering lines. I always got the best parts in every play or movie reenactment we attempted. But despite his flawlessness, Alberto rarely got to share the stage with me and usually only got a few boring lines. It was like Duvo — short for Duvauchel — was deliberately trying to keep us apart. Though I could appreciate the trivial obstacles thrown our way, now that the end of the year was near, I was getting fed up with it.

Once called off the stage, I ruminated on my chair, my gaze fixed on Alberto's nape, as the minutes dragged by. Watching him for too long always crumpled my resolve. Once alone in my room, I could well imagine us together, holding hands and smiling stupidly at each other while strolling around the latest Renoir exhibit. Once out there in the wild, however, with his diaphanous skin a mere fingertip away, my thoughts began fluttering in every direction, suddenly unsure what to exactly tell him. When the time came and the bell rang, like every other time, I froze. My bottom remained stuck to my chair, my shoulders stiff. And I could only watch as Alberto rose from his seat with a yawn, checked his phone for the time, and shoulder to shoulder with Sander, walked out of the classroom and into the bustling crowd.

Baffled at my own uselessness, I stared at the empty chair in front of me. Perhaps it was for the best that I didn't get to speak up today. My original plan wasn't great anyway. Who cares about casually asking him about his summer? It wasn't romantic. It sucked, even. His delicate artistic tendencies might have been singed by such idiotic behaviour.

No, no. I would have to do something more drastic if I ever wanted to succeed. It wouldn't be so good if it was too easy. I clenched my fists on my knees. Only then I heard an annoyed voice behind me.

"Zak?"

Duvauchel, at the door, shook his set of keys.

"Do you think I live here?"

I blinked. "Don't you?"

His gaze darkened. Before he could spin out of control, I took my cue and dashed out.

The corridors were busy with students rushing to their lockers, huddled together in tight clumps, hurrying to check their phones, making my life difficult. It was already seven in the evening, but between people's extra-curricular activities, late users of the library, fellow Drama Club members and their relentless friends waiting to pick them up, the narrow hallways were already suffocating.

Colette was a good high school. Pompously named Colette International School for Bilingual Students, it was mostly filled with French people like me earning their Baccalaureate in English in the hope of becoming fluent enough to invade foreign universities after graduation. But schools like Colette were also bustling with foreign kids whose parents had moved to France temporarily or permanently and didn't feel right about sending their kid to a normal school when they didn't know a word of French. About fifty per cent of Colette's student body were from different nationalities, making it an overall interesting experience, and turning the corridors into a cacophony of languages dominated by Frenglish.

Keeping my head down, I slithered my way through the crowd using the skills I'd acquired after a lifetime of avoiding people, combined with my embarrassingly lightweight frame. I succeeded in getting so close to the exit, I could feel the hot summer air on my face, but before I got to the door, I slammed head first into the person in front of me.

It wasn't his fault. He himself had hit a wall, or a guy leaning in the doorway, filling the entire space and making it difficult to get out. In his surprise, the boy in front of me dropped his bag. The contents tumbled out and went rolling between everybody's legs, causing laughter, sneers, and a lot of annoyance.

Recognising one of the objects on the floor, I knelt down to help before his copy of *The Ladies' Paradise* got stepped on by others. Looking up, I was met by a pair of grateful, round blue eyes and recognised Arthur, another student from the Drama Club.

"Thanks, Zak!"

I cast him a faint smile. Arthur was often pushed around. Tall and lanky as he was, he wasn't much to stand up for himself. Not that I was so great at it myself, for that matter, but I benefited first from being basically invisible, and second, from having a terrifying sister who used to own these corridors.

The prat who had caused this chaos hadn't even registered what he had done. He was pushing people back into the building when they wanted to get out, shouting: "C.H.!" Sticking two fingers in his mouth, he whistled by my ear just as I was getting up. I glared at him.

"Can you not?"

He threw me a look that said how little he thought of me, then raised his hand, almost swatting me in the process. "C.H.!"

"He's looking for Charles-Henry," Arthur said.

I watched in horror as he punched his maltreated copy of *The Ladies' Paradise* into the bottom of his bag.

Charles-Henry elbowed his way through the crowd, a confused look on his face. He, too, was in the Drama Club, though I couldn't exactly understand why. All he did was the bare minimum. He was more renowned for being part of the official Colette football team, and the tall, athletic annoyance in front of me was one of his teammates. I only knew they loved to wear their stupid jerseys even when they were not kicking their ball around. As if the Colette football team held any importance whatsoever in the world or even Paris.

Needless to say, I did not associate with these people.

"What!?" Charles-Henry asked, his cheeks red from exertion — or embarrassment.

His rude friend was still blocking our way out, and the people in the back were starting to shove. I had to duck to avoid getting too closely acquainted with that prat's armpit.

"Come on!" Prat said. "We're going to Eric's."

Arthur folded his arms over his chest with a sly grin. "So that's the reason you felt compelled to just keep us hostage in here?" He glanced down at me with an "amirite" expression.

7

"Get out of my face," Prat said.

At last, he removed his arm, and Arthur and I could slip out. I opened my mouth to breathe, only to choke on a blast of stifling air. This terrible weather did not agree with me, or my usual dark clothing. Fanning myself, I trudged toward the front gate, my hand shielding my eyes.

With a jolt, I realised Arthur was still following me, his long legs catching up with me in no time. Inwardly cursing the length of my limbs, I hoped he wouldn't try to strike up a conversation with me. I feared how it would go before it even started.

Him: *Thanks for your help.*

Me: *You're welcome. I couldn't let such a beautiful work be trampled by the masses.*

Him: *What? You like this boring book? You like... Zola?*

Me: *Sure. Would you like to sit tight while I explain to you why this book you hate is important to me?*

Him: *I'd love to. But I have to go, my time-sensitive triple-pass heart surgery is scheduled for right now.*

Me: *Farewell, see you never.*

Him: *Bye, loser.*

Thankfully, it never got to that. No sooner had I passed the gate, I heard my name spoken through a familiar voice. Arthur and I both stopped, and his jaw dropped.

It could be because Yasmine, my sister, was undeniably beautiful, with her thick black hair and clever dark eyes that glinted in the sun. Or it could be because her dog, Rufus, a fierce Malinois, was already pulling at his leash and snapping his fangs at our feet.

I didn't wait long for my answer. Arthur took one look at the dog, muttered some incoherent words, and quickly disappeared. Yasmine stared after him with a smirk.

"Here, take this." Squeezing a half-empty iced latte close to her chest, she clumsily handed me a plastic cup filled to the brim with clinking ice cubes and bubbly iced tea, all the while clicking her tongue at Rufus, whose snarling made everybody around us step aside in fright. "What?"

I must have looked a little surprised. "You came to pick me up?"

"Of course. For once, I had a mom—" Her cup popped open and some beverage fell on top of the dog's head. "Oh, damn."

Gratefully slurping on my iced tea, I waited as she mopped Rufus's head affectionally.

"So!" Now she sounded business-like. "Was this wide-eyed boy the love of your life?"

I frowned. "Who? That guy? No, not at all."

Yasmine laughed and leaned against the gate. "Then show him to me."

I decided to indulge her. Since she'd entered Sciences Po, she was swamped with her studies, and I'd seen way too little of her. She never had the time to pick me up before. So, I wasn't just surprised; I was really happy.

Yasmine and I had always been close, even by sibling standards. For instance, she was the first and only one I came out to. And she also was the first I ran to a few months ago, when it became clear that Alberto wasn't just a crush, but my soulmate. So, I also leaned conspicuously against the gate to scan our surroundings. Alberto usually slacked by the library entrance with Sander and their friend Oliver for about fifteen minutes after every Drama Club session. I knew that because I had stalked him mercilessly, and Alberto was a man of routine.

I looked beyond Charles-Henry and his prat friend. They and their mates were still hanging around the schoolyard with some girls I recognised from the Drama Club and from class. Behind the one called Melissa and her fluffy hair, I caught a glimpse of my Alberto. My cheeks turned hot. I waited until he was clearly in sight and pointed excitedly. "There. There he is, by the fire exit."

Yas leaned forward, squinting. "Which one?"

My heart sank. It was really insulting that she needed to ask. Sander and Oliver looked like decaying mummies compared to my living and breathing pharaoh. Yasmine needed glasses urgently.

"There. The tall, white one, with dark hair and blue eyes. In the yellow shirt."

"The yawning one?"

"Yes."

Yasmine made a sound of appreciation. "Mm. And I thought you had exaggerated his beauty."

My fist closed tightly around my cup of iced tea. "I did not!"

"He really could be a model."

"I know, right?" I let myself slump against her shoulder. "He's the most beautiful human being that was ever born. And the most brilliant too. If I can't have him, I will probably die."

Yasmine chuckled. She took my arm and steered us away from the gate. Rufus leapt ahead of us, pulling on his leash.

"You sound just like another hopelessly gay friend of mine."

I rolled my eyes. "What about you?"

"What about me?"

"That guy from last summer is still texting you, and I know it, despite your attempts to hide it from me."

Yasmine pretended to be shocked for a second, then shrugged. "I'm not hiding anything, I'm just not interested."

"You're never interested."

"I have other priorities. And so do you, by the way, if you recall."

She meant work. I was always going on about my five-year plan and how I'd become a respected actor by the time I turned twenty-one years old. There was no time for slacking. Between that and my regular studies, I had almost no time to fool around. But right now, I needed to concoct a plan to talk to Alberto before school was over. I only had two sessions at the club left. Because the gods were cruel, Alberto was not in my class, and I could only see him once every Thursday.

"You're right. And on that note… Let's pick up the pace so I can start striking items off my evening to-do list."

Yasmine put her hand on my arm. "I was only joking."

"So? You're still right."

She shook her head. "Zak, brother mine, you're all work and no play. It's almost the end of the year. You have no exams. Go and have fun a little."

I looked away, defiant. "It's a good thing my priorities and Alberto's are the same! We're both actors, we're both artists, we're both picky and moody and… you know it. We are aligned... like the stars..."

The streets were packed with people going about their business, walking briskly, clothed in colourful summer attire, like spots of bright paint on a blank canvas. Ignoring the outraged looks of passersby, Yasmine stopped us in the middle of the busy sidewalk.

"Goodness, Zak. You're in the pit."

Sensing the turn of the conversation toward something serious, I spoke carefully. "What is that?"

"You'll know when you try to claw your way out of it." She reached out with two fingers to tuck a strand of unruly hair back behind my ear. It was a lost cause; my hair had a mind of its own. "Promise me you'll take care." Yasmine pulled my arm. I followed slowly, the concrete pavement hot beneath our feet. Her apparent worry had already triggered mine.

"What exactly are you saying?"

"I'm saying Alberto is too beautiful for your own good. He'll wipe the floor with you if you're not careful."

It was my turn to stop us in the middle of the sidewalk. I ignored Rufus's resentful look. "I'm surprised that you, of all people, would react like this. Didn't you say I should have a little fun?"

Yasmine walked on with Rufus bounding ahead, parting the resentful crowds before her. "I did. That was before I realised you're taking this way too seriously. I just don't want you to get hurt, that's all." She looked over her shoulder with a grin. "Your boyfriends will all have to answer to me. I'll break their legs if they hurt you."

Pouting, I nestled against her arm. "Now you're just saying that..."

"I'll do it." Yasmine wrapped her arm around my shoulder and pulled me close. "I'll send Rufus after them too."

"I hope it doesn't come to that…"

Yasmine laughed, but she still looked fearsome.

I didn't see Alberto until six days later. But I didn't stay idle during that time. I spent it building up the courage the speak to him.

Time spent on various forums put me in contact with several movie students who were looking for actors for the summer. You've got to start small. I eventually got a chance to play the second lead in a short film.

I couldn't wait to tell Alberto. This was the perfect occasion to drop in and start a conversation. *What are you doing this summer? Oh, impressive. Me? I'm going to shoot a short film in July. Sure, of course, we can talk it over around coffee sometime. By the way, did I mention how gay I am? Because I'm pretty gay. Kiss me, you'll see.*

Except nothing happened the way it was supposed to. Barely through the school gate, I noticed two strange things despite this fine morning of high clouds and mild temperatures: first, I couldn't find Alberto anywhere, despite spotting his friends Sander and Oliver sharing a cigarette by the fire exit, as usual. Then, as I spun slowly on my heels to check if Alberto was simply running late, I saw Camille talking to a bunch of football players in their stupid jerseys.

Camille was like a VIP member in our Drama Club. She was a writer, a talented one at that, and a dedicated person. She wrote brutal plays and some mildly erotic poetry at times and was never afraid to read it out loud or staple it to the classroom doors to piss the most conservative teachers off. I quite liked Camille, even though we rarely spoke. So I paused when I saw her in the middle of the group of football players and their groupies, looking agitated. I never thought she would be associating with them.

Suddenly, she took off toward the gate, her flowery skirt swirling around her legs, attracting interest from the guys in matching jerseys. Hoping Alberto would make an appearance later today, I carefully walked around the group to make my way inside the building, when I heard my name spoken in a posh English accent. I froze at first, then, upon hearing my name called again, I couldn't pretend any longer and stomped over to their group. The one who called me was a British girl named Joy, who was both a student in my class and part of the Drama Club.

Joy was all right, but I didn't really associate with her either and knew little about her. She was best friends with Elodie, the most popular girl in our class and/or school, who was dating some football player and probably wished to be an all-American cheerleader. Because of that, Joy was always surrounded by footballers. She was also friends with another girl from the club, Melissa, whose awesome hair I could see from the corner of my eye.

"What do you want?" I asked.

Calling me to her group of friends was not the greatest idea. Already I felt on me the eyes of Elodie, her blond football player boyfriend, and of course, the tall prat who had pushed Arthur a week ago and whose eyes glinted with mockery. Charles-Henry cast me a wan smile which I returned in kind.

"Drama Club's cancelled," Joy said.

I looked at her, stunned. I'd have felt the same if she'd slapped me in the face. How was I going to speak to Alberto now?

"... Why?"

"I don't know, but Camille asked me to tell everyone, and I can't. I've got to go." She opened her bag and started rummaging through the mess inside. "So, can you tell everyone else? And also give the geography teacher my homework for me. I've decided not to go, but don't tell him that."

"All right." I extended my hand with a sinking heart.

"What's the Drama Club anyway?" a guy in their group asked. He could have been handsome if he didn't have dumb, vacant eyes.

"It's exactly what it sounds like," Elodie said with a mild sigh. "It's a drama club, where people do theatre and stuff."

"It's a club for losers, Xavier," the tall prat said, looking at me.

But Xavier — or the one with vacant eyes — was not listening. He was staring toward the gate. Elodie made a face, retreated to the arms of her boyfriend, and said, "Some guy once tagged the door to the Drama Club and almost got suspended. Guess what he tagged? *Loser Club*."

"That wasn't me," Prat said.

"Of course, it wasn't you." Elodie chuckled, the corner of her eyes crinkling. "I'm just saying. You could be suspended for this shit."

"*Almost* suspended," Prat added with a smirk.

Joy was still rummaging through her immense bag. "Sorry Zak, can't find the stupid thing, give me a second."

"Unless you want to spend a whole month cleaning up and doing chores for the club, you better think again," Melissa told Prat, a warning in her voice.

"That's true," Joy confirmed, and she triumphantly whipped out a wrinkled piece of homework.

It was true. I couldn't remember who did it and didn't really care about it. With some mumbled words of thanks, I grabbed Joy's homework and briskly walked away. I had just spotted Alberto passing the gate and was hoping Camille hadn't dropped the news yet. After a quick run, I skidded to a stop in front of him. "Hi, Alberto." I really hoped my voice didn't betray everything I was feeling for him. I wasn't sure he could deal with that level of intensity yet.

Alberto briefly looked down at me before glancing over my head to where his friends were waiting. Then his perfect lips parted. "Hi."

The gentleness of Alberto's voice couldn't be described by words written by mortals, so I wouldn't attempt to do it here. Or… Fine, I'll try. It was like a sigh, but not quite, not unlike a whisper then, almost a caress, really, and it often sounded languid, and always intoxicating, at least to me.

I knew not to screw up and say too much, especially not some sort of "I love you, you're the one for me" nonsense. Telling him about the club would be enough; I assumed a nonchalant tone. "Drama club's cancelled. I thought you should know."

He peered solemnly at me. We had never seen each other so close. His face was even more beautiful from here. His eyes, more brilliant. His lips, fuller. "Thanks."

He moved past me, elegant as a cat. I turned around, thinking, hoping, he would turn around too. He went straight to his friends this time. And why not? He didn't know who I was, how perfectly matched we were, and that one day he, too, would long to hold me in his arms.

Going inside the building, I noticed Camille now talking to our young History teacher and wondered, with great frustration, why on earth they had cancelled my second-to-last opportunity to speak to Alberto. Now I would have to go all-in during our last ever meeting before the three-month holiday.

I couldn't fail next time. It was my last chance.

2

HANDS OF FATE

My family and I lived in a nice Parisian district called the Fifth. Twenty years ago, my father, a pretty reasonable guy himself, met my mother, his opposite in everything. They fell in love, got married, and soon after, welcomed my sister Yasmine into their lives. I followed two years later, and that's when they went in search of the perfect family home.

My father's only weakness was my mother. So, when she found the most unpractical and atypical flat on the top floor of a sixteenth-century building in the heart of the 5th, he probably sighed before putting his head down to sign the papers.

The flat had rooms on two floors. On the third floor, my sister Yasmine had established her quarters since we turned too old to share a room. The office space next door was full to the brim with my mother's art supplies, so much that we couldn't even see her when she was painting inside.

The top floor was underneath the roof, which provided great lighting throughout the day, and a cathedral ceiling like no other. The open kitchen was an explosion of colours and represented my mother more than any other member of the household. Above the back rooms, my parents shared a mezzanine. The ceiling was terribly low but offered a full view of the living room below and the streets of Paris. Every morning, my father banged his head against the exposed wood beams and still managed to outperform everyone at work.

Tucked behind the kitchen, exposed to all sorts of cooking smells and noise, was my bedroom. To compensate for its small art studio look, I made sure that everything was in its place and never moved, including Bugs Bunny, my pet rabbit in his ginormous cage.

During dinner, it was clear I was distracted. Tomorrow was the last session at the Drama Club, and the director of the short film had confirmed that I was cast after all. My brain was coming up with several scenarios of how to start a conversation with Alberto. As a result, I could barely focus on my dad and Yasmine's conversation. She was talking about those extra books she had picked up for the holidays. Getting through them unscathed were her summer plans for this year. Shutting my eyes briefly, I imagined Alberto standing on a quiet beach, the wind dancing through his hair, my hand reaching out to caress his back...

"What about you, Zak?" my father asked, dragging me out of my reverie. "What are your plans for the summer?"

Fall in love.

Yours?

Of course, I couldn't say that, though it burnt the tip of my tongue. But I had better tell them I got plans of my own this year. "So, I've been thinking..."

"Lord help us." My mother's black eyes were twinkling with mischief.

Both my father and my sister, sitting next to each other around the dinner table, looked eerily familiar in posture, gazing at me seriously with their eyebrows drawn together.

"I was thinking of working this summer."

"But we're going to Tunis for the holidays," my mother said, alarmed.

"That's in August. We're only in June."

My father helped himself to some salad. "I keep forgetting you've got so much free time this year."

Yasmine took the serving spoons from my father's hands. "What kind of job are you thinking about?" She dropped a portion of salad, which completely missed her plate. "My friend François used to work at Happy Beans. He could get you a job there." She lazily picked up the lettuce leaves and shoved them into her mouth.

My father hurried to wipe the seasoning off the table. "What's Happy Beans?"

"A coffee place."

16

"I love Happy Beans," my mother said. "They have dancing beans on the facade, on the windows. They look so happy. The employees sing a song too if it's your birthday."

I tried not to gag at the thought of singing happy birthday songs to customers. I hoped these poor employees were paid handsomely.

"That's not the sort of job I was thinking of."

"A coffee place is a good place to start, Zak."

"It's not what I meant."

My father sat up straighter. "Do you want to come with me to the office, then?"

My father was a civil-rights lawyer, and despite all the respect I had for his profession, the idea of working for his office for the next two months was enough to make me want to jump out of the nearest window.

"No, better! With me!" my mom said. She and my dad started laughing.

As a painter, Mom had asked me to pose for her several times, and I always ended up in some kind of cubist purgatory that actually gave me nightmares at night. To this day, I still steer away from the cubists when I go to the modern art museum.

I waited patiently for them to stop laughing, while Yasmine watched me placidly, her mouth full of salad. "Are you quite finished?" I asked. After a few scattered hiccups, Mom and Dad fell silent. "I already have the job," I added. "I'm going to act in a short film."

My father frowned. "Are you sure you don't want a real job instead?" I stared at him in disbelief. He put his hands up. "Joke! I'm only joking! Of course, we support you."

"I don't know…" my mother said, her eyes fixed on the ceiling. "Don't you think you should enjoy part of your summer with your friends? At least a little?"

"But I don't have time for fun, or for friends," I spoke in a stubborn tone. "I want to have as much experience as possible if I want to enter the Cours Florent[1] and be taught by the best. I have to make sure my reel is good enough to get in."

My father shrugged. "You're mature enough to do what you want. But I still think you should keep your options open. You're smart. You could do anything."

"But acting is what I want."

---

1. Cours Florent: International drama school based in Paris.

Mom sighed. "My baby wants to be a movie star."

I shirked away from her attempt to stroke my cheek. At almost sixteen and a half, I wasn't a baby anymore. I was going to become a respected actor, and I'd go to red carpet events, and then who would follow me out of the limo and squeeze my hand as the Césars[2] host announced the award for *Best Actor in a leading role?*

Yes, of course, Alberto. It was always Alberto.

"I just think that's sad," my mom went on, obstinate as a mule. "These are some of your best years, and you spend them so much focused on the future and with your head down. You must look up to the sky at times and admire the clouds. I think you should spend more time with your friends, that's all."

I glanced up at Yasmine for support, even mouthing the words "What friends?" with a smirk on my lips, but her serious face surprised me. I was reminded of the words she spoke to me last week, of the fact that she agreed with my mother. I felt cornered.

When dinner was over, I locked my bedroom door behind me and went to pick up Bugs Bunny. He accepted the carrots I brought him and munched noisily as I stroked his fur. When I received Bugs for my birthday, my mum wanted to call him Sir Floppington, but I'd managed to put my foot down. She was always full of crazy ideas like that. He did have massive floppy ears, though, but Bugs Bunny was a pretty reasonable name for my pet rabbit. And I was, by all standards, a pretty reasonable person.

Perhaps I wasn't fun. Or I didn't know how to have fun. But I'd have fun later, when I'd have made my reputation as a respected actor and when Alberto officially accepted me as his soulmate. I couldn't let my guard down now.

Now that my parents knew of my plans for this summer, all that was left was to tell Alberto. I was fifty to fifty-five per cent certain he'd offer to help me with my lines. Tomorrow, I'd know for sure.

The next day, I entered the drama club classroom with my breath stuck in my throat. That was it: Last chance. All in or get out. Or something like that.

I didn't play poker; I didn't gamble; I didn't play games of any

---

2. César: French equivalent of the Academy Award.

kind. The most dangerous thing I ever did was pick up a book at random in one of the discount crates at the Shakespeare and Co. last year, and it ended up being a Salinger book and I tossed it right back in the bin.

Gambling's for people with too much to lose. I had nothing I could part with, nothing of real value. So, to get Alberto, I'd have to sacrifice a piece of my soul. Thinking of how lyrical I got every time I thought about Alberto, I couldn't help but laugh at myself. It was like he was arousing my brain. Not that I knew much about arousal and such things; but I assumed it was the same.

In the sheltered darkness of the Drama Club, I felt immediately at ease. Even the chaos on Duvo's desk pushed to the back of the room didn't bother me anymore. At the front, the makeshift stage was dark and empty and yet inviting, waiting for us to climb on and breathe life into the classroom. Today, the world would be my stage. My lines were memorised last night. All I had to do was act casual, even if that meant speaking up in front of Sander. Only my hands were slightly shaking.

Since it was the last session of the year, nobody here expected to do significant work. I took a seat at the back knowing Alberto, who also favoured sitting as far as possible from the stage, wouldn't be far from me.

It was stifling hot. The hard back of my chair was already sticking to my back. Students poured into the classroom all looking more or less comfortable. Camille and her impossibly flowery dress stomped proudly ahead of the red-faced Joy and the elegant Melissa. Nadia plucked a flyer from the corkboard on the way in to fan herself with. Charles-Henry looked much smaller without his goons. As for Arthur, he came in with his head held high, grinned when he saw me, and for some mystical reason, took the chair next to mine.

"All right, Zak?"

I absently accepted his offered hand. Alberto had just arrived, flanked by Sander. Alberto wearing white, in such hot, sticky weather, was almost indecent. Of course, not one of his hairs was out of place, and his shirt magically wasn't glued to his skin either. I was pretty sure Joy shivered when he ran his hand through his hair, and Joy already had an attractive boyfriend. When Alberto sat in the chair right in front of me and swiped his tongue over his shapely bottom lip, I, too, raised a hand to touch my face but only to wipe a pearl of sweat off my brow.

Arthur fanned himself. "Hot, isn't it?"

Another nod. Small talk was not my strong suit. To be honest, communication, in most of its forms, wasn't. Snarky comments and relentless nodding, sure. That's why I was never surprised when people moved on with their lives after a few sorry attempts to get to know me. Arthur's eyes lingered on me a moment, then he settled in his chair and mercifully became silent. Eventually, all of us arrived.

Duvauchel came in late as usual, and his hair a mess, as usual. I quite liked him, his glasses a bit askew, his untidy stubble, his French lit. teacher vibe that didn't really match with his newly fit body. He had started the year with the hint of a beer belly, and now I could almost feel the definition of his abs through his flannel shirt. Perhaps I wasn't the only one whose life had been shattered by an Alberto. I could only hope it wasn't *my* Alberto who had prompted this change.

Duvo sat on the stool set in the middle of the stage, joined his hands as though he was about to engage in some kind of prayer, and waited for the room to turn silent. It took a while since we were not much better than animals at this age, but eventually, we got there. "I have a surprise for you," he said. Already, gasps and sounds of excitement fluttered throughout the room. "But! I will tell you only near the end of our session…"

Cue the sounds of disgruntled students.

"… if you behave."

Immediately, no one wanted to behave. Everybody started chatting and ignoring him.

"What do you reckon?" Arthur asked, his round eyes looking at me.

I couldn't nod my way out of this one. "He might take us to the movies or something."

Arthur laughed. "You don't like to get your hopes up."

"I won't be holding my breath, for sure."

But my breath hitched anyway; Alberto was stretching. He inadvertently flung his arms too far back, and his fingertips almost grazed my hair.

"Could you tell us now?" my beloved said in his adorable Italian accent. "I've got to leave early today."

Duvo threw him a dark look. "Please accept our apologies for colliding with your private life, Alberto."

Alberto didn't react, but others were already agreeing vehemently with him and began to shout for Duvo to spill the beans right now.

"Yes, why wait?" I said out loud.

Arthur nodded beside me. After a while, Camille got up from her seat in the front row, her face serious. "Best to tell them now. Then we can make our plans."

Duvauchel hesitated. "Is that what you want?" He seemed disappointed that his great announcement wasn't going the way he planned.

Fool! No amount of planning could stand against the power of youth. He never seemed to learn his lesson. Every month he came up with an idea for a play or project; every month we tore down his original plan and injected it with nonsense, and every month he had to admit defeat. That's how it was.

"Very well, since you're all pestering me." He sounded dramatic, which didn't surprise us in the least. Duvo was a drama queen; we all knew it. He took a deep breath, hoping to stretch the tension a little more, before dropping the news. "Camille here has won a small literary prize for the play she wrote last year."

Some gasps in the room, some murmurs of admiration. Nothing much.

Of course, I felt different. Camille had done well for herself already. *Very* well. I stretched my neck to look at her face, and she did look a little pink. I remembered her play, of course. She'd asked me to play the leading male part. It was fun.

"We have talked about it," Duvo went on, "and have decided to turn it into a short film!"

There was a silence, only broken by gasps of excitement. Duvo being overly dramatic most of the time, no one dared express themselves too much, worried that it might just be a fake announcement to force us to draw some genuine acting bullshit thingy he was fond of — Duvo was insane. But right now, he looked almost giddy, a rare sight.

"Anyone free and of course, motivated, can join this project. We'll film in the countryside. I'm warning you: there's no room for slackers." He flashed us a terrifying fake smile. "Slackers will be shot."

But he wasn't the Colette headmaster; no one actually believed him, and we all started laughing. Duvo was smiling at first, unable to contain his joy, even as the others pelted him with questions. But soon his teacher ways galloped back, and he sat back on his stool, his lips pinched together, an unshakable haughty air about him. "One at a time, please!"

"When exactly is this?" Joy asked.

Duvauchel flipped open his planner; that old thing with rings and tiny boxes to fill, which I was certain belonged to a museum.

"From the 10th to the 28th of July."

"Awesome!" Joy said, while everybody took out their own planners and calendars — paper or otherwise — and checked the dates.

The girl next to Joy made a disappointed sound. "I can't at this time. I'm going on holiday with my family."

"I understand," Duvauchel said. "But I cannot change the dates."

"Why not? Let's do it in June, then."

The fake smile returned. "I cannot change the dates."

"Hold it! I can't in June either!" a guy named Bob said, quite aggressively. "How about August?"

People started snarling and yelling at each other about their summer plans, while Duvo tapped his foot on the stage while staring at his nails, obviously giving them thirty seconds before he'd blow up. In front of me, my divine Alberto was very quiet on his seat, as though the concerns of mortals had no effect on him.

"Why not next year, then?" Bob insisted.

Duvo made a funny face. "How about ten years from now, while we're at it!" His voice sounded like a slap when he was angry, and Bob fell silent. Immediately, Duvo softened. No one reacted; we were used to our drama teacher's antics. "I'm sorry. This was very short notice. That's because I was able to secure the location to shoot the film. It belongs to one of my relatives, and I couldn't get another chance to get it."

"Wait," Nadia said, always pragmatic. "You're the one who's going to care for us for over two weeks?"

"Yes, yes."

People gasped — in horror, this time. Duvo jumped from his stool, his hands up. "I won't be alone, don't worry! Binta will be accompanying us. Some of you know Binta, don't you?"

There were murmurs of approval. Binta was one of the most liked teachers at Colette, and though she was young, she was a sensible person. That would be needed to counteract Duvo's mind-boggling split personality.

Duvauchel pulled on the collar of his hideous shirt. "I'm going to pass around parents' authorisations and such, for you to give to your family if you're interested in coming."

Melissa raised her hand. "Where are we going to shoot, then?"

"A place called Aurons, near Nantes. It's lovely, you'll see. Quiet French countryside. I went there this weekend to drop off most of the equipment. It's perfect."

My heart sank. He said *lovely* and *quiet*. But to me, it meant crawling bugs, sneaky bats, and blood-curdling spiders.

"Where would we be staying?"

"Same place as our shooting location. It's an old mansion. The owners are opening some of the rooms for us to live in, and some to shoot the movie in. The maintenance staff will help keep an eye on the place, so no shenanigans."

An old mansion in the countryside; it sounded like my own personal nightmare. On top of bugs, spiders, and bats, it meant hot weather, squeaky and uncomfortable mattresses, cold water in outdated bathrooms, and of course, the dread of sharing a room with strangers. Who wanted to spend the summer in a decrepit and crowded mansion, seriously?

In front of me, Sander turned to Alberto. "Will you go, then? I won't go if you don't."

"Maybe," my beloved said. "I like old mansions."

Damn if I wouldn't sign up after hearing that! I could very well battle a few spiders for over two weeks of uninterrupted time with Alberto. I suddenly felt a deep and passionate love for old mansions.

"Is there enough space for everybody?" Joy asked.

"It's a mansion. You'll share rooms, and I'm sure once we have sorted who can come and not come…"

"What's the movie about?" I asked, not caring one bit about who could come and not come now that Alberto had shown interest.

Camille threw a glance over her shoulder, a smile on her lips. Duvauchel motioned her to approach the stage.

"Best to ask Camille about this."

"We've already played snippets of it," Camille said, walking over to the stage and climbing up with one frank step. "For those who don't remember, the play was about the secret and forbidden romance between a rich lady and her footman."

Some people giggled, some nodded respectfully.

"Camille is really impressive," Arthur said in a breath.

I stole a glance at him; he was watching Camille with eyes so bright I was worried they might burst into flames.

I agreed, her play was interesting. I had played the footman on stage, and Joy was the lady. She was terrible, but she had this amazing English accent and all the manners of posh people. Still… Fat chance of me impressing Alberto if this was the direction in which we would be going.

"Are there enough parts for everybody?" Charles-Henry asked.

"No, only a few. And the rest will be focused on tech."

"Yes!" Arthur punched the air next to me.

Joy stood in her excitement: "Hair and makeup needed, I assume?"

"Absolutely."

Joy and Melissa screeched with delight.

"Who's directing?" Arthur asked.

"What's with that question!" Duvo barked, offended. "I'm direct-ing! And not alone. A young student from the top film school in the capital will be joining us to be my assistant."

"Are you going, then?" Sander spoke in front of me, looking nervous. "I think I'm gonna be asked to be the boom operator. I'm always the boom operator. Still, it could be fun to go. Especially if the girls are going."

"Beats spending the month at home with my mum and her husband," Alberto said. "His daughter and her giggling friends are giving me headaches."

Sander laughed in his fist. "Only you could say that."

I made note of Alberto's lukewarm reaction to spending time with giggling girls and smiled to myself.

"I'm sure no one will ask *you* to be the boom operator," Sander said. "They'll probably want you to be in front of the camera. You should audition for the main part. That'd be fun."

My heart thudded in my chest. I almost got up and hugged Sander right there.

"You think so?" Alberto said mildly. "I'll think about it."

Two weeks of close quarters with Alberto, shooting a movie, my field of predilection. It was the perfect opportunity to sway him. Obvi-ously, I would need the best possible part. And for that, the best was yet to come.

"Are you going to sign up?" Arthur asked me.

I held a finger in front of my lips. Duvo was talking casting.

"And of course, we'll hold castings on arrival, to give the best parts to the best actors…"

"Oh, so you haven't cast the lady, yet?" Joy asked, her face bright.

"About that!" Camille lifted her hand to command our attention. "I have made a slight change to my play. Nothing much, really. But I turned the lady into a lord. Anna has become Adam. The forbidden love story will now be between two men."

Of course, there were exclamations of surprise and laughter. But, "nothing much"? This changed everything. I cast a quick glance at Alberto. He was yawning behind his hand. But by then, my heart was already pounding in my ears.

It really couldn't get any better than this. I knew what I had to do now.

I would secure myself the role of the footman, and Alberto would obviously be selected to play the other, on account of his otherworldly physique and his passion for movies. He looked regal even when he was slumped on a chair with his hoodie up. He would definitely be cast as the lord, and I would become his footman, and then, during the kissing scene, he would have a revelation.

I would be his revelation.

Just then, Alberto stretched once more. I perched myself on the edge of my seat so his fingertips accidentally brushed my forehead. He turned around with a start, and our eyes locked together.

"I'm sorry," he said.

The rest would become history.

3

OPERATION ALBERTO

After putting my name down on the list of the volunteers to make the movie, I knew not much was standing between me and true love. All I had to do was make sure I was ready to woo Alberto with my hard work and expertise. After all, I had little else to commend myself with. Dating, men, all of this was new. Alberto was my very first love.

My strengths were not physical, at least not in my opinion. As I was barely past the 1.70 m mark, Alberto, at already 1.85 m[1], towered over me. My eyes were too large, too dark, my eyebrows too full, my body too skinny, my hair too black and too unruly. My brain was the only thing that never seemed to fail me, and it's only because I never gave it the chance.

Mom hugged me when I updated her about my summer plans. Certain that I heeded her advice this time, she was so delighted, I didn't have the heart to correct her. I immediately dropped out of the short film I had been cast in and decided to dedicate myself to learning my future role by heart. Camille's script practically never left my hands.

My Summer of Love and Woe was the short tale of two men falling in love at the wrong time and in the wrong place. It ended poorly, in heartbreak and suffering, which was realistic for the era and gave the movie a powerful feel. I was to play Thomas, the young and inexperienced footman — who was logically terrified of losing his job — while

---

1. Zak is about 5'6". Alberto is already 6'0".

Alberto would be the young lord falling for his servant and tearing his household upside down to get a taste of the forbidden fruit. The funny thing was, the characters spent more time avoiding each other and fighting than actually falling in love, but Camille was the writer and I was here to perform, not criticise.

However, for a love story, there was a certain lack of kissing and touching. And I needed a kissing scene to make Alberto realise his love for me. There was only a chaste, miserable peck on the lips near the climax, so I was making notes in the corner of my head, hoping to convince Camille and Duvo to add a little passion to that scene, so that Alberto and I could smooch leisurely during and in between takes.

Alberto's name was already on the list when I got hold of it to sign up a minute later. Now our names were written one below the other on this piece of paper. A fated document. I would ask Duvo for it later, to frame it.

∾

A week or so into the summer holidays, I was stalking out of my bedroom to get a cup of coffee, the script still in my hand, when I heard a croaky voice coming from the living room behind me.

"Must be good," the voice said.

I turned around. Yasmine was having breakfast — or a war council — at the dinner table. She was practically invisible behind a pile of tedious-looking books.

"What did you say?"

"I said it must be good!" She brushed the hair out of her face. "You never put that thing down."

I walked over to her, blowing on my coffee. "Look who's talking." I gently poked her. "You slept here, didn't you?"

She stretched her stiff limbs. "Don't tell Mom."

"I won't."

"So, tell me about this movie that obsesses you. Is it going to be your breakthrough?"

In more ways than one, you could say that. I hesitated to tell her about my grand plan to seduce Alberto, which could result in more affected pleas about taking care, etc. As tedious as her books. I didn't want to hurt her feelings, but Yasmine, despite her best intentions, had a way of charging headfirst into what she deemed to be nonsense, and unfortunately, she saw romance as kind of nonsensical. It was best not to tell her.

"It's okay," I said soberly. "It's going to be a fun experience."

Yasmine's clever eyes fell upon mine, narrowing slightly, and I was about to get out of her sight as fast as possible when the telephone rang, saving me. When I sprung on it to answer, my sister's eyes widened in shock. Admittedly, I wasn't a big fan of answering the phone, but this was better than the alternative.

"Khoutifa residence."

"Zak! Excellent. It's Laurent— I mean, Mr Duvauchel."

"Hello, Mr Duvauchel," I said, rolling my eyes at Yasmine.

There were two kinds of teachers at Colette: First, those who wanted to be called by their first name, but knew it was inappropriate to ask. They secretly hoped to be cool, but they weren't. Then there were those who were cool enough so that we immediately started calling them by their first name, while the other teachers stood back and watched with envy.

Duvo clearly belonged to the first category; he longed to be called by his first name. Aware that we all called him Duvo behind his back, he pretended to like it, since it made him look slightly cooler. Binta, our laid-back but smart History teacher, was of the second category. Which explained why Duvauchel always looked at her with envy.

"What can I do for you?"

"Obligatory calls." Duvo sounded nervous at the end of the line. "Just wanted to check in, make sure you were still coming with us."

Yasmine was making gestures. Duvo was her teacher a few years ago, and she apparently liked him enough to want to say hello. People volunteering to be on the phone; how odd. With a grimace, I turned my back to her.

"Of course, I'm still coming next month. Why wouldn't I?"

Duvo let out a long sigh at the other end of the phone. I had to step away from the handset. "I've already had two cancellations! We might not have enough people to do the lights. Can you imagine?"

"Yes... I mean no."

Direct questioning worked terribly on me. I was either too startled that people would ask me for anything, or simply compelled to tell the truth at all times, resulting in saying things no one wanted to hear.

"So, ahem..." Duvo said. "You are definitely coming."

"Yes." I loved that he asked me twice. It made me think I was already his choice to play Thomas. Then something horrific came to mind, and I gripped the phone and whispered feverishly, "Did you just say two people have cancelled? Who are they?"

"Paulina!" Duvo shouted, making me flinch. "She said she would take care of the food. Not enough people are volunteering to help with food, I'm telling you—"

"Who else?" I asked again.

"That's the worst part. Are you sitting down?"

Normally I could appreciate my teacher's flair for drama. Today, not so much.

"Who else!"

"My young FEMIS student who was supposed to be my assistant. To get another student now will be next to impossible."

What would I have done if Alberto had cancelled? I let out a quiet breath of relief as Duvo went on. "They're all wrapped up in their own projects, and this boy used to be my student, and I really thought—"

"Oh no, that's really bad news," I said most convincingly, shrugging for Yasmine who was listening in wonder. But I obviously didn't care about some obscure FEMIS guy. What I cared about was to get perfect conditions to find myself with Alberto. "But the mansion, is it still ours?"

"Yes, the mansion is still ours. I'm going to have to spend the next five Christmas holidays at my aunt's to repay her kindness, but it's a sure thing."

"And everybody else is coming?"

"You were the last one on my list. Everybody else has confirmed. I still have a million things to worry about, however—"

"That's great, Mr Duvauchel. But I have to go, I'm still learning my lines. Super busy. I'll speak to you later, then." I hung up before he could add anything, turning around with a coy smile. However, my shrewd sister was still around, lurking behind her pile of books.

"What's happening? What did the old Duvo want?"

"Don't mind him. He's in a panic because Paulina cancelled and his FEMIS guy too. Apparently, Paulina was supposed to take care of the food." I paused. "Come to think of it… Knowing Duvo, we might actually starve to death."

"Lovely," Yasmine said. "And what's a FEMIS guy?"

"A student of the FEMIS, the film school. He was supposed to be our assistant director, but he dropped out."

"Isn't that bad?"

"It's going to suck for Duvo, but even more for the one of us who'll have to take on that role." I nipped a piece of toast from her plate. "Duvo's a drama queen and not so much of a director, as far as I know. He'll need all the help he can get."

"You don't sound very upset about it."

"Why would I be?" I said, my mouth full of toast. "I have so much on my plate already. You know, with my own job... Acting."

"Because," Yasmine said, blinking slowly. "Having a bad director or a bad team means a bad movie, which will reflect badly on you and your performance."

I immediately stopped chewing. "Well, now I'm upset. Thanks!"

She made a face. "Sorry. I'm sure you'll manage. After all, it's only a tiny, short film."

I stepped away from her with a haughty look. "There are no such things as tiny things when it comes to art."

"And you're definitely doing it for art, right?"

She was teasing me. She could, she was the only one allowed. But still, I answered with a growl and returned to the safety of my bedroom to add some notes about a much-needed kissing scene.

A week before departure, I was making myself a well-deserved snack when the phone rang again.

This time, it was Camille. I couldn't believe my luck. "I was just reading your play."

"Really?" She sounded excited. "Do you want to meet? I would like to say a few words."

I checked the clock above the oven, then realised I had literally nothing to do today, besides reading her script for the millionth time. Might as well meet the artist and tell her about my suggestion for an extra kissing scene.

"Sure, we could meet. When?"

"I was hoping you'd say that. I'm already at the Manga Café. You can join me there."

I wish I could say I didn't know where the Manga Café was, but I did, and I had read my fair share of BL[2] mangas by the time I entered high school. In fact, I read so much of it that the manager of the book-

---

2. Refers to Boy Love mangas or Yaoi, a Japanese genre that depict homosexual romantic relationships.

store and I were on a first-name basis. But she wasn't supposed to know that. *No one* was supposed to know that.

"Sure." I sounded innocent. "Where is that?"

"Look it up and meet me here. Now." She hung up. Truly authoritarian. She'd make a fine author one day.

I met my sister on the lower floor on my way out. She was just coming back from her favourite coffee place, wearing her sunglasses, proof that she had studied all night again and was not fit to be seen.

"Where are you going?" Her voice was thick with sleep.

"Out."

"In the sun? Watch out, it's about 25 degrees[3] out there."

She was pulling my leg. I replied in kind, gesturing at her crazy hair. "I bet you envy me and my first-year status right now. No homework, no sleepless nights…"

She yawned and smiled at the same time. "I bet you'll envy me soon enough when you land in the middle of nowhere. No mosquitos, no sharing bathrooms…" I looked at her in horror. She laughed and pushed her giant sunglasses up my nose. "There. I know you hate the sun."

"I don't like the heat. That's different."

She pushed me outside. "Off you go. Have some fun."

"It's not for fun!" I let myself be thrown out of my own flat. "It's for work! I'm meeting the author of the script."

"Wouldn't have guessed!" She slammed the front door in my face, and I made my way to the Manga Café.

Camille was near the cash registers when I came in, flicking through mangas on sale, a frown on her face. "You're late," she said when I approached. She didn't even lift her nose from the books.

I looked around, confused. "You just said to come in now."

"Yes, I did—"

"Hey, Zak!"

She was interrupted by the manager of the Manga Café, who was waving at me from behind the cash register. I pretended not to have heard.

"That guy is talking to you," Camille said.

"I don't think so." I put Yasmine's sunglasses back on.

"He said your name."

"You look tired. Don't you want to sit down?" Seizing her arm, I

---

3. 25°C is about 77°F

31

dragged her toward the tables in the back. Camille was forced to look at me, and her face broke into a smile. I dropped her into a chair and sat across from her. "I didn't know you were into mangas."

She shrugged. "I'm into anything with a good story."

I discreetly waved at the employee of Manga Café behind her back, and he gave me a clumsy thumbs up. I hoped he didn't imagine I was on a date with Camille, especially after he saw me purchase so many BL mangas. That would be awkward.

"So?" I said, "What did you want to say to me?"

Camille stared at my face, her bottom lip stuck between her teeth. "Nice glasses."

"Thanks. They're my sister's."

"I'm cool with that." She leaned forward and lowered her voice. "I need to tell you something."

This was getting a bit dramatic. My curiosity piqued, I moved closer to her.

"Someone vandalised the Drama Club."

"What?" I leaned back, surprised. "Why? Who would do that?"

The club was my favourite spot at school. Where Alberto sat, and performed, and sometimes adorably fell asleep under my watchful gaze. It was *the* place.

Camille considered the question. "I don't know. Someone either hates the Drama Club or loves theatre and is aware we totally botched Shakespeare when we did that thing back in April."

"What did they do exactly?" I asked, worried the classroom would be unrecognisable.

"Graffiti on the walls."

"What did the graffiti say?"

"You botched Shakespeare back in April."

My jaw went slack. "Really?"

"No, of course not." Camille laughed. "It said stupid stuff, I don't know what exactly. Duvo told me, he was all pissed off."

It was concerning. Being ridiculed by idiots is never a pleasant thing; high school was a breeding ground for bullies. But at the same time, some idiot spray-painting the club wasn't my priority at the moment. I had to stay focused on my goal.

"Is that why you wanted to meet me? To tell me that?"

"No." She waved her hand. "Who cares about that?"

I decided I liked Camille.

"I don't see anyone else but you for Thomas's role. So, you better ace that casting."

I decided I *really* liked Camille.

"Don't worry," I said with confidence. "I'll ace it."

"You want it?"

"Oh yes."

"You want to be Thomas?"

"I already am."

Her eyes lit up. "That's perfect."

Seeing how she was a little bit of a fan of mine, I got excited and decided to push my luck. "Who do you have in mind for Adam?"

Camille gazed out the window at the pedestrians outside. "I don't know. I guess we'll see after the casting."

"You really don't have a clue?"

I was surprised. Was I the only one with eyes in our group? How could she not be thinking of Alberto?

"Thomas is my favourite," she said. "He's more important to me."

My eyebrows shot up. "Why?"

"He's got the most to lose in this affair."

"Does he?"

I had never seen it like that. What did Thomas have to lose, apart from his job? Since I couldn't understand, I promised myself to read the script again tonight.

"Why?" Camille asked, scanning my face. "Do you have someone in mind?"

Camille was growing on me by the second. I wanted to see if I could nudge her in the right direction a little bit.

"I do, I mean… I thought it would be fairly obvious."

"I see what you're thinking." She pointed her finger at me. "Bob-Rob, right?"

"What?"

"BobRob. Robert."

"Robert?"

Who the hell was Robert?

"Belgian Robert. American Robert is just Bob."

"No…" She had it all wrong.

"Good, because neither of them can make it."

"But—"

"I know, BobRob would have been great."

"… You think?"

She nodded enthusiastically. I tried to think of Belgian Robert, but all I could remember was that he was tall.

"So… who do you have in mind, then?"

"Well…" I scratched my chin. "Alberto?"

Camille had frank eyes and knew how to hold a gaze. Her lip disappeared again between her teeth. "Alberto, huh?"

I nodded carefully, anxious not to look desperate.

"I didn't think of him," she said. "But if you've been considering it, it's probably for a good reason. I'll think about it."

"That's all I was suggesting," I said with a feigned detachment.

"We'll hold auditions for everyone interested. Is he interested?"

"Yes. Or so I heard."

"Okay then, perfect." Camille then saw someone through the window and jumped up. "That's Joy! I've got to dash. She lost her script, can you believe it? I told her I'd give her a new one." She slapped me gently on the shoulder. "Learn your lines, don't let me down!"

"I already did!" I shouted after her, hoping she would understand I was talking about the lines.

The manager of the Manga Café came strolling, holding a book. "Something really good just came in. Do you want it?"

Glancing at the entangled figures on the glossy cover, I let out a quiet sigh. I considered myself serious about my job, like an athlete. Didn't need anything distracting me now. So, I graciously refused the offer and left the café before I regretted it.

On the day of our departure, I awoke as the sun rose, several emotions bubbling up inside me. Anxious about going to the countryside, which I hated; excited to spend over two weeks with Alberto and thrilled to shoot my first short film.

Whenever I thought too much of cramped, smelly bedrooms and squads of mosquitos, I screwed my eyes shut and thought of Alberto, his eyes, his accent, and his lips… it was pointless to try to sleep at this point. But the real chaos began after breakfast, with my mother fussing all over me as though I was about to depart for college in the States and wouldn't return for years.

"I'm only going for two weeks," I said, rolling my eyes.

"Longer," Mom corrected.

"I'm sure you'll survive."

"Will you?" Yasmine chimed in. She sauntered into my room and stopped halfway through sipping her coffee. "Damn, your room is tidy. It does look like you're moving out forever."

I flashed her a grimace. "Not everybody's a slob."

"You're going to hate sharing a room with smelly boys, trust me." She made a face. "Or maybe not."

I warned her with a glare. Her eyes widened, and she mouthed words of apology. Whether they suspected it or not, my parents didn't know about my awesome gayness, and I had no desire to start the conversation at nine in the morning before my departure. Thankfully, my mother was nose deep into my backpack.

"You're not taking anything personal?"

Forcing down a curse of alarm, I snatched the bag away before remembering my racy mangas were stashed under the bed. "What do you mean, personal?"

"Anything to remind you of home, should you feel lonely."

The ideas she had sometimes. Ridiculous. All the same, I fished *The Ladies' Paradise* out of my backpack and bumped it gently against the tip of her nose. "I've got my book, I'll be fine." I tossed it back into the bag and handed it over to her. She clutched it as though it was a newborn baby.

"Don't forget to call us every day."

"Mother!" Yasmine said, feigning shock. "Will you let him breathe a little? He's not gonna call you every day. He'll be too busy having fun, and flirting—"

"Flirting?" My father stuck his head in the doorway. "Zak is flirting?"

"Thanks, Yas," I said in a dark tone. "Now you can all be certain I'll never call, and never come back."

"Don't joke about that!" my mother cried. She waited until Yasmine left my room to grab my shoulders and force me to look at her. "You must call me if you need anything at all. Or… if you want to leave. I will come and get you."

I wriggled out of her grip. "Why would I need something like that?"

"Just know that it's no trouble for me. I'll do it."

She still looked anxious when she plopped a kiss on my reluctant cheek as I put on my shoes. It was embarrassing. But it was also endearing, so I gave her a few affectionate pats on the head.

"Take care of my rabbit for me, please?"

Mom nodded and kissed my hand. "Sir Floppington's safe with me." She hugged me tight to stop me from uttering words of protest. Yasmine and my dad exchanged knowing smirks. When Mom let go, her eyes were misty. "Don't forget your iPod."

"I haven't. It's in my bag."

"I'm gonna miss you so much."

"Enough, now. I'm leaving. Please learn to survive without me."

Yasmine had offered to take me to the station. Nobody needed to know how relieved I was that she was coming with me. It wasn't as embarrassing as having your mother or father with you, while still providing some moral support. Still, I was surprised when she insisted to take me. After another effusion of kisses and hugs from my parents, and some excessive barking from Rufus, I met her downstairs and we set off toward Jussieu.

As we entered the metro station, I couldn't help asking, "You're not coming with me because of some ulterior motive, are you?"

She frowned. "What do you mean?"

"You wouldn't be having a crush on Duvo, would you?"

My sister had a thing for older men. And I mean *older* men. Even Duvo was young in comparison, and I knew him to be *thirty* years old.

My sister erupted in laughter, causing quite a few heads to turn. "Where on earth did you get that from? You and your crazy ideas. You're like Mom."

"I'm nothing like Mom."

"If you say so."

"But the other day, you wanted to talk to him on the phone…"

"I talk to a lot of people on the phone. Honestly, do you see me paired with Duvo?"

I hesitated. "He would be lucky to have you."

"Please, don't try to be nice now. I could eat guys like him for breakfast."

"Yes, but I suspect he would like it."

"Yikes. I wouldn't."

Good. This trip promised to be perfect. Everything was going in my favour, and I needn't worry about my sister having a crush on my teacher. She was right: I did nurture some crazy ideas at times when I was swept by my imagination. But only sometimes, and nothing too drastic. Most of the time, I had my head on my shoulders.

When we reached Montparnasse station, Yasmine led the way

through the bustling crowd toward the right platform. I immediately recognised the other students from the Drama Club, huddled around Duvo, and after stretching my neck, Alberto came into view in his V-neck T-shirt from Balenciaga. My pulse quickened. He was gazing down at the rail tracks and didn't see me approach. But when I got closer, my sister on my heels, I saw something that shouldn't be here, sticking out like a sore thumb. I first recognised Camille, Arthur, Nadia and Sander, then Joy and Melissa on one side, in great conversation with Binta. And I wasn't too surprised to see Charles-Henry had made it, but why on earth was he accompanied by a trio of his football player friends, including the nasty prat and the one with the vacant eyes?

The moment Yasmine left me to speak to Duvauchel, I dragged Camille aside. "What's going on? Why are they here?"

Camille pulled on the straps of her backpack. "They're coming with us."

"What?" My voice cracked. "Why?"

How could a trio of football players and bullies participate in our art project, except to ruin everything? I wasn't one to panic for no reason, but the prat seemed like the perfect specimen to push people's heads down the toilet, and I was the perfect specimen to be on the receiving end of his antics. There was still time to retreat; to get back home and reconsider. But Alberto was here... so close... and my plan was bulletproof... I looked back and forth between the train, Yasmine, and Alberto in anguish.

Then Binta clapped her hands and summoned us to get on board. Nadia appeared out of nowhere and pulled Camille toward the nearest coach.

"I'll explain later!" Camille said, leaving me.

My sister walked over, pushed her giant sunglasses into my hands, and pulled me into a hug. "Take these. Safety first." She paused, then whispered in my ear. "I left you a present."

"Where?" I asked with surprise. "In my bag?"

She did that thing, that smile she reserved only for me. "You'll know soon enough. Now get in and have some fun."

Jerking my chin in the direction of the four guys getting onto the train, I made a face. "I hope it will cheer me up. There are already problems."

"Difficulties keep things interesting. Your victory will only be made better by it."

My eyebrows shot up. "Why do you sound like a motivational PowerPoint all of a sudden?"

"Duvo literally just said that to me, talking about the same boys."

The *boys*. Call them boys all you want. I call them prats, thugs, ruffians… Troublemakers, mostly. But I steeled myself, thinking it was all for Alberto. And I only feebly protested when Yas pushed me toward the coach.

"Have some fun!" Yasmine repeated, and a glint of worry flashed across her dark eyes.

"Yes, fine!"

The train alarm rang, and the door began to slide shut behind me. Yasmine waved from the platform and I waved back, feeling oddly nervous.

Hanging by the luggage rack, Prat was blocking the way to the coach, his arms folded over his chest, and his muscles stretching the short sleeves of his polo shirt. "Was that your mother?" he asked in a taunting voice.

Can you even see the ball with such poor eyesight? I wanted to ask. But I clicked my tongue instead. "She's my sister."

"She's hot." He joined a crude gesture to his words.

I couldn't help snorting, imagining how my sister would have dealt with the situation if she were here. Or *Rufus*.

"Did I say something funny?" Prat bent down, trying to intimidate me, but Binta called out to us and ordered us to sit down. He lost interest, but a sour feeling lingered in the back of my throat. Almost three weeks in such company… I could only hope these idiots wouldn't make my life too difficult.

4

WELCOME TO LONGCHAMPS

Being last to enter the coach, I didn't have much of a choice in regard to seats. I first passed the four-seater spots. The football gang had already claimed that one, and I quickly looked away in fear of catching the prat's attention again.

On the other side, Alberto and Sander were sharing another four-seater with Joy and Melissa, who were throwing hopeful glances at the football players. I guess these guys didn't look too unpleasant when you weren't worried they might punch you in the face or stick your head down the bog for no reason.

Eventually, I found empty seats across the aisle from Binta and Duvauchel. When he saw me drop my backpack on the seats, Duvo glared at me.

"Why don't you sit with Arthur? And leave the adults alone, hm?"

Why don't you mind your own business, old man? I showed him my book, and his eyebrows rose. He turned away to speak to Binta in a whispered voice. Naturally, I could hear everything.

"This one loves classic literature. He never gets enough of it."

Binta had her own nose plunged into a novel. "It's an odd book of choice for a boy this age."

"What do you mean?" Duvo sounded surprised. "It's in the program."

"The program isn't exactly adapted to the needs or wishes of teens."

Duvo huffed. "We all know what their needs and wishes are. Thank goodness the books in the curriculum don't reflect *that*."

Binta chortled.

"But I agree," Duvo continued. "He's an odd one. Likes to keep to himself. Don't be surprised if he asks to be left alone."

"I know," she said gently. "He's the same in my class."

Funny how adults who went past the trying years of school automatically believed that when they whispered and gossiped, no one could hear them. I placed my small suitcase in the overhead compartment and settled down, but their words stayed with me. So what if I was an odd one and I kept to myself? It was my way of being. But in all fairness, I couldn't help worry a little. How would I fare over there? Sharing rooms, bathrooms, meals? No privacy, no Yasmine, and being watched 24/7? I once again ventured a look ahead at the four-seaters and saw Alberto was making himself comfortable against the window, gazing out as we left the suburbs of Paris. Never mind the obstacles life was throwing my way. It would all be worth it in the end.

Remembering Yasmine's parting words, I emptied the contents of my backpack on the other seat, but there was nothing I didn't expect to find in there. The surprise she talked about had to be in my suitcase. I'd find it later. Setting aside my iPod for now, I opened my favourite book, *The Ladies' Paradise*. But it was difficult to focus on Denise's trials and the impossible love she felt for the unattainable Mr Mouret while catching furtive glimpses of Alberto's godly face. There wasn't much to see, however: Alberto was already asleep by the time the train reached full speed, and I spent the rest of the journey reading to my heart's content.

A few hours later, my body light from relief, we exited the train at Gare de Nantes. My head was now the size of a cruise ship because of the incessant chattering and laughing of some of the silliest people I would ever spend the next weeks with. Trying hard to keep my eyes on the prize — or else take the risk of faltering and jumping back into the train straight to Paris — I kept my distance from the group while keeping within earshot of Duvauchel.

Our teacher was looking confused when he stepped out of the train station. He used his hand as a visor to shield from the brutal early-afternoon sun and spun around in the middle of the forecourt. "Where's our bus? It was supposed to be here ten minutes ago." He fished around in his pocket for his phone. "They said the driver would be waiting right outside."

"I'm sure it's nearby," Binta said with her usual cool. "Have you tried the bus lane?"

Inspired by Binta's suggestion, Duvauchel whipped around too fast and lost balance. He didn't see the poor guy who was walking toward him and smashed straight into him.

"Ouch, sorry!" Duvo stepped back, his glasses askew.

"Laurent?" the stranger said, surprising us all.

Duvo seemed even more confused, pointing at his own chest as if he wasn't sure of his first name after all.

"It's me, Michael."

The guy spoke French with a British accent. I couldn't see his face, but I watched as he extended his hand. Then, getting closer, I saw who was attached to the hand and did a double-take.

It was Michael. My sister's Michael!

Her British best friend, to be correct. All dark curls, dimpled smiles and sparkling green eyes, and wearing an oddly intoxicating apple-scented aftershave. As far as I knew, this living eye-candy studied directing at a film school in London. What the hell was he doing here?

"Hi, hi!" Duvo shook his hand gratefully. "Are you the bus driver?"

"No," Michael said, his face barely showing any surprise. "I'm your AD."

"My AD? Oh, my God! I had completely forgotten!"

While Duvo was apologising profusely to an amused Michael, everyone gathered around them. In a somewhat satisfying turnaround, even Joy and Melissa stepped away from the gang of footballers to take a good look at the newcomer. The prat's pale eyes narrowed in distaste. Nearby, Arthur and Sander also gazed at Michael curiously. Standing between them, Alberto peeked at Michael between two yawns.

"How can you possibly forget a guy like him?" Nadia giggled, and Camille joined in, her cheeks pink. I looked at them and chuckled: Michael was as gay as they make them. I knew it because, well, my sister told me.

Though he was no Alberto, he was undeniably pretty, and his arms and stomach more defined than the last time I saw him. From the look Duvauchel tossed him, he agreed with me. Binta hurried to shake his hand, apologising for the confusion, switching to English.

"Sorry Michael, we were a bit out of sorts, we couldn't find the bus."

"It's right over there." Michael gestured toward a white bus that was parked clearly in plain sight this whole time.

"Brilliant," Duvo said, giving Michael a once-over that said anything but.

Two options offered themselves to me here: introduce myself to him, or more like re-introduce myself to him, which would focus unwanted attention on me, or just ignore him, which he might consider rude because it was, in a way, rude. But who was I to claim acquaintance with him anyway? He was an adult. If he wanted to acknowledge me, then he would. So, I trudged behind Alberto, Sander, Camille, and Nadia toward the bus.

Inside, I took a seat right in the middle, by the window. Of course, the gang of footballers aimed straight for the last row so they could all sit together. Sticking my earphones into my ears, I was about to turn on some Massive Attack when a long and lightly-tanned hand invaded my field of vision.

"Hiya!" Michael bent over to be at eye-level with me.

Damn that cute face! I looked at him, wide-eyed, at a loss for words. And I wasn't alone to think so. Behind him, I could see Joy and Melissa stretching their necks to get a better look. Michael, oblivious to all that, gazed at me with a serene smile.

"How are you, Zak?"

I removed my earphones and gave him a somewhat lame handshake that turned my stomach. "I'm awesome," I mumbled, torn between shame for avoiding him and pleasure that he actually remembered me. A seat or two away, Camille was observing us from the corner of her eye, not missing a bit. "It's good to see you."

Michael was about to say something else, but Duvauchel, now settled, summoned him dramatically to the front row. Michael made a face that screamed, *'Is he for real?'*

"Sorry, duty calls. I'll talk to you later." He returned to the front of the bus.

I stared after him, intrigued. I never expected Michael to be here. Now that the surprise had passed and the awkwardness of the introduction was dealt with, I could see how great it would be to have him around. As a friend of my sister and fellow gay man, he was probably going to be a tremendous help to survive this trip. I had gotten myself an unexpected ally. Not only was everything going according to plan, but I kept scoring points in unexpected areas.

Camille appeared out of nowhere and plopped down next to me, her mini-shorts offering me such an extended view of her thighs I didn't know where to look, so I focused on the seat in front of me.

"So, you know the Assistant Director?"

"Mm?" I got distracted by Nadia who came to listen in on our conversation. Arthur, whom I didn't know was seated in front of me, turned around to listen as well. I had never had such attention thrown at me, including at the Drama Club. I swallowed a small lump. "He's a friend. Of my sister's." Great. I was stammering now. "A friend of my sister's."

"How old is he?" Nadia asked.

Honestly…

"I don't know… More or less like my sister, I guess."

"Which is?" Joy asked, joined by Melissa.

"Twenty, twenty-one?"

They pressed themselves against Nadia in the narrow aisle just as Alberto attempted to walk down to the back rows.

"I can't get through," he told Melissa. She didn't hear him, too busy exchanging laughs with Joy.

"Your sister's hot," Prat said behind me, and I started to find the whole football team standing behind me, listening. One of his less idiotic friends had the decency to swat him over the head for the comment, but what was better was the look of disgust Camille threw his way.

"Piss off," she said, her eyes dark.

Prat was about to reply, but his friend pulled him down to sit, leaving us alone.

"Michael's so pretty," Melissa said, a dreamy look on her face. "Does he have a girlfriend?"

Behind her, Alberto was poking her shoulder. "I can't get through."

Arthur made a resigned face. "All hail the intellectual hottie every girl dreams of putting her hands on."

"And boy," I said, thinking to settle the matter immediately to get these girls off his back. "Don't bother with Michael. He's gay."

Melissa and Joy made an "Ooooh" sound of surprise.

"What kind of gay guy is he?" Melissa asked.

What kind of gay guy, really? What the hell was that about? Did she think we came assembled with different options, like Barbie dolls? What kind of gay guy… The kind who sleeps with men, I assume. He wasn't Alberto, that's for sure. And that was a relief. I didn't think I could handle having another crush of that intensity for anyone else.

"He's just… the normal kind, I guess," I said.

Impressed with my small talk abilities, Melissa and Joy gave me a

43

look of boredom and returned to their seat. With a sigh, Alberto followed, but not before throwing a glance at me that made my heart jump. I wasn't sure he'd ever looked at me so voluntarily before.

"Tell me more about him," Camille said, making herself comfortable, much to my dismay.

"Why?"

"He's going to direct my movie."

"I thought Duvo was your director."

Camille tilted her head. "I think you'll find out soon enough why we needed a competent AD for this project."

Fair enough. Fair enough.

"So, how is he?"

I could feel Arthur's round blue eyes fixed on my face, in addition to Camille's. It took me a moment to think about what to say.

"I don't know him that well… My sister calls him the most patient man in the world."

"Why?"

More questions… I just wasn't used to that. Or having anyone swinging their bare legs so close to me. I flattened myself against the window.

"Hum… He's dating a crazy person. Well… More than dating, actually—"

"How crazy is he?" Camille laughed when she saw my dumbfounded face. "Sorry, I'm curious about people. And I like the crazy ones." Uninterested, Nadia also returned to her seat. But Arthur and Camille were both staring at me, waiting for me to answer.

"I don't know what to say," I said with a shrug. "I've only briefly met him once or twice. He's always acting weird around my dog."

Camille gasped. "Dog hater alert!"

"Yes, well, he isn't, really… I think it's a little more complicated than that…"

Camille looked relieved. "Who doesn't like dogs, seriously…"

"Is he hot at least?" Arthur asked.

Camille snorted.

"He…" I was at a loss for words. "He's all right, I guess."

In fact, I used to play that game when I realised, around age twelve, that I was into other boys. I liked to sort the guys in my neighbourhood. I remember electing Louis Mésange most likely to be a closeted gay hottie. When two years later, my sister told me he was dating Michael, I treated myself to a reward at the Manga Café.

Plot twist: I don't even like blonds.

"That explains it, then," Arthur said.

Camille made a face. "How often do people lose themselves to a pretty face? I hope that I'll be different."

My thoughts fluttered toward Alberto, and I shifted in my seat.

"And yet, you're sitting here asking questions about Michael," Arthur said in a resentful tone.

"Oh!" Camille tossed around in her seat. Her shoe collided with my tibia, bringing me close to tears. "No! I wanted to tell you something else." She leaned in, and Arthur did the same from his spot. "You were wondering why these guys are here." She gestured toward the back of the bus.

"Yes, please!" Arthur said, raising his hands to the sky. "What the hell are they doing here? Way to spoil the mood."

I couldn't have said it better. Camille looked around and, satisfied nobody was listening, said in a low voice, "They're here as punishment."

"Pun—" I shook my head. "For what?"

"*They* vandalised the Drama Club!"

Arthur stole a glance at the back of the bus. "They did? But why?"

Camille shrugged. "Don't know. But it's definitely not because we botched that Shakespeare play back in April. I know for a fact they didn't see it."

"No one did," Arthur said.

"Yeah, that's how I know it."

"I'll tell you why," I said darkly. "Because they're idiots."

"Don't underestimate the tall one," Arthur said in a gloomy voice. "He's a bully."

"He doesn't seem very nice, no," Camille said. "From what the graffiti said on the classroom's wall, we are nothing but a bunch of losers." She bit her lip. "But really, I didn't think Charles-Henry was that stupid. I mean, he's really okay once you get to know him—"

"They're all the same," I said, a little too fast. "You are who you associate with." Camille and Arthur nodded hesitantly.

"Anyway," Camille said, "Headmaster Van Bergen wanted to suspend them, I mean, literally suspend them from the ceiling like in medieval times, but Duvo said he wouldn't punish them if they came here and helped out with the film."

"You think they're capable of it?"

45

"I don't know about the others, but I heard Charles-Henry has volunteered to help with cooking."

"No way." Arthur glanced back up toward the gang, a look of wonder on his face.

Duvo bleated Camille's name from the head of the bus. After a lamenting groan, she gave the teacher a thumbs-up and rose from her seat. "Zak, are you ready for the audition tomorrow?" she asked.

I met her gaze head-on. "Born ready."

"That's what I like to hear." With a delighted smile, she left to join Duvauchel and Michael, who looked like he'd just realised he'd made a huge mistake.

To my surprise, and before I could protest, Arthur jumped off his seat to occupy the one Camille had just left. "It's going to be an eventful trip," he said, looking happy at the prospect.

I decided to let this slide, for once.

The best thing about the ride was that it was a short one. It wasn't long before the bus slowed down and turned onto a narrow country road, followed by a long, gravelly driveway that led us to the mansion called Longchamps. We all glued our eyes to the windows to take a look at the place.

The house stood three storeys high, glorious in the sunlight, surrounded by tall, majestic trees. Vines covered the walls almost protectively, but not the grey slated roof or the two imposing chimneys. Countless windows larger than man, flanked by elegant white shutters, looked like so many unblinking eyes peeking at the newcomers. A long, narrow terrace stretched along the front of the house. An old woman waited there atop the marble front steps, her hand resting on a wrought iron railing, a tranquil smile on her face. Behind her, the double doors of the mansion were open and reminded me of a mouth about to speak. I immediately felt a sense of relief. This place looked rather comfortable, better than I expected.

"There we are!" Excited, Duvo slapped Alberto's back, catching him off guard and sending him flying straight into Michael's arms. Alberto looked indignant, but Michael laughed and told him that it was quite all right.

So, it seemed Duvo's time with Michael aboard the bus had already chilled him out a bit. Yasmine had warned me her friend had such superpowers. Perhaps he could use them on me, turn me into a loose, sexy, sophisticated person, the sort Alberto would fall for naturally.

"There is plenty of space to shoot the film, plenty of green space for you to do some reading..." Duvo hesitated when he saw Binta's incredulous face, then got the hint. "... or playing games, of course, *once* we're done with daily filming, this goes without saying. There's even a pool in the back."

"A pool!" Joy and Melissa squeaked in unison.

Once outside, I was engulfed in the oven-like heat pressing on me from all sides, and my good mood somewhat dimmed, but I knew myself to be tired from the journey. Nothing a glass of water and a night spent in the bed next to Alberto's wouldn't fix. I hoped the bedroom window would be open at night, a gentle breeze swaying the curtain, letting in the melodic hoots of an owl, stars visible from the corner of my eye while Alberto and I were locked in an amorous gaze. I hoped, I hoped, I hoped.

Michael emerged from the bus and stretched with ease, revealing two inches of a golden, toned stomach, and causing Joy to choke on the cigarette she had just lit up.

"Use the ashtrays!" Duvo barked. "This place must remain spotless, or my aunt will have me killed."

"But, sir——"

"No excuses!"

Melissa tossed Duvo an outraged look as she gently rubbed her friend's back. Duvo didn't get it; even Michael didn't. He was admiring the house, oblivious to his own sexiness.

"I'm warning you, Michael," I said, in an attempt to be helpful. "Duvo's a handful. No one knows how he is outside of school, but it can't be good."

"That's okay," Michael said gently. "I've got one of those at home. I'm pretty sure I can handle it."

"About that..." I couldn't help asking. "How did you get wrapped up in all this?"

"Your sister got me into this."

Of course, now it all made sense. "Are you my... surprise?"

Michael's green eyes widened. "What was that?"

"Sorry, nothing." I took on a disinterested air. "How did she get you into this?"

"She told me your teacher's AD dropped out. Since I had nothing else to do this summer, I thought I could use the experience."

"But aren't you studying to be a director?"

"I am." Michael swung his backpack over his shoulder. "But I can learn a lot from working as an AD. I think it's important to do all kinds of jobs. Besides, I really liked the text."

Xavier, his suitcase rattling after him, sniggered past us. "Why? Because it's gay?"

"No…" Michael's eyes narrowed briefly. "Because it's good."

If he was made uncomfortable, he didn't show it, but I was. I flushed all over, thinking with shame that to get the girls off Michael's back, I'd told them he was gay, but anyone could have this information now — including this batch of bullies. I hoped it wouldn't cause too much trouble in the future.

Near the front door, Binta was talking to the old lady with the smile. She wore an old school apron and was probably part of the maintenance team Duvo had mentioned. When she was done, Binta whistled with expertise, reminding me of Yasmine, and summoned us inside the house.

Delighted at Michael's comment about her script, Camille shoved me aside to talk business with him, while Duvo stared at them with suspicious eyes. Following in their footsteps, I kept my head down. I thought I was doing Michael a favour. It's not like he lived in the closet; he and his boyfriend were not hiding their relationship. But the bad taste in my mouth didn't leave me until we reached the house, and something far worse got my attention.

Inside, the hall felt breezy and cool, pure relief after the stifling heat. Our steps clattered on the black and white checkered floor. Facing us was an interesting spiral staircase with an intricate iron-wrought railing and wide marble-like steps. Duvauchel turned to us, his face beaming.

"The mansion was erected on the base of a castle built in 1668—"

"This is your castle?" Prat interrupted.

Glaring at him, I accidentally made eye contact with his other friend and turned away immediately.

"Huh…" Duvo was taken aback. "No. It's my aunt's. And it's not a castle anymore, hasn't since—"

"If it's your aunt's, then it belongs to the family, doesn't it? So, it's yours."

Duvo scratched the back of his neck in a rare show of patience. Which could only mean Prat had tiresome parents and teachers had to walk on eggshells around him.

"My aunt bought it when she retired. It doesn't belong to our family."

"My father is a baronet," Prat's friend Xavier said, his vacant eyes gazing at a spot in the ceiling.

We all stared at him in silence. Outside, a blackbird chirped from one of the trees. Standing on my left, Camille popped her gum loudly.

"Okay!" Binta clapped her hands. "Let's see the bedrooms, shall we?"

She nudged Duvo, and he led the way up the circular, otherworldly staircase. He was still trying to teach us a bit of history in a slightly pompous tone while Binta looked on with an amused smile.

"This mansion itself was built in 1842 by the Earl of Achonne for his great-niece Marie-Louise as a wedding present..."

He droned on and on as we climbed up. Joy groaned as if she were in pain, and Melissa let out a vocal yawn. On the other hand, Michael looked like he was drinking in Duvo's words.

"This staircase is so beautiful," he said to himself, caressing the railing.

Melissa saw him and turned to Joy with a grimace. Alberto was standing next to Michael. He tilted his head. "If you like this sort of thing, you should go to Napoli. There are plenty of beautiful houses in the region."

"Are you from Napoli?"

Alberto nodded.

"My mother's family is from Florence," Michael said, and they both looked enchanted. "What's your name?"

"Alberto." My loved one extended his hand.

Michael took it, his smile deepening. "Michael."

My heart swelled. I felt really lucky. My ally and my crush were already becoming friends. Of course, it would have been better without the brutes sniggering and mocking Duvauchel behind his back. But my brain was already thinking fast. Alberto, wanting to get to know Michael better, would surely turn to me since I knew him from before. Then, we would start hanging out, just three gay guys chilling in the countryside, chatting and tanning around the pool. Except I usually hid from the sun, and I didn't care for pools, but it didn't matter so much at the time.

When we reached the carpeted corridor leading to the bedrooms, Duvo stopped and faced us all with a solemn air. Binta snapped her fingers to get some silence.

"Okay, so you'll share rooms, and since you're more numerous than you were supposed to be—"

"Hang on," Alberto said in his languid voice. "We're in a mansion, and there isn't enough space for everybody?"

"There is, but we'll have to adapt. Some rooms are not opened to the public, some are reserved for filming, like the master bedroom, and some rooms are reserved for Binta, Michael, and I…"

There were some groans and some shrugs. I said nothing, shaking with impatience at the thought of sleeping right next to Alberto for the next couple of weeks.

Duvo pointed to the rooms at the end of the corridor. "Girls, you will share two bedrooms, and Binta's room will be right across the hall."

"We're not sharing with the girls, then." Xavier sounded disappointed. The look Binta gave him sufficed to silence him for now.

"Boys, it's a different matter. With the addition of our three friends here" — I didn't even bother turning around to look at them — "there are eight of you, so you will be four per room so I can keep an eye on you. The staff has already made arrangements."

He gestured to two bedrooms — one right in front of us, and the other closer to the right end of the corridor — then walked off toward the girls' room. Prat, Xavier, Charles-Henry and their friend rushed toward the room on the darkest side of the corridor, while I followed Alberto and Sander into the nearest room.

Alas, I wasn't as lucky as I'd hoped, for Alberto and Sander dropped their bags on the two twin beds on the right side of the room, and I was left to pick a bed on the left side. I dropped my backpack on the bed opposite Sander's, so I could glance more easily at Alberto during the night. Yes, like a total creep! We could always switch later, after exchanging our vows.

Arthur walked over to the bed next to mine and dropped his own bag, a happy smile on his face.

"Where's the bathroom?" Alberto asked around to no one in particular. I berated myself for not knowing, especially when his feline eyes fell on my face. "Nevermind, I'll just look around." He turned on his heel and left.

Sander didn't waste time; he opened his suitcase, and started unpacking. I anxiously watched the door to witness Alberto's return and was disappointed when Duvo's head appeared in the doorjamb.

"Are you settled?" We nodded, and he left. But no sooner had I opened my own suitcase, he returned, his cheeks red, and followed by the band of ruffians. "Okay, sorry, guys, but this won't do." He nudged the others inside the room. They were all holding their luggage. "I can't possibly let you share a room together, you know full well why you're here."

Prat let out an ostensible sigh and looked over his shoulder at his friend, smirking with pride. Xavier grinned stupidly.

"Therefore," Duvo said, "I require two of you to switch, right now."

My heart lurched in my throat; behind me, Arthur let out a fearful gasp. Duvauchel was wearing his most serious face. Prat stared into it for a second, realised he was serious, then turned to his friends and, after a silence and with another sigh, he took charge. Snapping his fingers at Charles-Henry, he spoke in a bored voice. "Come on, C.H. Switch with…" He gave us all a quick once-over, then smiled when his eyes fell upon Sander. "You. Come with us."

Sander didn't move, too dumbstruck or intimidated. Duvauchel waved feebly.

"Come on, Sander, go with them."

Sander quickly packed up his stuff again and went to stand near the thugs, while Charles-Henry, looking perfectly indifferent to all this mess, laid his own backpack on the bedspread with a serene smile.

Alberto came back and stared at the scene with a confused expression. I wanted to scream at him, *Quick, get out!* I knew there was no chance Duvo could force me to stay in the same room as these guys. I would invoke every power available to me, including deities, *not* to sleep unprotected next to Prat. That meant Arthur would have to go, and Alberto and I would have a reason to stick together.

"Good?" Prat asked with a quirked eyebrow.

Duvo managed to look at him with contempt. "No, not good. Charles-Henry didn't participate in your little criminal act, so no, not good. Another one has to go. And don't think I won't be keeping an eye on you. I'm sleeping right across the hall, and Michael will be sleeping right across the other room."

"What's going on?" Alberto asked.

"One of you has to switch to the other room."

"I'll go," Alberto said without skipping a beat.

My heart plummeted to the depths of my stomach with a *clunk*. It took all of my willpower to not slap my own forehead.

"Oh, good," Sander said, relieved.

Alberto didn't react. Prat glanced over at Xavier with a hint of sympathy, no doubt to command him to stay in this room, but before he could speak, his other friend stepped forward and dumped his suitcase on the bed.

Prat's smug face morphed into pure dejection. "Dude, what the fuck!"

"Language," Duvo said in a tired tone.

His friend answered with a shrug and patted the quilt on Alberto's bed. I watched in horror, tears of resentment stinging my eyes.

What the hell just happened?

The guy dropped heavily on the bed, his blond hair catching the light, and smiled at Charles-Henry with perfectly aligned white teeth.

And just like that, my foolproof plan began to fall apart.

5

THE AUDITION

I woke up early with my eyelids stuck together, my thoughts in disarray, unsure of my surroundings. The smell of unfamiliar sheets. Narrow beds with plain bedding. Tired, if not gawky, wallpaper. Dark wooden furniture lining the walls. Two handsome windows, currently shuttered closed. I finally remembered that I was at Longchamps, that the annoying snoring sounds I thought I'd imagined in the night were in fact coming from Arthur, and that the fiend who stole Alberto's bed hadn't even bothered to sleep in the room he so unfairly claimed as his own.

After a short while of stretching in silence, I decided to snap out of it and pushed down my self-pity. Yesterday was already wasted. From the moment of our arrival to dinner, my foul mood never left me. When the three football players, after all here as punishment, were sent back to the kitchen to help with the dishes, Binta proposed some games before bed and led everyone outside. I quietly retired before I was asked to sit around the fire pit and sing "Kumbaya" or worse.

On my way to bed, I saw Michael unpack in his room. His bedroom was indeed right across from where Alberto would be sleeping. Michael heard my sigh of envy and came to the door.

"Are you nervous about tomorrow?" His face looked anxious in the dimmed light of the corridor.

I shook my head. I couldn't tell him what ailed me. Not now anyway.

He insisted. "Is it a bit too much, too many people?"

I was worried that oversharing would cause me to lose control, so I muttered some vague response and disappeared into my room. When the others came to bed, I pretended to sleep so I wouldn't be bothered, but even after the others settled, the usurper was still noisy. Eventually I opened my eyes and, in the darkness, saw him grab a jacket and his backpack and sneak out of the room. Anger rose in me. He was surely up to no good with his prat friend and the other dumb one. Too good to play by the rules like the rest of us. The sort of people that really got on my nerves.

Now fully awake, I blankly stared at his empty bed. I wouldn't let this drag me down. Today I was going to nail my audition and get cast as Alberto's love interest. Everything else was unimportant.

I was the first one down. I didn't know what I was allowed to touch, so I just sat in the dining room and waited for the others to come down. Sunlight poured from the two massive windows, illuminating the modern white tiles and the less modern sets of tables and chairs. The coolness of the walls, painted in pastel shades of blue, mixed with the long, flowing white curtains and thick tablecloths, gave the room a soft but crispy clean atmosphere.

Not five minutes later, Michael trotted into the dining room, looking freshly rested. He took a seat opposite me, his aftershave wafting into my unaccustomed nostrils. "Are you alone?"

I replied without thinking. "Always."

Michael gracefully pretended I didn't sound so emo. "I'm going to make coffee, then."

"Good idea." I got up to help him.

Little by little, people trickled down the stairs and into the dining room, their brightly-coloured summer outfits clashing with the simplicity of the dining room, making them appear like exotic little birds. Under the leadership of the old lady we met yesterday, and who appeared to be the master of the kitchen, breakfast was swiftly organised with a special treat of croissants served still warm, and so buttery they melted on the tip of our tongues.

I ended up sharing my meal with Michael, causing certain looks of envy from the girls. There wasn't much to be envious of, however. Michael spent more time typing on his phone than paying any attention to me. I didn't mind either, my brain full of lines from Camille's script.

The football players, led by Prat, eventually made their appearance, causing Joy and Melissa to divert their attention to their athletic figures instead. My unwanted roommate was among them, eating a banana with a gleaming smile, the picture of innocence. As though he didn't spend the whole night screwing around while my loved one had to sleep on the other side of the house.

"Morning!" a voice boomed at my side, jolting me back to reality. Arthur, deliberately joyful as always, took the chair next to me. "Ready for casting?" Michael and he shook hands and exchanged smiles. I guess friendships blossomed while singing "Kumbaya" around the fire last night. But the vague answer I had planned to give got stuck in my throat because Alberto appeared, slightly dishevelled, causing my heart rate to accelerate shamefully.

To my surprise, it's toward our table that he walked, holding a cup of coffee. He lightly pulled the chair next to Michael and made himself comfortable, while Sander looked at him confusedly. Arthur immediately brought an extra chair for him, and he sat down with a grateful expression.

Alberto still looked sleepy, but it suited him very well. I decided not to touch my food anymore, worried I would forget how to chew or swallow and embarrass myself.

"Good morning." His voice as usual was gentle, a little flat, giving away nothing.

"Are you going to audition, Alberto?" Arthur asked.

With a long finger, Alberto tapped the rim of his cup. "Yes."

"That's great," Michael said, his tone pleasant but his eyes still glued to his phone. Alberto gave him a furtive glance but didn't say a word, so Arthur swallowed a mouthful of cereal and went on.

"Zak's gonna get the part. Aren't you, Zak?"

The corner of Alberto's mouth twitched. He was — sort of — smiling at me! My heart did its best not to hop out of my throat and land on my plate.

"Isn't he, Michael?" Arthur insisted.

Michael finally took his head out of his phone. "Mmh?" He tossed a look around the table, and his eyes widened. "Oh! I can't be talking about this with you! That's unfair to the other applicants."

Arthur pointed his spoon at his face. "Who are the other applicants? Give it up now!"

He meant it as a joke, but Michael was already gathering his coffee and his notebook. "Sorry, kids." He left the table in a hurry.

Arthur redirected his spoon at Alberto. "Did he just call us kids?"

Alberto nodded. "He did."

Michael didn't get far. Out of nowhere, Camille jumped right in front of him, her own notebook in hand, and took his arm to lead her to her own table.

"So, I guess the AD is incorruptible," Arthur said, his mouth full.

"Apparently so," I muttered.

Alberto watched Arthur eat with a blank look. Arthur didn't notice anything and swallowed noisily.

"Don't be so tense, Zak." He clapped a hand on my shoulder. "Camille pretty much wrote the part for you."

"I doubt that. I'm nothing like Thomas."

Thomas was a meek and frightened creature and stubbornly refused to fall in love with the dead-on gorgeous Adam. A victim of his times and circumstances. I wanted to be nothing like him.

"Well, you're a great actor. You can play anyone."

A quick glance at Arthur's face told me he meant it. "Thank you," I said, surprised. I felt Alberto's eyes on me and gulped.

"When is your audition?" His expression was unreadable.

It was the first time he'd addressed me. I cleared my throat to make sure the next sound coming from me wouldn't be an embarrassing squeak.

"Late. Half-past twelve."

"Mine is at a quarter to one."

Made sense. Thomas followed by Adam.

"Tomorrow we might be partners on screen, then." Alberto got up with his empty cup of coffee, and Sander followed him without a word. At the last second, he turned around. "Good luck."

I laughed nervously, while internally, a nasty part of myself was rubbing its hands. Alberto had no idea how determined I was to be his partner on screen. Should he have wanted to play Thomas, I would have auditioned for Adam, and if I hadn't been able to be his love interest, I would have auditioned for his valet, his chauffeur, his cook, even his maid. Anything would have been worth staring into his hypnotic blue eyes.

Arthur was gaping at me. I quirked my eyebrow, and he plunged back into his cereal with the air of a told-off child.

～

"And that's a scene!"

Sitting behind an imposing desk, Duvauchel concluded my audition with a satisfied smile.

I stood still in the middle of the study, a little bit disoriented as always when I left a character and returned to my normal self. On Duvo's right, Michael was scribbling down on his notebook. Camille, seated on his left, was chewing the end of her pencil, her eyes bright.

"Thank you, Zak! Results will be announced tonight after dinner."

The audition was not the hassle I had been worried about. The scene I'd just performed, in which Thomas must make the difficult decision to break up with Adam, was easier to perform without Alberto around, at least for now.

"You can go." Duvo was already back into his own notes and gestured vaguely at me. "Please let the next one in."

Feeling slightly lightheaded, I picked up my bag and left the room with my head down. "You're up."

"Thank you," a familiar voice said.

Surprised, I looked up and stopped abruptly. The next candidate was none other than Alberto.

"You're... up?" I repeated.

"Yes, you said."

I shook my head to clear my thoughts. "Are you... auditioning for both?"

"No..." Alberto checked his script to make sure. "No. It's a quarter to one, you know."

"But that means..." With Alberto looking at me like that, it was more prudent to stay silent. "Never mind. Good luck in there."

Alberto shuffled into the study. The door squeaked shut behind him, and I was left alone with my thoughts.

So, I was the only one to audition for Thomas after all. I should have been pleased to secure the part. But winning by default only felt like a tainted victory. Even if I was almost certain to get the part, it would have been nice to have a little competition. On the other hand... Now I was certain to be Thomas. Alberto would be Adam. It was going to work out just as I hoped.

Keen on showing Alberto support, I took a seat on the bench in the hallway. I sat with my back straight, then dropped my shoulders. I didn't want to look too stiff but didn't want to appear too loose either. For a while, I tried different positions, until the sound of laughter coming from the other side of the wall distracted me.

Lunch was over; people running around the house was to be

expected. But those voices belonged to the football players, and I didn't want to see them. Evidently, those clowns respected nothing, not even Alberto's audition, because they stumbled into the hallway, their guffaws bouncing off the mansion's walls, oblivious to my presence in the corner. What were they doing here instead of doing their chores? There was plenty to do in the kitchen, especially after lunch. Were they already breaking the rules they had agreed to?

Eventually, I took a chance and stole a glance at them. My eyes immediately fell on Charles-Henry, who stood a little more quietly on the edge of their group. He was technically one of us, but more likely one of them. I didn't know much about him, except that he entered a Drama Club session by mistake and decided to stay, and that there was always a crowd waiting either for him, or Joy and Melissa, after each of our club meetings. Charles-Henry never volunteered for anything and never said much during our times together.

I started to worry that he had taken a leap of faith and was actually waiting here to audition, and he had brought his posse to support him. Charles-Henry, playing Adam. He must have been out of his mind if he thought he stood a chance, especially against Alberto.

Then, the door to the study squeaked open, and Alberto emerged, his expression unreadable. Excited, I ran after him.

Duvo gave us the rest of the day. Already, our group had split into tiny little gangs. It was unavoidable, after all. The football players liked to stick together, Melissa and Joy liked to stick to them. Camille and Nadia seemed to have begun a friendship based on proximity, while Alberto and Sander never left each other. And I was watching them from my newly found hiding place.

At the end of the long corridor serving our bedroom, I found a storage utility closet with shelves stacked with maintenance products and a dirty window overlooking the backyard and the pool. From there I could read while observing people, and nobody knew where I was. I was pretty proud of myself for finding such a gem so rapidly. However, I kept obsessing about what I saw when I was waiting for Alberto. Did Charles-Henry audition? Where was he now? Unlike his prat friend and the baronet's son with vacant eyes, he wasn't at the pool trying to impress the girls. It left me feeling uneasy the whole afternoon. Eventually, I fell asleep right against the window frame and jumped out of my skin when a bell announced dinner.

I got down to the large kitchen, modern in function but outdated in style, which had been reorganised so that we could pick up any available dishes we liked, help ourselves, and carry a small tray to the dining room to eat.

"You've got a big mark on your face," Joy said when we were standing in line. Her tone was almost reproachful, as if I should have done my best to prevent it. "What is it?"

"Window frame," a voice said, "from the look of it."

It was Alberto! I hadn't noticed he was right behind me. Even Sander, behind him, was looking closely at my face. I slapped my hand to my cheek to hide my shame but only managed to flinch in pain. Alberto stared at me with a blank face.

"What? It's not a window frame?" He bent down to take a proper look. I shrunk onto myself, embarrassed, and gave an awkward smile. The line moved, and I followed breathlessly. Behind me, Alberto was mumbling, "I could have sworn it was a window frame."

"Are you specialised in windows or something?" Joy asked, her tone teasing.

"He's a specialist in falling asleep against things," Sander replied in a resentful tone. I threw a perplexed look over my shoulder, but Alberto didn't react, and it was my turn to pick up a plate.

Dinner tonight was a homemade quiche and mixed salad. After the soggy pasta from last night, I couldn't help a sigh of relief.

"Definitely an improvement on last night's dinner," Alberto said.

"Charles-Henry made it," Joy said, helping herself to some salad.

"He did?" I asked, surprised.

"He likes to cook," she added with a shrug, as though it was mental but couldn't be helped, as opposed to the mark on my cheek. "He spent all afternoon in the kitchen in there with Janine and Eric."

Since I had no idea who she was talking about, I quickly helped myself to some food and returned to the dining room, where the table I liked best, the one nestled in the deepest and darkest corner, was still available.

Charles-Henry spent hours in the kitchen. That meant he didn't audition. Or perhaps it only meant he cooked as he waited for the results, instead of hiding in a storage closet and falling asleep against a window. There was no way of knowing; I'd have to wait. Hopefully, not for long.

When Duvo, Binta, and Michael came down together with Camille, a tired but satisfied look on their faces, I jumped up, expectant. Michael dragged along a rolling whiteboard on a stand, which he left in view of everybody. The surface was still blank, but soon enough, he'd write the names of the definitive casting for the movie.

"Don't be so nervous," Arthur said, inexplicably sitting next to me again. "You know you're Thomas."

"Did you know I was the only one applying for the job?"

He gave me a sheepish look. "Even so, Camille had you in mind the whole time."

"Right." I tried not to sound disappointed. "What about you? Did you audition for anything?"

Arthur shook his head. "I said I wanted to do the cinematography and I gave them my references. Acting's not my thing. I want to be her eyes, you know. Make her vision happen." He pointed at Camille.

Wow. He was really into her stuff. I wondered if she knew she had a massive fan. "I wish they would announce it now," I said, holding my tummy.

"Monsieur Duvauchel!" Arthur bawled at the top of his lungs. Everyone in the room stopped eating and chatting to look at us. Duvo had just returned with the others, holding his plate. He stared at Arthur in shock while I rubbed my traumatised ear. "We want to know the results."

"Can't you let me eat first?" Duvo asked, staring down at his quiche.

Arthur looked at me, uncertain. I nodded. "I guess so."

Michael glanced in our direction, clearly amused, but at the same time pulled out a chair and sat down to eat.

I watched each and every one of the bites they took, until Binta, the slowest eater I'd ever seen, put down her fork. Immediately, I slammed my fist down on the table in victory, and Arthur sprung up.

"Sir!"

Duvauchel had just turned to tell something to Binta. He glanced at Arthur, looking annoyed. Binta said something in his ear.

"Do you really want to know now?" Duvo asked.

There was a wave of murmurs across the room. Of course, everybody wanted to know. To my surprise, even the imposters stretched their necks to give Duvo their attention.

"Can you hurry, please?" Prat said in a bored voice. "You said we could watch the game when this was over."

That explained it.

Duvo glanced at Prat in confusion. "The what?"

Binta grimaced and patted Duvo's hand. "I told them they could watch their football game. Today's the… It's the World Cup final."

Duvo looked bewildered. "Who cares about such things?"

"Everyone!" Melissa cried.

Most people burst out laughing at her words. Even Michael gave a small smile, but Alberto's lips didn't even twitch.

"Very well," Duvo said, looking at Binta's hand on his. "If Binta gave permission, that's fine with me. Michael?" Michael was already up and was opening a marker. Duvo took on a dramatic air. "The basics first. I'll be the director."

Just the way he said *director* should have been a sign he was not ready to assume that role. But I didn't care. My heart pounding in my chest, I waited to hear our names.

"Write it down, Michael," Duvo said with an anxious glance at Binta.

Michael obliged without a word.

"Binta is the producer," Duvo added.

"I'm the boss," she said. "You must obey me."

"Well technically, I'm the boss." Duvo laughed nervously.

"Not in this case," Binta assured him.

"Well…"

But Michael had already scribbled down in ridiculously large letters: Binta = boss.

"Michael, here, is going to be assistant director, and he's going to do everything I ask…"

Michael made a funny face behind Duvo's back, causing general hilarity. Duvo turned abruptly, but Michael's face had gone back to looking innocent.

"And Arthur will be our director of photography, pretty much doing everything I ask."

Arthur's face turned red when Camille turned around and gave him the thumbs-up.

"Now, starting with the technicians…"

Camille would be in charge of supervising the script, Joy was in charge of wardrobe and makeup, Melissa of hair and wardrobe. Sander and his unusual size were put to use as boom operator. Then Duvo said, "Nadia, you and Charles-Henry will be in charge of catering."

Sounds of guffaws echoed around the room as Prat and Xavier slapped C.H. across the back and congratulated him, calling him a woman and laughing stupidly. C.H. didn't seem deterred at all, even wearing a serene smile, and I breathed for the first time since the auditions were over. I knew now he would not be Adam, whether he applied or not.

"In charge of lights, we have Kevin."

Michael turned to the board and wrote the name in large letters. From the twisted look on his face, Kevin was the one I'd been calling Prat this whole time. As Michael was finishing writing down his name, Xavier began to clear his throat to get his attention.

"Excuse me!"

"Yes?" Michael turned to him with a smile.

Xavier, his eyes animated for once, pointed at the board. "That's not how you spell his name!"

Prat's shoulders sagged. He elbowed Xavier in the ribs.

"Oh, I'm sorry." Looking slightly disoriented, Michael wiped the offensive letters from the board. "How do I spell it, then?"

An elbow through the ribs apparently wasn't enough to silence Xavier. He went on happily: "K - A - Y - V - I - N"

Prat — or Kayvin — stared around defiantly, daring people to say anything, but there was nothing but silence in the room as Michael fixed his mistake. Meanwhile, I was trying my best not to chew my nails, should my hands appear on camera, under the watchful gaze of Arthur.

"Wasn't that complicated," Xavier sneered.

"How was I supposed to know?" Michael mumbled, dropping his arms to his sides. But Kayvin looked murderous, as if he profoundly abhorred his own name. I would have felt sympathetic, since no one can ever choose their own birth name or the diverse and sometimes silly ways to spell it, but since he was a super prat, I found my well of empathy was running a tad dry.

"Let's move on!" Duvo barked.

He switched to announcing the small parts. Joy and Melissa would be the maids, Camille the kitchen wench... Even Xavier had gotten a part: the gardener. He seemed delighted, probably because he hadn't read the scene yet, in which the kitchen wench beats him with a wooden spoon for spying on their master.

"But who plays Thomas and Adam?" Arthur bellowed.

"You're ruining the suspense!" Duvo shooed him. "All right, let's end the torture. There's only one of us who could play Thomas... and it's Zak, of course."

People clapped. People actually *clapped*. Politely, out of habit, I don't know. Binta and Michael were clapping too. I would have blushed if I wasn't so nervous. Duvo didn't, probably because he thought the claps were for him.

"And now, in the role of Adam, after, I must say, a very impressive audition..."

My chin trembling, I sat at the very edge of my seat, waiting for the news that would seal my romantic fate.

"In his first role ever..." Duvo opened his arms, beaming, "I give to you the... ahem... surprisingly talented Eric!"

I blinked.

Cheering noises reached me as though my head was underwater. Through blurry eyes, I saw people clapping vehemently, including Arthur. My heart, like an anchor, sank to a depth which I knew not existed. My neck twisted and turned as I sought something to pin my gaze on, a culprit, *the* culprit.

My eyes found a head of golden hair in the middle of a trio of cheering football players. The head turned to me, flashed me a beaming smile. Completely bewildered, I could only stammer words of incomprehension until all my shock and heartache, desperate for relief, rushed out of my chest and I blurted out the words:

"Who the fuck is Eric?!"

6

WHO THE FUCK IS ERIC?

In the short span of my life, I can confidently say I'd never been so inappropriate in public. I sure knew how to pick my moment. Not only did Duvo and Michael hear my words, shouted in a broken voice, and glanced at me in shock, but if they heard it, that meant that Alberto did too.

I didn't dare to look in his direction at first. When I finally stole a glance, his cold expression felt to me like an unappealable judgment. I had managed to react more poorly than him despite the fact that he was the one who was actually rejected. But if Alberto was too classy to display his reaction, I, on the other hand, had completely exposed myself.

When people returned to their conversation and noise filled the room once again, Arthur, always genial, squeezed my arm.

"You're gonna play Eric's boyfriend. You're lucky."

"Excuse me?" I blinked fast, trying to gather my thoughts. "Who! Who is Eric?"

Arthur was grinning. "How can you not know Eric? He's even sleeping in our room."

"Huh?"

That… that blond-haired guy?

Turns out, Eric was the imposter who stole Alberto's bed.

And now Alberto's role!

When I slammed my fist on the table, Arthur flinched, slid out of his chair, and ran out of the room as though I'd turned into my sister's dog.

This decision made no sense, no sense at all. How could Alberto fail this audition? How could a football player be better than him? Who was this person, and how could I get rid of him? There was no way I would make out with anyone other than Alberto. No way.

My plan was completely ruined!

"Can we go watch the game now?" Kayvin's voice boomed over the others' chatter.

Duvo waved his hand. "Keep it civil, please, unless France is playing."

While everyone rushed out of the dining room to go watch the World Cup Final — in which France was definitely not playing — I extracted myself from the table with difficulty and hobbled toward Duvauchel. Barely waiting until Michael left the room, I slumped onto his table.

"Sir! You got it all wrong!"

Binta looked sympathetic. "What did we get wrong, Zak?"

I turned around and pointed at the imposters leaving the room. Slapping themselves across the back, Prat — I mean Kayvin — was hugging his friend, who looked almost just as shocked as me. Clearly, he himself didn't even expect to be picked!

"This. These guys. You're not serious, right? They're supposed to be punished. *Punished*."

"Yes."

"Then why am I the one being punished?"

"You?" Binta and Duvauchel exchanged looks. "I don't get it, Zak."

"Why do I have to put up with him? What happened to Alberto?"

"Alberto?" Duvo gave me a funny look. "To be honest, he didn't impress us during his audition. Whereas Eric really gave us something."

How bad was Alberto, that this stranger overshadowed him? Did he accidentally slip on a banana peel or something? Insult Duvo's outdated outfit? How could he not be better than what's-his-face, who didn't even know the script and probably put something together at the last minute?

"Perhaps Alberto was sick. You should give him another chance."

Duvo snorted. "He doesn't want another chance."

"We haven't forgotten Alberto," Binta said with a side-glance at Duvo. "He's got a small part in the film if he wants it."

A small part? For my Alberto?

"I told him he could participate in the making of the movie in any way he wants," Binta added. "He could assist Arthur, for instance. Or Melissa."

"You… spoke to him?"

"I will, if you give me a minute." Duvo was losing patience. "Everyone had the opportunity to audition. Alberto didn't seem motivated. Eric's audition was better. End of story."

I refused to believe such nonsense.

"Don't worry, Zak, Eric's great! You should have seen him. He was so… How do I put it… effortlessly good."

"Effortlessly… good," I repeated in a thick voice.

"Look, Zak." Duvo seemed annoyed now. "It was a democratic decision. We all decided. Camille and Michael chose him too."

Traitors, I thought abruptly, before realising something was really wrong with me. My head felt dizzy.

"So, relax! Why don't you head over there and watch the game with your friends?"

Fuck the game. And fuck democracy! I was tempted to call my sister, who could unleash hell and overthrow this regime in about five minutes. Duvauchel saw violence in my expression and urged me to calm down.

"Fine, don't watch football. Go to bed, then. Tomorrow, rehearsals begin. You want to be an actor, don't you? So do your best, right?"

Binta smiled kindly at me. With a sigh, I dragged myself to the living room where everybody was gathered. Most people were sitting in heaps near the television. Alberto was alone on the side, his eyes riveted to his phone, slurping a soda straight from the can with a straw. I lumbered toward him, desperate to speak to him but unsure of what to say.

"I'm sorry you didn't get the part, Alberto."

Alberto sucked on the straw in an otherworldly way, then slowly raised his eyes to me. "Why?"

I didn't expect him to say that; I hesitated. "I… I think you would have been a great choice."

Alberto stared at me for a long time. I began to feel hot and really self-conscious, my feet itching to take me out of here. When I glanced away in agony, he spoke. "Thank you." His voice was as soft as a kiss. Without another word, he returned the straw to his lips and his eyes to his phone.

Through his silence, I interpreted he was really hurt and didn't want to expand on the subject. I wanted to tell him that I would work diligently to fix this injustice, but I didn't. Instead, I stomped upstairs in search of a true artist.

I found Camille in her room. When I barged in, Nadia, already in bed, shrieked and threw the blanket over herself. Camille was standing in her bra in front of the mirror and stared at me with her mouth wide open. "Oh." Her face relaxed when she recognised me. "It's only Zak." She turned around to fish something out of her suitcase.

Nadia emerged from her blanket, her hair a real mess. "Could you possibly knock next time?"

I raised a fist to my mouth. "Didn't I? I was sure I did."

"You certainly didn't." Nadia was seething.

"I'm so sorry." Averting my eyes, I grabbed the long-sleeved shirt left on the bed and tossed it to Camille. She didn't catch it. "I need to talk to you."

"Well, talk, then."

I pointed at the shirt on the floor. "I can't talk to you when you're like this."

She glanced at my reflection, amused. "When I'm like what? Half-naked? But you barged in!"

"Honestly..." Nadia said. "If it had been anyone else, they'd be dead right now. Well… Except Michael, of course, but—"

"See, you're privileged." Camille nevertheless put on the shirt.

In my impatience, I was certain she meant we were between fellow artists, so I exhaled a sigh of relief and told her of my grievances, how ridiculous all of this was. To my surprise, Camille didn't seem to agree with me. Nadia began to protest, but Camille silenced her with a finger over her mouth and said: "Let me handle the talent."

I glanced over at Nadia haughtily. I was *the talent*.

"Zak. Eric auditioned and was great. He was better than Alberto. Honestly, he floored us all."

"That's impossible. He's a football player. He plays football."

"Plays really well too!" Nadia chimed in, earning herself another glare from *the talent*.

"And he can act. Miracles do happen. He was… How did we put it… Effortlessly good! One can only hope to be a natural like that."

A natural? Oh, so he was a natural now. I dropped on the nearest bed, causing Nadia to hiss at me. Camille gave me a pointed look.

"He's really popular, you know. Everyone loves him and says he's a darling. You're lucky to play his boyfriend."

Okay, this was getting ridiculous.

"He's a thug! And I'll never get along with him! And I can't believe you'd do this, Camille."

"Do what?"

"Sabotage your own text for a popular guy."

I knew I went too far immediately. Camille's eyes darkened; she pointed a fierce finger at the door. "Get out. And think about what you've done."

Before such a display of authority, I could only comply. Nadia kicked me off her bed, almost foaming at the mouth, and Camille slammed the door in my face before I could add another word.

Perhaps I shouldn't have barged into their room like that. I really thought I'd knocked… My attempt was doomed to fail. Who else could help me now?

Remembering something, I retraced my steps in the direction of Michael's room and was about to knock on his door when I heard Alberto's voice up the stairs. Tailed by Sander, as usual, he appeared slightly perkier than before.

"He's not in here," Alberto said when he saw my hand hovering over Michael's door. I stuck my hands in my pockets instead.

"Going to bed already?"

"I don't like football."

Neither did I, Alberto. You and I were soulmates, and if only you knew…

With a sigh, Alberto added, "Duvo said I could do anything I want, you know, to assist the production."

"And?"

"And it's great," he said without enthusiasm. "It will be nice to be behind the camera for once."

I didn't believe this for a second. Perhaps he was deluding himself, like a coping mechanism. He still looked disappointed to me.

"Still," I muttered, "why should you have to step aside for… I mean… Who is this guy anyway?"

Sander, in an uncharacteristic manner, rushed forward. "It's Eric! Eric's awesome!"

Alberto's blue gaze glided over his friend. "Sander likes football."

"Honestly, he's really good!"

I was getting pretty tired of hearing that.

"One day he'll be in Premier League, and we'll all be able to say we shot a movie with him. A gay movie too. You'll be able to say you made out with him."

"There are no making out scenes," I said darkly.

Alberto tilted his head, distracting me.

Sander went on. "And he's dating Elodie, the hottest girl at school!"

"He's dating Elodie?"

Oh, so that's why I thought he looked faintly familiar! He was Elodie's boyfriend. I must have caught a glimpse of him the other day. Haha! Hilarious! A guy so effortlessly great, I'd never even noticed his existence. I would shove that in his face the first chance I'd get.

Sander, his biggest fan, was still talking. "Rumours are he'll go to Harvard after Colette."

"Who would want to go to Harvard?" Alberto said, turning on his heel and disappearing into his room.

I gathered Alberto didn't know anything about Eric either and smiled tenderly at his back.

"Hey, wait, give me your charger first!" Sander went after him into the room and closed the door behind them.

So, Eric played football, was really popular, dated the prettiest girl at school, and was going to Harvard for some reason, probably on account of his athletic prowess. He was a jock. A proper jock. I started to feel like I'd just been transferred to the movie version of an American high school where everyone was wearing either varsity jackets or cheerleading outfits. Where would I fit in there? With the nerds, I guess. Or worse, the glee club.

It was definitive. I couldn't let that happen. There was no way I could ever kiss that guy, let alone pretend I was in love with him.

Thankfully, Michael came upstairs just as I was about to go down in search of him. He glanced wearily around as though he expected some burglar to jump him, then opened his bedroom door with a key. Seeing me hovering outside his room with my face set, he pinched his lips.

"Do you… want to come in?"

"Yes."

I charged inside the room, determined, and sat on his bed. Looking frightened, Michael didn't close the door after us, and moreover, stood as far away from me as possible, making me feel like I'd just been diagnosed with the most terrifying infectious disease.

"What's wrong? Do I scare you or something?"

He smiled, at last, left his awkward post by the door, and sat on the edge of his own bed. "What's up, Zak?"

Michael had a nice face. By that, I meant, he seemed kind, and caring. A nice guy. Someone you could trust, I guess. Trusting people wasn't really my thing, but Yasmine vouched for this guy.

"The casting…"

Michael smiled. "You must be happy."

I slapped my hand on my forehead. It's like no one could understand me. And of course, they couldn't. It was like we were characters from different rom-coms. They were all in love with this guy, while I was the only one fighting for Alberto.

"Actually…" I looked away to avoid Michael's incredulous stare. "I don't understand how you picked this guy, Eric, over Alberto." Crumpling Michael's sheets within my fists, I waited for his answer.

"You wanted Alberto to get the part?"

"Not wanted…" I almost spoke too fast, but I recovered in time. "I thought he should get it. He's the better actor."

I hated to see the small, dubious look on Michael's face. "Eric was better during the audition."

"Alberto was probably nervous."

"Even so, Eric was just better." Something suddenly flashed in Michael's eyes. He edged a little closer. "Zak…"

I shifted away from him. "Perhaps you could talk to Duvauchel for me. He's encouraged Alberto to participate in the movie either way, but I could see that—"

"And then tell Eric what?"

I reacted hotly. "Tell him that he still has football and that he doesn't need to get in on other people's stuff."

Michael frowned. "Really?"

The way he looked at me made me feel really bad about myself. I spoke my next words in a gentler voice. "This is important to me. To… us. People from the Drama Club."

After a short silence, Michael patted my shoulder. "I'm sorry, Zak. There's nothing I can do except reassure you that you shouldn't worry about Eric screwing things up. He was terrific during the audition. In fact, he was—"

I held up my hand to stop him. "Don't say it." Michael gave me a look of surprise. I heaved a sigh. "Don't worry about me. I just thought… I was hoping you'd understand."

"Understand what?"

"Nothing."

Michael slapped his hands together as if in prayer. "Zak… Listen to me. If you really are serious about this movie, then Eric was the better choice. Tomorrow you'll see. He was very pro. And you're a pro, right? There's no reason why it wouldn't work."

These wise but unwelcome words sent a faint shiver down my spine. Michael rose and stood by the door, a silent invitation for me to leave. I had played all my cards, and I had lost. Nothing was left for me but to be forced to perform with Eric the next day. I left without thanking him, absorbed by my own thoughts. When I noticed my mistake, I turned around to apologise, but his door was already closed.

The next morning, I found myself side by side with the football player in the drawing room, my hands clutched behind my back, the tip of my shoe tapping the surface of the ancient wooden floor, waiting for Duvauchel's signal.

Behind me stood Eric, doing god knows what. I was doing my best not to give him any attention and was doing so well, that not only did I not introduce myself to him, but I couldn't describe what he actually looked like, even at gunpoint.

Camille, Duvauchel, and Michael were staring at us, aghast, after our fifth attempt at rehearsing a scene which I was positive I could do with my eyes closed… before Eric was cast.

Interior - Drawing room - Day

Adam meets Thomas for the first time as he cleans around the drawing room. Adam silently goes around the room, unnoticed, while Thomas feels someone is watching him. Eventually, Thomas is aware of Adam but pretends not to notice him.

He knows what his master looks like, the script said.

He knows and he's subtly afraid both to look and to be seen.

On the first take, I did okay. Nothing too terrible. Duvo made idle threats about having me flogged, nothing serious. But the more we tried, the more I felt disoriented, the more Duvo tore at his hair and threatened the lives of my whole family.

"No, no!" Duvo screamed in French after the fourth attempt, crum-

71

pling his script into a ball. "You're supposed to vaguely be aware of his presence, not throw angry looks over your shoulder."

"English, please, Mr Duvauchel," Camille said for the fiftieth time, while Michael was slowly slumping down the wall, a dead look in his eyes.

"Yes, yes," Duvo conceded grudgingly. Then to me, in English: "You're doing everything wrong."

"Yes, well... I'm just... I just want to know where he's standing."

Eric was getting on my nerves, lurking about and chewing gum during rehearsals. What an ass! Even though I had woken up with wishes to act professionally, what I heard over breakfast had sent me in a rage.

Earlier today, and while sitting glued to his side, Joy had asked Eric why he auditioned to play a gay lord, and Eric replied with a wide grin as he peeled a banana: "As a joke."

He said that in a flawless, *don't-mind-me-I'm-an-American* accent.

Of course, he had to be American.

"As a joke?" Joy insisted.

"Yeah, it seemed fun, whatever."

Everybody at his table laughed except for Kayvin, who didn't think playing gay was a joking matter at all, and Alberto, who was staring out the window with a blank expression, forever deprived of being my lover on set.

So funny, haha. Whatevs. Hearing that, I squeezed my muffin until it crumbled in my fist and made myself a promise not to acknowledge him at all. I wouldn't give him the pleasure. Anyway, an hour and a half later, after much effort and another failed rehearsal, Camille approached me, a thin smile on her face.

"Good on you not to look so angry anymore!" She hesitated. "But remember, you do find him attractive, not terrifying." Hearing this, I finally dared a glance at the creature behind me. I saw a pair of loose, grey shorts, a blue T-shirt, and some seriously dirty sneakers, and focused back on Camille. "So please, Zak, can you do that for me?"

I looked down at my feet in silence.

"But..."

I flinched, hearing Eric's voice. Camille tilted her head toward him. "Yes?"

"Doesn't it make sense... that Thomas is afraid of Adam?"

Was his *football-slash-acting-slash-Harvard-alumni* resume not enough for him? He also had a degree in psychology? But Camille approached, pencil balanced on top of her ear. "What do you mean?"

"Thomas is a footman," Eric said. "Adam's his powerful master." I snorted; he ignored me. "Thomas would be uncomfortable around him. After all, he's afraid he's gonna get fired."

"That's true," Camille said, and I reluctantly agreed. "And I thought his reaction, as I wrote it, implied the same thing. He'd definitely be wondering if he's in trouble. But, Zak... I wrote 'subtly' on the script, and you... just now... you acted like you saw a T-Rex in your rearview mirror."

I felt that one deeply.

Duvo nodded. "Can you take it down a notch, buddy?" An amused smile crept over Michael's face, who was standing behind him.

"Sure, sure."

But nothing would do. The next take was also a bust. The blame was still on me. Apparently, I looked repelled, not attracted.

When Xavier came in with a refill of snacks and beverages, Duvo slumped into his makeshift director throne — it was just a chair, really — and called for a break. Everybody in the room sighed in relief. I followed behind them with my head down, longing for iced tea.

"Is the scene wrong after all?" Duvo said, helping himself to a cup of coffee.

Camille changed colours. "Is the scene *what?*"

"The scene isn't wrong," Michael said, with a quick look toward me. "Zak just needs to relax a little."

"Zak!" Duvo turned on his heel. "You need to— ah!" He noticed I was right behind him, put his hand on my shoulder, and sighed. "Relax!"

"I'm fine," I said in a low voice. "Just tell him to stop chewing gum. It's distracting."

"Tell me yourself." Standing behind me, Eric sounded amused.

Camille and Michael's worried looks reminded me of my mother and father's. Eric walked over to the edge of the snack table. From the corner of my eye, I saw him dump his gum in the trashcan. Surprised, I almost looked up to meet his eyes. I pulled myself together and faced the exit instead.

As though things weren't bad enough, Alberto showed up, looking absolutely dashing with his dishevelled hair pulled back. He trotted up to us, the hint of a smile on his face. Had he come here to witness my shame? To my shock, it was in front of me and Michael that he stopped.

"How is it going?"

My heart sank. What could I say? Let's see, Alberto. Personally, I think even the *Titanic* did a better job staying afloat than myself, but how about you? How's your day so far?

Of course, I didn't say that. I just stared at Alberto's face in awe and muttered something insignificant.

"What are you doing here, Alberto?" Duvo asked, looking down at the script. "You're not supposed to be in this scene."

How rude. In my opinion, if Alberto wanted to crash the set, or even set it on fire, he could very well do it every minute of every day.

Alberto threw his head back and spoke in an impassive tone. "I'm to be Michael's assistant."

"Really?" Camille and Michael spoke at the same time.

Alberto gave her a frustrated look. "Duvo said I could do whatever I want. And I want to be here." Our eyes met, and he gave an awkward, almost embarrassed smile that weakened my knees and strengthened my resolve to hate Eric forever.

"Oh, that's nice!" Duvo said, without looking up from his notes. "Michael needs all the help he can get."

I seriously doubted that from the way Michael swallowed and his jaw clenched, but his pleasant demeanour remained the same.

Honestly, I didn't feel too hot about it either. Alberto was to become the witness of all my failures. And he'd have to watch me kiss and touch the one who stole his thunder. I began to feel sick.

I'm no fool. I knew today's failures were all because of me. But how could I help it? Nothing felt right and everything *he* did was rubbing me the wrong way.

A coffee and two failed rehearsals later, Duvo, looking ten years older, ordered another break. Camille had sunk so low in her own chair that her hair had fallen over her eyes, making her look like a revenant. After the next break, Duvo, Camille, and Michael reached a conclusion. They summoned Eric and me with a dejected air.

"This is clearly not working," Duvo said, adding to his words a long dramatic sigh.

I folded my arms over my chest. "I told you the casting was all wrong."

"Eric's fine," Camille said simply. "But—"

"But…"

74

"You're both good actors. But…" Camille looked crestfallen. "Am I the only one who thinks you have no chemistry?"

"Zero," Duvo agreed. "Ze-ro che-mi-stry. Never seen such lack of chemistry since Rachel Green and Ross Geller."

Behind him, Michael and Alberto exchanged a look. I emphasised with a nod, trying not to glance at Alberto. "See? This could have been avoided."

"No. I'm still sure of them," Camille said, sounding *super* unsure.

Then a voice spoke from a corner of the drawing room. "Maybe we should do something else?"

We all turned around, searching for the owner of the voice. It was Xavier, who had managed to remain completely unnoticed this whole time.

Duvo looked about to throw in the towel. "What do you mean?"

Wringing his hands, Xavier approached. "I'm just saying maybe we should do another movie!"

"What's wrong with this one?"

"Let me guess…" Camille began.

Xavier looked at all of us like his point was making a lot of sense: "It's gay! It's offensive!"

Alberto's cool gaze swept over him with indifference. Michael's eyes shut. Duvo slammed his hand against his forehead. "Offensive? Who's offended?"

Facing a lack of enthusiasm from all, Xavier lost some composure. "A lot of people."

"Who, especially?"

"Me, for example. I'm offended. My father is a baronet. When he hears about this, he—"

With a beastly roar, Camille sprung from her seat. "And I'm offended by your dumb face, but I was told to put up with it and I will, so you will put up with our gay film!" Her nostrils were flaring danger-ously. "Maybe we'll both learn something, who knows."

Shock succeeded in making Xavier's face look even dumber. He retreated with his hands held up, his gaze fixed on Camille as though she had just descended from the heavens to smite him.

"Camille, come on," Duvo said mildly. "I can't let you speak to people like that."

"Why? You scream all the time."

"That's because I'm an adult and a teacher. I have all the rights and you have none. That's how it works."

Clicking my tongue with impatience, I turned to Eric, about to tell him to take responsibility for his stupid friend, but he was already pushing him out of the room, so I let it go.

Michael, indifferent to Xavier's outburst, was frowning in the distance, looking thoughtful. He finally spoke. "I think I have an idea." Duvo looked torn between intense gratefulness and jealousy. "I think the problem is that these two don't know each other at all," Michael said. "They should rehearse together, away from everyone else."

"That's a stupid idea," I said, alarmed.

"I'll do it," the football player said behind me.

Camille didn't look convinced. "What? The two of them, without supervision? They might kill each other."

"I don't see how it could hurt," Michael said.

"I don't want to!" I knew how childish I sounded, but I really, really didn't want to spend hours, let alone days, alone with this guy.

Duvo smiled at me. "You can rehearse with this one, or you can ask maintenance for a shovel and go dig your own grave in the backyard. How about that?"

Our teacher had spent too much time with Colette's headmaster and had learned some of his ways. This was totally inappropriate.

Ignoring him, Camille took me aside. "You're going to have to work together," she said in my ear. "This is my movie, and I'm not going to let anyone ruin it for me. I don't understand what you're going through, and if you want to tell me, I'll listen, okay? But why are you acting like this? Why is Eric more professional than you are?"

Camille's words had the effect of a truck crashing at full speed into my ego. I looked into her eyes and only saw my own resentful face reflected in them. She was right. I wasn't being professional at all. In fact, I'd put my anger before my work. It was unacceptable.

"Fine," I said quietly. "I'll do it."

7

CAT FIGHT

The moment we left the drawing room, the football player took charge and led the way outside. The hot sun fell upon me like a curse, and I quickly put my hand up like a visor.

"We should get back inside. It's too hot out here."

From here I could hear people splashing around in the pool and laughter coming from the kitchen. Eric scratched his nose.

"I'd rather be outside."

"Well, I'd rather be inside."

His fingertips twitched, but he didn't seem angry. "If we stay inside, everyone will be able to see us."

"Oh."

That was actually a good point. Sneaking a glance at his face, I caught a blinding flash of hair, pure gold against the azure sky.

"Fine," I said. "But… I can't stay in this heat. I'll die."

Eric bounced on the balls of his feet for a moment, then pointed at a thicket of trees on the side. "Follow me." He marched into the grove with confident steps. When he noticed I wasn't following, he stopped. "Come on. It's really nice, you'll like it."

Not really convinced, I followed nonetheless. Rows of trees sheltered us against the heat as we walked, twigs crunching under our feet. Sunlight filtered through the canopy, falling on colourful patches of wildflowers. Something brushed against my ankle, startling me. Instinctively, I quickened my pace and hid behind his back. Embarrassed he may have noticed, and not quite sure where he was leading us, I tried my luck at small talk the best way I knew how.

By saying weird things in a muttering tone.

"You're not going to murder me, are you?"

Eric chuckled faintly. "Shouldn't I be asking you this?"

Good point.

He wore shorts and didn't flinch when vegetation and bold insects brushed against his shins, while I was cursing every blade of grass or flying monstrosity coming my way. He advanced happily while humming to himself a popular song, something I should have recognised, but didn't.

We walked for less than ten minutes, the birds overhead making conversation for us, when a flash of light forced me to cover my eyes.

"We're here," Eric said.

I removed my hand. The blinding light came from an expanse of water nestled between rows of trees. Reeds and long grasses grew all along the shore, but the surface of the lake itself was clear and reflecting the cloudless sky, glittering like a perfect blue gem cushioned in a bed of lavish green velvet.

Slightly astonished, I left the cover of the grove and walked a few steps toward the bank. Butterflies busied themselves over a rainbow of wildflowers, and the birds hiding in the trees were chirping with vigour. Who knew Longchamps hid such a treasure?

When Eric turned to me, I realised my mouth had fallen open. I turned my head away and coughed in my fist. "How... How did you find this lake?"

Eric approached me. "I just found it."

"When?" I stepped aside. "We've just arrived."

"On the first day." He shrugged. "And anyway, it's a pond."

"Ahem." I cleared my throat. "It's a lake."

"It's a pond."

What was the difference again? I had no clue, but I didn't want to ask him. His assurance was infuriating, however. It could very well be a lake. How did he know for sure? Huffing and puffing, I sat on a patch of fluffy wild grass by the edge of the water and hugged my knees. Eric hovered uncertainly for a while, then pulled a wrinkly set of sheets from his shorts pocket.

"So, where do we start?"

I said nothing and simply stared at the still surface of the lake in great turmoil. I had made such a mess of things this morning that I didn't even know how to act anymore. I could have been done with rehearsals for today and back into my utility room with my book, and now I was stuck with this guy for an entire week. Karma might be a thing, then. Served me right for acting like a fool. But now what? It was really awkward to have this intruder hover behind me. His eagerness started to make me feel uncomfortable. I felt his gaze on me for a long time, then his hand appeared in my field of vision.

"Do you want to do this scene, then?"

I shot a glance at the wrinkled, destroyed copy of the script he pulled from his pocket. What a slob. The front page was missing. He had scribbled notes all over the script as well, but his handwriting was so terrible that I suspected no human being could possibly decipher it.

EXTERIOR- DAY

ADAM CORNERS THOMAS AND THEY SHARE THEIR FIRST CONVERSATION.

THE SUN IS BEATING HARD ON THEM, AND THOMAS IS UNCOMFORTABLE IN HIS LIVERY...

I squinted at it a moment, then lowered my head. Eric retrieved his script. He walked over and stopped in front of me. I saw his legs up close. They were very toned, as expected of a football player I guessed, and covered with a layer of downy blond hair.

Just as I thought he was inappropriate to stand that close, he suddenly crouched in front of me. If I hadn't been so experienced at lowering my gaze ultra-fast, I'd have ended up face to face with him.

"What are you doing?" He sounded amused.

"Just taking a break."

"Ah." He rose and I looked up tentatively, only to meet his knees. But then he squatted again, and I barely looked down in time again. "Are you shy?"

"No."

"You weren't shy back there."

"I'm not shy."

"Then—"

"Give me five minutes, I'm on my break."

My stupid promise to not pay any attention to this guy was proving unfeasible, but now that I'd made a perfect idiot out of myself, I didn't know how to get out of it. If he could give me a few minutes to collect myself, I'd be fine.

"Okay. I'll be over there."

"Yep."

Poring over his script, Eric edged along the *lake* and headed toward where the sun was the brightest. He soon sunk low among the tall grass, disappearing from my view. I immediately fell apart, hiding my face in my hands with a groan.

Camille was right. I was being unprofessional.

I was here. I knew the script backwards. Every one of my lines and his, every movement around the set, every little gesture, even those Camille hadn't thought of yet. But then my plan went out the window, and I couldn't adapt.

This Adam, he didn't look and didn't feel the same as the one in my dreams. His version of Adam would be like a dashing American compared to Alberto's old and romantic Italian sophistication.

What was Alberto going to think of me, however, if I kept acting like a child and flunked this movie because I didn't get what I wanted? Moreover, this project wasn't just a springboard to my future relationship with him. It was supposed to open doors for me. As it stood now, I had little chance of impressing Duvo, let alone the jury of the Cannes Festival.

Perhaps Eric wasn't that bad after all. Perhaps he wasn't as thick as Xavier or as horrible as Kayvin. Perhaps we could actually work together. With a sigh, I opened my backpack and searched for my bottle of water. My fingertips found my iPod. I retrieved it and stuck the earphones in my ears. Five minutes of peace could do me some good. Turning it on, I stretched my neck to get a better look at Eric. He was still hidden, swallowed by wild grass, enjoying an impromptu tan.

How much fun was he having at the present? Rehearsing alone under the oven-like sun, stuck with a sourpuss like me? I bet he regretted his decision to audition already.

The first song coming out of my iPod was awfully vintage and had no business being in there. I skipped it.

Eric hadn't moved. Perhaps he had fallen asleep and would wake up sunburnt. His white face would be flushed, his arms crimson, and his hair almost white. That would mean an impossible job for Joy, our makeup artist. Could Adam even be a red-faced monster? Wouldn't that alone be a reason to cast Alberto back? Alberto, though Italian, never spent too much time in the sun. His pale skin was almost transparent at times.

Another song began playing, a tune I hadn't heard for a long time.

I skipped forward absently, my gaze fixed on the spot where Eric had disappeared. Another sixties song by Zouzou.

Wait, Zouzou?

What the hell was she doing on my iPod? Skipping forward, again and again, I was met by yet again more sixties songs. Brigitte Bardot. Françoise Hardy. Even the king of has-beens Dave was in there, for heaven's sake.

Now alarmed, I looked down at the iPod and could only find the same songs over and over. These were all my mom's favourites, not mine. I used to love them and sing them with her when I was a small kid, forever ago. A closer look confirmed it was indeed my device, but my mom had clearly tampered with it. For some reason, she wanted to put this playlist on my iPod, and as a result, had deleted everything else I had in there. My own music was gone, and all I had left was Dave and Zouzou.

...

And to think there was a time when I thought I was going to enjoy myself at Longchamps. I flung the iPod aside in frustration and slammed my forehead against my knees.

"What are you doing?" Coming from behind me, Eric's voice made me jump in fright.

"Wha—" I clutched my chest. "Did you just sneak up on me?" Bewildered, I glanced back at the spot where I had seen him disappear.

"Not intentionally," Eric said. "I thought you might be ready to rehearse now." He approached the spot where the iPod had landed. "What were you doing?"

"Leave that!"

If a guy like him put his hands on this thing and spoke about it, I'd never outlive it. Alberto didn't need to know that I knew Zouzou's songs. No, no, no.

"That's your iPod." Eric picked it up. "Why would you throw it?"

"Just leave it!" My voice broke in panic.

Eric looked at me, then the iPod, then back at me. "What's this?"

To my horror, we both realised I hadn't successfully turned the damn thing off. Zouzou was still singing, and I could hear it from here. With a childish expression, Eric picked up an earbud and brought it to his ear. It took less than half a second for him to register what the song was. His jaw fell open.

Lunging forward, I tried to recover the iPod. Eric lifted his arm in defence, looking thoroughly entertained. I snatched the iPod from his hand, but by accident, the corner of my watch split the skin on his arm.

"Ouch!"

As he stepped aside with a grimace of pain, I snatched the iPod back. "I told you not to touch it!" I haphazardly shoved the thing in my pocket, trembling all over from anger and embarrassment.

"Sorry," Eric said, clutching his arm and not looking at all sorry.

That was the last straw.

"I'm going back," I said, stomping toward the house.

"What? But what about the scene?"

I threw a look over my shoulder. "Rehearse on your own."

Eric let his arms drop by his sides. The angry-looking mark stretched over his arm like some wild animal had come at him out of nowhere. Unsettled, I picked up the pace and only allowed myself to breathe once I reached the cover of the trees.

Once back inside the house, I paced in my utility room, biting my nails.

Now what? Eric would tell Kayvin, Kayvin would stick my head down the toilet, or… he would tell Duvo that I was impossible to work with, and I might get kicked out of the film. Everything was suddenly too much to bear. With trembling fingers, I pulled out my phone and disturbed my sister.

Yasmine picked up on the third ring and listened in silence, even when I shamelessly brushed over my disproportionate reaction when I found out Alberto had been replaced, both in my bedroom and in the movie, by some popular jock who just wanted to have some fun.

"You should see the scratch that Grandpa's watch left on him."

Yasmine chuckled. "He's been branded, for sure."

"Branded as my enemy." I tried to laugh, but I just coughed instead.

"Where are you now?"

My sister's voice was warm and soothing. For the first time since I arrived, I allowed myself to relax a little. "I'm hiding in some utility room. But, hey! It's got a view of the pool."

"Mmm. I bet you have a nice view."

"Alberto's not around. So no, not really."

On the other end of the line, Yasmine knocked something over and cursed. "Sorry about that. Honestly, Zak, you sound more depressed than angry. What's going on?"

"It's nothing." I pinched the bridge of my nose. "I just wish I hadn't hurt him." I couldn't tell Yasmine I was afraid Kayvin would punch me in the face. I didn't want her to think I was that much of a baby.

"It seems you have it all figured out already."

Sticking my cheek to the window, I saw Alberto approaching the pool, dressed in linen. He looked fantastic. Michael followed him shortly after and Melissa, Joy, and Nadia fought to give him the best seat. He gracefully sat in the middle of them all, causing me to smile.

"Oy!" Yasmine's angry voice brought me back. "You're the one calling me. Can't you listen?"

"Sorry, what?"

"Zakaria."

Oh. She was being serious.

"You acted like an asshole. And you feel bad about it because you know it."

"But he's—"

"Athlete or no athlete, he's your partner throughout this movie, isn't he?"

"I never said he was an athlete." The word athlete automatically conveyed respect. "He's a football player."

"Sorry to burst your bubble, brother, but football players at his level are athletes."

I couldn't help laughing. "What do you know of his level?"

"I googled him."

"You what?"

In surprise, my legs kicked out, slamming into a giant tub of paint.

"Of course I did!" Yasmine said, ignoring my moans of pain. "His club is huge! and he's one of the kids who's expected to have a brilliant career. I have the picture of his team under my nose. What does he look like?"

I tried to recall. "He's got blond hair. And blond legs."

Yasmine laughed. "You're useless."

"Hey!"

"Just treat him with respect. He didn't mean anything by taking the iPod. And he sure didn't mean anything by taking this role." She yawned, distracting me from my thoughts.

"Are you even getting some rest?" I felt ashamed to disturb her with my stupid problems when she was so busy.

"Yes," she said. "Don't worry."

"You're working too much."

"Zak, listen. Don't worry so much, all right? You're in a strange place with people you barely know. It's normal that you act a little crazy. But think about your goals. What do you want the most from this trip?"

Alberto-Alberto-Alberto said a sneaky voice in my heart. Of course, Yasmine couldn't hear that.

"Is it squabbling with your co-star or producing your best work? You'll never see this guy again, but the movie might be an important step for your career. You never know."

As always and even exhausted, Yasmine was right. I let out a deep sigh. "I miss you."

"Baby." She snorted. "Okay, I miss you too. But you can do this. And don't be jealous of him. You're a good actor. Show him how it's done."

"You're right."

"Now…" Yasmine's tone changed. "How's Michael?"

"Michael?" I hadn't given him that much thought. "He's fine, I guess. He's very popular with the girls."

"Tell me about it."

"But Duvo seems to drive him a bit crazy."

"Pff! He's used to it, his boyfriend's the worst."

I smiled behind my phone. "Speaking of, how's Rufus?"

"He's a good boy. Tried to charge at some loser who was catcalling me the other night."

"Watch out, be safe."

Yasmine laughed. "That's exactly what I told the guy. He's probably moved to another planet by now."

My sister had to get back to work, so we hung up. But I remained perched on my shelf, staring outside the window into the pool below. A bell rang, announcing lunch.

Yasmine's words had been a comfort, just as hearing her voice was. But I still came down to the kitchen with my head down, figuring either Camille, Duvo, or Kayvin would bite my head off. When nothing happened, I was a little surprised. I passed Camille as she was getting back from the kitchen with her tray, and when she smiled at me, my shoulders relaxed. My moment of respite wasn't long, however. Lulled by the voices of Joy and Melissa who stood in line behind me, I realised a little late that Eric, Charles-Henry, Kayvin, and Xavier had joined the line as well. They couldn't see me, thanks to Sander standing behind Melissa, but by straining my ears, I could hear them.

They were talking of punching someone. My heart stopped in my chest.

"Just hit him right here, right there."

Kayvin even mock-punched Xavier in the stomach while Eric looked on, biting at his nails.

"No, *you* do the dishes!" Xavier said. I realised they were probably talking about Duvo. Xavier let out a harrowing sigh. "How come we do the dishes while you're having fun all day?"

Eric moved, and I couldn't see his face, but Kayvin's features twisted into a mean smile. "It can't be that fun to spend all your time with those losers."

Xavier guffawed on cue, though his vacant expression turned vaguely concerned as he looked around the room. Meanwhile, Kayvin was still mock-fighting, throwing light punches at Eric to, I assumed, rile him up to do the same.

"Hey," Kayvin said eventually, "what's that on your arm?"

"What's what?"

I held my breath.

"What happened here? Did you get into a cat fight or something?"

Xavier laughed stupidly again. "He—he tried to kiss a girl, and she defended herself."

"Ha-ha," Eric replied in a blank tone.

"Which one did this to you? Which girl?" Xavier asked, the funny frown back on his face.

"What?"

"Which girl?"

I braced myself.

"There's no girl. It was a cat."

"A cat? I don't believe it," Xavier said in a surprising show of intelligence.

I knew all too well that there was no cat. Just me.

"You…" Eric playfully shoved Xavier. "You really think I go around assaulting girls?"

Kayvin punched Xavier much harder in the other shoulder. "You're so fucking dumb." Then he looked at Eric. "But why would you fight with a stupid cat?"

"I didn't mean to fight it, I—"

"You wanted to strangle it or something?"

"No—"

"Anyway, you better sterilise this shit."

There was a silence. Then Melissa poked me in the arm.

"Food's gonna be cold by the time you're done staring at it."

"Sorry!"

It was my turn to pick up food. I hastily threw some mixed salad onto a plate and stepped aside.

Eric lied. He didn't say anything about my rotten behaviour. And more importantly, they believed him. Perhaps he wasn't so bad after all.

When I walked slowly back toward the exit, I noticed Kayvin was staring at Eric with an odd expression. "Remind me why you wanted to do this stupid movie again?"

Eric shrugged, a wide grin on his face. "Didn't want to be stuck doing the chores for two and a half weeks like you two losers."

Kayvin gritted his teeth and punched a laughing Xavier in the shoulder again.

After lunch, I returned to the lake, my hands clutched behind my back, wondering how I'd be received. Eric was already there, his hands on his hips, his shorts slightly askew, staring at me. I still couldn't meet his eyes, so I looked down. His messy script was lying in the dirt at his feet.

Yasmine's words were bouncing around in my head, so were the words I heard him speak back in the kitchen. Should I apologise? I felt it was appropriate. Keeping my head down, I stepped forward and gestured toward his arm.

"Look, about this morning—"

"Should we rehearse?"

I was speechless. Now that I was ready to distribute apologies, he wouldn't even take it? I looked up, only to see a tennis ball flying toward me. It hit me in the chest with a thump.

"Catch!" Eric said.

Furious, I pointed a finger at him. "You're supposed to say 'catch' before you throw the ball, not after!" I kicked the ball toward him. It completely missed him and went rolling toward the trees. "You're the one who plays sports. Aren't you supposed to know these things?"

He went to pick it up. "I thought you saw it coming. You were looking at me."

"Not really, no." I flinched under his mischievous smile. "I hate ball games anyway."

Eric let out a laugh. It sounded like the spontaneous noise a toddler makes when you pull a face. The sudden child-like outburst, unexpected from a guy like him, froze me on the spot.

"What's—What's so funny?"

"Nothing." Eric tossed the ball up and down for a while before sticking it in his pocket. He picked up his wrinkled script. "Good thing we're not here to play ball games, then."

When I snuck another glance at him, his face was hidden behind his script. The mark on his arm flashed red, daring me to be rude again.

"Fine, let's go." I approached him cautiously. "Which scene should we do?"

"Let's do the one where they talk for the first time." Eric lowered his script, prompting me to look down at my shoes. "Don't you need your script?"

"I know my lines."

I expected him to show a little bit of, I don't know, awe or something, but all he said was, "Don't you want to make some notes?"

"Notes?"

"Yeah, notes about the scenes. We can add some stuff, right?"

I let out a dry laugh. "Please call me when you're going to tell Camille that you want to meddle with her script. I want to see her reaction. No, I want to film it, so I can watch it over and over again later."

Eric bounced on his feet as though embarrassed. "I've already asked her, and she's cool with it."

That… didn't sound right and completely threw me off guard. "Wait… Really?"

Camille had clearly fallen for his charms. I'd never speak to her again or welcome her to my table, which I never did, in hindsight.

"Yeah. Small things, of course, but she said we should, I quote, *allow for our chemistry to alter the scenes*. She's funny."

"Haha, yeah, she's hilarious." I forced my face to relax, knowing full well how murderous I could look with my set of eyebrows. "Okay. Let's do this."

And so, we rehearsed.

At the beginning, I was nervous, but I didn't show it. But even confronted with Eric's self-assured demeanour, I held my ground. I plunged into Thomas's boots and performed better than I expected. Eventually, we fell into a precarious rhythm.

Surprisingly, Eric adapted to my style, even when I diverted from the script to size him up. He just followed my lead, smiling pleasantly, as though he was really enjoying his time. His confidence conferred his portrayal of Adam with a sort of endearing insouciance which brought another layer of charm to his character. It didn't take long before I concluded that Eric wasn't a terrible actor, far from it. He was running the lines… effortlessly, just as casually as when he was throwing his ball up in the air and catching it with one hand.

It was maddening.

After a while, we became tired and sat by the bank to drink some water. I felt hollow. Eric was decent, and I was an idiot. I overreacted and prioritised my crush over the movie. I didn't have to like him. But at least I could be a pro and work with him. Unconsciously, I let out a sigh.

"Is something wrong?"

Eric's voice tore me from my thoughts. He finished a whole litre of water in a few gulps and wiped his chin with the back of his hand.

"No," I said in a thin voice.

"You look so serious."

"Well… That's the way I look."

"Like you have a lot on your mind."

"Yes, fine."

"You…"

I raised my voice. "Can you drop it?"

"Okay…" Eric pulled a great chunk of grass and began tossing blades around in silence.

"I'm sorry," I said. "I don't know why I raised my voice."

He shrugged. "I do."

"No, you don't."

Blades of grass flew in every direction. It was like he couldn't keep still for more than a second. I observed his hands while drinking more water. They were large, with long fingers and half-bitten nails, as if he'd just picked up this bad habit recently.

"But I really do," Eric said, unbothered by my tone. "You think I shouldn't have been cast, and you don't want to work with me."

His completely accurate assessment sent me into a fit of coughing, water spraying everywhere. Eric's hand reached toward my back as though wanting to help, but I waved him away.

"See?" Eric sounded amused. "I did pretty well there, didn't I?"

I said nothing, focusing on catching my breath.

"Do you think I'm terrible?" Eric said. "Like, really bad?"

"No, you're not bad." I choked on the words. "… Not bad at all."

"You seem surprised."

I didn't answer.

"You think I'm too dumb to act? Did someone tell you I play football and you just happen to think football players are morons or something?"

Another dart straight into the bullseye. What was with this guy? Could he read thoughts?

Sticking my head between my knees, I let out a nervous laugh. I was partisan of always telling the truth. That was my thing. So… I could save face by not responding, or I could be honest and maybe hurt his feelings.

"So you *do* believe I'm a moron because I play football."

"Honestly… I don't know anything about you."

He gave another burst of child-like laughter. "That's right."

"Why should I?" I said with some pride. "I told you, I don't like ball games. You won't find me in a football stadium. And I don't pay attention to who's popular and who isn't. The only people I know are from class or the Drama Club. You're not in my class. You're not even in my year. And you're not exactly famous for hanging around the Drama Club. Now you appear out of nowhere, and you got the best part without even trying, and it felt like…" I failed to find the right words.

Eric quirked an eyebrow. "Like?"

"You already have your thing. Can't you let us have ours?"

Eric squished the clump of grass in his fist. "Is that what you think?"

I wasn't so sure about what I thought, so I didn't speak. Eric picked up a small rock and tossed it into the lake.

"Charles-Henry does it and no one minds." He sounded frustrated.

"Does what?"

"Football and drama."

"Right." I scratched my chin. "But he's not really good at it."

"He's not great at football either, to be fair."

Eric was silent for a while. When he spoke again, it was in a voice full of childish resentment. "Why can't I have both? I think football is fun. And drama is fun. What's the problem?" He rubbed his hands. Blades of grass and dirt stuck to them, so he wiped them on his shorts.

Come to think of it, so far, he'd displayed none of the obnoxious behaviour I'd expected from him and his friends. After all, one of the reasons why I never noticed him was that he never bullied, insulted, or laughed at anyone in front of me. He'd treated me with respect even when I was acting like an entitled brat earlier and didn't even tell his friends where his scratch came from. Perhaps it was time for me to bury the hatchet and forgive him the irremissible crime of not being Alberto. After all, it wasn't his fault. No one could ever replace Alberto.

"I admit it," I said softly. "I made a mistake."

Eric immediately perked up. "Sorry. I think I misheard that." He put a hand near his ear. "You made what?"

Apparently, he was so good an actor that I'd genuinely fallen into his trap. He wasn't dejected at all! Still, now that I'd started my apology, I couldn't back down. "All right! I said I admit it. I was wrong about you."

Eric did not answer, and I started feeling a little insulted when suddenly his hand appeared in my field of vision. The hand waved, waiting for me to shake it.

"Huh…"

"Last night, in the dining room…" Eric lowered his voice, but it still sounded slightly teasing. "You said *Who the fuck is Eric*, didn't you?"

My heart thumped. "Oh, you heard that. Wonderful."

"Well, Zak…" The hand waved again. "I'm Eric."

My face slowly burning up with shame, I slipped my fingers into his hand. Eric gave it a firm handshake.

"It's so nice to meet you."

There was such candour in his voice. I suddenly wished to see him. Lifting my head a little, I saw a pair of striking blue eyes.

Part Two

'HE'

8

ALL ABOUT BEES

T he next morning, I went back to the lake with my script. I was a
little out of breath. Kayvin had threatened to kick my ass on the
way out, and I escaped by charging straight into the grove. It was not
the first time he'd made threats, but he was getting a little out of
control lately, especially toward Arthur, whom he particularly liked to
terrorise.

Aside from that, even though I initially thought I'd hate being stuck
in the countryside, I was doing better than Kayvin. However, it was
best to stay as far away from him as possible. That Eric, with his easy-
going personality, could be Kayvin's best friend was nothing short of a
mystery. But I'd only known Eric for a day; it wouldn't be right to make
assumptions.

I found him lying leisurely by the shimmering bank. He held in his
hand the same annoying tennis ball and seemed to be humming to
himself. His blond hair under the morning sun made him look like he
was wearing a golden crown. I realised I was feeling a little self-
conscious. It was probably because of what we talked about yesterday. I
wasn't used to having honest conversations with strangers.

A twig snapped under my foot. Eric saw me and scrambled to his
feet. "Nine o'clock sharp! You're very punctual."

"So are you," I said, surprised both by his good mood and his
punctuality. "And you… were already gone when I got up."

"Yeah…" He wiped imaginary dirt from his shorts. "I have to run to stay in shape."

Stay in shape? Oh, right. To play football, I assumed.

"You didn't wait for Charles-Henry. Or the others."

"No chance." He laughed and began playing with his ball. "They don't wake up early enough."

I recalled what Yasmine told me yesterday. Eric wasn't like his other friends, who only played for the Colette football team, or to put it simply, for fun. He actually played for a good club on the side. It probably meant he really had to stay in shape to perform well. Still… What time did he wake up, exactly? He was usually the last to get into bed. Well, it was none of my business, and it didn't matter. I was here to do my job, and now I was committed to doing it well.

We rehearsed all morning. I was getting used to Eric's style and his movements. The way his jaw tensed and his eyes grew serious when he slipped into Adam's shoes, such a contrast to his boisterous ways and fits of laughter in between scenes. And he was getting used to my ways as well. Especially, my surly attitude.

For someone like me, who lived pretty much secluded and enjoyed the quiet and reading books, a few hours around Eric felt like sticking my fingers in an electric plug. After rehearsing for a few hours, I dropped to my knees and wondered how the hell I was still alive. It was noon, and lunch was surely being prepped at the mansion. I was hungry but didn't really want to return there where I'd have to deal with even more people. Eric snatched the bottle of water I had just drank from and slapped his stomach.

"We should get lunch."

Do you actually *read minds? How does this work? How?*

"Give me my bottle back," I wheezed, exhausted. "I just need a minute before heading back."

"I finished it." He tossed it back on my lap — empty — but I was too tired to protest. "We could get lunch and eat it here, next time. We wouldn't have to go back to the house. We could just eat under the tree there. Looks comfy-comfy."

He was a mind reader now, I was sure of it. Hang on. Did the others know that? Was it possible he was so popular because he knew what people thought? The corner of my lip curled up.

"What?" Eric said. "What did I say?"

"Nothing," I spoke in a haughty tone. "But it's nicer inside the house at the moment. It's too hot out here."

Eric linked his fingers behind his head. "I like it here. It's nice. And I bet it's not too hot under the tree."

Truth be told, this place really was nice. But I didn't feel like admitting it and risk facing an onslaught of laughter or I told you so's. "How did you find this place anyway? You didn't say."

"I did. I said I found it."

"Of course you did. But—"

"I'm an explorer." Eric laughed, probably at my annoyed face, unwrapped a stick of gum and offered it to me. I declined with a grimace. Unfazed, he started chewing noisily, a dreamy smile on his face.

"I thought you wanted to get lunch?" I said.

"I wanted something sweet first."

The look on my face made him laugh even louder. I watched him, torn between annoyance and wonder. "Are you always this…"

"This what?"

Exhausting was my first thought.

Yesterday, I thought he was a little intimidated by me, and he acted less manic. Today, his boisterous ways were flattening. But that wouldn't be nice to start a conversation like that. After all, he was merely enjoying himself.

"Like that. You know… Happy."

Eric popped his gum and plopped down next to me, his shorts pockets rattling. Some sugar packets rolled out of the pockets and littered the ground.

"Why shouldn't I be happy?" He bent his head and recovered the fallen packets. The smell of strawberry chewing gum and some peachy shampoo reached my nostrils. "Everything about this place is awesome."

"Oh, really?" That sounded a little extreme to me. Borderline ridiculous, even.

"Yeah."

I tilted my head toward him. He stared back. His eyes were so blue that the cloudless sky above us looked dull in comparison.

"*Really?*" I used a mocking tone.

"You're looking at me like I'm full of shit. It's true. I like everything here. You don't?"

My perplexed face seemed to amuse him to no end. For the purpose of illustrating, I looked around and immediately spotted at least three buzzing creatures a far cry from *awesome*.

"These, for instance."

"What?!" His eyes widened. "Bees? Bees are awesome!"

"No, they're not, they sting. You're gonna tell me these make you happy?"

He nodded enthusiastically. "Yes, they're so cute! They wear little furry pyjamas."

"What?" I thought I misheard at first. "What did you say?"

"Bees wear furry pyjamas." He sounded really convinced too. "You've never noticed?"

"Sure, Eric. Sure."

"That's true. You have to watch closely, though." He lay on his back and waved his hand dismissively. "I'll show you later."

"Absolute nonsense." I felt the corner of my mouth ache and noticed I had been almost smiling against my will. He was watching me, so I focused on something else. "Then, this heat."

"Are you kidding? Summer is the best time of the year. Look how tanned I'm getting already." He extended his white arm under my nose. I tried to ignore the scar left by my watch and pretended to admire his nonexistent tan.

"Impressive."

Eric looked again at his arm, inspecting it with a little grimace. "Don't make fun. I'll get there eventually. My skin doesn't like the sun at first. I just have to keep at it a little longer than most."

"But..." I spoke seriously. "Exposure to the sun will only get you cancer."

Eric scoffed at my pessimism. "But I'll get a tan, first. And..." He shoved his finger under my nose. "I always wear protection."

Shocked at the sudden invasion of my personal space, I slapped his finger away. "Good to know."

"Look." He dug into his pocket and removed a full-size bottle of sunscreen. "SPF 50!"

I stared at the bottle in disbelief. How could that thing fit in his pocket?

"Are you wearing any sunscreen at the moment, Zak?"

I said nothing because I wasn't. But I was always doing my best to stay away from the scorching ball of fire hanging in the sky, while he was always looking for the sunniest spot.

"You're not, I knew it. Who's gonna get cancer, then?"

"Definitely me. Of my ears. If you don't stop talking."

But he laughed and went on, even going as far as sitting closer. "You don't even bother with sunglasses."

"Neither do you," I protested.

"I forgot mine at home."

"I don't have any. My sister gave me hers, but I never wear them."

Eric cocked his head. "Then you should lend them to me."

"Why?"

"Because your eyes are fine, but mine aren't. Look." He opened his eyes wide. The sight of the glittery gemstones made me blink harder than if I'd stared directly at the sun. "It hurts!" He rubbed them harshly.

"Fine!" I flinched away from him and his eyeballs. "You can borrow them as long as you promise never to do that again."

Eric pouted and returned to chewing his gum, humming absently. He was reminding me of Rufus when Yasmine got him. Four flailing limbs, all enthusiasm and no tact, and a very basic understanding of things. I could very well imagine Eric bounding down the stairs with his tongue lolling out for some reason.

"So that's why you're happy," I said. "Bees and a bit of sunshine. You're low maintenance at least."

He sniggered. "Wait till you see their little furry pyjamas."

He was messing with me again. "Bees don't wear pyjamas! I think you should also get a hat because the sun's been beating down on your head too hard."

"I'll show you one day, and you'll never be able to un-see it."

"Stop messing with me."

"I'm not! It's true."

"You're impossible."

Eric observed my face for traces of actual anger and saw me struggling not to smile, so he looked away with a satisfied smirk. It was a moment before he spoke again. "I'm happy to be on holiday in this cool place and meet some nice people too."

When I thought of whom he was considering nice people, like his shit friend Kayvin, I couldn't help laughing.

"What, what did I say?"

"Nice people. Okay."

"All right, so you don't like cool places or nice people either."

I snorted at my own moodiness. "Apparently not. I'm hopeless."

"Oh!" He punched his own knee. "I know something that makes us both happy!"

I watched him, curious. Was he dreaming of getting an Oscar for *Best Actor* too? Because we had literally nothing in common outside of a knack for acting.

Eric knelt on the grass and began pulling items out of his shorts pockets. There was a lot going on in there: the tennis ball, bottle of sunscreen — how? — a half-eaten lollipop, the old, crumpled sheet of paper scribbled with the messiest handwriting I'd ever seen which used to be Camille's script, a dozen small sugar packets, and a *whole* chocolate muffin still wrapped in plastic.

"You have really deep pockets," I said, amazed.

Eric turned to me, beaming. "Thanks!" He finally pulled out an iPod, *my* iPod, and stuck it under my nose. I was sure I had put it in my pocket after our scuffle yesterday and stared at it in wonder. "You dropped this." He tried to push it into my hands.

"Hm." I gingerly held it between two fingers. It was way too warm to the touch, being nestled into his pocket for so long. But thanks to my acting skills, I refrained from looking absolutely disgusted. "Thanks, I suppose."

Eric resumed his seat next to me, a little too close to my taste. I pretended not to notice but edged away from him.

"So," he said, getting even closer, "I listened to it."

I looked at him in horror. "What?! Why?"

His eyes bore into mine earnestly. "You know, when I picked it up—"

"Yes."

"— and this song was playing—"

"Yes."

"— and you freaked out, out of nowhere—"

"Yes! Whatever."

"Well, I liked it, so I listened to the whole thing, and there are some serious gems in there."

"You're messing with me, right?"

He shook his head. "Nope."

"This is, ahem… my mom's iPod. She switched it with mine by mistake."

"Oh." Eric looked disappointed. "I thought it was yours."

"It's not."

"Because it's written *Property of Zakaria Khoutifa* on the back."

I gulped audibly. "It used to be mine. My mother writes my name down everywhere."

Remember that time I said I wasn't a liar? Well, dump that out the window. I was just as shameless as the rest of humanity, it's just that I'd yet to learn it.

The disappointed look was wiped off Eric's face and replaced with the usual smile. "My mother used to do the same. She was sewing my name on my football clothes when I was a kid. I had to beg her to stop eventually."

I gave a nervous laugh. My mother was the same.

"Anyway," Eric said. "Tell your mom she's got good taste. And that I wouldn't mind listening to these again."

"You're serious?"

"Yes. I liked it." With a playful grin, he dug his elbow into my rib. "It was fun!"

I wriggled out of his reach. Eric's smile widened. "You're so shy." His hand moved toward my waist, either to pinch or tickle me.

"I'm not shy," I said, glaring at his fingers until they withdrew out of sight.

"Sorry. You're angry."

"I'm not! It's just my face. I have expressive eyebrows."

Eric became somewhat serious after that and watched me wrap the cable of the earphones around the iPod murderously.

"And I can't believe you took my iP—my mom's iPod!"

"I meant to give it back! I just forgot how long it was in my pocket."

"Well, lucky for you. Because I sure won't."

"See? You're angry."

"I'm not angry," I said in a cold tone. "You don't know me at all, so stop making assumptions."

Eric hugged his knees and rested his chin on top of them. I could see he was throwing looks in my direction, about to ask something. I felt agitated and didn't know why. I thought of going back into the house where it was cooler, but I didn't move.

In truth, I was annoyed that he saw me as a shy or angry person, but I didn't know how to defend myself.

Because I felt he was right.

"What are you, then?" Eric asked eventually.

"What?"

"You're right, I don't know you. You said you're not shy, and you're not angry, so what are you?"

I found the question preposterous in its intimacy. Any attempt by people to get to know me always profoundly disturbed me. As though we were playing Operation and I was the one on the slab, making all sorts of wrong sounds as they poked me with laughing faces.

I hesitated. Eric pouted and shook his head. "Uh uh. You don't get to do that. I told you things about me."

"When?"

"Yesterday! And, like, two minutes ago, not even!"

"Excuse me? You told me nothing. Nothing important anyway."

"Ouch." He turned his head away. I thought I vexed him, so I spoke in a gentle tone.

"Sorry, Eric. I don't do well with——"

His head snapped back, his blue eyes twinkling. "Conversations?"

"Yes, and——"

"People!"

"Especially those who interrupt me all the time."

He rubbed his neck. "I'm sorry, I just get excited about things."

"Yeah, I saw that… Bees, really?"

"Bees are awesome!"

I added nothing, thinking he would drop it, but this was a guy who wasn't in the habit of dropping anything.

"So? What are you? If you don't tell me, I'll stick to shy and angry." I gave him a good glare, and he started laughing. "Fine. We should return to the house. I'm starving."

Eric didn't look too disappointed. He got up and weirdly extended his hand to me. I wasn't so helpless as to need help getting up, thank you very much, so I got up by myself. At first, I thought he was a bit weird, but I tried to put myself in his football player shoes. In the rare games I'd seen, players often picked up their mates when they were laying flat and faking death on the field, or even when they were actually wounded. In his eyes, it was probably a nice thing to do.

The next day, I had to shoot some scenes on my own in the morning, so I didn't see Eric at all, and he wasn't with his horrid friends at lunch, so I headed to the lake with sandwiches, thinking I'd find him there.

Something buzzed behind my ear, and I swatted it away. I strolled into the grove, humming to myself. My scenes went really well. They were shot quickly and without Duvo barking at a nonplussed Michael. Everyone was pleased — and to be honest, a little relieved. On top of that, I was practically sure that Alberto smiled at me this morning.

Perhaps I was reading too much into it, but he saw me through the window when I left the house, and the corner of his mouth curled up. In any case, I was pleased.

Besides, though I'd never seriously considered getting close to Eric, I liked my times with him more than I expected. He was amusing even though he was exhausting, and I had to watch out for his hands at all times, or they'd end up trying to ruffle my hair or tickle my waist. Despite that, I was not too displeased with the situation. He was serious enough during rehearsals. And to my surprise, he never complained. He didn't seem to mind that I didn't talk to him between sessions, that I frowned a lot for no reason, that I called him out on his nonsense every time I did open my mouth, or that I didn't believe bees were wearing pyjamas or that the lake was a pond. He just couldn't care less about anything.

I finally made it to the clearing. Bathing in a spot of warm sunlight, Eric was lying on his belly with his eyes closed, his head bobbing up and down, an iPod resting by his hand.

My iPod, resting by his hand.

Instinctively, I slapped my hands on my pockets. How did that scoundrel get his hands on it since he gave it back yesterday? I must have dropped it again. My pockets weren't as deep as his, clearly. I approached Eric and nudged him with the tip of my foot. His face brightened when he saw me.

"Zak! You're back."

"Guess what?" I folded my arms over my chest with a proud smirk. "I'm officially in love with you!"

Ecstatic, he got to his feet. "Really?"

I couldn't help smiling this time. "Yes, I'm done with all my scenes. What have you done all morning? Aside from stealing my stuff again."

I attempted to snatch the iPod, but he closed his fist on it and moved aside. "I practised on my own. Made some notes."

"You and your notes!" I gave up on the iPod with a sigh. "So, let's hear it. What are they?"

Eric put on a thoughtful expression. "We should add a kissing scene."

"What? No! Why?"

That idea was mine, mine! But things were different now. At the time, I naturally wanted to kiss Alberto. But now that I had been cold-showered, of course, I thought adding an extra kissing scene was preposterous. The chaste little kiss Camille had written for the end of the movie was more than enough.

"Why not?"

His tone was suspicious. What if he thought I was some kind of homophobe? I had to find a good excuse.

"Clearly… It's too cheap."

Eric scratched his forehead, a slight frown on his face. "No, I think they should kiss. This looks like the person who wrote this has never been in love."

"Do not, and I emphasise that, do not ever tell her that."

Eric gave me a half-smile before turning serious. "Honestly, Zak. They're supposed to be in love and they're not even kissing. Who's gonna believe they're in love, then? She even wrote that passion is spilling over in one of the later scenes. Passion! Look, Adam here…" He pulled his derelict script from his pocket. Curious, I walked over to his side. "Look. This. *Adam obsesses over what he cannot have.* She wrote that, but the guy does nothing. Then, when he finally corners him, she wrote *passion spills over.* And yet there's no kiss. Have you ever been obsessed with something you can't have? The moment you get your hands on them, you're not going to lock yourself into a staring contest, trust me."

Our eyes met. I immediately looked away. "Okay, you have a point. But Camille wrote it this way for a reason. It's our job to portray passion without kissing."

My own shamelessness made my face burn. I was there, trying to convince Eric to keep the passion to a minimum when I myself obsessed about Alberto and imagined thirty different ways I'd kiss him given the chance.

Hopeless.

But in regards to the movie, there was actually a reason why Camille wrote it chaste. Without my desire to kiss Alberto, I really could see her point. I explained it to Eric patiently. "It's all about Thomas. In that case. Adam might want to kiss him, but Thomas would never do it. He's not as passionate nor as daring as Adam. He's frightened. At this point in the movie, he would never do it."

"Is that so?" Eric stared at me, an amused look on his face. "I'll simply tell Camille you don't want to kiss me."

I snorted all over his script. He clutched it to his chest, his lips pursed.

"Go ahead," I said, "and I'll tell her what you did to her script."

"Uh oh." Eric shoved the whole thing into his nonsensical pocket. "You're tougher than you look."

"You have no idea."

He pretended well to look impressed by me. Since the matter of the extra kissing scene was settled, I figured it was time for lunch. I gave Eric a club sandwich and began eating mine quietly, my thoughts agreeably drifting toward Alberto and the almost-smile we shared this morning.

Eric didn't enjoy this moment of silence, and after a few minutes, decided to break it. "So, were you amazing during those takes without me?"

"Yesh," I said through a bite of sandwich.

"So I have to be double-amazing, then."

"Yesh."

"I'll do it!" He slammed his hand on my shoulder. My knees buckled, and I dropped my food. "Oh no! Sorry, Zak."

Eric picked up my sandwich and put in it my hands, pretending not to notice my skewering glare. I wasn't really mad at him. More at myself after my confident outburst earlier. I wasn't, in fact, tougher than I looked. He was the opposite. Whatever he packed under his shapeless clothes wasn't what I'd expect from a football player. Aren't they supposed to have strong legs, not strong arms? Do they exercise every part of their body? What do I know?

Eric had already moved on to something else, his finger on his lip, seemingly staring straight at the sun. "I was thinking…"

Rubbing my knee, I looked up. "Did it hurt?"

"Huh?"

"Nothing."

His narrowed eyes bored into me, and I couldn't help turning away. Eric explained to me that he had an idea about an earlier scene. Since it didn't involve kissing, I played along, and he was right. His suggestion was an improvement. He made me realise I didn't have many suggestions myself. In addition, mine were small and not nearly as bold as his.

I always thought it wasn't really my place to question the script. But Eric didn't care. After all, he was doing it for fun. He saw this as an amusing activity to kill time during the summer, something he wanted to be good at, but mostly something to entertain himself with. The fact that he thought running around the countryside and kissing boys in front of a camera was the funniest thing was a little baffling to me. But after a few days in his company, I was completely resigned to the fact that he was my opposite in everything, and I shouldn't question anything too much because I would simply not get it.

At the end of the day, I watched him drink another litre of water in one go with astonishment. Eric didn't notice, clearly lost in thought. A little part of me warmed up at the sight.

"What is it?" I asked tentatively. "Do you have more notes?"

"More like…" Eric cocked his head. "A suggestion."

"Tell me."

He beamed. "Come to campfire tonight?"

Campfire was everyone's favourite activity after dinner. They lit up the circular gas fireplace which we called the fire pit located near the pool and sat around the flames to sing "Kumbaya" and probably braid each other's hair. Meanwhile, I was in bed with my book, lulled by the sound of their distant laughter, recuperating from a whole day of… Eric.

Did he really think I'd come down after dinner and let myself be trapped between him and his awful friends, a breath away from Kayvin's vicious glares? He couldn't be serious.

"That's a no."

"But why?"

I briefly thought of an excuse. I couldn't come up with anything else than *I hate your friends*. "I need my beauty sleep."

Eric laughed. "You're like that guy. He's always sleeping too."

I raised an eyebrow. "Who's that?"

"That Italian guy. He always goes to bed right after you. Always. Like clockwork."

My eyes widened. "Alberto?"

Eric's words lit a fire in my chest. Alberto was like me? So people were noticing our similarities after all! I didn't realise how wide my smile was until I saw Eric was staring at me.

"Yeah, that guy. You're the same."

I tried really hard not to laugh sneakily into my hands.

"So," Eric said. "Are you coming tonight or not?"

"No!"

He wrinkled his nose, clearly displeased. "Seriously, why don't you hang out with people?" He sounded impatient. "Just for a little bit. Won't kill you to have a little fun."

I turned my head away.

"I don't get it," he muttered.

"That's the thing. You don't get it. That's all. I prefer to be alone."
With a sigh, I rubbed my temple. "This… this is work to me. I want to
relax after work. I wouldn't be able to relax around your friends."

A frown appeared on Eric's face. "What's wrong with my friends?"

How did I get myself entangled in this unpleasant conversation? I'd
rather go back to negotiating a kissing scene. Wait, hang on, scratch
that. I'd rather get back to bed. Could he really not be aware of how
many of us disliked Kayvin?

My arms dropped to my sides. "Sorry, Eric… But are you really
that clueless, or are you just pretending?"

His expression crumpled. "Okay, okay. Fine."

Eric didn't insist. Nor did he speak to me for the rest of the evening.
After dinner, just like always, the others gathered together outside, and
I climbed up the stairs toward my room. But this time, stretching my
ears, I waited patiently and indeed, not ten minutes after I got into bed,
I heard shuffling footsteps down the corridor.

It made me feel warm inside to think it was most likely Alberto.

9

GRAB ANYTHING

The next morning, Arthur sat down next to me, grinning from ear to ear.

"Morning, Zak!" He took one look at my face and shrunk back in horror. "You... hum... did you sleep well?"

"Not really."

"What's on your mind?"

In truth... I tossed around in bed half the night wondering the same thing. Eventually, I came to the conclusion that I may have taken it a little too far with Eric. Perhaps he was one of those guys who was fiercely loyal to their friends, and my comment must have vexed him. If only I had explained to him that he seemed all right, but his friends... not so much. If only... if only... I had the social skills required to explain instead of putting up walls and pushing people away.

If Eric was a friendly puppy, I was a feral racoon. Possibly with rabies.

"Nothing, Arthur," I said quietly. "Everything's fine."

Eric only meant to make me feel included. It was nice of him. But after years spent by myself, I wasn't sure I was able to make sense of what people wanted. That was another reason why I was drawn to Alberto, who was known to be a person of few words.

Kayvin and Xavier walked by our table, and naturally, I tensed, but Arthur didn't turn white as a sheet this time. And Kayvin went by him without even a look.

"Seems he's gotten over you," I said, surprised.

Arthur plunged his spoon into his bowl of cereals with a smile. "Eric told him not to fuck with me anymore."

"What?"

"Yeah, he saw Kayvin messing around with me last night. He went up to us and told him to leave me alone. I thought Kayvin would at least defend himself, but no. He just looked like Eric had come from outer space and he left. That was awesome."

So, Eric had finally realised his friend was a nasty piece of work. It was about time. For a second, I wondered if I wasn't partly responsible for this change, then I berated myself for my presumption.

"Anyway, Eric is the best," Arthur said with gleaming eyes. "I might have accidentally fallen in love with him."

Camille was just on her way to our table when she heard him. She stopped in her tracks. "With whom?"

Arthur's face turned crimson. He glanced at me for support. I nodded.

"With Eric," I said.

Arthur kicked me under the table. But Camille didn't seem remotely surprised. She sat down — uninvited — with a longing sigh.

"Oh, yes… We're all head over heels among the girls as well." Noting my lack of reaction, she cocked an eyebrow and added, "By the way, how are you getting on with him?"

"We're okay."

She and Arthur exchanged a glance. "Do… you like Eric?"

"He's okay."

"Oh. Great. Not enthusiastic, but fair enough."

"Okay's better than nothing," Arthur said.

Watching them, I was actually entertained. Pleased, even. Everybody falling for Eric when Alberto was living and sleeping under the same roof was extremely amusing to me. It meant the whole competition was wiped away, and I had Alberto all to myself.

And summer was agreeing with Alberto. The sun had left a kiss on his pale skin, and he looked even better. Spending so much time working on the set with Michael had made him a little more animated as well. They were rarely seen without each other, and twice this week, I saw him casting Michael an actual smile.

Thinking of Alberto usually lifted my spirits. Now I was eager to find Eric and determined to be extra nice to him since he defended

Arthur last night. I finished my breakfast in record time, Arthur and Camille's dumbfounded eyes staring at my back as I walked away.

I found Eric throwing his other best friend the tennis ball up in the air halfway through the grove. The skin on his arms was still hesitating between surrendering to a tan or burning altogether. Since I hadn't seen him all morning, I was a little worried he would act cold toward me. But the moment he saw me, he gave me a bright smile.

"I was starting to believe you wouldn't come. That I'd done something wrong."

I looked at my watch. "I'm sorry. I didn't mean to."

Out of the blue, Eric crossed the distance between us and seized my wrist. "Oh look, that's the thing that got me!" He was talking about my watch. With a little laugh, he brushed his finger along the glass panel. "So, you still wear one of these."

I tore free from his not-so-surprisingly strong grip. "Nothing special about that."

"It looks old too."

"It was my grandfather's." His laughter deepened. I was confused. "What's so funny? That I care about family?"

"No! Nothing like that." Eric waved his hands in front of my face. "It's just... Between that, and the music, and your habits... also your attitude..."

I began sensing where this was going. "What's your point?"

My severe look only enlarged his smile. "You're like an old... soul."

"You mean an old man!"

"No," he said, clearly trying to hold back a laugh.

He did. He meant an old man. Plain as day. Of course, he would think that. Even my own sister thought that. It was true! It never used to bother me before, but now that Eric was mentioning it, I felt embarrassed for the first time.

"I know how to have fun, you know." My voice came out sounding a little weaker than I'd liked.

"Yeah, yeah, I'm sure."

"I do!"

Eric began throwing his ball up and down, a smug look on his face. "Let's hear it, then. What do you do for fun?"

"I read and I watch movies," I said proudly, thinking of the thrills I got when I read the first chapters of *The Ladies' Paradise* and discovered Denise had a disastrous crush on her inaccessible boss.

"Oh." Eric kept his eyes on his ball. "You go to the movies often?"

"No." I dipped my head. "I don't really like being around people."

"So much fun indeed."

"Not seeing people *is* my idea of fun. Okay?"

"Okay, old man." Ignoring my furious expression, he threw his ball higher in the air, twirled around, and caught it with one hand. "What sorta books do you read?"

"Nothing you'd know."

My thoughts somehow rushed to the collection of smutty mangas hidden under my bed, when it wasn't what I'd meant at all.

"Why?" Eric asked. "Do you assume I don't read?"

"Do you?"

He looked at me instead of his ball and missed the catch. The ball sank into the plush grass. Eric retrieved it with a frown.

"No. Not really. But I know some books, come on."

"Not the ones I read, I assume."

"You mean like the one on your nightstand?"

I snorted. "How do you know what I have on my nightstand?"

"We sleep in the same room. Anyone can see it." Eric took on a sly air. "I've seen it, and I can definitely tell you it's an old man's book. In fact, even old men would rather watch football than read this b—"

"Speaking of!" I rudely interrupted. Eric had managed to convince even me that I was, in fact, an old fart. At the ripe age of sixteen, I was anxious to lead the conversation elsewhere. "What's the deal with you and sleep? You're not around when I fall asleep, and you've already gone every time I wake up."

"I told you, I exercise." He ran in place as he spoke. "Do you ever listen to me?"

"No no, I heard you the first time. I'm just surprised. Do you exercise at night too?"

His expression turned a little mysterious. I could see he enjoyed the attention. He was one of those people. As expected of the most popular guy at school.

"At night," he said in a playful voice, "I sit around the fire with the others while you read like an old man… Oops. An old soul."

I squinted suspiciously at him. "But you always get to bed after the others. I've noticed."

Eric threw the ball really high. When he caught it, he buried it in his pocket. "You've noticed that, huh?"

Crossing my arms, I nodded severely, expecting him to explain his behaviour, but he didn't. Such a frustrating person to talk to at times.

Then I remembered that I had decided to give him a break, so I let it go.

Eric and I rehearsed all morning. Even though it went well, and he didn't even bring up adding a kissing scene for once, I was a little distracted. I couldn't stop thinking of what he did for Arthur, and if maybe, maybe, I didn't have a part of responsibility in this, even a tiny one. So, when we were walking back toward the house for lunch, I couldn't contain myself anymore and spoke up.

"Arthur told me what you did last night."

"Awesome!" Eric said. "What did I do again?"

My eyes rolled up to the sky inwardly. "You know. Telling Kayvin to leave him alone."

"Oh." Eric became uncharacteristically serious. "I didn't really know, you see."

We stopped in the middle of the grove.

"Know what?"

"How bad he was."

"You've never noticed Kayvin is really nasty?"

Eric gave an awkward shrug. "Not really. I mean, of course, he's a bit rough, you know. I got used to it with time. But he's not like that with me! He's a different person when I'm around. Not that I…"

"That you what?"

"Nothing." His expression twisted. "Last night, I observed him, and I noticed he was mean to your friend. You were right, I was clueless. So, I fixed it."

I said nothing; he avoided my gaze. We stood like that for a while. But that wasn't what was supposed to happen! When I started this conversation, I had the best of intentions, and now he looked completely depressed.

Well done Zakaria, you old man.

"We… ahem… We should get lunch."

Eric gave me a sheepish look. "So, you're not mad at me anymore?"

I stared back. "I wasn't mad at you."

"You sounded mad."

"I'm sorry. But I really wasn't."

"I'm glad!" Just like that, his whole face transformed, as if someone switched a light inside. "Because I wanted to show you something, and we don't have all day." Out of nowhere, he tried to take my arm. I jumped aside. "Come on." He gestured for me to follow him. "Let's go."

"Go? Where?" I trotted after him anyway. Without stopping, he produced a set of keys and shook them teasingly. "You're impossible," I muttered. But, my curiosity piqued, I followed in silence. Eric led me back toward the mansion at first but avoided the main house and circled around toward an old stone barn. He strolled in through the open door as if he owned the place.

The barn was clearly used as a storage facility of sorts. There was farming equipment and diverse gardening tools stacked around the place. The walls were lined with old wooden planks used as shelves for a jumble of old broken things, cans of paint, and bags of pesticides. It smelled of dust and fertiliser, so much so that I sneezed when we got in. Unfazed, Eric stopped in front of a battered scooter.

"Ta-da!" He stretched his hands toward the machine.

I blinked several times. "Can I be confused? Or is that too much of an old man's behaviour for you?"

"You can, but I'll explain."

He swung a leg over the seat, made himself comfortable, and patted the space behind him. "Hop on."

"No." He made a scrunched-up face; I replied with a haughty look. "Not before you explain."

Eric's eyebrows rose in impatience, but his grin never faded. "So Old Rich is the maintenance guy around here, right? He and his wife, Janine, they live in one of the dependencies, you know? The one with the vines." He looked at me as if I had any idea who Old Rich was and which house he was talking about. "His wife doesn't let him have sugar in his coffee." A cute frown momentarily twisted his features. "Or at all, for that matter."

"Oh."

Some things started to make sense.

"I told him I would give him ten packets of sweet-sweet diabetes if he let me drive his scooter to town. He asked for fifty. He's a tough negotiator, Old Rich."

My mouth gradually fell open.

"Then we settled for twenty-five and four chocolate muffins. Since I don't drink sugar in my coffee, and I don't eat chocolate muffins, because…" He pointed at his abdomen as though that was explanatory enough. "I had to be careful not to get busted stealing twenty-five packets of sugar and four muffins from our supplies, right?"

I nodded absently.

"So, it took a few days, and one little lie to Charles-Henry, who basically lives in the kitchen, and also hiding from that Nadia girl who's a zero-nonsense sort of person."

"She is…"

"Anyway, I finally got the count, gave my bounty to Old Rich, and he gave me the key to his scooter." Eric flicked his index finger, beckoning me closer. "Now we can ride to the village. So, let's go."

"But…" I said, feeling he had omitted something of importance here. "… Why?"

"Why?" He snorted as though I'd just asked the stupidest question. "Because it's fun!"

I stood rooted to the spot, too bewildered to move. Eric was insane. Befriending old men behind people's backs and… what… was that technically a kidnapping? I'd never been kidnapped before. I guess it would be if he took me against my will… I shooed that idea away.

"What about rehearsals?"

"Never mind that." He waved his hand. "We'll rehearse this afternoon. We're just going to the village, not to Mars."

"But…" I wrung my hands together. "What if we're caught?"

"Caught for what? It's not like we're in prison here." When I said nothing, he began laughing mercilessly. "Did you think we were in prison?"

"No!" I said, feeling stupid.

I didn't know what else to say. I had run out of arguments.

"Hop on!" Eric began drumming his fingers on the handlebars. "I'll be careful, I promise."

I didn't know why I was finding it difficult to just say no. I'd never been offered a ride on a scooter before. By a guy. I mean, a person. Any person. And I'd wondered before how it would feel to have the wind in my hair. Noticing my hand had already moved to rest on the seat, I removed it quickly. Eric saw that and smirked.

"Don't be an old man. No one cares what we're doing all day as long as we can do our job when we're asked. Trust me, I know." Eric bounced on his seat. "Come oooon!"

The cogs in my brains started working feverishly. Then they stopped altogether, and I let out a sigh. "Okay."

Eric made a victory fist and handed me a helmet which probably dated the Vietnam war.

"There's only one helmet."

"Put it on, put it on," Eric said, pushing it into my stomach.

"But what about you?"

He slapped on a pink bicycle helmet on top of his head, grinning. "Courtesy of Janine. I'm already in trouble, so a little more, or a little less…"

I had barely secured the helmet under my chin that he started the scooter. Only then I realised what he had just said. "Trouble? What trouble?"

"And we're off!"

The old scooter roared and lurched forward, but after a few meters, it stopped abruptly. I almost fell over. "Shit!"

A wave of Eric's child-like laughter assaulted me. "So, you *can* swear."

"Of course, I can!" *Dickhead*. "What's wrong with you! You almost killed me."

"Sorry, sorry. I had forgotten something."

He removed a small portable speaker from his enormous pocket and handed it to me.

"What am I supposed to do with that?"

"Play your music."

"My music?"

"I mean, your mom's music." He ostensibly pronounced "mom" to let me know what he thought of it.

I gave a dry chuckle. "You're crazy. I won't. I can't anyway. I haven't got the iPod with me."

Eric immediately took it out of his other pocket.

"How! What the—"

"Don't be mad. I found it on your nightstand and—"

"And you thought you'd just steal it."

"I thought it would be better to take it and use it than leave it to gather dust in your room."

"Right…" I felt that comment deeply. "And you want me to play that while you're driving?"

"Yes, yes, play that Harley Davidson one. And we'll pretend we're riding one. It's gonna be fun."

With a groan, I did as I was told, knowing better than to argue with him for hours while we were sitting in this awkward position.

"It's like you had planned for this," I commented as I turned on the speaker. Eric didn't reply. The moment the song began, we lurched forward again. "What am I supposed to hold on to?" I asked in a panic, sticking the speaker dangerously close to my crotch.

Eric shrugged. "Just grab anything."

Easy for him to say, whose fingertips always twitched in search of someone to tickle and torment. Gingerly, I put my hands on his waist. It felt hard and narrow and way too warm, so I gripped the fabric of his shirt for safety.

We drove past an old man with a wrinkly brown face on the way out. Eric waved at him excitedly. "Thanks, man!"

Old Rich, a limp cigarette hanging from his lips, waved right back at us.

"I hope all that sugar you gave him won't kill him," I said in a reproachful tone.

"What? I can't hear you at all!"

I knew he was lying because he laughed anyway.

The drive really was sort of fun. We bumped and lurched along a thin country road, Brigitte Bardot's rebellious voice reaching out to us through the speakers. Eric's shirt felt slightly damp in my hands. The wind did run through my hair, but not much since unfortunately, the scooter was probably closer to Bardot's age than my own and was getting near the end of its life.

On the way to Aurons, we only met two cars, but it was enough to drive Eric wild with delight. Like a maniac, he honked at them and waved at them as though they were old friends. The drivers stared at us bewildered, probably wondering if some unknown ruffian had stolen Old Rich's scooter.

"I guess scooters make you happy too, then…" I mumbled.

"I can't hear you, what?"

I didn't repeat my words, since they were meant only for myself.

On our journey, I discovered something Eric was terrible at: Singing. But what he lacked in talent, he made up for in enthusiasm. Singing his heart out, he happily butchered Bardot, and I laughed as I gazed up at a smiling blue sky. As this happened, I noticed Eric's French was much better than his singing. So good, in fact, that I couldn't hear an accent at all. I made a mental note to ask him about that later.

It took us about twenty minutes of country road on this old scooter to cross the seven kilometres[1] between Longchamps and Aurons. Eric

---

1. 7 km= 4.3 miles

stopped the scooter in front of a war monument in the centre of the village, near a small fountain, and waited patiently for me to get off. I struggled with the latch of my helmet, and he stretched out his fingers to help me. I slapped his fingers away.

"Don't need your help, thank you."

Unbothered, Eric turned around and walked toward a bakery with a pink awning. I followed him with both hands raised above my eyebrows, already uncomfortable under this glaring sun.

When Eric pushed open the door to the bakery, a little bell rang, and we were suddenly assailed by shrieks.

"Eric! It's Eric!"

"What are you doing here again?"

"We just saw you this morning!"

All in French. Stunned, I stood in the middle of the bakery with a dumb look on my face. The shrieks belonged to a middle-aged woman and two much younger girls of about our age. Their whole faces started glowing when Eric flashed them a smile. He was basking in their attention with obvious relish.

"Today you see me twice!" he said, in French. "You're so lucky!"

I took a timid step forward. "Hang on a minute, are you French?"

"Huh?" Eric flashed me a confused look. I closed my mouth and held my helmet closer to my chest.

The three bakers fussed around Eric as if they were family. One of the young ones was giving me curious looks. I had nothing to do with him, I wanted to say, but Eric had other plans.

"This is my friend Zak," he said, shoving me forward.

"Friend, that's a bit much…"

"Oh, Zak! Of course!" the woman said. "You're the other boy."

"The other what?"

Eric, confidently leaning against the countertop, seemed thoroughly amused by my awkwardness. "She meant the other actor. I told her about the movie."

"Who are these people?" I whispered through gritted teeth.

Eric flicked his hand. "This is Mona, this is Gabrielle, and this is Justine. Gabrielle and Justine are Mona's daughters. Obviously, they're bakers."

Easy peasy, his manner of saying this was, as though I should have known all along.

I turned to Mona. "How do you know this guy?"

"That's Eric! Eric Singstar!"

"Eric… Singwhat?"

"Well... Every day he—"

"I come in to say hello!" Eric interrupted in a booming voice. "I bought croissants once, since then I come here every morning."

"You're the one who bought croissants on our first morning? I thought it was Duvo."

"Please." Eric sucked his teeth. "Duvo doesn't wake up as early as I do. Only Mona does."

Mona agreed. "That's right."

Eric suddenly slumped on the counter. "I'm starving, Mona! You said you'd save me a sandwich, the best sandwich. Where is it!"

I was completely floored. Who really was this person? He knew everyone here and lived a whole different life while we were snoozing under the blankets. Befriending old men and bakers and getting weird nicknames. I'd never seen anything like it.

10

CONFESSION ON A STONE BRIDGE

M ona showed Eric a sandwich that really seemed to please him. Watching him spin around madly with an astonished smile, I didn't notice at first one of the baker's daughters, was again, observing me closely. When she saw me looking, she tucked a strand of gorgeous blond hair behind her ear, her cheeks pink.

"How is rehearsal?" she asked.

"Ahem… It's okay, I guess."

I didn't know what else to say. The girl's cheeks turned even redder. "You're so lucky… to spend all day with Eric."

I couldn't help smiling. "Am I?"

She clearly didn't know how exhausting, talkative, and tactile he was. But maybe that was her thing. *My* thing was Alberto. She had never met Alberto, or she wouldn't be into Eric. And that was a good thing, because she was really pretty, and you never know what damage a pretty girl can do.

"Could you tell him I like him when you have the chance?" the girl said. "He won't be here long. Better make the most of it."

I felt the slightest twitch in my eyelid. How could one be so brazen? Do people really do that sort of thing?

"He has a girlfriend," I said without thinking.

"What was that?" Eric appeared, brandishing his baguette in my face.

The other sister leaned on the counter with a smile. "He said your heart is taken."

"Mmh. He's right." Ignoring the blond sister's disappointed look, Eric took my wrist and pulled me to him. "What do you like? Ham? Turkey? Veggies? What sort of sandwich are you?"

"Maybe no ham," Mona said, looking closely at me.

I laughed nervously. "Turkey's fine."

She took out a sandwich and put it in a bag. "Anything else?"

"Could you add a bottle of water, please?" I asked. "Sparkling, please."

"Sparkling water?" Eric's eyebrows rose. When Mona turned around to get the bottle from the fridge, Eric casually leaned into me and spoke in a mischievous tone. "I knew you were a bit wicked."

Obviously, I didn't expect to hear anything like this, and the whole range of human emotions flashed on my face in about three seconds, until I forged a haughty smile.

"I thought I was an old man…"

Eric shrugged. "Old people can be wicked."

Feeling a little hot all of a sudden, I escaped outside. Even if the weather was stifling out there, I found it more comfortable than in there.

Despite the baker and her daughters' protests, Eric finally got out, after many promises of returning tomorrow. Once outside, he pushed the sandwich into my chest, cracking one of my ribs.

I looked down at that thing and grimaced. "Now I owe you money."

"Later. Let's try to find a good seat somewhere."

I nodded. "In the shade, please."

"Of course. Zak doesn't like the sun."

Without warning, Eric began swinging his arm over my shoulder. I jumped away with a furious glare.

"Why are you so…" I managed to suppress the vulgar word that came to mind "… tactile?"

Eric laughed. "I don't know. I just like touching people."

"I've noticed. Please stop immediately."

He looked at me with the air of a scolded child. Clearly, no one had ever told him that before. How was that even possible?

"You don't like it?"

"Being pawed by strangers? Unsurprisingly, no, not really."

A brief frown marred his face. "I'm not a stranger."

"I've known you two days—"

"Four!"

"Whatever. Stop touching me."

"Roger." He made a mock salute. "You know… you're a lot like Thomas. You think Camille wrote it for you?"

I shook my head vehemently in protest. "I AM NOT a lot like Thomas, thank you very much."

"He doesn't like being touched either. Also, he's really grumpy, like you."

"I'm not grumpy." I turned away, scowling. "Why do people always assume that?"

Eric waited a few seconds before he answered. "Because you act grumpy." Nothing ever fazed this guy. His amused smile never waned even as my scowl deepened.

"Well, I'm not. I'm just… on my guard."

"From what?" Eric scoffed and jerked his head at the monument two feet away. "Nazis?"

"This... is a World War I monument."

"Oh."

"And I don't have to justify myself to you."

"Fine, fine. I'll leave you alone." With twinkling eyes, he bounded toward the deserted main street.

After walking around for a while, we found a little stone bridge overlooking a canal. The sight of ducks paddling in circles in the glittering water down below made Eric almost jump off in excitement. The edge of the bridge was flat and large enough for people to sit safely. I bit into my sandwich with a sigh. The baguette crunched nicely under my teeth, and the sweet flavour of ripe tomatoes coated my tongue. I made an appreciative sound and swung my legs over the bridge to sit more comfortably.

"Why do those women call you Eric Singstar?"

"Mmh…" Eric looked up at the sky, chomping at his food. "I don't feel like telling you."

Asshole. Now he was playing secretive. How infuriating.

"Really? Just like that?"

He grinned. "*C'est la vie.*"

"Oh!" His words jolted my memory. "So, you're French?"

Eric swallowed noisily and gave me a strange look. Like he wasn't sure I was messing with him. "Am I French?"

"Come off it." I nudged him playfully. "I heard you sing Bardot earlier, and just now, you spoke French like a native."

Eric nudged me back. "Yet you still speak to me in English."

"So do you. So where are you from, Eric... What's your name again? Taylor?"

He pouted. "Tucker."

"Right."

"I'm from Paris, like you."

"Paris? Paris, really?"

"Yes!" He began laughing again. "Why do you look so shocked?"

"You're not American?"

"No." Then his face twisted in a funny grimace. "I mean yes!"

"Seriously?"

"It's easy." Eric raised his index finger. "My dad's American." Then he added his middle finger. "My mom's French." He made the two fingers touch and rub against each other, then intertwined them under my perplexed gaze. "One day, they decided to smooch. One thing led to another... Now I'm here!"

"Okay, enough. Drop the finger thing."

"And my name's actually Tucker-Régnier, by the way..." Eric sounded sightly resentful, as though I should have known that.

"So that's how you speak French..."

"Of course, I grew up here. Why d—" He paused, looking shocked. "Did you think I was an exchange student or something?"

I dipped my head, embarrassed. "I haven't really thought about it."

"Clearly!" Eric shook his head with a smile. "You've never heard me speak French?"

"No."

"Really? Never? Not even to Kayvin and Xavier?" He seemed completely floored. "To Elodie? You saw me with Elodie, didn't you? You told the baker I had a girlfriend. You saw us together."

"I saw you together, yes." I had a vague recollection of seeing her get into some blond guy's arms. "But the first words I ever heard you speak were on Monday, and they were in English."

"Oh, right," he said. "Of course."

"Then I heard you speak in English... again. With your footballer friends."

I recalled the conversation I'd overheard in the kitchen, when Kayvin interrogated him about the scratch on his arm, but I had no intention of letting him know I was eavesdropping at the time.

"Only when Charles-Henry's there. His French isn't very good, that's why."

Eric also swung his legs over the bridge and ate in silence for a while. He had just encountered the only person at school who didn't even know who he was. It must have come as a shock for him. And it amused me a little. I don't know why. It just did. Still, I didn't want any awkwardness between us. So I decided to break the silence and teasingly leaned toward him.

"Why are we speaking English to each other, then?"

"We don't have to!" He met my stare full-on. "It was you who started speaking to me in English, so I thought, fine! If that's what he prefers."

"Now I'm used to it anyway."

Eric rubbed his forehead, a sheepish smile on his face. "Me too. We get along so well in English. Why jinx it? Anyway, lots of people around us don't speak French, like Melissa, Joy, and C.H."

"Or Alberto."

Eric quirked an eyebrow. "Oh? I didn't know that."

"He's Italian, remember."

"Ha, right, of course."

Perhaps it was the peaceful setting. Or the delicious sandwich. Or the thrilling — slowest — scooter ride. But I felt a brief rush of warmth and trust toward this person that I'd never felt for anybody but Yasmine.

"How would you call it in French, then?" I asked in a teasing voice.

Eric threw an anxious look at my unusually smiling face. "Call what?"

"A bee's furry pyjama."

"Huh… Ah!"

His surprise passed, he burst out a laugh. I hid my smile behind my sandwich.

"That's easy!" He took an important air. "*Un petit pyjama duveteux*."

I bit my lip not to laugh. "That's actually adorable."

"I know. Bees are adorable."

"They're not."

"You're wrong."

"I'm not."

"You are."

I let it go this time again, only shaking my head in silence.

Minutes drifted by while we ate. All this food mixed with the heat and Eric's constant humming had turned me pretty mellow. I had to watch it, if I wasn't careful, this frivolous football player might become a friend. When I was done eating, I neatly wrapped the rest of my sandwich and put it on my knees, thinking I wasn't in a hurry to return to the house yet.

Eric stretched for a long time, then lifted his chin toward the sky. "Are we friends now?"

I stared at him, taken aback. Again it was like he was reading my mind. It was freaking me out! "No."

"Ouch!"

"Pff!" I took on a dramatic air. "Friendship requires more than sharing two conversations around a lake."

"A pond."

"Whatever. It demands time, and nurturing, and... trust. A lot of trust."

"Okay." Eric put his chin in his hand. "So you're saying we're not there yet."

"That's it."

He nodded quietly. I wondered if I hurt his feelings in any way. After all, he was exceptionally warm toward people. Perhaps he needed company just as I needed solitude.

"Why..." I flinched when he looked earnestly at me. "Why do you want to be my friend anyway?"

"Why not? I like having friends."

"Don't you have enough by now? Aren't you a football superstar or something?"

"A football superstar!" He exploded in laughter. "Call me Mister Football Superstar from now on. Or Your Highness. Works too."

"Be serious. Aren't you the new Cristiano Ronaldinho or something? People are all over you, it's disgusting."

Eric blanched and brought his hand to my mouth as if he wanted to silence me, but he seemed to remember I asked him not to touch me, so he waved his finger in front of my face instead.

"Cristiano Ronaldinho? Really? Zak, I like you, but I can't let you do that. It's criminal."

I gave a small laugh. "Sorry. What's his name, then?"

"I'm not even going to answer that."

I turned away to hide my laughter until his face came dangerously close to mine, cutting off my breath.

"Who is all over me?"

122

I jerked my head back. "What?"

"You say people are all over me. What did you mean?"

"Only that... that everyone seems to fancy you." Recalling Arthur's confession this morning, I almost laughed.

"Names," Eric said, pretending well to be serious. "I want names."

"Why? You have a girlfriend."

"NAMES!"

He laughed and leaned back, allowing me to breathe a little better. For the first time, it occurred to me that Eric was, in fact, a little slutty. His way with words, how he coaxed people like the bakers, and the constant touching and all. I was beginning to sense a little minx.

"Popularity is a curse," I said darkly. "It turns people into impossible flirts like you."

Eric snorted loudly. "Crap, you're really not holding back your punches with me. I'm glad words can't kill."

I hid my face in my hands. "And I'm glad you're not as violent as your friend Kayvin or you would have drowned me in the lake by now."

"The pond."

"Nope."

We exchanged a smile. Eric turned away first. He was thoughtful for another long moment, his gaze fixed on the canal below. I could almost see steam burst out of his ears.

"Zak."

"Mm?"

"Zak."

"What?"

"Can I ask you something?"

He was full of questions, this one. Questions about *me*. I tried to silence the part of me who relished his attention, but it had already grown to surprising proportions in a couple of days. All I could do was tilt my head curiously.

"Yes, you can."

He didn't smile, this time. "How come you don't have any friends?"

Hearing this, I almost protested. I could have claimed I had friends, that they weren't here, but back at school, or perhaps in Canada. But that would have been a shameless lie.

"Oh, that."

I saw in his face he meant no harm by asking. And the surge of warmth I felt toward him was still here, lingering, whispering to me that I could talk to him, that it would be fine. So, I began talking.

"Basically, I found out pretty early that it's easier for me to be alone than to be around people."

"Really?" Eric's eyes widened. "That's so strange. I'm the opposite."

"Yeah, I saw that."

His expression turned worried, as though he thought I was a pitiable thing.

"I'm not a pitiable thing, Eric. I'm happy with the life I've had so far."

"You are?"

"People exhaust me. I have a hard time making friends. Then when I make one, I start caring too much and having crazy expectations, and it's too much work for both of us… I'd rather focus on other things."

He was watching me with an expression bordering on terror. A life without friends! A guy like him would never understand.

"I'm not completely alone, mind you. I've got a great sister."

"The one we saw at the station?"

"Yeah. We're really close. She's my best friend."

Eric took a moment to ponder my words, but then his expression crumpled again. He had another question. "You've never had another friend, in all these years?"

"Oh…" I scratched my nose awkwardly. "I did, once. A few years ago."

"You're not friends anymore."

"No, we're not."

"What happened?"

With a sigh, I tried to recollect my friend's face. It was useless. "We got along when we were kids, but then I got a little too weird, and a little too gay—"

"Pfffft!"

Out of nowhere, Eric spat the last bite of his sandwich straight into the canal below. I stared at him, aghast.

"What the hell is wrong with you?"

"Excuse me." He coughed a few times, his eyes glistening. "Did you say a little too gay?"

I hesitated. "… No?" I rewound a little, then slapped a hand over my mouth.

I did say that!

124

My eyes bulged to the level of pain. Did I just accidentally come out to freaking Eric the football player?

"I... I... I..."

I came out! To a guy I'd known for four days! Why on earth did I do that? My parents, even my parents didn't know that... that...

Flames of mortification crept up my neck and burned my face. I even considered an emergency retreat by jumping into the canal. "Could you forget I said that?" I said through the deepest blush of my life.

Eric was staring at the ducks fighting for his unintentional donation below. "I don't get it."

"You—"

"I don't get it," he repeated. "How does one become too gay for his friend? How does that happen?"

Between blinks of stupor, I observed his face intently. He looked back, expecting an answer. It was just as though I'd never said anything peculiar. Perhaps he wasn't surprised after all. Or perhaps he didn't care. I didn't know which was best — or worst.

"Hum... I don't know."

Eric wiped his mouth thoughtfully. "Did he think you were into him or something?"

"I don't know..." I frowned. "Good question. He... he never said."

"Oh. That's a shame."

I stared at Eric, amazed. I'd just come out to him. His initial reaction was pure shock, which was a little weird, honestly, but not as weird as his lack of reaction now. It was like I'd just confessed to preferring tea over coffee. Not a big deal. It made me wonder if I'd get that lucky with everybody else in the future. My heart gave a little jolt; I even returned his smile.

"When I asked him about it, he said he was sorry to feel this way, but that's how it was. He said: 'You are who you associate with.' So I guessed I was either too weird or too gay. Because these are the two things I definitely am."

I got momentarily lost in thought while Eric stretched his arms toward the sky. His shirt lifted and revealed the narrow waist I'd had my hands on earlier. I averted my eyes.

"Okay," Eric said. "Sounds like something his dad would have said and he just repeated the words to you. Sounds made up. I don't know."

Maybe. All I know is that I had repressed the memory of my friend's face in my rancour. But his words, I still remembered.

"If it makes you feel any better," Eric said softly, "it's the same for everyone, you know. We all get through the same stuff."

"What? Being too weird and too gay?"

We both laughed. My timid chuckle was drowned by his boisterous laughter. Then his face became serious again.

"No, but losing touch with a friend, putting some distance, all that."

I could hear in his tone, see in his face, that something similar had, or was happening to him. Perhaps he would tell me if I'd ask.

"Can *I* ask you a question, then?" Eric blushed furiously. I couldn't help laughing. "Don't worry, it's just a question."

"It's just the way you asked. I'm not used to it, that's all."

"You're not used to questions?"

Eric shook his head, smiling. "Just… ask."

"Okay. Here goes." He was flinching in anticipation. It was kind of cute. "Why Kayvin?"

His jaw went slack. "Why… Kayvin?"

"Yes. Why is… Kayvin? What's the… Why?"

Eric closed his mouth but still looked confused. "I don't get what you mean."

"You don't get that he's a massive asshole? And you're, like… not?"

Eric clutched his heart, his eyes glittering with mirth. "Good Lord in Heaven, Zakaria!" He suddenly spoke in an inexplicable Southern drawl. "Did you just compliment me?"

I gave a resigned sigh. "I was insulting Kayvin, remember?"

"Yes."

"And you're not mad."

Eric groaned and kicked his feet together with even more vigour, like a child who doesn't want to cooperate.

"He wasn't so bad, I swear. He's changed. I've changed. We've all changed. It's like I told you."

I was right, then. He was going through the same thing, with that asshole.

"What happened?"

Eric appeared very uncomfortable. I didn't know if he wanted me to shut up or not. I decided that after I accidentally came out to him, he owed me a small embarrassing confession to make us even.

"Are you not friends anymore?"

"We are, we are," Eric said darkly. "But… We met on the football team. We spend most of our free time together. Then we ended up in the same class. I guess it does qualify as 'best friends by default'. But

I'd like to do other things than talk about football and girls all the time."

Perhaps there was more to his decision to audition for Adam's role than meets the eye after all. It was possible that even Eric, the most popular guy at school, needed a place to escape.

Oblivious to my thoughts, Eric gave a wan smile. "I just got to a point where I started to feel like a trope."

"A trope? Like a movie trope?"

"Yeah."

"Really?"

"A high school jock, wearing a varsity jacket and dating the cheerleader."

"Oh. Elodie would like that." I turned my face away.

Again, it was like he was reading my mind. I had called him all those things. It was insane! And really embarrassing for me.

"You're not alone, you know," I said, in an effort to relate to him. "I feel like a trope too."

"You do?"

Once again he attempted to meet my eyes, but I found it more comfortable not to look at him. "Of course. I'm in high school, and I'm—"

"No!" He jumped off his seat, suddenly excited. "Don't tell me. I'll guess, I'll guess!" He thought about it for a moment, then pointed his finger at me triumphantly. "You're the tormented artist, right?"

"... No."

I was amused, though. Alberto was the tormented artist. How laudable that Eric would think that.

"Okay. Wait." Eric leaned on the stone bridge thoughtfully. "Hm... The lonely genius who's great at maths, but sucks at making friends?"

"No." I snorted. "But I am good at maths."

"Except when it comes to calculating the days of the week."

"Shut it."

"Make me." He stuck out his chin. "Go on, tell me what it is."

I stared into Eric's smiling face, the truth ringing inside my head, desperate to come out, to be spoken out loud, to have someone to share it with. *Will you still want to be my friend if I tell you that... If I tell you...* "I'm the nerdy teen in love with a bombshell, but the bombshell doesn't even know he exists."

Eric's expression seemed torn between confusion and disbelief. "What do you mean?"

I snorted. I didn't know why I found his face amusing. His reaction now felt more normal than the one he had earlier when I dropped my gay bomb. I leaned a little closer to him. "That's the real reason I was so mean to you."

Eric's eyes widened. "That you…"

"I'm in love with somebody from my Drama Club, somebody who doesn't know I exist."

"Wow…" Eric hunched himself over the bridge, dangerously close to falling over. When I nervously extended a hand to grab him, just in case, he whirled around and propped himself back on the edge, light as a feather. "Is that true?"

I chuckled. "Yes, it's true."

He looked thoughtful, as though my news were a complicated equation he had no idea how to figure out. "I don't know what that's got to do with me, but I don't think there's anybody in your class who doesn't know who you are."

"Are you messing with me?"

"No."

"Sure. Let's see. Does Elodie know who I am?"

"Yes."

That actually surprised me. "How do you know?"

"I was on the phone with her the other day. Of course, she knows who you are. You're in the same class." Eric lunged at me, almost gripping me by the shoulders, but stopped himself at the last moment. "Hold on, are you in love with Elodie?"

"No. Eww. No." I removed his hand from my shoulder with a click of my tongue. "Are you high? I just told you I was gay."

"But then, why——" Eric's face was funny to watch. It was like he was trying really hard to think and couldn't make sense of anything. Then he took a deep breath. "That's fine. You don't have to tell me who it is. Just… what does that have to do with me?"

Of course, it didn't make any sense to him. Poor thing. I had to clarify it for him.

"I was supposed to tell him I loved him even though he doesn't even know I exist yet."

"But how?"

I made a face. "By making sure to be cast in the same film and declare my feelings at the most opportune moment?" I suddenly found the surface of the canal deserving of all of my attention. Though he said nothing, I could feel Eric's eyes burning into the side of my face.

"You're in love with Alberto."

I said nothing. But when he clapped his hands, I jumped.

"Bombshell!"

He burst into a laugh so loud, the whole village could hear it. I watched him, stunned. At least he could put two and two together. Yes, Eric, the bombshell from Drama Club could only be Alberto.

"I know, I know. He's perfect in every way, and I'm, you know, me. Doesn't make much sense, at first glance. But that's how it is."

Eric thoughtfully looked up, his eyes bluer than the sky. "So that's why you hate me."

"No." I shook my head in haste. "I don't hate you."

"That's why you hated me then."

With a pang of shame, I pursed my lips. Eric went on, his eyes narrowed, "Because you thought Alberto would play Adam…"

"Yes."

"And that you'd be able to smooch him during the kissing scenes!"

I cleared my throat. "*The* kissing scene. There's only one."

"Yeah… I still think we should add one more."

"Anyway—"

Eric stomped his foot. "You should have told me before!"

"What difference would it have made?"

"I wouldn't have auditioned if I had known."

I paused, surprised by his words. Then I waved my hands in his face. "First, I only learned you auditioned after you got cast. And how would it have looked, me approaching you even though we had never even seen each other before, and telling you to drop the audition because I was in love with Alberto?"

Still. Deep inside, I appreciated the thought more than he knew.

Eric put his chin in his hand and sighed. "Anything for true love, isn't that what we say?"

His words stunned me. "Thank you, Eric. But don't worry about it. I'm not mad anymore, okay? It was never your fault, to begin with. I was just…"

He held up a hand to silence me. "I destroyed your perfect plan. I get why you were a little annoyed with me."

"But that's over," I said decidedly. "I'm okay with you… being Adam now."

His face brightened. "So, we're friends now?"

"You… You don't ever listen to me, do you?"

He sniggered. "Should we go back? We need to rehearse now that we're stuck together. For better or worse."

"Right. For better or worse."

Once again, he held up his hand for me, but I didn't take it. We walked back to the scooter, but Eric was humming along, and I was grateful to step in his shadow in silence.

"Alberto, huh?" Eric said when we reached the scooter.

I looked at him with eyes I knew were full of sparkles and was met with an incredulous frown.

"What?"

"Nothing." Eric swung his leg over the seat. "Let's get back."

The rest of the day went by really fast, as though nothing happened. If any change occurred, it happened within me.

Once back at Longchamps with the others, the safety and excitement I felt around Eric which made me confess to intimate things didn't last. All I could see was a crowd of teenagers who spent most of their days gossiping. Not only did I entrust my secret to the most popular guy at school, but he was also an unstoppable chatterbox and looked at his happiest when other people showered him with attention.

Why on earth would he bother keeping my secret when there were so many people to tell?

At 2 p.m., this idea was merely a passing thought.

At 5 p.m., the thought had turned into a nagging voice constantly whispering in my ear.

By 8 p.m., it was all I could think about.

Why, why did I feel it was okay to share my secrets with Eric? What consequences would I face tomorrow if he couldn't keep his mouth shut? From Kayvin's bullying to the other's sneers, I think the worst could still be... Alberto's reaction. This was not the way I intended him to know I loved him. My insides churned unpleasantly when I thought of what the others might talk and laugh about around the fire pit. I flinched every time I heard anybody burst into a laugh.

In the middle of the night, as I lay in bed, the fear that Eric could weaponise my confessions was wrapping like a coil around me, choking me. As a result, I was still awake when Eric came to bed a while later. Immediately, I squeezed my eyes shut and pretended to sleep. Doing his best to be quiet, Eric tiptoed his way around the bedroom but couldn't suppress a giggle when he heard Arthur snoring.

When he got under the covers, we both heaved a sigh.

11

NOT RIPE YET

It's once again glueing myself to the walls that I came down to breakfast the next morning, with bags under the eyes. To cement my fears, the first person I came right across on the way down was Kayvin.

I didn't know what I expected exactly. Not necessarily the dreaded homophobic slur, but at least something. But all he said was "Get out of the way" with a sigh. He could afford to be a little rude, since Eric was most likely out there flirting with the baker's daughter, unable to scold him.

It felt like everyone was watching me at first, then I realised I was just being paranoid. Back in the dining room, I slid into my chair in my preferred spot at the table located at the very back of the room. I would know straight away if Eric talked, because Alberto would know. Though he was usually restrained in his displays of emotion, this time he was bound to react.

But it's Arthur who first sauntered toward me and took his seat on my left, as usual, thoroughly uninvited. Both he and Camille really had no consideration for my sensibilities.

"Big day, huh?"

"What? Why? What have you heard?" My tone was too aggressive. After a sleepless night, I was all nerves. Arthur threw me a fearful look.

"Duvo and Binta said they had a major announcement to make later today."

"What announcement?"

"I don't know, but there are rumours flying around, if you know what I mean?" He winked at me. A layer of cold sweat began forming on my neck.

"What are you saying?"

Before he could answer, we were interrupted by the last people I wanted to see: Camille and Duvo. Behind them, Michael followed with his head down, typing on his phone.

What did I do to deserve the whole squad charging at me so early in the morning in the middle of rehearsal week? Did Eric talk? Did he? What would I do if they wanted to blame me for trying to get Alberto cast? I was close to hyperventilating when Duvo, who wouldn't let Camille speak first, put his hand on her shoulder and pushed her out of his way.

"Zak!"

The grunt I gave him didn't deter him at all.

"We just spoke to Eric. Congratulations are in order."

Silence around the table. Camille nodded empathically, while Michael was frowning at his phone. Eric's stupid grin flashed in my mind. That sly… He must have talked.

Exhaling slowly, I dumped my spoon into my untouched cereal bowl and braced myself for the rest. "Thanks, I guess."

"You really showed some maturity. I'm sure the movie will be better for it."

"… Did I?" I couldn't see the point he was making here.

Camille approached, her cheeks pink. "The movie's already better for it, or so Eric said."

I gave a nervous chuckle. "Eric said what, exactly?"

Michael was still standing behind Camille. He didn't see my frantic looks at him for support, so engrossed with his phone that he didn't even notice his notebook was slipping down his grip.

"Anyway, check in with Michael." Duvo waved his hand over his shoulder. "He's the best suited for this stuff. Keep it up, I'll see you later."

Camille nodded. "Thanks for being awesome. Between the two of you, and him," — she discreetly pointed at Michael — "I'm starting to dream awards!"

Leaving me stunned, she followed Duvo toward the kitchen, and they immediately started fighting about something. Michael absently sank into the chair opposite mine.

"Hey, Zak." He sounded tired. "Everything all right?"

"Yeah, I guess…"

He finally looked up. Seeing my confused face, he gave me a thin smile. "Sorry. I've got a lot going on at the moment."

"Tell me about it."

"So…"

So… So? Was he supposed to give me the big talk or something?

"I think I know what this is about," I said with reluctance. "Apparently, you're the best suited for the job. But don't worry, I know all about it. I've known for years, and my sister is… well… Yasmine."

Michael gave me a weird look, but then his phone vibrated, and he pounced off the table to pick up. "Sorry, gotta take this." He turned his back to me, his phone stuck to his ear. "Hey, Louis."

Only then I realised Michael looked odd. He kept running his hand through his unkempt hair, messing it up even more. Was it that Duvo was really getting to him? That would be extraordinary. My curiosity piqued, I intended to listen to the call, but Alberto made his entrance, pushing all other thoughts away.

Fresh out of the shower, looking both elegant and windswept, he made poor Sander, lumbering behind him, look trollish in comparison. My heart jumped into my throat. I could only wait.

Alberto scanned the room until his eyes fell upon my little corner. Luckily, Michael was standing in front of my table, partly hiding me from view. But upon noticing Arthur getting up and walking away from our table, Alberto said something to Sander and walked alone toward us in a decided manner. I felt at this moment I was going to die. Right here and now. Either Alberto rejected me, or he'd confess his love to me. Either way, I'd die. All that was left to know was which epitaph would be written on my tombstone.

When he came close, Alberto accidentally bumped into Michael's shoulder, then plunged right onto the table, bathing me in the fresh scent of his shampoo. Mint with a hint of lavender. Nice.

Sprawled over the table on his elbows like that, he was giving everyone around a perfect view of his… assets, while I stared, gulping like a fool, into his blue eyes.

No. His *grey* eyes. Grey and cool like a polished steel blade.

Wait. Alberto's eyes were… grey? How could I not have noticed before?

Perhaps because we'd never been so close. If I stretched my hand, I could have touched his hair. It looked so soft, very tempting.

"Hi, Zak."

His voice was so gentle, almost like a whisper. I found I couldn't breathe anymore. My heart was thundering around my ribcage, making me dizzy.

Alberto started picking at his cuticles then, noticing my lack of answer, glanced up at me. "So, is Eric any good at all?"

"You… you don't know?" I blurted out.

Alberto's eyes fell back to his cuticles. "How would I know…"

Stunned by this revelation, I was rendered speechless. But Michael saved me when he hung up the phone, pulled back his chair, and dropped on it heavily.

"Hi, Michael," Alberto said, still absorbed by his cuticles. Michael didn't answer him either. He was still staring at his phone, looking numb. Alberto looked up at him, at me, at him again. "What's up with you two this morning?"

Michael woke from his daze with a start. He took notice of Alberto and plunged his nose back into his notebook. "So, Zak, where was I?"

"Ahem…" I was momentarily distracted when Alberto propped himself up on one elbow. Blinking fast, I tried to ignore how gorgeous he looked like that, but he flashed me an unexpected and enigmatic smile. "I… I have honestly no idea where you were."

"Right!" Michael came to his senses. "Duvo asked me to check with you which scenes you and Eric rehearsed yesterday, because last night Camille was 'struck by genius' as she said and made some changes, so you might have to rehearse some… new… things." Michael slowly turned his head to peer at Alberto, who was drumming his fingers on the surface of the table, his expression unreadable. He stared at him until Alberto stopped and rose with a sigh.

"I'll see you later, then."

Yes, you will! said the little slutty voice living shamelessly within me. I gave him a feeble wave. My heart was so full; minutes ago, I was wracked with anxiety, and now I could float about the room like a balloon. Michael and I watched him leave, then I felt Michael's eyes on me, so I quickly looked down at my soggy cereal, a sheepish smile stuck to my face.

I was feeling reborn again. Alberto didn't know. No one seemed to know.

Eric had not betrayed my confidence.

The balloon soared even higher.

Michael was still observing my face when I looked up. "Hang on," I said, suddenly remembering something. "Changes, you said?"

"Yeah."

My pulse quickened. "Is that anything to do with a kissing scene?"

"Among other things," Michael said. "The kissing scene at the end has been—"

"Removed?"

"No. Modified. Camille's still working on it. Have you rehearsed that one already?"

"No, we were…"

We never even approached that scene. I always dodged it, asking Eric to rehearse something else first, and he never complained, even looked just as eager as me *not* to do it. Everything else we did many times, including the post-confession awkward hug, which had Eric roaring with laughter. Eventually, we would have to get down to business and do that. But I had a feeling Eric was more nervous about it than he let on.

When I stumbled outside after breakfast, I tore across the secret path to the lake with a racing heart. I had not been betrayed. Eric wasn't like his football buddies. Eric was a person I could get along with. Eric was… a friend.

I had a friend.

My heart swelled when I finally caught a glimpse of him, standing with his back to me by the edge of the lake. He was the same. Nothing had changed. Unflattering clothes and dirty sneakers; gilded hair and sculpted legs; inappropriate hands with bitten nails. But now he was my friend.

In my haste to reach him, I wasn't careful. My foot bumped against a root, and I almost fell flat on my face. Eric heard me and lunged forward to help. Slapping his hand away, I bent over to catch my breath.

"Be careful, Zak. No one needs a footman with a broken leg."

"You…" I blurted out without thinking. "You didn't tell anyone I love Alberto."

Just as I wasn't prepared to say it, he wasn't prepared to hear it. He blinked several times, confused. "Of course not. Why would I tell anyone?"

"I don't know. I just thought… I expected you to."

"Have *you* told Alberto?" His tone was teasing.

"No."

"Pff. You're gonna have to. Or he'll never know."

"I'm not gonna tell him today, that's for sure." I straightened up. "So thank you for your discretion."

"Just call me 'My Lord' from now on, and we'll be even."

I ignored his nonsense. "What did you tell the others, though? Camille and Duvo were acting weird just now."

Eric scratched his chin with his finger. "That's because they're afraid of you."

"Why are they afraid of me?"

He didn't answer.

"Are *you* afraid of me?" I asked in horror.

He considered the question, a childish look on his face. "Not all the time, no."

"Come on!" I stepped forward, aiming to shove him out of my way. He extended his arm in defence, and I ended up hurting my wrist. I didn't show it, though.

"Relax. They just wanted to know if we were getting along," Eric said.

"Oh." I looked down at my feet. Then I rushed forward and gripped his arm. "But what did you say?"

He studied my face with a delighted grin. "I said everything was going really great, and that we had all sorts of notes that would blow their minds. Also that our chemistry was off the charts and stuff like that."

"But… you lied." I dropped his arm and watched it fall limply to his side.

"It wasn't a big lie though, was it?"

Eric's expression was somewhat fearful. Hating the idea that he might be frightened of me, I decided not to tease him on this matter.

"What if Camille asks for the notes? What do we do?"

Eric's face relaxed. "She has, of course, but I told her I would show them later. I also winked, so it added some mystery around the whole thing."

I looked down, finding it hard not to smile. "But now, we have to produce some notes."

"Easy! Just say you think Thomas wouldn't say this or that but should say this or that instead. Also, there should be an extra kissing scene."

"I thought we went over this." I gave him a reproachful look. "Approximatively fifty times."

"But, Zak! Zak. Listen."

Shut up, shut up. Can't even rehearse the one kissing scene but wants to add another? He was crazy. I tried standing my ground, but he kept calling my name and clicking his fingers together until I faced him.

"Zak. Trust me, I keep thinking about this!"

I folded my arms over my chest. "You don't say."

He spoke excitedly. "They're guys. Guys! They're not going to flash their ankles or swoon or whatever stupid stuff you find in old movies."

I vaguely wondered what sort of old movies he had been watching. Not the same ones I had, evidently. In any case, his agitation reminded me of something. Here was my chance to ask him a burning question.

"I'd been meaning to ask you about that," I said.

"About what?"

Eric retrieved his tennis ball from his pocket and gave it a long look, probably pondering whether to play with it or not. I hoped he wasn't wondering if I would play catch with him like with a dog.

"The kissing scene at the end. Are you not even a little bit bothered by that?"

Originally, I meant to say "nervous" not "bothered". But I chickened out. Eric glanced up from his ball.

"Why would I be bothered by that?"

I merely looked at him.

"I'm an *actor*," he said, with a dramatic accent.

This sounded like a jab at me. I deserved it after my rotten behaviour at the beginning of the week. I wanted to add something, but in the end, I said nothing, suddenly frightened he would deflect with one of his jokes and make it look like I was the one afraid to rehearse a kiss. I was, after all, the actor. I wasn't afraid. Even if…

No, I wasn't.

Eric knelt down on the grass; his appalling script splayed over his knees. "I'm just gonna write it down, and then we'll see."

"Write what down?"

"Second kissing scene."

"You're impossible!"

His child-like laughter split the air, causing a few birds to take flight in fright. Watching him write some scribbles on his crumpled piece of paper with the tip of his tongue sticking out, I felt a sudden rush of affection for this exuberant person.

"Okay," I said.

Eric looked up from his script. "Okay what? Okay to add a kissing scene?"

I shook my head. "Okay, we can be friends, I guess."

"Really?" He flashed me a sly grin.

"Yeah, I guess. You didn't tell my secret after all."

"Not my secret to tell," he said firmly. Then he added, mumbling, "And you said it yourself, friendship needs trust."

I turned away because I didn't want him to see me smile. But he looked so happy, he made me feel… appreciated.

We mentioned the kissing scene once after that, only to agree we would not rehearse the dreaded scene until Camille delivered the updated script.

At the end of the day, after rehearsing for hours, we walked together back to the house. In these days I had already gotten used to Eric's persistent humming, so when he became quiet, I couldn't help turning around, slightly alarmed. He was staring up at a tree, his eyebrows drawn together, apparently deep in thought.

"You like apples?" I asked.

"Hm?"

"You're staring at this apple tree. You want one?"

Eric's smile softened. "They're not ripe yet. See?" He pointed to the fruits, small and green and nowhere near edible yet.

"What do I know about fruits?" I mumbled.

He gave me a weird look before grinning. "So… we're friends now."

"I guess."

Eric scratched his chin as though he was trying to think of some mischief. "That means you'll hang out tonight maybe?"

I gave a sigh. "We already spend most of our days together."

"We could spend the nights too." Noticing my expression, he shook his head with a laugh. "I only mean like, chatting around the fire together, you know?"

"Will Kayvin be all right with this?"

"Who cares?"

"I wouldn't want to end up punched in the face."

"Zak…" Eric looked confused. "I'd never let him touch you."

I dug my feet into the ground for fear I might just float about. Besides my sister, no one had ever stuck up for me. For some reason above my understanding, his statement made me feel self-conscious and shy. My intuition warned me to be careful around Eric, and that perhaps it wasn't wise to spend so much time alone with him.

"Then, hum… What about Arthur?" I said, marvelling at my own coyness. "He's always following me around."

"Yeah, I know Arthur!" Eric flicked his wrist. "He's cool. Let's hang out together."

Of course, he knew Arthur. This guy had found the time to befriend everybody, including the baker, her daughters, probably her third cousin once removed, while I still didn't know anything about Arthur outside his first name and that he was our DOP.

"And Camille too," Eric said in a firm tone. "She's great. She should hang out with us too. And then we can talk about Alberto."

Upon hearing my beloved's name, I blinked several times, not sure I heard right. "We can what?"

The tip of Eric's ears turned pink. "I think… I think you need help with Alberto."

"You want to give me dating advice?"

"You need it, don't you?"

I had to hold my ribs to suppress my laughter. "Eric, you have a high opinion of yourself if you think you can give me dating advice."

He cocked his head. "Am I not a football superstar?"

I leapt forward to swat him. He dodged effortlessly and buried his hand in my hair, making a terrible mess of it. While cursing and attempting to push him away, I considered his offer.

Indeed, Eric was the most popular guy at school, while I was… well… Zak, forever single and, up until a few months ago, perfectly fine with it.

"All right," I said, willing to play a little. "Let's see how good you are."

He perked up just like Rufus did whenever he saw Yasmine holding a ball.

"Answer me this simple question." I sounded serious on purpose. "How did you and Emily get together?"

"Elodie," Eric said with a faint smile.

"Sorry. What did I say?"

"You said Emily."

He turned slightly away from me. At first, I thought he was vexed, so I felt bad about my mistake. Then I realised he was thinking. Thinking so hard I could see the cogs turning in his head.

"Hang on!" I sounded a little too gleeful, so I cleared my throat a little. "You… don't remember how you met her?"

Eric shook his head, his lips pursed, as though I was spouting nonsense. "Pff. Of course, I remember. It was after class. We were playing football, and Elodie came with her friends to watch us play."

Boring, I thought. Naturally, I didn't say it.

"All right. Then how did it happen, you know… the… seduction part."

"I'm not sure." Eric licked the corner of his mouth. "She gave me her number. I texted her, I think. No! She texted me. Can't remember."

I stared at him, astonished. "So romantic, you don't even remember."

"What?"

"It's lame! It's shit! Worst meet-cute story ever! And you want to give me advice?"

Not at all bothered by my comments, he giggled like a toddler. "It's not my fault if that's how it happened. Okay, it's not romantic, but it's high school."

I chortled. "What do you mean, it's high school?"

"It's high school, it's supposed to be fun."

"Meaning?"

"Meaning, if someone asks me out, and I'm free, then I generally say yes. It's as simple as that."

So unromantic! Flaunting oneself at the first one who asks you out like that. Yikes. I knew he was a flirt, but now, it was confirmed.

"Romance is dead." I sighed.

"I get it." Eric gave me an appraising look. "You're a grand gesture kind of guy."

"There's a world of difference between grand gesture and 'Oh! No! I don't remember, she texted me, I couldn't say no, you know, it's high school'… Awful!"

Eric exploded in laughter. "Is that what I sound like?"

I didn't answer.

"But it's so hard to resist when someone nice and attractive comes to you and all they want is to hold you and kiss you and tell you nice things…" For a moment, Eric seemed lost in the memory — or fantasy — of countless young maidens throwing themselves at him. Watching him got me thinking too.

"I guess that's what Alberto must experience all the time."

Eric landed back on earth. "Then why is Alberto single, if he's all that?"

"I don't know. He's a tormented soul, you know?"

He let out a snort powerful enough to be heard back at the house. "A tormented soul." He clutched his ribs. "Alberto's just a guy, with a face."

Oh, hang on! Seemed like Eric needed urgent training if he wanted to be my friend. First rule of friendship: no one was allowed to diss Alberto. Everything else was more or less irrelevant.

"Have you ever talked to him?" I said, scandalised.

Eric looked unimpressed. "Have you?"

I harrumphed in anger. "I have heard him speak many times. He's not just incredibly beautiful. He's charming, clever, sophisticated."

"Okay."

"Everything I dream of."

"Okay!" Eric threw up his hands and leaned against a tree. "I hope he'll appreciate your loyalty when he finds out about your hopeless crush on him."

With my hands behind my back, I cautiously approached him. "What... do you think he'll do when he finds out?"

"Hopefully, he'll take you out back to smooch you."

I lost myself in pleasant thoughts when he said that, all the while getting closer. When I came to, I was standing right in front of him. "Anyway..." I tried my best to sound casual. "Have you ever kissed a guy before?"

Eric shook his head with fervour. "No."

I expected this answer. The opposite would have surprised me. Eric tilted his head, the sly grin back.

"You have, I suppose."

"... Yeah."

His smile widened when he noticed how flushed I was. He probably thought I was embarrassed. And I was. But it wasn't because we were talking about kisses. It was because I lied.

I was only sixteen. Okay, and a half. But it wasn't unusual, I guess, to never have been kissed at that age. I was the only gay guy I knew of, besides Alberto. Once I came really close, back in Tunis, on holiday. But close meant nothing.

I shamelessly lied.

Eric had most likely kissed plenty of girls by the time he reached my age. I didn't want him to think I was a loser. Only lying about it right now made me feel like a loser. To shake away the feeling, I stuck my chin out, defiant. "Nervous?"

Eric shrugged. "Yes."

This time, I did not expect that answer. Surprise forced a laugh out of me. "Afraid it will turn you gay or something?"

He snorted. "No chance."

But the tip of his ears turned bright pink. Mesmerised by the sight, I didn't want to let it go. I was drawing closer, ready to tease him some more, when we heard some rustling coming from the nearby thicket of trees. Eric tossed a curious glance in that direction, and I froze, anxious.

"Hello, ladies."

Kayvin emerged first, holding a large stick. Xavier stumbled after him, looking clueless as usual. Not reacting to the dubious joke, Eric smiled and walked over to them. Their fists met, bumped, and rubbed against each other in some complicated combination I couldn't decipher.

"What's up?"

"We were looking for you," Kayvin said in French, hoisting the stick over his shoulder.

I found that quite threatening, but Eric was completely unimpressed.

"Are you afraid of bunnies or something?" Eric pointed at the stick.

Ignoring his questions, Kayvin looked around the grove with a dubious expression. "Is this where you hang out all day?"

My lips instinctively tightened. Eric giggled and spread out his hands.

"Yep. Right there, with the apple trees."

"It's not comfortable in here." Kayvin glanced at me briefly with a frown.

Xavier approached and pointed at his foot. "I stepped into a hole!"

Kayvin punched him in the shoulder.

"We make do," Eric said, making eye contact with me. "Why were you looking for me?"

"It's late." Kayvin stood between me and Eric. "Dinner is starting soon, and we couldn't find you anywhere. That loser Duvo's losing his mind, he thinks you've been kidnapped."

I checked my watch; he was right. It was time for dinner. We had completely lost track of time, conversing out here.

"Binta said we wouldn't get the surprise if we didn't try to find you," Xavier said with a sniff.

"What surprise?"

"They're making an announcement and they didn't want to start without you."

"Figures. We're the superstars after all." Eric winked at me. Kayvin looked even angrier after that.

"Don't you need to shower before dinner?" he asked.

"Not as much as you do," Eric replied pleasantly. "You look like you were trampled by the evil bunnies."

They turned around and started walking back in the direction of the house, their banter sounding like a foreign language to me. With my head down, I followed them a short distance away and in silence.

12

LET'S HANG OUT

To my surprise, seconds after they got into the house, Eric ran back out alone, shouting my name.

"Zak!"

Standing on the front steps, I blinked several times. "I'm right here."

"Zak, Zak." His hands pawed at my shoulders. "Are we hanging out tonight?"

The sight of Arthur hovering nearby, an expectant look on his face, distracted me momentarily. "Hum…"

"Yes! Say yes!"

"… Yeah, okay." I followed him into the hall. "I'll hang out."

"Yes!" In his joy, Eric slapped me hard across the back, bending me over. "Sorry, sorry!" He patted me all over with an apologetic look, then gestured upstairs. "I've got to go. I'll meet you later."

I stared after him. Was he really going to shower with his footballer friends? Just a bunch of bros casually showering together naked. *No homo.*

Perplexed, I rubbed the shoulder Eric had crushed with a grimace. Of course, Alberto strolled by at this exact moment, right when I looked worse for wear. "Hey, Alberto," I croaked.

To my surprise, he walked over to me. "What's wrong with your shoulder?"

"Nothing. Came across a mad dog." You could give me a massage, I almost added.

Alberto glanced at me curiously. "Anyway... Duvo wants to tell us something, but Michael said to wait for you." He looked exhausted by the mere trials of having to wait. He was so adorable.

"Lead the way, then."

We entered the dining room side by side, him tall and handsome, and me short and nervous. Everyone's attention turned to us. Of course, it was because they were all waiting for Eric and me to return home and defuse Duvo, but I liked to imagine it was because Alberto was by my side, right where he should be, and that we looked mighty handsome together.

I spotted Michael sitting alone at a table, looking miles away, and waved at him. Nearby, Duvo almost fainted when he saw me.

"You're alive!"

"Of course he's alive," Binta said in a patient tone.

I felt myself blushing when Alberto leaned dangerously close to my ear.

"Are you? Alive?"

"Barely," I muttered.

He chuckled, sending my nervous system into panic mode.

"Where's the other one?" Duvo barked.

I feigned stupidity. "The other one?"

"Yes, your partner. What's his name again? The loud, sporty one."

"Eric!" everybody yelled, out of patience.

"Yes, Eric."

"Ah, this guy!" I pointed a finger at the ceiling. "Upstairs."

"Thank God." Duvo slumped in his chair. "The less I interact with parents, the better."

Binta laughed heartily. I didn't know what to say to him, but then Alberto nudged my arm.

"Come sit with us."

"Me?"

Naturally, I followed after him with starry eyes. I expected Alberto to lead me to Sander, who sat by the fireplace with his Nintendo DS, but he walked right to Michael's table and took the seat opposite him. Surprised, I stood frozen on the spot. Alberto pulled the nearest chair with his foot and invited me to sit down. I did so with my heart in my throat, thanking him with a smile.

Michael woke up from his daydream when the legs of my chair gave a nasty scraping noise. "Where's Eric?" he immediately asked.

"Showering with his manly friends, I think," I said, attempting a joke.

"Oh, okay."

Astonishing me once more, Alberto answered my joke with a knowing smirk. My heart bounced around my ribcage. The first joke Alberto and I ever shared! I used to dream about it. It finally happened. I could already hear the bells.

The *wedding* bells.

"What's the surprise, Michael?" Alberto's voice was smooth like velvet.

Michael cast a gentle smile. "It wouldn't be a surprise if I told you, would it?"

"I don't like surprises." Alberto leaned forward on the table. He gave Michael a look which, if addressed to me, would have made me give up all sorts of information, classified state secrets included. "Please, tell me."

"No." Michael turned his head away. "Be patient, Binta will tell you after dinner."

Alberto pouted his lips. A pout looked cute and childish on Eric's face. On Alberto, it was a fire hazard. Breathless, I scanned around the room for a fire extinguisher.

"What do you think it is?" Alberto said, turning to me.

"I… ahem… I don't know."

He blinked slowly. "Use your imagination."

Too shellshocked to answer, I glanced at Michael to beg for support. He looked amused and was beginning to smile, when his phone emitted a loud beep. His face tensed; he jumped off his seat and walked off. I stared after him in wonder.

"Trouble in paradise." His chin in his hand, Alberto was looking at me.

"What do you mean?"

"He and his boyfriend are having problems."

"They are? That's impossible."

"Why would it be impossible?" Alberto yawned and rubbed his face. "Sorry."

"Because. That's impossible. And…" I said, with another look at Michael who had his back to us, "… he could be on the phone with a million other people."

I hesitated. If Michael was having problems, it wasn't a good thing. And if he was going through it alone, it was even worse... But if Alberto was right, then he wasn't going through it alone...

Alberto's feline eyes didn't leave my face. Under the table, my hands shivered slightly. "Okay, whatever you say." As he spoke, Alberto's hand came dangerously close to my face. I tried hard not to hyperventilate when he picked up a piece of fluff from my shoulder and swiped it clean with the side of his hand. "But soon you'll see I was right."

"Okay," I said, stunned.

When my gaze returned to Michael, I found him staring at us with such sadness, I thought with some anguish that Alberto might be right after all.

"Gotta go," Alberto said abruptly.

He rose from his seat and hurried back to Sander, leaving me alone and sweating. Seeing how he accidentally collided with Xavier on the way there, I expected him or Kayvin to give him a hard time, but Xavier only laughed and squeezed his shoulder affectionally. I first exhaled a breath, relieved. But before long, I was scratching my head.

Alberto was... flirty? Was this considered flirty? Or was it appropriate behaviour between two Drama Club students? And what about Michael having problems with Louis... And then... the way Xavier touched Alberto... Was that appropriate? I mean, they weren't even Drama Club buddies. So, what did it mean?

On the other hand, so what if Alberto and Xavier were surprisingly friendly? They shared the same room. Perhaps Xavier hadn't noticed how gay Alberto was yet.

After a while, I finally noticed Arthur standing near my table looking all shy, and I smiled. "You can sit with me if you want."

"Really?" He approached, his eyes bright.

Yes, really. Since you're gonna do it uninvited anyway, might as well.

Arthur and I went to the kitchen to grab dinner together. Arthur updated me on the shooting of the movie. Everything was going pretty well, considering. Xavier had even stopped complaining about the offensive nature of the script. That it happened after they shot the scene where Camille, as the kitchen wench, beat him with a wooden spoon was probably not a coincidence.

We returned to the dining room. Our butts had barely touched our chairs when Camille dropped her own tray on our table. Arthur's face immediately started glowing.

"Zak, are you and Eric ready?" She sat opposite him. "Eric said you were practically done. Please tell me you're done?"

I hesitated. "We aren't, we're fighting over notes."

If I'd told her we were done, then what would happen tomorrow? I was quite happy spending all day rehearsing with Eric, away from everyone else. Why change anything? And it wasn't exactly false, mind you. We *were* fighting about a certain scene.

"I'll be the judge of your notes," Camille said, fighting with her carrots.

"Yes, of course."

"What's the big fight, anyway?"

I gave a little cough. "An extra kissing scene."

"A kissing scene?" She dropped the carrots. "Are we kissing now?"

The pointed look she exchanged with Arthur made my mouth twitch.

"Actually…"

"I'm so relieved!" she cried, shocking me. "With all your pointless struggling on Monday, I was that close to scratching my original scene because I wasn't sure you'd be comfortable with it."

"That *I* wouldn't be comfortable with it?" I poked my chest. "I'm the actor, here! And Eric's the… the…" I kind of lost track here. With the way she was looking at me, it seemed like I was a diva who needed special care. "Eric's the football player. He's the one you should have been worried about."

"Of course." She slipped another pointed glance at Arthur. "Let me ask you something. Who suggested an extra kissing scene?"

I stabbed my piece of chicken. "He did."

"So what's the problem? You don't want to kiss him twice?"

"Why do you assume I don't want to kiss him?" I asked, scandalised. "Why not assume it's Eric who doesn't want to kiss me?"

Arthur nodded adamantly.

"Didn't you just say he's the one who suggested it?" Camille said. "Besides, Eric's up for anything. Don't you think we asked him during his audition? He said it. He said," she lowered her voice in a terrible impression of Eric, "I'll do anything you ask."

"So that's why you cast him!" I slammed a triumphant fist on the table, sending pieces of chicken, peas, and carrots everywhere. "He said he'd do anything you ask, and you couldn't resist. Classic."

Camille patted the hand of a pale Arthur. "Calm down, Zak, or I'll have to spray you with water."

"Oh. Of course. Sorry."

"I'm not the one with the super-sized ego here, trust me." Camille tilted her head toward Duvo. Already done with his meal, he was showing off his stretching exercises to Binta while Michael was staring right at his ass, lost in thought.

"Eric is devoted to his work," Arthur said.

"I am devoted!" I said, feeling jealous for some reason. "I spend every hour of every day with this guy because you asked me. Isn't that devoted enough?"

Arthur sniggered. "Can't be too bad to spend all day with Eric. I'd love to spend all day with Eric. He's really cool, and he—"

"Yes, thank you." I glared at him.

"Just saying…"

Once again, Eric was the best. It was maddening. Even his devotion was better than mine. If what Camille said was true, then I had never seen anyone so desperate to get cast in a student movie *ever*.

Well, except for me, of course.

"You know, Camille, you didn't even ask me if I was up for anything."

"Aww," she said, now patting my hand under the envious gaze of Arthur, "my little Zak is feeling insecure."

I removed my hand and hid it under the table.

"Zak. Don't be upset. I simply assumed you were, actually, up for anything. I didn't feel the need to ask."

"Why?" I asked suspiciously.

"Because you're an actor, you said it."

Arthur nodded almost fearfully. "Definitely."

I gave them a smile that I assumed looked smug and hid my mouth behind my hand. They were really terrified of me! And I should have felt awful about it, but they were just so cute, it couldn't be helped.

"I understand they have to kiss at the end," I said. "I really do. But Eric thinks the guys are burning with passion and wants to add a kiss after Adam confesses, while I think Thomas isn't ready. Adam is coming at him too strong. That's what I think."

Camille looked thoughtful. "You're not wrong. I tend to agree with you. But you have rehearsed everything else, right?"

I looked away. "Yes… But one or two more days together wouldn't hurt."

She smirked. "I actually thought you would murder him at first. I'm glad you warmed up to him."

"He's… he's all right."

I had gone from *Fuck this imposter* (➢_◅) to *Eric's my only friend* (❍⚲❍) in less than a week, but no one needed to know about this.

"You'll have more to rehearse soon," Camille said. "I'm still reworking the climax. It lacks something. I think we'll shoot two endings: a happy one and a sad one. Send your notes tomorrow and I'll look at them over the weekend."

"Ask Eric. He has everything."

"Fine. Then you'll rehearse the climax together next week after we're done filming the other scenes." I nodded. Camille turned to Arthur. "What about you? Everything ready on your end?"

Arthur smiled confidently. "Yes. I know fuck all about life, but I know how to use this camera." He turned to me. "I'll make you beautiful, Zak."

What an odd thing to say. I shifted in my seat, embarrassed. But Camille looked satisfied.

"Campfire tonight, Zak? Binta's announcing the surprise."

Arthur spoke in a whisper. "Eric already asked him, so…"

"It has nothing to do with Eric!" I said, knowing full well it had everything to do with Eric. "And you were eavesdropping on a private conversation."

"But you're so lucky, I want to hang out with Eric!" Arthur said.

I clicked my tongue. "If you love him so much, why don't you ask him out?"

"I might!"

Camille laughed, but I looked at Arthur, surprised.

"I didn't know you were into guys."

"I'm not!" he said, with a quick glance at Camille, who missed it. "That's how cool Eric is. He told Kayvin to leave me alone, and since, Kayvin hasn't even spoken to me once."

"He's a darling, isn't he?" Camille said. "Joy and Melissa always said so, and once I saw his girlfriend, you know, *the* Elodie, who's also a darling, and she said he was the best boyfriend and the best…" Camille trailed off when she saw me rolling my eyes. "What, do you have a problem with Eric?"

"No, I don't. But come on, he's not perfect either. Trust me, I know."

"Tea!" Camille bounced on her seat. "Spill it! Now!"

"Okay, let me see…"

Faced with their enthusiasm, I couldn't help chortling. Being fond of Eric myself, I wouldn't go too far naturally. But a part of me wanted to shatter their fantasy. It wasn't healthy to idolise people the way they did. I only meant to help.

"For instance…" I straightened up and feigned to think about it for a second. "He's got zero sense of propriety."

"I know!" Camille put her hands on her cheeks, her eyes sparkling. "Melissa met him out of the shower with only a towel around his waist, and he didn't even look bothered."

"Nothing wrong with that," Arthur said. "I would be comfortable with my body too if I looked like him."

"And forget about personal space!" I said, pushing unwanted thoughts of a half-naked Eric out of my head. "He doesn't respect that either. He always sneaks in closer, with no regard for—"

"This is rubbish!" Camille barked. "What else?"

I paused. "He… he's got grabby hands."

"…"

"…"

"It's true…" I scratched my head, disoriented by their reaction. "He's always trying to tickle me or worse, to pinch and hug me… And that… that… that doesn't seem to shock you at all!"

They were both staring at me with… *envy*.

"So he *is* perfect," Arthur squeaked. "And we're lucky to have him."

"Lucky, lucky, let's not exaggerate here. He defended you from his friend, okay. He wouldn't have had to do that if his friend weren't a real piece of—"

"Shit," Camille said.

Work, I meant, obviously, but I did not correct her.

"*And* they wouldn't be here if they weren't punished for vandalising our Drama Club, a place which they clearly despised."

"About that…" Arthur tapped his finger on the table. "It has to be Kayvin's work."

Camille nodded. "It has to. Charles-Henry is absolutely delighted to be stuck in the kitchen and away from them. Nadia doesn't seem to mind being stuck with Charles-Henry. And Eric practically went on his knees and begged us to let him be an actor. Now, which ones are left?"

"Kayvin and Xavier."

"A shame Eric got dragged into it," Arthur said.

"But… on the other hand…" Camille's smile faded. "What is it that you said, Zak? You are who you associate with?"

"I…" I hesitated. After all the things Eric said to me, I wasn't willing to associate him with Kayvin any longer. "I said that, yes. But perhaps that's what convinced Eric that he's better off without his friends."

"That's why he wants to hang out with you tonight," Arthur said, his eyes wide. "You're nothing like his friends."

"He wants to hang out with you too, you know," I said, remembering our conversation.

"He does? With me?"

"Both of you. For some mystical reason, he seems to think we're cool."

Camille made a little screeching sound. "Look at me, I'm gonna spend the evening around the fire with Eric Tucker-Régnier."

I frowned because it never occurred to me that Camille could be anything other than a talented artist, a courageous writer, and a badass. In my opinion, it wasn't that she was lucky to hang out with Eric, but the opposite.

"Oh my God," I said, teasing, "you even know his full name."

"You're the only one at Colette who doesn't know Eric, Zak."

Not the only one… Alberto didn't know him either.

"I don't care for football. I've never seen him play and I don't intend to."

"Neither have we," Camille said, carefully scooping the last of her carrots. "But his dad made a donation to Colette so seniors can have a prom ball after their exams, like American students."

I pulled a face. "That sounds even worse than attending a football game."

Eric then interrupted us, smelling of peaches, his blond hair still damp from his shower. Grinning, he hoisted himself on the table and nearly sat into Camille's empty plate.

"Are we still hanging out tonight?"

"Sure, why not?" Camille said super casually, as though talking to a boring old friend.

I admired her skill in respectful silence and stole a quick glance at Alberto on the other side of the room. My beloved was staring out the window with a dreamy look on his face. If I could act as cool and detached with him, we'd be married already.

Arthur began laughing nervously. Eric flashed us all a gleaming smile.

"Then I'll see you—"

"Eric!" Duvo's angry voice made us all jump. "Get your ass off this table!"

Eric didn't move. "What's the announcement, sir?"

"You won't know if you don't get off this table this second!"

Binta put her hand on Duvo's arm, distracting him. Eric pointed at the plastic-wrapped brownie laying by Camille's plate.

"Are you going to eat that?"

Camille flung her hair back. "Nope, not at all."

"Mind if I..."

"Go ahead."

"Eric!" Duvo screeched. "*Getdownthistablethisinstant!*"

With a wink addressed to me, Eric slid off our table and returned to his own.

"Just wow, Camille," I said. "You've really perfected the casual-indifference look."

She gave me a seductive smile. "That's how it's done, baby."

I pointed to her empty plate. "But he took your brownie."

"Yeah, that's a shame. But he looked like he really wanted it."

I watched Eric slide into a chair between Xavier and Kayvin and immediately get hounded by Joy. "You're all so crazy about him. I don't get it." Yes, he was my friend. But still, why the fangirls everywhere? They clearly didn't know how bouncy, chatty, and handsy he was.

"I don't fancy him, silly," Camille said with bright eyes. "Yes, he's nice to look at, I'm not stupid. But that doesn't mean I fancy him."

"He's got abs like a chocolate bar," Arthur said, causing Camille to snort into her water. "*Despite* stuffing himself with brownies. That's not fair."

"He's got what?" I asked, confused.

"Abs. Nice ones." Arthur frowned. "But that doesn't mean I fancy him either."

"How the hell would you know that?" I said, weirdly annoyed. "He always wears these shapeless T-shirts and these oversized shorts with insane pockets."

Camille tut-tutted me. "You have to hang out with us by the pool, Zak! That's where the good stuff happens. The guys play games, and the onlookers enjoy... well... the game."

"Xavier never wears a shirt if he can help it," Arthur said resentfully. "And Joy almost fainted the other day when Michael finally agreed to play badminton and almost stripped."

"Almost," Camille said. "He got all shy at the last second."

"Probably because Joy's tongue was hanging out!"

"You're all insane," I whispered.

"And you spend all your time cooped up in your room or god knows where," Camille said haughtily. "That's what's insane."

After dinner, everyone gathered around the fire, as planned. Low garden chairs and puffy cushions were dragged around the circular fireplace, and citronella candles were lit to protect us from evil mosquitos.

After half an hour or so of idle chatter, I was already looking up to the first-floor window where my room was and thinking about my bed and my book, but then I saw Eric on the other side of the fire, rolling on the floor with laughter at something Xavier said, and I thought I could at least stay a little longer. Next to me, Arthur and Camille were trying to have a conversation with Nadia about which Coen brothers movie was the best and not realising I was sitting right next to them with the answer. They never asked.

Finally, when everyone else got bored and began ganging up on Duvo, Binta rushed to his defence to announce, her eyes glowing, the most anxiously awaited surprise.

"To thank you for your hard work… We'll have a party tomorrow night!"

Arthur whooped, Camille gasped, Joy and Melissa squeaked with delight. Even Kayvin's eyes brightened. I saw from the corner of my eye that Eric was scratching his chin, thoughtful.

"Just for you," Binta added, raising her voice above the commotion. "Because you've all been amazing this week, and half the movie is shot, Charles and Nadia have been great in the kitchen," — there were sniggers around the fire — "and even Kayvin and Xavier have proven particularly helpful."

Kayvin's eyes narrowed, but Xavier beamed when he heard her. "Binta! Say, can we drink at the party?" he asked.

Duvo frowned at him. "Drink?"

"Yes, alcohol."

Duvo barked out a laugh. "No."

"So it's not a real party."

"Little shitheads, you're minors!"

"So?" Xavier crossed his arms over his chest, pouting. "We're in France, not Siberia, as far as I know."

"I'm pretty sure we'd be allowed to drink in Siberia," Kayvin said darkly.

Duvo rose from his seat. "Do you want me to lose my job?" He looked like he was about to tear Kayvin to shreds, but again, was distracted by Binta's gentle touch on his arm.

"Charles-Henry, Nadia, and I will make preparations in the kitchen if you're okay with that, and Kayvin and Xavier will help with the equipment in the main living room."

"Why us!" Kayvin snapped.

Duvo pointed a judgmental finger at him. "Do I have to remind you that you're here as punishment?"

Kayvin became red with rage or embarrassment. "What about Eric, then?"

Binta hesitated. She looked at Eric, who had retrieved his tennis ball and was tossing it in the air, his tongue stuck out. "Eric is…"

Kayvin got up, eyes flashing angrily. "What about Eric?"

"I'll do it," Eric said calmly, with a look at his friend. "I don't mind."

Kayvin stared him down for a moment, then satisfied with the result, sat back and returned his gaze to the fire. But then, Eric shoved his ball into his pocket and began slowly making his way toward our group. Kayvin's eyes burned brighter than the fire with anger.

"Why is he so mad at you?" I asked, when Eric sat next to me, plunging me into a cloud of peachy shower gel and firewood.

"Because I'm spending all day with you instead of doing chores."

"Serves him right for destroying our Drama Club."

Eric waited, then as though he couldn't help himself, said, "Nothing was destroyed. It was just a bit of spray paint."

"I don't care. The Drama Club is like my second home. Attacking it is a direct attack on me. He won't get any pity from me."

Eric linked his fingers behind his head. "It was dumb, granted, but not so big of a deal. You won't even notice. We've cleaned it all up already."

"You should not have let him drag you into doing something you didn't want to do."

Eric gazed into the fire and said nothing. I thought perhaps I shouldn't give him a hard time. This was how I ended up scaring people and having

155

them think I was no fun, or an old man. Seeing how Arthur, Camille, Nadia, and now Charles-Henry were still fighting about the Coen brothers' movies, I scooted over closer to Eric to isolate ourselves from them and turned the conversation to something more agreeable instead.

"Guess what?"

"Wait, don't tell me." Eric put his fingers on his temples and furrowed his brow. Then he opened his eyes, laughing. "I can't. I can feel your impatience and I can't focus."

I bumped against his shoulder. "Alberto invited me to his table."

"When?"

"Earlier. When you were upstairs."

"What happened?"

"Nothing, really, he wanted to know about the announcement. But!" I added, seeing Eric was losing interest, "I think he may have flirted with me, but I'm not sure, since I've never been flirted with and I don't know the difference. How do you know if people are just being nice to you or if they're flirting?" Eric opened his mouth to answer, but I kept talking. "I don't even generally know if people are being genuinely nice to me or just polite."

Eric smiled. "Just assume everybody is flirting with you. Makes life so much funnier."

"That's because, in your case, I can honestly say everybody *is* flirting with you."

"*And* it makes life so much funnier."

I shook my head. "But back to Alberto—"

"Yes. About that. I've watched him a bit and I've been meaning to ask you." Eric made himself comfortable first, then spoke close to my ear. "What's his deal?"

"What do you mean?"

"What is he? Does he like girls? Or boys? Does he—"

My shoulders slumped. "Why do you say that? Do you know anything about him that I—"

"I don't." Eric gave my nape a reassuring pat. "But you'd be surprised with people sometimes. I've asked around…"

"You what?"

"Don't worry. I was discreet. It's just that no one could tell me anything for certain." He momentarily looked baffled. "Not even Joy…"

"He's secretive, that's all…" I racked my brain for the clues I'd collected about my beloved over the year. "I can tell you he's never looked at a girl, as far as I know."

"That's good."

"But... he's never looked at a guy either."

"That's..." Eric made a face. "... That's not good."

"I always assumed he was shy."

"Or... he thinks everybody's beneath him."

I shook my head vehemently. "Alberto wouldn't think that."

"How do you know? I mean, have you spoken for more than two minutes with him over the course of your life?"

I tossed Eric a dark look. "Fine, no need to rub it in."

"Not my intention. I'm here to help you. But if he's not into guys, there's nothing you can do about it. Just be ready."

"He's gay, he's gay. I know he's gay." I remembered him leaning across the table in front of everyone this morning. No straight guy would dare display their ass like that. But that was only as far as I knew... And in all fairness, I didn't know many people who were not fictional characters.

Eric seemed to read my mind and tilted his head. "Only one way to find out, Zak. You should go and ask him."

"How would that look? You're insane!"

"Then I'll do it."

"Oh, because *that* wouldn't be weird at all. You coming up to him and asking him if he's gay?" I couldn't help snorting.

Eric chuckled. "It would definitely be weird. He might think I'm interested in him."

I began laughing behind my fist. "That would make quite the scene."

"If it amuses you so much, I'll do it."

I stopped laughing but couldn't wipe the smile off my face. "No, no, it doesn't amuse me. Let's drop it."

"What are you going to do, then? Alberto knows who you are, and he was flirting tonight, so are you going to talk to him, then?"

"Perhaps. Eventually. I'll have to talk to him eventually, but—"

"Ask him out during the party."

Eric looked serious. Even more so with the shadows of the flames dancing across his face.

"Ask him out... I was thinking more along the lines of asking how his day was and stuff."

"How else are you planning to tell him you like him?" Eric leaned

157

forward in secrecy. "Keep stalling and he'll be taken by the time you make your move."

Horror struck me. Eric was right. Suddenly everyone around me looked like contenders.

"I wasn't planning on telling him anything, remember?" I said, biting my nail. "He was supposed to fall in love with me while shooting the film. I had it all planned in my head." I poked my temple with my index finger.

"And I ruined it." Eric pulled my wrist to stop me from chewing my nails.

"And you ruined it." I pushed him away with my other hand. "So now you must fix it." I was clearly joking. But Eric's expression was still focused.

"I told you I'd help you."

"So you were serious, then? If yes, then I accept your help. You're clearly good with people. And I'm not. So perhaps I should heed your advice."

"Good boy." Eric swung his arm over my shoulder. "Tomorrow night, you go to him and you ask him out."

I frowned. "Is that how you would do it?"

Eric took some time to consider my words while I shrunk under the warmth of his arm on my neck. After noticing my discomfort, he swiftly removed it.

"I guess I'd make sure he liked me first."

I gave a frustrated groan. "See? I don't know that he likes me! The whole point is that I don't know if he likes me!"

Eric didn't seem worried at all about my predicament. "Then ask him something small first. Like… to dance?"

"Dance?" My eyes bulged. "Dance?"

"Sure. It's going to be a party after all."

"But do people really do that? Dance at parties? It sounds so old-fashioned."

"It's not like you have to waltz or whatever people did in the old days! Just shake your ass, you'll be fine."

I gave Eric a shrewd once over. "Do you? Dance at parties? Shake your ass?"

"Hell no! I don't have to do any of this stuff." He pointed at his own chest. "I'm a football superstar."

He laughed like an idiot for a while. I waited, my mouth hanging open.

"Are you happy? Proud of yourself?"

"What? Your words, not mine! You should have seen your face. All the love you have for football was right there—"

"Alberto hates football too, you know."

"And so… that's a good thing I'm not the one asking him out, then. But the thing is, if you don't make him notice you, he might never will."

I briefly pondered his words. "He invited me to his table today. He does notice me."

"Noticing a guy from a crowd of ten people isn't so hard. Seeing him as a potential boyfriend is another. Now you have to find out if he likes you." He spoke as though he had infinite knowledge on the subject, which made me feel a little bitter somehow.

"I guess you've never had that problem." I saw Eric's lip curl up from the corner of my eye. "Yes, yes, you can laugh at my ignorance, but no, I didn't know playing football granted you automatic sex appeal."

Eric's sneaky smile turned into a laugh. "I like how you say sex appeal." Seeing me roll my eyes, he added, "But, but! It's not as easy as you think. Like, if I missed all my shots, no one would care about me. Just like you thought Alberto wouldn't notice you if you were just an extra. People really couldn't care less about you if you don't perform to certain standards. It's annoying, but it's what it is."

It seemed Eric was capable of some wisdom despite looking like a newborn pup. I looked up, feeling like flattering him, and accidentally met Kayvin's murderous gaze on the other side of the fire. The sight made me forget what I had intended to say.

"Why did you lie to Kayvin earlier?" I asked. "About the lake?"

"You mean the pond?" I reached out to swat him, but Eric easily seized my wrist and returned it to my lap. "I don't feel like sharing it with them. And their sticks."

"That's a good point."

In truth, I had no intention of sharing that place with them either. I quite liked having it to myself and Eric. It felt like having a little secret, and this place was peaceful and safe. The thought of watching Kayvin and Xavier trampling the wildflowers and jumping headfirst into the lake made me feel nauseous.

"So…" Eric leaned in my side. "You'll talk to Alberto tomorrow, right?" My face must have betrayed my terror, because he slammed his hand on my shoulder and gave me a coaching look. "Zak. You can do it. I know you can. Asking someone out is no different than ripping off a Band-Aid."

"I'm not so sure about that. The Band-Aid thing. Hurts like a bitch for a second, but then you can toss it in the bin and forget about it. Alberto isn't someone I can get rid of or forget instantly."

Eric gave me a look which implied he was perfectly capable of forgetting all about Alberto in less than a second.

"Zak. You are brave."

"Am I?" My voice sounded weak.

"Yes. Anyone who seriously wants to become an actor really has to be. Tomorrow, you will do it. You will get ready, put on your best clothes, walk into that room, go straight to Alberto, and you will ask him out."

"I will?"

Eric's fingers dug into my shoulders, kneading it. "Yes. But don't worry. I'll coach you. And I'll be there for you all the way."

Eric's eyes were twinkling in the firelight. His touch was warm on my shoulder. But this time, I didn't flinch.

13

MY CRUSH AND MY COACH

Eric was taking his coaching mission pretty seriously.
After boasting he wouldn't let me out of his sight, he was already tutoring me in the line to get breakfast the next morning. His confusing bits of advice sounded an awful lot like the lyrics of a Katy Perry song. I was in dire need of a cup of coffee.

Suddenly, Eric gasped and clutched my wrist.

"He's here!"

"Yes, I can see that. He's hard to miss."

Alberto entered the kitchen, looking like he could use a strong cup of coffee himself. I smiled at his sleepy appearance and noticed, amused, that Eric was observing him keenly, his lips parted.

"Admit he's got good genes," I said, cunning.

"Pff. That's nothing to brag about."

I rammed my elbow into his ribs. "Then stop staring so intently! He's gonna notice."

Ignoring Eric's sob of pain, I moved along the line and felt him move closely behind me. I turned around, exasperated. "Why are you standing so close?"

"I'm your coach, I need to be close to give you all my secrets."

Yes, okay, but his breath was tickling my ear. I felt like swatting him, but I didn't want to do it in front of everyone, so I gritted my teeth and said nothing. After a second, a voice boomed in my ear.

"Zak. Zak! I was just thinking…"

I rubbed my ear. "What?"

"Let's make him jealous!"

Without warning, Eric roughly hooked his arm around my neck, pulling me to him. His other hand, searing hot, ended up on my waist.

"Hang on a minute…" Pinned against his warm chest, I tried my best not to gag.

"Hold still." Eric's laughter reverberated through my back. "It's an old trick, but it always works."

I was about to kick him in the crotch, but what he said made sense. It really did wonders in books and movies. It was worth a try.

"Can you see him?" I couldn't move my neck, considering our awkward pose. "Is he jealous?"

"Not yet."

"And now?"

"Nope."

Everyone else, however, was beginning to look our way.

"Now?"

"If only he looked in our direction!"

"Having fun?" a deep voice asked behind us.

Eric whirled around, and I turned alongside him, still glued to his chest. Kayvin, also too tall and too large to be considered good news at this instant, was looking at us, his lips pursed. I stared into his disgusted face with wide eyes, hoping Eric would come up with an explanation, — like for example, that he simply meant to put me in a headlock to teach me a lesson — but Eric didn't relax his grip and chose to remain silent.

"What the hell are you doing?" There was a flash of confusion in Kayvin's pale eyes.

"Rehearsing," Eric said, deadpan.

"Man… Is it really worth not doing the dishes…?" After a weary shake of his head, Kayvin helped himself to some toast and jam and slunk away. Just as I looked up toward the exit, I noticed Alberto glancing in our direction and gasped.

"He looked!"

"He did!"

Breathless, I wrenched away from Eric. "Him and everyone else…"

"I still call that a success. And look! Bananas!"

Eric hurled himself at the serving table. Every portion was to be shared among us, and there was a strict one item per person rule, except for fruits. I looked at Eric gather half a dozen bananas, several apples, and a small brownie into his arms, grinning like a child, not at all bothered by the fact everyone present in the kitchen had seen him grab another boy and hug him to his chest. I guessed confident guys didn't think about these things. I knew how we looked; clearly, he didn't.

"Are you never uncomfortable?"

Eric glanced down at his bounty, confused. "I mean, in general, or this morn—"

"Everyone was staring!"

"Ah." He shrugged. "I said we were rehearsing, and it worked. Don't worry about it."

At least he was trying to help. But did his body have to be so warm? My skin felt hot and tingly now.

Eric slammed a plastic-wrapped brownie on my tray as I was turning around to leave. "You forgot this."

"But I don't want it."

"Oh, I'll have it then, thanks!" He put the thing in his pocket and disappeared to his table, leaving me dumbfounded.

I scanned around the room, but no one was looking at us anymore, and Eric's hands were busy dipping into Joy's breakfast as she laughed. It was likely that everyone was resigned to the fact that Eric's hands ended up pretty much everywhere, and that was nothing to concern themselves about.

Naturally, no one cared where Eric put his hands, because the only thing on anyone's mind that morning was tonight's party, and the conversation over breakfast was centred on the fact that no one had anything to wear. That was hardly true, as proven by some of the girls, who miraculously produced enough garments to dress an army and had dumped a pile of clothing onto their table, exchanging ideas. Even Kayvin was all up in arms, thinking himself likely to get smooched tonight. His friend Xavier had grown quiet, for everybody's benefit.

Personally, I was a little out of my depth. Aside from family gatherings, I never socialised, so this would be my first party. I didn't know the rules or how to conduct myself during such events. With my real agenda tonight, it would be preferable to look my best. The stakes were high.

Thankfully, I wasn't the only one worried about looking stupid.

"What are you going to wear?" Arthur asked in anguish as we returned to our room. "I have a feeling I should make an effort tonight."

I silently agreed with him. Sitting on my bed, I opened my suitcase and started rummaging through the contents with a small lump in my throat. Getting dressed was actually the easy part; confessing my feelings to Alberto would be much harder. But Eric said he'd be with me all the way, right?

Screams of delight filled the corridor and our bedroom through the open door. I clutched my best shirt to my chest. "What the hell was that!"

"It can only mean one thing." Arthur sighed longingly. "Michael is out there. He's so popular among the girls. I wish I were a pretty gay guy sometimes."

"I'm sure you do," I muttered back, recalling his man-crush on Eric.

What would Alberto be wearing tonight? I had never seen him outside of school. It was unlikely that he packed an Armani suit, but something told me his suitcase contained an *Open in case of casual party* emergency pouch, while mine seemed to contain nothing but underwear.

My thoughts drifting agreeably toward Alberto wearing Armani, I started when someone dropped heavily onto my bed.

"Do you mind?" I spoke harshly, expecting to see Arthur.

But Arthur was gone, and I found myself staring at Eric's earnest face. Everyone else had magically disappeared.

"What are we angry about now?" Eric asked, his voice smooth and teasing. He smelled of bananas mixed with the faint artificial scent of peaches.

"*We* are not angry, *we* are nervous."

Eric squirmed a little closer, and I scooted away. "What are you nervous about?"

The sweet, fruity smell became overpowering. I began to wonder if he actually ate the half-dozen bananas he'd taken from the kitchen.

"Alberto always looks flawless, and I'll look like a troll compared to him."

"That's not true."

"Don't start with the empty words." I pointed at my suitcase with a helpless look. "Help me find something to wear instead."

"Yes, m'lord." Eric slid off the bed and knelt by my suitcase. With a disengaged expression, he began to move around a few clothes. When he encountered the stack of underwear, he scratched his chin and pushed the suitcase away. "Dressing up isn't really my thing, you know?"

I believed him and still couldn't comprehend his complete lack of effort in that department. But after learning last night what he was packing under his unflattering clothes, I couldn't help but tease.

"I imagine you could just stroll down there naked, and you'd make a certain effect."

Eric lowered his head. "Wouldn't work on our target, though."

Staring at the outline of his body, I tried to imagine what it was like under his shirt. "No, Alberto wouldn't like it at all," I said with mounting doubt.

Eric heaved a sigh. "Sorry, can't help after all. You should ask Joy, or Melissa, perhaps."

"Yes. I'm sure they'd love to dress me up like a doll."

"No, trust me." His smile returned. "Tell them the reason and they'll kill themselves trying to help you."

At this moment, the girls' unbridled laughter rang out in the corridor, full of mirth and confidence. I had no intention of requesting their help. But before I could answer, a silhouette appeared in the corner of my eye, and I let out a gasp. Eric's head jerked up toward the object of my surprise.

Alberto was standing in the doorway.

He hovered on the threshold, seemingly hesitant to step in or not. In my flustered state, I threw my good shirt into my suitcase, but it landed straight on Eric's face.

"Hey, Zak." Alberto finally stepped in. He did a double-take when Eric emerged from under my shirt. "What are you doing?"

"Tidying up," I said stupidly.

I expected Eric to laugh, but he got up, all serious, with his hands on his hips.

"What do you want?" His tone was harsh, unwelcoming.

Such rudeness toward the object of my affections! I almost hit him with the bedside lamp. Alberto was gracing me with a visit for the first time and this was how you treated him?

Then I recalled how Eric was playing at making him jealous earlier, and my heart thundered in my chest. We were still playing that game, then? Well played, Eric.

"Just wanted to talk to Zak, that's all." Alberto stared into Eric's eyes with such indifference that I felt a little vexed for my new friend.

But Eric held his own, didn't even move an inch. I had to pretend to cough for him to get out of the way.

"I'm going to ask Michael," he said suddenly.

"Ask him what?" Alberto and I said together.

I begged him with my eyes not to say anything embarrassing. Eric stared back, his blue irises glinting.

"Clothing advice, for tonight."

He passed Alberto on the way out and left with a last look at me. Alberto stared after him, a blank look on his face.

"He's gonna need it," he mumbled.

"Need what?"

"Clothing advice."

I looked at my shoes, embarrassed a little, and pleased also, because this all meant that Alberto was impervious to Eric's charms, which was a blessing because I was totally *the opposite* physically. But I still felt the need to protest, however weakly.

"He's all right, you know."

"Is he?" Alberto strolled over to Eric's bed and even put his hand on his bed frame.

Did he sound jealous? I couldn't know for sure. Alberto was usually mild spoken. No one at the Drama Club had ever heard him raise his voice.

"Yeah, once you know him." I hesitated. "He's really into bees for some reason."

Alberto ignored my comment. He ran his hand along Eric's bed frame and went as far as to spy on the contents of his night table. Was this the behaviour of a jealous person? I just couldn't tell for sure.

"His friends are okay, too," Alberto said, turning away from Eric's bed.

"Really?"

"Mm-mh. Xavier's all right. Kayvin's a little…" He paused, thoughtful. "He's an acquired taste, I guess."

He almost smiled, and I dropped on the bed.

"His father's a big deal," Alberto spoke as if that settled the matter.

He walked toward my bed and looked into my suitcase absently. Was he stalling? Was that what it was? Imagine if he were the one to confess his feelings… and before the dreaded party! We could elope immediately instead of worrying about how to dress.

A twisted smile tugged at the corner of my lip. Alberto didn't notice. He closed his eyes for a moment, then opened them, frowning.

"Did you say Eric was into bees?"

"Huh? Oh. Yeah."

"I thought I heard wrong."

"No, you didn't." I held my breath. He was getting ridiculously close to digging up my underwear. "He says all sorts of ridiculous things about them."

Alberto blinked slowly with the faint hint of a smile. The temperature in the room rose.

"What brings you here anyway?" Stretching my foot, I snapped the suitcase shut. "Can I help you with anything?"

A girl screamed somewhere down the corridor. The sound was followed by general laughter.

"There are a lot of screeching girls out there," Alberto said, his voice flat.

It was like the gods were on my side. I couldn't think of a better chance than that to gather information about his... proclivities.

"Is that... ahem... not your thing?"

"Hm-hm," was all he said, but the shake of his head told me what I needed to know.

Not.

Into.

Screeching.

Girls.

Gay. Gay! Alberto was gay. And he must have wanted me to know. He was, after all, wandering in my room with nothing to say. My heart bounced around in my chest with such vigour that for a moment I wasn't sure if it was from love or from terror.

Alberto then opened his mouth, but unfortunately, I never got to hear his words, because darn Michael swooped in. Closely following him was Eric, but he didn't enter the room and stayed at the door.

"Hey... Zak..." Michael's voice trailed off when he spotted Alberto. "Alberto? Are you helping Zak dress?"

Alberto's perfect eyebrows drew together. "Zak doesn't need my help to dress. It was Eric." He lowered his voice and said in my ear. "Clearly."

His words, though falling like an intoxicating caress into my ears, made me turn away from him. Seeing that Michael was staring at him, Alberto put both hands on my shoulders. I blinked helplessly.

"Oh, I mean..." Alberto said. "If Zak... If you want my help, I'll help you."

He could help me get out of my clothes, that's for sure.

Quickly, I smothered the slutty voice in my head with a mental pillow and coughed in my fist.

Michael shrugged. "If you don't need any help, I've got to go. The girls are putting together a fashion show and they asked me to be the judge!"

He seemed outrageously pleased at that. The two adorable dimples which made his reputation as the ultimate cutie made their appearance. Alberto gave my shoulders a faint squeeze and stepped away, leaving me feeling strangely dizzy. Just then, Xavier and Kayvin barged, panting, into the room.

"We just heard!" Xavier said.

Kayvin nodded. "We want to be in the fashion show!"

"Michael!" Xavier clung to his sleeve. "Do you have to be gay to be a judge?"

"Not necessarily." Michael put his hand over his eyes. "You have to be liked, though."

Slow as he was, Xavier understood Michael's jest, and he blushed, vexed. Kayvin, in vengeance, blocked Michael's way out of the room, forcing him to squeeze himself out by flattening himself against the door frame. Michael did so with a neutral face which forced my admiration. My sister would have probably head-butted Kayvin on the way out, and I felt strangely tempted to do the same.

Alberto also rushed for the exit, but Xavier stopped him.

"We're going to play badminton. Are you coming?"

"No, I don't think so," Alberto said quickly.

In a display of unbelievable familiarity, Xavier grabbed his bicep with both hands. "You need to start exercising."

Alberto merely smirked. "I think I would die in the attempt."

Xavier laughed and followed Alberto out of the room. Eric and I exchanged an astounded look. Were these two becoming friends? What an odd pair they'd make. Eric seemed to agree, because the corner of his lip twitched, and he quickly made his way toward me.

Not missing any of that and with a dark expression, Kayvin pulled Eric to him and whispered something in his ear. First showing surprise, Eric shook his head, a frown on his face.

"No, no."

"No?"

"No, not this time."

"You've got to get over it." Kayvin's hand tightened around Eric's shoulder. "Now's the chance!"

Again, Eric shook his head, his face set. "Tell him not to do it."

Kayvin looked surprised. Remembering I was in the room, he quickly set his face back to a smirk.

"Are you coming down to play badminton, then?"

"No." Eric looked smug. "I have to help set up the party, remember?"

Kayvin remembered and seemed at a loss for words. With a last disgusted look in my direction, he left the room. Everyone's behaviour was particularly strange today. So strange that I was starting to feel like the only normal one. Kayvin had a secret, Xavier was friendly with Alberto, and Alberto was in my bedroom alone with me just moments ago!

Eric called my name and snapped me out of it. "Camille said she'd also look at your clothes for tonight." He bounded toward me, looking quite excited and pink in the cheeks, and grabbed both my elbows. "I went out there to find Michael, and I got into their room!"

"Their room?"

"Camille and Nadia! Only Joy and Melissa were there, and they were in their bras, though Michael kept begging them to cover themselves, and they said they didn't mind since he wasn't a pervert, well at least not with girls, Joy's words, not mine!" Eric's eyes were glittering with delight. "But he kept saying he was still in charge of them, and no one showed him any respect as a responsible adult, so, unfortunately, she put on a T-shirt, but before they noticed I was in there, I saw every-thing!" He dropped flat on my bed. "Oh, the things I've seen…" Reaching for my pillow, he buried his head in it.

"You're impossible," I said, retrieving my pillow with a disgusted grimace.

He watched me, giggling. "There's no harm in looking."

I couldn't deny how his rosy cheeks were a good look on him. The warm feelings I occasionally felt toward him came rushing back. I sat next to him.

"What happened then?"

Eric pouted. "They saw me, and Melissa screamed." Seeing my severe face, he waved his hands. "It wasn't a scream of horror! It was surprise, I think."

The corner of my mouth curled up.

"Anyway," Eric went on, "Camille said to leave it because I was, I quote, a darling, and Michael gave me the look!"

"What look?"

"This look." He wiggled his eyebrows.

I chuckled.

"I think he meant that I was indeed, a darling, and they all love me dearly," Eric said, sliding closer.

For a second, I felt like patting the top of his head and calling him a good boy, which was weird. Then I remembered he had a girlfriend, and his promiscuous ways were intolerable.

"Remember, Eric," I said, with a strict countenance, "you can look, but you can't touch!"

He blinked earnestly, even going as far as making the sign of the cross. "Of course not. I'm not a beast."

Wasn't he, though? Seriously. While we were speaking, he had slithered so close to me that I could see the tiny scar on his chin. He really had no sense of boundaries.

"Immediately I said we needed help to dress——"

"We?"

"Yes, I said that I needed help too, so… so that I wouldn't throw you under the bus, you know."

I gave him an appraising look and bowed my head a little. "Much obliged, your lordship."

He bowed his head right back. "Don't mention it, Thomas."

"Wow. Your British accent got better."

"Thanks to you." Eric kissed the air. "But I convinced Camille to come help us. And Michael wanted to help too, because he said he'd do anything for you. He said, 'Anything for Zak, of course', and the girls were like, *Aww*, and you would have loved it."

Tut-tutting, I shook my head, but secretly, I did love it. "I'm glad you had a good time in the apparently mystifying kingdom that is a girl's bedroom."

"It was awesome." Eric gave a long, satisfied sigh. "It smelled nice and there were pretty things scattered everywhere. A lot of ink stains on Camille's stuff. A *lot*. But what about you?" He became more serious. "What happened with Alberto?"

I gave him an account of what transpired.

"You interrupted too early. We might have been engaged already, if not for you."

Eric's enthusiasm faded. "I keep blowing this up for you."

"Not at all," I said with a smile. "You've helped me enough. I now feel I have the confidence to talk to him about my feelings tonight." I got up and stood in front of the mirror. "As soon as Camille teaches me how to dress."

"Perhaps _you_ should get down naked," Eric said, linking his fingers behind his head.

"There are enough scarecrows outside."

I saw in the reflection that Eric was staring at the ceiling and registered that he didn't disagree.

The day went on. While Eric went downstairs to help Binta, the girls performed for Michael, and the others played outside. I watched them from my faithful hiding place, the utility closet at the end of the corridor. As the clock advanced, so did my anxiety. From my perch, I could see Alberto, soundly asleep on one of the lounge chairs, sheltered by the large shadow of Sander. Even when he looked like this, at his most vulnerable, I still found him dangerous, unapproachable.

When it was almost time for the party, I reemerged from my closet and came face to face with Eric.

"So that's where you're hiding," he said, stretching his neck to get a look inside.

With a disapproving click of the tongue, he pried my book from my fingers and dragged me by the arm toward our room. He was already dressed, in jeans and a simple T-shirt, his cheeks still pink from a recent shower, smelling of flowery aftershave. I followed him without complaint, only smiling awkwardly at Charles-Henry as we entered the bedroom arm in arm. Seeing me so obedient, Eric hesitated before pushing me onto my bed. Arthur, who was sitting on his own bed, looked at us and laughed.

"There you are! Eric called you a little chicken."

"Did he now?" I said, squinting at him.

Eric's expression, a mixture of mischief and warmth, threw me off guard. I closed my fists and looked away, feeling his weight as he sat on the edge of my bed.

Then Camille barged in, her face flushed. We all startled, but Arthur sprang up like a rubber band and began to straighten his clothes feverishly.

"What's up, boys?"

She looked very nice tonight in one of her flouncy skirts and a lacy white top which gave her a romantic air. With a longing sigh, Arthur sunk down on my bed right next to Eric.

"Is Nadia downstairs?" Charles-Henry asked.

"She's in our bedroom."

Charles-Henry immediately headed out. Eric noticed Arthur was fidgeting with manic eyes and slammed him headfirst into my bedspread. Arthur re-emerged looking shaken but less demented.

"You look real nice, Camille," he said, his voice squeaky.

"Thank you, Arthur!" She did a little twirl, and we all saw a flash of her pink underwear. Arthur moved quickly in front of Eric whose mouth had dropped open. "So, Zak, what can I do for you?"

I put my hands on my hips. "I don't know… Make me look handsome?"

"No problem. Which effect are we looking for?"

"That one?" I pointed at Eric, whose mouth was still open.

Eric closed his mouth and blushed when he saw me pointing at him. Strolling lightly toward the clothes I had laid on the bed, Camille let out a long sigh.

"Oh, Zakky-Zak!" She bumped into my suitcase and almost landed face first in Eric's lap. Arthur let out an impressive yelp of horror, but Eric had the situation under control.

He seized her shoulders and began shaking her.

"Girl, you are drunk!"

She looked at him cross-eyed. "A little."

"She can barely stand on her feet!" Eric said, horrified.

"That's because you shook her like a god damn coconut tree!" I pulled her close to me. "Back off, beast!"

Eric backed off.

"When? Why? How did this happen?" Arthur sounded anguished.

Camille, on the other hand, looked like she was riding on a cloud. "Xavier gave me some of his rum. It was disgusting. Then it was delicious."

Eric frowned. "Is he trying to get you drunk?"

"Don't worry," Camille said. "He just gave me a little, and the other girls too. He poured most of it in the punch so everybody can enjoy it."

"I told them not to do that," Eric said with a look at me. "Duvo's gonna kill us."

Camille didn't care for such trifle things at the moment. She threw her arms around my neck and laid her head on my shoulder. "I like you, Zak."

"I've got to get some of this punch!" Arthur said and ran out of the room.

"You smell really nice," Camille said.

I gently pushed her away. "So do you, but—"

"Don't you worry about clothes. You have a great body."

"A great body?" I looked down at myself. "Please let me know when you stumble upon it."

Eric laughed and reached out to ruffle my hair. I couldn't defend myself because Camille was still hugging me. Suddenly motivated, she kicked my suitcase open.

"Listen to me. I know everything." She quickly picked up a selection and tossed it on the bed. "Your skinny frame is perfect to wear just about anything. Girls starve themselves trying to look like you."

"Starve themselves?" I threw Eric a panicked look and found him staring at my skinny frame. His gaze lingered on a certain part. "Stop it!" I hissed.

"Stop what?"

"Stop staring at *it*."

Eric cocked an eyebrow. "You can stare at mine if it makes you more comfortable." He turned around, and both he and Camille made some crude dance moves before giggling like two toddlers.

"She's drunk!" I barked, reminding myself of Duvo. "But you, you have no excuse!"

"What?" Eric looked hurt. "You don't like my butt?"

He was playing the impossible flirt again, and as always, I was a victim. It was insufferable, trying to make me uncomfortable at this precise moment.

"Yes, fine. You, too, have good genes. Just stop shaking it in front of me."

Eric was looking at me with a frown. "It has nothing to do with genes."

"Sure."

"There," Camille said, shoving the pair of jeans and the shirt I had planned on wearing all along into my arms. "Wear this."

I'd vexed Eric, evidently, because he left the room without a word, and Camille's drunk face split into a grimace.

"What did I say?" I asked, more to myself than to her.

"I guess you hurt his feelings." She twirled around inexplicably.

"What? How?!" I had never seen Eric vexed by anything ever. "I don't understand. This morning I said the same thing about Alberto, and he didn't bat an eye."

"Shhhh!" Camille pressed her finger to my lips. "Guys don't like to be compared to Alberto, Zak. Alberto has it easy."

I removed her hand. "But Eric has it easy too!"

"Do you really think so?" Camille took on a serious air. "Guys like Alberto don't have to do anything, while Eric works really hard."

"Oh, that's why…"

"It's vexing when people play down your efforts. Don't you think?"

Camille was right. How could I have been so insensitive? And after he told me he was waking up early to exercise, and that he didn't have much time for anything outside of football. I hugged the pile of clothes close to my chest. I, too, was enraged when people doing nothing got better results than hardworking ones. I always said Eric and I were vastly different, but we had this point in common.

"All right. I'll make sure to apologise to him."

"I'm sure you're forgiven anyway. Eric's got a soft spot for you."

"I don't see why," I said, dumping the clothes on the bed. "Unless he's into feral raccoons for some reason."

"Feral what?"

"Forget it. I'm just spouting nonsense." I gestured for her to turn around so I could change quickly. She blew a raspberry but complied.

"Eric said he'd stick together with you tonight and made us all very jealous. Joy seemed really disappointed. She said that drunk Eric is particularly interesting."

She meant loose, probably, considering the sober version already had the grabbiest hands in recorded history. I shivered to think what the drunk one could do.

"Joy's got some nerve," I said haughtily. "Isn't she Elodie's best friend?"

Once dressed, I poked Camille's shoulder. She gave my outfit a thorough check and gave me the thumbs-up.

"Very handsome." Her eyes narrowed. "Is that on purpose?"

I played innocent. "What do you mean?"

"I don't know. Anything you want to tell me?" She wiggled her eyebrows like Michael.

That beast had been going around teaching the eyebrow game to everyone, and I was the only one he hadn't taught anything.

Music started playing downstairs, drawing a sound of delight from

Camille. She gave me a quick hug before rushing out to join the others. I stood alone in the middle of the room, waiting for Eric. I waited a long time, but he didn't return.

14

PUNCH AND PUNCHES

Eric kicked the door of the utility closet down, catching me in the act of moping while listening to my mom's playlist. The fright sent me flying to the edge of the table on which I sat, and he grinned from ear to ear.

"As I suspected. You *are* hiding."

Discreetly, I turned off the iPod and tucked it in my back pocket. "Sorry. I couldn't make it down in the end."

"Why?"

I didn't want to say that I couldn't do this without him, but he had left the room in a hurry, looking upset, and didn't return. And I definitely didn't want to add I was hoping he would come back for me. Looking at his open expression, I had a hard time recalling how much I resented him a week ago, so I furrowed my brow and mumbled, "You said you wouldn't leave me."

Eric's eyes widened. He closed the door behind him and put his hand behind his ear. "What's that?"

"Nothing."

"No, no, I heard right. You can't do anything without me, that's what you said." Laughing at my scowling face, he hoisted himself beside me. "What's wrong? Nervous?"

"Yes."

There, I confessed I did go down shortly after Camille left. Spotting Alberto in his black slacks and white shirt, talking to Michael in whispers, I got flustered, ran back up with my tail between my legs. Eric laughed so hard he almost slid off the table.

"You're mocking me," I said.

"I'm not. I think it's cute."

I hid my face in my hands, embarrassed.

"What about me, then?" Eric shifted in his seat. "I was waiting for you like an idiot this whole time! I told Camille, 'What's he doing?' She said she didn't know, that you were ready when she left. That she dressed you herself."

I gulped. "She said what? Don't listen to her. She's drunk. I dressed myself."

"I gave you an hour, but that's enough. By the time you come down, it's gonna be over. People are already tipsy and some of them are dancing *really* badly. Duvo and Binta are gonna find out eventually, and then the party will be shut down."

He was talking fast, his eyes on his sneakers, as though he was impatient to go downstairs. I tilted my head toward him.

"You were waiting for me?"

"Of course!"

"I thought..."

"What?"

"You weren't mad at me, then?"

He gave me a puzzled look. "For what?"

"I didn't mean to say you had only good genes, I just..."

"Huh?" His eyes were as round as his tennis ball. "I had completely forgotten about that."

I was speechless. Of course, he had forgotten. With the attention span of a ten-day-old pup, Eric wouldn't be troubled with such things. Instead, he took advantage of this moment of confusion to pinch my waist through my shirt.

"So, you're afraid to see Alberto? There's nothing scary about him. He's downstairs, guarding the snacks, glaring at us all."

"He's glaring? Why?"

"Who knows? Maybe because you're up here."

My stomach wouldn't stop hurting. I looked at him, eyes pleading. "I just have this feeling... Perhaps I'm not ready to tell him. Now's not the right time. I'll tell him next week. Or when we return home. Or never. How about that?"

"No." Eric shook his head. "It's just your nerves talking."

"Yes. Nerves. Do you even know how that feels?"

Eric heaved a sigh. "Zak, it's great that you think I'm Superman, and I love that you're my biggest fan, but I'm human too, you know."

What the hell was he talking about? I wasn't his biggest fan at all. Then I saw his grin and understood he was pulling my leg. I rewarded his efforts with an elbow in the ribs.

"Ouch. That's the spirit." He rubbed his side. "Now listen to me. I'm your coach. The key's to get in there. If I stayed on the bench every time I was nervous, then I wouldn't be a football superstar like Cristiano Ronaldo."

"Ah, there's the name."

Eric slid off his perch and tugged at my sleeve. I resisted and he let out a groan of frustration. "You'll never get better at acting if you stay cooped up in here for the rest of your life. Go downstairs, get some experiences, see how dumb we all are after a few drinks."

I hesitated a moment. "That's actually… a good point. You're full of those."

"Am I not amazing?" His smile was so bright, it shamed the light-bulb overhead.

A silly urge suddenly shot through me. The closet was small, and if I extended my arms a little, they would be around his neck. I wondered how he would react then. Scared? No. Nothing ever scared him. If I tried to toy with him, I'd probably end up being the sorry one. The silly urge passed as fast as it came.

"All right. I'm going."

Satisfied, he opened the door, and with a longing look back, I left the comfort of my secret haven. Side by side, we descended the stairs, following the sound of the music, and entered the drawing room where the party had been set.

"Do you like it?" Eric asked, spreading out his hands.

The ceiling lights were off, replaced by diverse smaller lamps, which gave the large and cold room a feeling of warmth. Eric, presumably, had pushed sofa and armchairs into a corner to make room for a dance floor. On the side, a large table offered a variety of snacks in plastic bowls, pizzas in cardboard boxes, and a large bowl containing the spiked punch Camille was telling us about. And in front of the table, Alberto stood expressionless and watched the others engaged in conversation. He gave a purple balloon drifting toward him a lazy kick and sent it floating toward us.

Dozens of these party balloons of various sizes had been tossed around the room with more or less of an effort. A few were hanging off the walls and curtains rods, but most of them were left abandoned on the floor for people to kick and fool around with — and trip over — reminding me of ball pits at kids' restaurants. It was a good thing I hadn't been invited to parties before and couldn't compare with other memories. However, I wanted to humour Eric for being so nice to me, so I nodded politely in approval.

He put his arm around my shoulder. I flinched but didn't wriggle away. Under his protection, I'd do the impossible and finally tell Alberto I loved him. He just had to not leave my side at all. Because with him, I felt quite safe.

But then Eric's unruly hand left my shoulder to travel down to my waist, and to my right buttock. I felt his fingers slide into my jeans pocket, in full view of Alberto, no less. All the blood contained in my body rushed to my cheeks.

"Nice butt."

Eric's words, breathed into my ear, made the small hair on my nape stand up. Before I could react, he had already left me in the middle of the room to join Joy by the sound system.

I threw panicked looks around, anger rising in my stomach. More than an impossible flirt, and a tease, he was also a traitor. Not ten seconds had passed, and I was left to fend for myself while he attended to a girl. Fuming, I retreated to a corner of the room under an ugly painting of a hunt, ignoring Alberto babysitting the snacks. A drop of sweat sashayed down my collarbone. I could still feel the warmth of Eric's fingers like a searing handprint on my ass. This... Was this also to make Alberto jealous? It felt so hot in this drawing room. How could I declare my feelings drenched in sweat?

Picking up a napkin from a side table, I dabbed my forehead and composed myself. What was I getting worked up for? Either way, it didn't mean anything. Eric was never serious. And when I'd spent an hour berating myself over a few misspoken words, he, on the other hand, had forgotten all about it. We really lived on different planes, he and I.

And then, I heard it: France Gall's infamous Eurovision hit, booming through the speakers. With trembling fingers, I dug into my back pocket and found only empty space; my iPod was gone. Wide-eyed, I turned to the sound system, only to find Eric watching me smugly, my iPod in his hand. My jaw dropped, only deepening his smile.

I should have been mad. But I found I couldn't. Eric had no intention of leaving me after all. Such a relief! He could have my iPod and his way with my ass, as long as he stayed by my side tonight. My heart settled somehow, and if I turned away from him haughtily, it was to conceal my smile.

Booze, sugar, and a vintage playlist can have quite an effect on people. Duvo and Binta were talking and laughing loudly. Michael was dragged to the dance floor by his flock of little birds, while the boys, first looking at them in envy, dropped their surly act and went dancing with them. If you could call it dancing. They flailed their limbs and bounced off the floor with more or less style.

Alberto hadn't left his spot. He sometimes swept a cool gaze over the variety of snacks as if he were tempted, only to turn away from them with a sour expression. I found his attitude to be helpful; after all, if he were dancing over there with the others, I wouldn't be able to approach him. Eric walked over to the table and exchanged a few words with him while I watched, breathless. His warm smiles and playful jests had no effect on Alberto, who looked away with indifference. Eventually, Eric returned with a small plastic cup of punch.

"No, no, no," I said, waving my hands. "Get this thing out of my face."

"Just one cup. You look like you're about to explode. One cup will make you feel better. And I had some earlier. It's really not strong."

I looked once again into the cup. The red liquid was swirling with promises of laid-back conversations with Alberto. I could imagine the merits of being a tiny bit more relaxed around him. And if drinking this cup could get me there, then why not?

"It really isn't?"

Eric shook his head. "Xavier's really cheap."

"Watch out. His father is a baronet."

Eric snorted into the plastic cup. "He didn't put much stuff in it and probably stashed the rest elsewhere. You'd have to drink lots of it to get really buzzed. Duvo's gonna feel it, though. He must have drunk half the bowl already."

We looked around at our teacher who had given up on trying to look cool and was gesticulating with the others, to Binta's enjoyment.

"I'm not gonna get embarrassing like him?" I asked.

Eric tilted his head. "Have I ever done anything to embarrass you?"

"You've just put on my fucking playlist!"

He slapped a hand over his mouth. "Oops."

Scowling, I gripped the cup with both hands. "Give me this, then."

Eric watched me down that thing with an amused smile. The drink tasted sweet and nice on the tongue, went down really easy. I smacked my lips.

"It's good!"

"Yeah…" He felt his chin. "Just don't make a habit of it."

"Now what?" I asked, bouncing on my feet.

I felt a little different already, but that could also be because of the insane amount of sugar present in the drink. Eric balled his fists and started walking around me in circles, very coach-like.

"Stand straight. No, that's too straight. Yes, better."

"How's my hair?"

"Perfect."

"My face?"

"What do you mean, your face?" He laughed. "You can't change your face."

I grabbed his wrists. "But this is such an important moment in my life!" Staring into Eric's earnest blue eyes, I sought to find strength and confidence in them. But as of now, they were just impossibly wide.

"Go to him," he said, his voice firm. "I'll keep Sander out of the way."

"How?"

"I'll figure it out."

"Of course, you will." I squeezed his wrists. "You're an actor."

He smiled, first with his mouth then with his eyes. "Good luck, Thomas." He gave me an unexpected and quite affectionate hug.

"Thanks, Adam."

Alberto was glowing like a lighthouse among the tumultuous sea of people dancing in the centre of the room. He didn't register me at first. He was gazing at the spot where the girls were surrounding Michael with a faint trace of a smile. On the side, Camille was dancing alone in a brutal manner, with Arthur hovering around, looking nervous. Binta seemed to approve of her style and jumped into the crowd of girls to do just the same. She was met with delight, while Duvo stared at Michael resentfully.

I approached Alberto, trying to think of a way to strike up a conversation with him. He seemed like he was not having fun. The only explanation had to be that he didn't enjoy parties. So, I spoke in what I felt was a steady voice, all the while wringing my hands behind my back. "What is the point of parties, right?"

It took a second for him to notice me standing by his side. "Sorry," he said, pointing at his ear. "Did you say something?"

He couldn't hear me over the sound of the girls singing over the music. I raised my voice.

"What is the point of parties?"

"Oh." He frowned. "Hooking up."

"Hoo—Hooking up?" My cheeks grew hot.

Oblivious, Alberto folded his arms over his chest. "Duvo only came up with this whole thing because he wanted to shag Binta."

"What?" My eyes widened. "Duvo wants to shag Binta?"

Alberto gave a dry chuckle. "Are you blind?" Then he gave me a second look, more serious. "Have you not realised yet this little excursion was all because Duvo wanted to shag Binta?"

I shook my head. It didn't seem right to me. After all, Duvo was a teacher. An adult. Adults are not like us; they're wiser. I told Alberto just so, but he shrugged.

"Adults are just as horny as we are. Or worse."

We, he said. I turned away to hide my face from him.

Was I horny? Was he? Did Alberto harbour improper thoughts toward other men? Even though I was madly into him, I sort of imagined he was pure and beyond these matters, a little like an angel of sorts. I had to keep my cool. Yes, he was Alberto. But I was Zak. We were very similar. There's no way I couldn't talk to him, be honest, speak my mind.

"People wouldn't go through such trouble just to sleep with someone," I said, feeling a tiny bit like a hypocrite. In my defence, my fantasies about Alberto involved holding hands and walking up red carpets together, the occasional wedding, and holidays on the Italian coast. It wasn't anything as improper as whatever smut I hid under my bed.

Alberto's eyebrows rose slightly. "The world's history is made of things people did to impress the people they wanted to shag."

He sounded like the whole concept was beneath him. Something felt a little off. I hesitated, felt like retreating. It was probably just nerves, I told myself. Nerves. I was so close to him, I could hear my heart beating madly.

Turning around, I searched for Eric and found him on the opposite side of the room, attempting to throw his arm around Sander's shoulder to distract him away from Alberto, but Sander being freakishly tall, Eric's hand could barely reach his shoulder. I snorted despite myself.

"They're having fun."

"They're all drunk," Alberto said. "That's why they're dancing so... Oh. There you go." Alberto pointed at Duvo who, looking possessive and fierce, was dragging Binta into a dark corner. To my surprise, she allowed him to kiss her.

"You were right!" I said, impressed.

Alberto's shoulder half-lifted in a shrug.

"And Michael?" I pushed on, now that I had his attention. "Is he drunk?"

Michael looked cheerful enough tonight, being twirled around the makeshift dance floor by his devoted fan club. Behind his back, Melissa stretched on her toes, was burying paper umbrellas into his curls. Every time she turned around to fish another one out of her pocket, he stuck one of his right back into her own hair, unnoticed. Joy was trying hard not to laugh.

"I should think so," Alberto said. "But it's not the same. He deserves a little bit of fun."

I assumed Alberto was talking about Michael's alleged problems with Louis. I still found it hard to believe and didn't want to get into the subject.

"What about you, Alberto? Not drinking?"

"I prefer to keep a clear head."

For some reason, he seemed to think he said something particularly amusing, and he glanced at me as he laughed.

"Me too," I said, struck dumb by his laughter.

I must have looked particularly intense. Alberto quickly looked away.

"What is Sander doing?"

Following his gaze, my eyes nearly popped out of their sockets. Eric had jumped onto Sander's back. Sander, huge but placid, began spinning around, confused.

"Oh, huh, that's Eric. If he doesn't put his hands on somebody every five minutes, he might actually explode."

The smile Alberto conceded stabbed right through my heart, leaving me breathless. Turning my flushed face away, I saw that Kayvin and Xavier had rushed to Eric's side, followed by Camille and Arthur. I had to make it quick before Eric lost control of whatever the hell he was doing.

"Alberto, look…" He didn't look. "I want to tell you something." There was an urgency in the tone of my voice, and Alberto heard it.

"What?"

His tone was gentle, at least. Still, I couldn't find my voice.

"What is it?" Alberto insisted. His gaze never left the others.

Eric had somehow convinced them all he wanted to play piggyback. Sander looked like he couldn't believe the football player he admired was wrapped around him like a koala. Camille jumped on Arthur's back. Xavier tried to do the same with Kayvin but was slammed straight into the ground by his friend. Duvo and Binta, busy in their corner, didn't pay any attention to us. I turned my back to all of them and faced Alberto.

"I…"

"I can't hear you, you have to speak up."

Until then, I had never felt crushed by our size difference. How fifteen centimetres could feel like fifty when pinned under the gaze of the person you've liked for too long.

Brave. Be brave. Don't stay on the bench… or whatever.

"I wanted to tell you…" I took a steadying breath. "That I would like it if you… If you wanted to hang out, someday."

Horrified by my delivery, I didn't dare to look at him. I didn't. I wanted to look at Eric for support, but I was afraid to lose my grip.

"I'm not sure I understand what you're saying," Alberto said.

How ruthless of him. Did he want me to draw him a picture or something? My hands were sweaty. I clenched them into fists.

"I guess what I'm saying is, it would be great if you wanted to go out. With me."

"Oh." Alberto finally looked at me. His Adam's apple bobbed as he swallowed. "You mean…" His fingers twitched. "That."

Yes, that. Holding hands, kissing against trees, calling each other dumb names, but not too dumb. All that.

Alberto's posture changed. His shoulders tensed, his hands found the depths of his pockets. "But I'm not… You see, I'm not…"

I broke out in a cold sweat. "You're not what?"

Don't tell me he isn't gay after all?

Alberto briefly narrowed his eyes. "I'm not exactly… out, yet."

I breathed out a sigh of relief. So, he was gay. He was just a little embarrassed. Alberto pointedly looked away, straight at the dance floor, where everyone was now piggybacking except Michael who was staring around confusedly.

"This is nice…" he muttered. "I mean… I'm flattered."

My heart sank. Nothing good ever followed those words. Even I knew it.

As if they knew what Alberto was about to add, my legs shook with the desire to dash out of here. I had no conscience of my surroundings. It felt like Alberto and I were all alone on the world's stage, that I was kneeling by a chopping block, and Alberto held an axe over my head. Not once did he look at me in the eye. After a moment, he lowered his head.

"The thing is, I can't throw myself away like this to the first one who asks."

I wasn't sure I heard right. His words… they… sounded an awful lot like *No*.

Just like that, the word "Rejected" was lowered onto my head like a crown of shame. I could only blink stupidly. Amidst all that, I heard Alberto mumble the word "Sorry". Then he turned to leave but collided with Sander who had finally lumbered back to the table, Eric still wrapped around him.

I was stunned. The music had long faded to the background, and for a moment, all I could hear was the dull yet resilient thumping of my heart.

Of course, Alberto wouldn't want me to be his first. Of course, he had higher aspirations than silly little Zak with his silly little fantasies. Of course, I was insignificant, and he shouldn't throw himself away to the likes of me. It just made a lot of sense.

It still hurt like a bitch, however. When I thought of a Band-Aid, my eyes began stinging.

Dazed as I was, I hadn't even noticed when Sander and Eric had arrived. But from the look of Eric, he had heard Alberto's words and didn't like them at all. His face twisted in anger, he slid off Sander's back and blocked Alberto's way out.

"Why would you say something like that?"

Alberto blinked. "Something like what?"

A vein popped on the side of Eric's forehead. "Why would you say something like that to someone who— who just told you they liked you!"

Cringing, I retreated behind him and pulled the hem of his shirt. "Let's go, Eric."

"No. Why did you have to say something like that?"

Alberto's nose wrinkled. He seemed out of patience. "Would you rather I lied to him?"

"Lie?" Eric seemed thrown off by that argument. "I don't know. Maybe! Anything would be better than this!"

Eric had raised his voice. It got the attention of his loyal friends. When Kayvin and Xavier began to approach, I tugged harder on his shirt, and he snapped out of his rant. He noticed his friends and waved at them in an offhanded way to send them away. Then he dragged me, still stunned, back to our spot under the hunting painting and pushed me down on a chair. Camille and Arthur rushed to our side.

"Is everything all right?"

"What happened?"

Eric seemed unwilling to reveal anything that might embarrass me and said nothing.

It was his stupid idea to confess to Alberto tonight. I should be furious at him, and I really wanted to be. But it was impossible. And looking at his expression right now, how he was still trying to be on my side, his ears still flushed by his bout of anger, I could feel nothing but a mumble-jumble of gratitude and a deep feeling of humiliation.

Camille was holding a cup of punch. I snatched it from her hands and drank it all in one go. My eyes inadvertently drifted back to the snack table and I flinched. Alberto was looking at me, his face completely closed. We both quickly turned away. A feeling of sadness drifted over my burning shame. Because of what happened tonight, even friendship between us might become too wild a fantasy, even for me.

"What happened?!" Camille asked again, kneeling by me. Her concern only made my eyes well up some more. I started twitching on my chair.

"None of your business."

"Stop." Eric gently kneaded my shoulder, then turned to Camille to speak, but Arthur spoke first.

"You asked Alberto out, and he said no because he's an idiot."

A brief silence fell on us. Camille, Arthur, and Eric exchanged a knowing look. Just how obvious was my crush on Alberto, exactly? Did everyone here know I was in love with him?

"What?" Arthur said. "Am I wrong?"

"No," Eric said.

"He's not an idiot!" Tears clouded my vision. The drink was getting to my head. "I just... I came out of nowhere, and he just... he never thought of me that way and that's not his fault, how could it be his fault? It's my fault. For thinking for a minute that I was in the same league."

"No," Eric said flatly. "He's an asshole."

"I love him," I said fiercely. "Saying awful things about him won't make me love him less. It will only make me mad."

Seeing that Arthur also had a cup in his hand, I grabbed it and drank it too.

"Easy now," Eric said, putting the empty cup away.

Camille gently patted my wrist. I felt all of their stares, and their care for me just made me even more pissed off somehow. I pushed Arthur away, and from here, I had a good view of the dance floor. People were enjoying themselves, dancing without a care. At least not everyone had noticed my humiliation. I let out a sigh. "You should not have played this music."

Eric's fingers were still digging in my shoulder. "I thought it would make you happy."

"How?"

"Because everybody loves it! Look at them."

I slapped his hand away. "Fine. It doesn't matter anymore."

"It's your music?" Camille hopped up and down. "How cool! Everyone was asking."

I had nothing to say. Everything felt insignificant, just like I was. I didn't want to look at Alberto ever again, and yet the first chance I got, I snuck a glance. His gaze had returned to the girls on the dance floor, to Michael, who looked out of breath and was wiping his forehead. Alberto's eyebrows drew together in a slight frown. Michael laughed at something Melissa said. Alberto's hands curled around the edge of the table. Michael glanced toward the table.

Their eyes met.

They exchanged a smile.

It finally hit me. I sprang from my seat. "Michael!" I choked out a cough.

"What's with Michael?" Camille jerked her head to look at him.

Michael felt it was the perfect opportunity to stop dancing. After an amused look at Binta and Duvo hugging in the darkest corner of the room, he approached us, his face glistening.

"Are you having a good time?" he asked, stretching. "Everybody seems to be having a great time."

I almost bit his head off. How he stood there before me, my

supposed *ally*. Handsome and smart, golden and sexy, and what else... *Taken* too!

He was good enough for Alberto, that's for sure. Of course, I had recognised the look in Alberto's eyes, because I had looked at him the same way for almost a year.

While I thought this man was on my side, he had spent the whole time getting closer to Alberto while his boyfriend was left behind. All the embitterment in me swirled around madly, shrouding me like a poisonous cloud. Before I could stop myself, I spoke words in a sharp tone.

"How's Louis?"

Michael was smiling. Upon hearing that, his smile died down a little. "What?"

I raised my voice so he could hear me over the music. "How's your boyfriend?" Michael saw my clenched fists and gave me a blank look. I pressed on. "Is it true that there's trouble between you two?"

Camille and Arthur looked at me, then Michael, shocked. Eric didn't move.

"No. Who said that?" Michael tried to speak in a clear tone, but he looked too agitated to be honest. "Yasmine?" he insisted. "Did Yasmine say that?"

I shook my head coldly.

"Louis and I are just fine," he said, his eyes frantically searching around the room. "I don't know where you got that... that idea..." His voice trailed off. While he was scanning around the room, a frown disturbed his handsome features. "You all... You all seem really weird. Why are you all acting so weird?"

"Oh, that!" Arthur shrugged happily. "We're all drunk!"

"Someone spiked the punch." Camille drunkenly threw her arms around Michael's waist. "It's delicious. Did you have some?"

Michael stared at her in disbelief. "How...." His expression changed; I could almost see the lightbulb spark to life over his head. "Xavier! I'm gonna kill him." He made to turn but then changed his mind. "No, I'm gonna let Duvo kill him." He walked away in search of Xavier.

"Snitch," Camille said through half-closed eyes. She hiccupped.

Alberto followed Michael outside. I slumped back onto my chair. Did something already happen between these two? That would be so gross!

"Who told you Michael and his boyfriend were having trouble?" Camille asked with a quirked eyebrow.

"Alberto."

"That's none of his business," Eric said. "And he was wrong. Clearly." Though he didn't sound so sure.

"Why are you mad at Michael?" Arthur looked confused.

"Ahem." I cleared my throat. "Alberto."

"Oh…" Arthur nodded pensively. "So he wanted to separate them?"

"Alberto wouldn't do something like that."

"You never know with him." Arthur snorted. "He's weird."

"No, he's not," I said darkly.

Arthur was about to retort, but Camille took his hand.

"Let's get more of this punch before Michael snitches."

"Great idea!" Arthur held on tight to her hand and led her toward the buffet.

Michael reentered the hall, followed by Alberto. They stood in the middle of the drawing room, talking. I watched them with bated breath, expecting something to happen, but nothing happened. Useless tears began to prickle my eyes. I rose from my seat and left the room in a hurry. I wanted to take refuge outside, as far as possible from the others, and emerged in the backyard by the pool. Out there, it was quiet. The fire was not lit tonight, and the silver moonlight reflected gently on the surface of the water. I took a seat on a lounge chair and buried my head in my hands.

It was hopeless to hope for some time alone, though. Arthur and Camille came stumbling happily toward me, followed by a more cautious Eric.

"Zaaaak!"

Those two drunkards had thought to bring me some punch. I thanked them with a wan smile and drank both cups under Eric's worried gaze.

"Please, watch out with that stuff." Eric dragged a lounge chair alongside mine. He sat so close I could feel his heat.

"You're not going to leave me alone, are you?"

"I said all the way, remember?"

His kindness was both a caress and a slap on my face. I didn't really understand the feeling. I was probably drunk.

"Why are you so nice to me anyway?" I asked drily.

Eric opened his mouth to answer, but Camille spoke first.

"What was that funny game you played earlier, Eric?" She stood by the pool with her hands on her hips.

"Yeah," Arthur said, "why were you piggybacking Sander?"

They were slurring. I glanced sideways at Eric and noticed the gleam of mischief in his eyes.

"It's a trust thing," he said, as though talking to two very dumb children. "I have to piggyback people before I can move on to the next stage of our friendship."

In their state, they were ripe enough to believe his stupid lie, and they made sounds of awe.

"Climb back on," Arthur offered Camille.

My stupid playlist could be heard even from here. An appropriate tune of heartbreak reached me, solemn and mournful.

"Fuck," I said.

Eric spoke softly. "I'm really sorry it didn't work out."

"Thanks."

"But I'm really impressed that you did it."

"Stupidity and bravery go hand in hand. I was really stupid to believe I had a chance."

Eric looked terribly sad for me. Not long ago, *he* was the source of all my woes. Then he wasn't. Now I realised *I* was the source of all my woes. I was solely responsible for nurturing crazy fantasies about Alberto. When I thought of him inside, loving another, while I sat there, wretched, bitter tears welled up at the corner of my eyes.

"Don't cry," Eric said, looking distraught. "Please don't cry. I don't know what to do when people cry."

"I'm not crying," I said, gritting my teeth. "I have an eye allergy." Eric tried to dab my cheek with a cocktail napkin. "Leave it!"

He jerked away as though I was a vicious cat.

"I'm such an idiot." I buried my hands in my hair in despair. "Of course, he doesn't want me. How could I have been so delusional! Alberto, with me. You know, I never seriously considered he wouldn't want me, because I… I was certain we had so much in common, and that, of course, I wasn't like him, but… still, I thought we made sense. And Michael… I didn't see a thing. I'm sure everyone else did. You did, didn't you?"

Eric looked confused after my muddled speech. "Me? No! I… I don't know."

"You won't tell me not to hurt my feelings, I get it." I let out a groan. "How could I have been so insane? I feel so embarrassed now!"

"But…" Eric hesitated. "He's an idiot—"

"No need to bother with the usual platitudes. 'He's an idiot. You deserve better'. What if I don't want someone better? I want this idiot!"

Eric dared to wave his hand dismissively. "Don't worry. You'll like someone else. I can promise you that."

"Looking forward to it. With my delusions, I'll keep aiming at people who don't even care if I exist or not." I was getting quite depressed. "You know, I always thought I wasn't good around people. Now I think it's best if I remove myself from the world."

Eric gave me a perplexed look. "Hang on a minute."

But I was on a pathetic drunk rampage, there was no stopping me.

"It's like I knew it all along. I'll never go on a date. I'll never walk around, holding hands." I gasped. "I'll never be kissed." Eric's eyes widened. I gave a dry laugh. "I lied to you. I've never been kissed. I'm already the only one in my class who's never been kissed. Even the weird ones got themselves some weird boyfriends and girlfriends, and all the action I'll ever get is gonna be from other people's stories." Satisfied with my outburst, I snuck a glance at Eric and my breath hitched in surprise. That dog was laughing in his fist. "Do I amuse you?"

"Yes! A bit."

"Why?"

His body was shaking from trying not to laugh. "You're such a dramatic drunk!"

He let me grab him and shake him without flinching. "Let me be drunk!" I snapped, tears clouding my eyes. "And let me be dramatic!"

I sprang up, wishing to kick him, but again he read my mind and got to his feet just as fast. Then we heard Camille scream.

"Wai—aaah!"

I whipped around. Arthur and Camille's game of piggybacking was taking a turn. Stumbling under her weight, Arthur crashed face-first onto a lounge chair while the unlucky Camille fell straight into the pool with a great splash.

Arthur yelped. "Holy shit!"

I turned back to Eric. "Do something!"

He pulled me to him and smashed our lips together.

"Holy shit!" Arthur repeated.

My mind had turned completely blank. When Eric released me, I panicked and shoved him so hard he tumbled backwards into the wall. He grunted in pain, his wide eyes fixed on my awestruck face.

"Now you've been kissed!"

Stroking his own back, Eric went over to Camille, who was laughing hysterically in the middle of the pool. Trembling fingertips rose to my face, circled my tingling lips. I could only stare dumbly after him, the tears on my cheeks already dry.

15

DON'T YOU?

The sun rose over Longchamps. Blackbirds shook themselves awake and broke into song. Eric's bees left the hives for another hard day of work. Down the corridor, Alberto slept soundly after rejecting me.

I woke up with a start and the feeling I hadn't slept at all. However, I didn't notice the others coming to bed. It must have happened after I passed out, exhausted, my pillow wet with bitter tears. The other beds were already empty. Looking at my watch, I saw it was quite late already.

People who drink often say they can't remember what happened the night before. Unfortunately, that wasn't the case for me. If only I could forget. But Alberto's embarrassment, his demeanour, and his cutting words were burnt into my memory.

So was Eric's lousy kiss… and his expression when I shoved him into a wall.

I really outdid myself last night. Destroyed my hopes of a relationship with Alberto, lashed out at Michael, left Camille in the middle of the pool to run away upstairs in a panic, and pushed away the person who'd been the most helpful, even as he was trying to comfort me in my drunken state.

That was it. I would avoid parties from now on, and rum.

And Alberto.

And everyone else.

From the looks of sympathy coming from Joy and Melissa to the way Alberto and Sander teleported out the dining room the moment I came downstairs, there was no point denying it: everybody knew.

It didn't matter so much, I noted as I stood in front of the breakfast buffet, trying to muster an appetite. Who outed me? Alberto? Michael? Arthur? Camille? Eric? Not that it mattered.

It didn't matter at all.

I wasn't ashamed of being gay. Nor was I ashamed of loving Alberto. Who in their right mind hadn't stopped before him at least once in the corridors of Colette, submerged with envy? Envy to possess or to become him for a day? I wasn't ashamed. Irritated that people talked behind my back, maybe. But it couldn't be helped.

Still, I felt hollow. For once, I'd have liked to share my thoughts with someone, but to talk to Yasmine now would be unbearable. She'd warned me Alberto would wipe the floor with me, and he did without even meaning to. I didn't listen. And now, I couldn't face her.

It ached to be soundly rejected, and with such strange words too. Now I was doomed to remember this moment forever. Alberto's sentence would be the whip with which I'd lash at my self-esteem in the years to come. For a second, it occurred to me to take my mom up on her offer and get the hell out of here. And then I thought I was really being immature. We were shooting a movie here, and they relied on me to do a good job. Eric too.

Speaking of, was Eric even okay? I suspected he'd be pretty mad by now. He'd taken such good care of me, even treating me a little bit like a child at times. All of his efforts amounted to nothing, and I shoved him into a wall for good measure. He was a nice guy, but last night I also noted he could get angry when he thought people were rude. And I had been especially rude.

Why did he kiss me but to stop me from whining? He said it himself, I was a dramatic drunk. If anything, my first kiss was born out of pity. A pity-kiss.

What a mess I'd made of things. I never meant to hurl him into the wall like that. But who wouldn't be surprised to feel their friend's lips suddenly pressed against theirs? It came out of nowhere. I wasn't prepared.

Next time, he should definitely give me a warning.

One absent step after another, I dragged myself to my usual table and looked down at my breakfast. I had forgotten the milk for my cereals and was holding a fork instead of a spoon.

A great *clang!* made me jump. Arthur slammed a spoon on the table as he filled the chair next to mine.

"This morning sucks! I wish I could just stay in bed all day!"

Following him, Camille pulled out a chair, causing a racket that had Joy and Melissa cry out and put their hands over their ears. I saw, dumbfounded, that Camille looked as fresh as a daisy despite her heavy drinking and her midnight swim.

"Binta said the day is ours," she said, staring at my dry cereal with a quirked eyebrow. "Everyone wants to take a dive in the pool. Some said something about going to the village. What do you think, Zak?"

Currently, I was thinking of death. My own, hers, the bees, the Amazonian forest, as well as the end of the universe. I couldn't possibly answer. The dark cloud floating above my head was probably visible even to their untrained eye, because Arthur made a frightened face and Camille lowered her voice.

"You all right, Zak?"

"Yep." My voice sounded just as gloomy as I felt.

"My God," Arthur said. "What a night. It was crazy, wasn't it? I'm not sorry to say Xavier is a national hero. Though he might pay for this with his life."

Camille took the fork and attempted to scoop a handful of cereal from my bowl. "Eric said Duvo looked murderous this morning."

I lifted my head. "Eric? You've seen Eric this morning?"

She nodded. "Passed him in the corridor. He was in a hurry. Said with all that happened yesterday—"

"What?" My heart jumped in my throat. "What happened yesterday?"

"Xavier spiked the punch, remember?" Arthur frowned. "You *do* remember, don't you?"

"Yes. Of course, I do."

I wasn't sure whether Arthur saw Eric kiss me or how I reacted, and I didn't want it to become a subject of conversation. Not today, not ever.

Camille twirled the fork around my bowl of cereal, a pensive look on her face. "Alberto saw Eric in the corridor and said hello, but Eric wouldn't say hello back."

"No!" Arthur said, his eyebrows shooting up. "Perhaps he didn't hear him."

"Oh no, he heard him all right."

The embarrassment I experienced last night came rushing back.

Half of my face felt hot. But if Eric was still mad at Alberto this morning, then did it mean he wasn't mad at me?

"Where's Eric?"

"I don't know." Camille tossed a look over her shoulder and beamed. "Hey, Michael!"

Seeing Michael and his annoyingly nice face standing in front of me, I sprung up, knocking my knee into the table as I went.

"I've got to go."

"But you haven't eaten anything!" Camille said.

Ignoring her, I hurried outside. I didn't want to face Michael; not now. There were too many things I was keeping bottled up, and I didn't want them to explode in his face. It was best to avoid him.

Other pressing matters were swirling around in my mind. If Eric wasn't mad at me, could he be waiting for me at the lake? I had nothing to lose after all. I rushed over there with a beating heart, but I didn't find him, so I retraced my steps toward the house and emerged from the grove to find Camille and Arthur staring at me.

"Why are you following me?" I spoke in a most unwelcoming tone.

Camille showed me what she was cradling: a pear, an apple, and a banana. "Brought you breakfast. You didn't touch your food."

Would I have to contend with these two following me around all day? I wouldn't be able to bear it today. Not with Eric missing and Alberto trampling on my heart. I stomped toward them. Arthur gasped when I took the fruits from her hands and threw them over my shoulder.

"I asked you a question. Why are you always following me?"

"We—"

"Do you pity me or something? You were the same last night. Everywhere I looked, the both of you, always following me. I thought perhaps you were after Eric. But Eric's not here, and you're still here, so I guess you really are following me. Why?"

"Sorry, we…"

"We what! Don't you have anything better to do?"

Seemingly by accident, Camille stomped her foot straight onto my toes. "Like what?"

I retreated with a curse. "Don't you have friends to hang out with?"

But Camille did look really angry this time. "Friends? What friends?" She advanced on me, readying to stomp on my foot again. "Haven't you noticed? We're from the Drama Club, we don't have friends."

Arthur folded his arms against his chest, looking almost proud. "I don't have friends either."

I watched them for a moment. They both looked fierce — and also a little pathetic, to be honest. It was like I was looking in the mirror; I saw myself in them. Immediately, my anger disintegrated, replaced by regret at my bad temper. I turned around and picked up the fruits Camille brought me.

"We really are a loser club," I said. "Just like the graffiti said."

Camille exhaled a breath, the flash of anger vanishing from her eyes. "If being cool is being a bully, then I quite like being a loser."

Arthur nodded. "Hell yeah. Look at us. We're making a movie ourselves, based on a play you wrote, we live in a mansion, we have a pool, and last night we had an awesome party. Losers have it pretty good."

"Awesome party, indeed," I said darkly.

Camille shook her head, thinking herself discreet, and gave Arthur a pointed look.

"I mean, the party was awesome, to a degree," Arthur said, stammering. "It wasn't that great. It was okay." His face contorted in a grimace. "I mean, it sucked, you're right. It was the worst."

I smiled despite myself.

"So, is that why you're following me around all the time? You want to be my friends or something?"

"I thought we already were." Arthur sounded helpless.

Camille's blue eyes were full of determination. "Zak's playing hard to get. You think you're too good for us, is that right?"

"Oh no." I shook my head. "It's only that... *Friends*. Didn't expect to make so many friends within one week. It's a new experience, for sure."

"Losers must stick together," Arthur said.

Camille pointed at herself. "Not a loser."

Arthur bowed. "The Not-A-Loser club officially has three members."

The three of us stood there awkwardly for a while, feeling like the air around us was slightly different. I didn't know what to say. Eric was the one who always had something to say, even if it was stupid stuff about bees and whatnot.

Confused at how often my thoughts drifted toward him this morning, I forced him out of my head. Using my T-shirt, I wiped the apple carefully and took a bite. "Thank you for breakfast. I'm sorry I yelled at you."

Camille huffed. "You're such a loser."

Together we decided to go for a walk toward the village. Camille picked up wildflowers along the way, and Arthur was trying really hard not to stare at her colt-like legs sticking out of her shorts.

"I'm just gonna say it," Camille said, brushing my arm.

"Say what?"

"We knew you liked Alberto and we never had a problem with it. It's cool, I mean, not that you'd need our approval or anything, but…"

"That's fine." I forced a clipped smile. "Cat's out of the bag. Or more precisely, the gay's out of the closet. Wait— I was never closeted. But I'm out. What am I out of, then?"

"I really can't answer that," Camille said. "Let me know when you find the answer."

"Do you think everyone knows? About my crush on him?"

"I think so, yes."

A sinister thought bloomed in my mind. I tried to push it down, but it kept coming back.

"Do you think Alberto outed me?"

That he didn't like me was one thing, but that he would tell everyone I liked him was indecent, and not at all what I imagined him to be. The mere thought was twisting my heart.

"Can't say," Arthur said. "I knew you liked him because you were literally shaking every time he was physically close to you."

"Perfect," I said.

Camille hesitated. "Personally, I've had some serious doubts since the Manga Café. It felt to me you were pushing me to cast him despite…"

"Despite what?"

She exchanged a glance with Arthur. "Alberto really isn't a great actor, Zak."

I laughed. "That's nonsense. He's perfect."

"He doesn't even bother learning his lines. He mistakes rehearsals for sleeping sessions—"

"Nonsense! He's perfect."

Arthur's lips moved, and Camille gave a nod. "Okay, then. He's great. But I was suspicious, and I guess I got confirmation when you learned Eric was chosen instead."

I screwed my eyes shut.

"Isn't Alberto straight, anyway?" Arthur asked. "I know you were angry at Michael last night, but Alberto and I are in the same class. I know the way girls are looking at him."

"You're in his class?"

"Yeah."

"You see him every day?"

"Yes…"

"Lucky you."

Another glance was exchanged between them.

"I've heard people say both," Camille said. "Girls saying he's gay, guys saying he's straight, it's really confusing."

"I can safely say Alberto isn't straight. He's got a crush on—"

"Michael," Camille said. "Yeah, it's possible."

"You knew?"

"First, we all have a crush on Michael." She started giggling, then abruptly stopped. "Seriously, though. We shot scenes with them every day. Alberto is glued to Michael all day long, they're almost tripping over each other."

I looked down at my shoes with a sinking heart.

"I didn't notice a thing," Arthur said, awed.

"That's because you're looking into the camera, not behind. Which I'm grateful for, because you're serious about my movie, while others…" Her voice trailed off when she saw my face. "And that's why we're here. The movie, right?"

Blushing shamefully, I pretended I didn't hear a thing.

"So, Alberto said he didn't want to date you because he wants to be with Michael?" Arthur said with sympathy.

"Actually, he said he couldn't throw himself away like that to the first one who asks."

"Hell," Camille said. "That's harsh."

"Wait." Arthur looked shocked. "You're telling me you're the first one who's ever asked him out?"

"I know," I said slowly. "I must say I'm surprised now that I think about it. He didn't say much to me, and what he said, I'll remember probably until my dying day. This line keeps coming back to me. How is that possible that I'm the first to ever ask Alberto out? He's sixteen and more beautiful than anyone else in the world."

Arthur snorted and Camille elbowed him.

"Worse, even," he said, caressing the spot where Camille hit him. "He's seventeen. He repeated a year."

I stared at him in disbelief.

"Yes, he's older than us. I'm not surprised he repeated a year, honestly."

"Why?" Camille asked.

Arthur actually laughed. "He's always told off for sleeping in class. He only gets by because he's so pretty and most teachers let him get away with everything. Life is so unfair! Good looking people really benefit too much from their luck. There should be laws against that."

I didn't like these new bits of information. They didn't sound like the Alberto I knew... or that I imagined.

"Still. Can you seriously believe I'm the first person to ask him out?"

Camille bit her lip. "Possibly because he never hangs out with anybody but Sander and Oliver, and they're both straight."

"Sander and Oliver resent him, you know," Arthur said. "Girls are always inviting him here and there, sometimes right in front of me! And he never goes to any of their parties. I've been to a couple and I've never seen him."

"Alberto's got a taste for finer things," I muttered.

"And Michael is finer things?" Arthur said. "He's not related to the Queen, as far as I know."

"His mother is Anne Landi-Parker," Camille said.

"I don't know Anne Landi-Parker."

"She's an actress, and Alberto has seen her on stage a few times."

Arthur stared at Camille, looking impressed. "How the hell do you know that?"

"Because I'm stuck shooting the movie with those two and I overheard their conversation! They were talking about it between takes."

Arthur sniggered. "The real surprise is that Alberto can hold a conversation with someone without falling asleep halfway through it."

"Shh!" Camille said, with a side glance at me.

But I was lost in thought, consumed by sadness. "Alberto and Michael..." I sighed. "So, it's real, then... Poor Louis."

"Who's Louis?" Camille asked.

"Michael's boyfriend."

She grabbed my arm and gave it a shake. "Michael's not going to date Alberto!"

"How do you know?"

"I just know it!"

"... Okay."

"No, really! I think Alberto scares him a little. I told you they were tripping over each other? That's because Michael always seems in a hurry to get away from him."

"That makes no sense… No one in their right mind would reject Alberto."

"I would," Arthur said. "I definitely would."

I shot him a glare. "That's because you're not gay, Arthur!"

"Well… maybe so. But if I were gay, I wouldn't be into Alberto."

Camille and I looked at Arthur while he appeared lost in thought about who was his type of man. I ostensibly clicked my tongue and returned to the subject at hand.

"Alberto said there was trouble between Louis and Michael. And Michael reacted strangely when I confronted him about it."

"Yeah, but Alberto has an agenda. So, can he be trusted?" Arthur said.

"And you were coming onto him so aggressively! Michael was probably scared of you," Camille said.

"I saw them together many times," I said. "Talking closely, and I never thought…"

Camille shrugged. "Alberto probably thought the party was the perfect occasion to make his move."

Arthur flashed a sneaky smile. "Worked for Duvo. He's with Binta now."

"That's the only reason why Xavier is still alive."

They both sniggered.

"Anyway, he shouldn't have said these things to you," Camille said. "It was rude."

"It was only the truth." I dipped my head. "How can I blame him for that?"

"Apparently you can't, but Eric can. He was still pissed off when we went to bed."

"He was?"

It was likely that he was pissed off at something else, something they didn't know, which had to do with a drunken fool throwing him into a wall.

Suddenly, I didn't want to talk about Alberto anymore. Forcing a smile, I turned to Camille. "Have you gotten over your fall into the pool, Camille?"

"I've learned a valuable lesson," she said after a fit of laughter. "I'll stay away from Satan's liquor from now on. But did you see how Eric pulled me out of the water? With one hand!"

"Yes, that's because his other hand was already on your ass!" Arthur said angrily.

"He was fixing my skirt, actually, because it was stuck to my back. He was never improper."

"Oh. Sorry."

I remembered Eric's hand being not so gentlemanly with my own buttocks last night. The memory brought a little smile.

"If you weren't so shellshocked," Camille told Arthur, "you could have pulled me out of the water and done the same!"

"I was confused!"

"Where the hell is Eric anyway?" I interrupted them. "I'd really like to speak to him."

"He went to town with Duvo," Camille said.

"What? Why didn't you say something?"

"I didn't know you were so impatient to see him, Mr Sulky. Duvo made a show of taking the whole gang to the bus stop in town to threaten them. I think the plan was to kick Xavier out, but Eric convinced him not to be too harsh."

"How did he do that?" Arthur asked.

"Beats me. But they should be back by now. We could head back."

We all agreed to go back and began retracing our steps toward the house.

"How do you know all this?" I asked. "Are you in touch with Eric?"

"Yep."

Camille gave me her phone. The screen was so scratched I could barely read the text she was showing me.

"Eric's playing Adam! Do you think I wouldn't try to find out what happened? I've got my eyes on the both of you. You can't escape me."

I squinted at Eric's messages. They were so short and neutral. He clearly didn't like typing.

"He's more talkative face to face."

"Yeah, maybe." She took the phone away. "Or Duvo was breathing down his neck."

Arthur let out a frustrated sigh. "Eric had nothing to do with Xavier's stupid idea!"

"Duvo is only doing what he can," Camille said. "After all, they trashed the Drama Club. If our parents find out about the booze, he could lose his job. We all made a pact last night of not telling a word to protect Binta and Duvo."

My eyebrows rose. "And everyone agreed?"

"Not really. Kayvin wasn't too hot about it. But Eric convinced him that this would protect Xavier, so he relented."

"It's more because Eric also said he would do something in exchange," Arthur said. "Can't remember what. He didn't want to do it, but Kayvin won in the end."

"I didn't hear any of that."

"You, huh…" Arthur blushed furiously. "You had fallen asleep on my knee at that moment."

"Haha! Sorry about that." Camille looked away. Arthur's gaze softened behind her back.

"No problem. No problem."

I stared at them for a while, pondering. I felt like something was happening, but I couldn't put my finger on it. I made a note to ask Eric later about these two.

~

Sharp and crystalline bouts of laughter reached us as we returned to Longchamps. When we got closer to the front steps, Joy and Melissa, returning from the pool wrapped — mercifully — in towels, walked over to us with gleaming smiles.

"You missed a good one!" Joy said to Camille.

"Oh? Did Michael finally remove his shirt?"

"Haven't seen him, but Eric did earlier." Joy made a fainting motion and landed in Melissa's arms.

At the mention of Eric, my heart thumped in my chest. "Eric's out there?"

"Yes he is, Zak."

Something about the girls was off. Joy and Melissa were both looking at me with misty eyes, as if I were an abandoned kitten on the side of the road. I gave them a frosty look.

"You know, Zak…" Melissa began.

Camille hurried over and clapped her hands. "Let's get inside! Tell me everything you saw today."

Joy waved her hand. "There's nothing to say. They were shirtless, that's all."

"That's enough apparently," Arthur mumbled on the side.

After a sympathetic pat on Arthur's shoulder, I turned on my heel and made my way around the house.

I heard Kayvin and Xavier's guffaws before I saw them. Sitting on a patch of grass, his racket by his feet, a serene-looking Charles-Henry was putting on his shirt, but the others were still playing.

Eric was already dressed. His hair was pure gold in the late afternoon sun. He lifted his chin, the tip of his tongue sticking out, the sky overhead trying its best to imitate the colour of his eyes. Eric waited for the shuttlecock to come his way. Xavier hit the thing too hard; it flew toward me and landed at my feet.

"That's it for today!" Kayvin said, turning around. He noticed me and smirked.

"I'll get it," Eric said.

He betrayed no emotion as he walked toward me. The absence of the usual teasing smile made me feel uneasy.

"There you are," I said. "I looked for you all over."

Eric glanced around the backyard with a frown. "I was here the whole time."

Not the whole time, I thought out of the blue.

Eric picked up the shuttlecock and stuck it in his pocket. He retrieved his worn-out tennis ball from his other pocket and began bouncing it off the badminton racket.

"How are you?"

Something twitched inside my chest. Despite what I did to him, he was asking how I was? Was he serious?

"I'm actually okay."

"Yeah?"

"Camille and Arthur made sure of it."

Eric's eyes narrowed playfully. The sight filled me with delight, but I kept a straight face.

"Zakaria," he said. "Have you been making friends behind my back?"

"Shut it."

His childish laughter triggered a wave of relief. I was so happy, I didn't notice his friends approaching.

"Let's go inside," Kayvin said, squeezing Eric's shoulder as he went.

"Just a minute."

Kayvin's mean eyes fell on me. "It's gonna take more than a minute."

As he walked by me, he balled his hand into a fist, lifted it to his mouth, and pushed his tongue into his cheek in a really crude gesture. Eric waited until they were out of earshot, then returned his attention to the tennis ball, bouncing it off his racket with a focused frown.

"Don't mind them. They're idiots."

"I know that. It's not like I wasn't expecting this to happen."

Eric didn't look away from the ball. "What? These idiots?"

"No, I mean, people finding out about me. It's not like I wanted to keep it a secret forever."

"I didn't tell them."

"I know. Alberto probably did."

The ball missed the racket, but Eric snatched it before it hit the ground.

"He didn't, actually. Kayvin saw you two talk and put two and two together. Then Melissa and Joy said they always suspected you had a crush on him."

"Oh, great."

"They really admire the fact that you even approached him in the first place."

"Hm."

"No one's blaming you, you know. Joy said practically everyone had at least thought about asking Alberto out."

"Why don't they, then?" I mumbled, remembering Alberto's words.

"Joy has concluded that the only interesting thing about Alberto is his face."

"Harsh."

Alberto was more than a dazzling face. I was certain of it. Even if I didn't know that much about him, I always believed I was attracted to more than his features.

"I think she was vexed because he never even spared her a glance." Eric accidentally sent the ball flying at my face but caught it in time. "Oops!"

I snatched his wrist to get his attention. "Listen. I'm sorry about last night."

Eric's blue eyes widened. "What are you sorry about?"

"Being drunk. Being rude. Throwing you into the wall, that sort of thing."

Eric didn't answer. I released his wrist, and he returned to his game with more fervour. The bouncing ball was beginning to get on my nerves.

"And not just for yesterday, actually. You're always nice to me, and… and… For fuck's sake! Will you stop for a second?"

Eric caught the ball and tossed it over his shoulder. The ball landed in the pool with a splash, a bit like Camille last night, but slightly more dignified.

"Anyway, I'm really sorry," I concluded. "I'll be nicer from now on."

At that, Eric put his head in his hands and laughed quietly. I waited anxiously until he spoke again.

"You have nothing to be sorry about. Alberto's the one who should be sorry."

That again.

"You keep saying that…" I said. "But I think I caught him by surprise, and he didn't know what to say. He was in a hurry, you know… to get back to Michael."

Eric slammed a warm hand on my shoulder. "He's not going to get Michael." Taking one look at my face, he read my disbelief. "He's not. Michael's responsible, is he not? Messing around with a high school student, can you imagine? Also, he's so not interested."

"He does have a boyfriend," I said weakly.

"Yeah, Louis. I know."

"He told you?"

"Yeah."

When did Eric find time to chit-chat with Michael? How much time did they spend together, how often did it happen, and how could I stop it? Michael sure had a way of going from boy to boy…

I pinched the bridge of my nose, annoyed at myself. I had to stop my rancour from spiralling out of control. But just to be safe, I'd better not let Eric out of my sight from now on.

Eric thought I was still worrying about Alberto. He drew closer and dug his fingers into my shoulder. "There's no chance of Alberto getting in the middle of that. Michael's too hung up on his guy."

"How do you know?"

"Do you know how many pictures of his boyfriend I've had to look at? A word of advice: never, never ask Michael to see a picture."

His traumatised look made me chuckle. "Louis has been called handsome, you know."

Eric twirled the handle of the racket between his fingers. "You think he's handsome?"

"Sure, I'm not blind."

I didn't want the conversation to stir awkwardly toward the fact that they were both white, blond, and blue-eyed. It wasn't like I suddenly found Eric attractive just because he took pity on me last night. The fact that I noticed how toned his arms were when he raised the racket above his head earlier had nothing to do with it.

Eric leaned on his racket and let out a groan of relief. "You're not mad at me, then. I thought you might be."

"Me? Why should I be mad at you?"

He pressed hard onto the racket, plunging its butt into the lawn. "Because I kissed you, maybe."

Our eyes met. His were unflinching, mine not so much. I waved my hand dismissively.

"Oh come on, I'm not going to be mad at you because you threw me a pity-kiss."

He barked out a laugh. The racket plunged into the ground by another thumb.

In my opinion, there was no need to talk about this anymore. We could move past this and remain friends. That was enough of a relief for me. But Eric looked all serious when he said, "Zak, you're the lead in Camille and Duvo's movie. You're friends with the writer, the DOP, and the hot AD. Binta calls you the smartest student in her class. Even Duvo cuts you some slack. Trust me, no one sees you as this pitiable thing. To almost everyone here, you're the equivalent of the captain of the football team. The fact that you're moody and cooped up all the time only makes you cooler. If anything, I'm jealous as hell."

I stared at Eric blankly. "You're joking, right?"

"No. Everyone thinks you're cool, and Alberto's the weirdo."

"… Thanks, I guess."

"For what it's worth…" Eric plucked the racket from the grass. "I'm sorry you're sad. But I'm here. I'll distract you until you're not sad anymore. I'm *really* good at distracting people. You'll see." He looked so determined that I couldn't help but smile.

"Oh yeah?" My tone was teasing. "How are you going to do that?"

"Hm…" He didn't seem too sure of himself for once. "I'll come up with something."

We returned to the house. Eric was walking at my side, behaving normally, which I found abnormal. When we entered the hall, I stopped, a question on my lips.

"Why did you kiss me, then?"

Eric threw a longing look toward the kitchen. "What?"

"If you didn't pity me, then why did you kiss me?"

Silence fell between us. Eric looked down at his feet, his face scrunched up in a grimace.

"… Thought it would cheer you up."

Our eyes met. We both snorted.

"Idiot! It almost got you punched in the face!"

"Yeah, I've noticed!" Eric laughed some more. "I never thought you'd come after me with your tiny fists—"

"There's—hey!" I protested, outraged. "My fists aren't tiny."

He waved his hands in front of his face. "No, no, you're right."

"What the hell!"

"Sorry." Then he laughed again. "I didn't know you'd be so fierce!"

His eyes gleamed. He looked almost possessed. I had a hard time looking away.

"Pff! Of course, I am." The way he was staring at me was making me feel a little hot. Unwilling to fall for his flirty tricks, I escaped toward the kitchen, and Eric followed. We were walking shoulder to shoulder, so I stretched my neck to appear taller.

"Just how short do you think I am, compared to you?"

"Shorter." He pressed his hand on top of my head. "Even shorter now."

"Cheating already! You'll go far in this life."

Eric stopped in the doorway, the sly grin back on his face. "Anyway, I was going to have to kiss you eventually. So I thought, why not get it out of the way?"

"When I was drunk and helpless," I said, an eyebrow quirked.

"I wouldn't call you helpless, ever…" Eric laughed.

"Come to think of it… That was technically an assault!" Seeing his sheepish air, I couldn't help smiling. "Don't worry, it's not like…" I coughed when I realised what I was about to say. "It's not like I'm gonna call the cops or anything."

He looked both relieved and frightened at the same time. To hide my own fluster, I decided to tease him further.

"So you *were* afraid to kiss a boy."

"I told you I was!" He gently shoved me aside. Then he glanced once more into the kitchen, full of noise and laughter, then back at me.

"So, did it work?" I said. "Or are you still nervous?"

"Of course I am. Do you recall what happened last night?"

"Okay, I apologised for that. You took me by surprise. And I won't be drunk when we shoot the scene. *Hopefully.*"

"But…" He looked at me earnestly. "You want me to be good, don't you?"

Perhaps it was the way his eyes bore into mine, so frank and unwavering. But when he said that, I felt a strange and sudden longing which left me speechless.

The others poured out of the kitchen amidst sounds of laughter and bickering, their trays in hand. Immediately, Kayvin swooped down on Eric.

"You're coming with us," he said with authority, pulling him to his side.

"I haven't got my food yet."

Still, Kayvin dragged him along with him, not forgetting to glare at me for good measure as though I was a dangerous influence on his precious captain.

"Eric." Joy slithered between them. "I managed to save you a brownie." She waved it under his nose. "I noticed how much you love them."

My eyes narrowed. Joy, you minx. I had it on good authority Eric didn't eat this sort of thing. She knew nothing of him. And what was with her honeyed voice and the way she glued herself to him? She clearly had no respect for boundaries.

But Eric looked pleased. His eyes lit up, and he eagerly pocketed the brownie. After an apologetic grimace to me, he let himself be pulled toward the dining room, leaving me still throbbing from what I'd almost let slip out earlier.

His kiss had at no point been unwelcome.

Part Three

'YOU'

16

CHEMISTRY

The day had finally come.

On this bright Monday morning, Eric and I were to begin filming our scenes together. All the work achieved last week during rehearsal would come to fruition, and I felt nervous about it. Could we reproduce the chemistry I'd felt between us when we were hanging out by the lake? I was certain to be the only one asking myself stupid questions, of course, and I was right: it was clear during breakfast that Eric didn't have a care in the world.

Everyone was running around purposefully this morning, doing their jobs. Even Xavier looked extra-focused, but that could be because Binta threatened to throw her phone at him when she caught him laughing with Melissa instead of helping set the lights.

Eric, however, was too busy flirting with Joy.

I'd never really thought about Joy before. I knew she was British, that her best friend was Elodie, and her front teeth vaguely gave her the air of a rabbit. At Colette, she was regarded as pretty. Here, at Longchamps, with Elodie out of the picture, she was definitely considering herself the best catch among the girls, and therefore found it somewhat acceptable to flirt with Eric.

Camille, who always seemed to know everything about everyone, informed me at breakfast that Joy had ditched her boyfriend of six months to get some fun during the holidays. Joy said she wasn't to be blamed — this summer was particularly hot, and she was thirsty.

Coming out of the changing room with my footman livery on, and escaping whistles and screams from Melissa and Camille, I arrived for hair and makeup to find Eric and Joy in great conversation. Even worse, Joy had her bony hand in Eric's hair and was stroking it while smiling at his reflection in the mirror. The light pouring in from the window illuminated Eric's face, making his eyes glitter. Of course, that impossible flirt appeared to relish the attention.

And to think he was my first kiss. I was glad I pushed him into the wall. Served him right.

As for Joy, well… I'm usually not one to badmouth British people, but between her and Michael, I just *had* to get out there and say it: they are bloody thieves, and the British Museum proves it.

It upset me that no one seemed shocked about her partiality toward him. She was best friends with his girlfriend and acted like she couldn't remember it. Such betrayal should not be forgiven, in my opinion. Eric seemed to have forgotten too, the way he was chuckling as she caressed his hair. They were so cosy they didn't even notice me standing in the doorway.

Melissa, in charge of hairstyles on the set, let out an audible gasp when she saw the scene and shoved me out of the way to charge at Joy.

"I just did his hair," she barked, her nostrils flaring. "Did you have to mess it up?"

"I didn't!" Joy said, her face scarlet. "I was just fixing it."

"Fixing *what*?!"

Melissa took Joy aside, and they seriously began arguing about their friendship. Without a look at them, I sunk into the chair beside Eric. He was fixing his hair, humming to himself. I gave him a look that spoke volumes and he grinned.

"Morning, Thomas!" His eyes immediately fell on my outfit. I ignored his appreciative pout.

"You seem to be having a very nice morning yourself."

By that, I meant to tease him about his unbearable flirting with Joy. But Eric's smile widened.

"So, you really weren't joking when you said you'd be nicer to me from now on!"

Because I was about to call him a dirty little strumpet next, I decided to bite my lip instead. Glancing sideways, I realised he was already dressed as Adam, in a grey check suit which really complimented him. The sharp blue eyes noticed my struggling expression, and of course, he didn't miss this opportunity to torment me.

"Just how much nicer did you intend to be?"

I had lived sixteen and a half years in this world, and no one had ever spoken to me this way. His voice had lowered by several octaves and sounded almost like a caress. In any case, it was obscene. A seasoned flirt like this knew how to use every possible trick to make their target sweat, but I wouldn't fall for this. My name wasn't Joy. I bit down harder on my lip.

Eric leaned ridiculously close to me, his breath tickling my ear, and locked eyes with my reflection in the mirror. "How... much... nicer?"

"Back off, hussy!"

The words tumbled out of my mouth unrestrained. Instantly, Eric erupted in laughter, pounding his fist on the table, sending makeup brushes flying everywhere.

"Did you just..." His eyes were streaming. Joy and Melissa returned, having solved their crisis. Melissa approached him with a comb. "I'm good, I'm good." Eric pushed her hand away.

"Stop crying, Eric," Joy said in her honeyed voice. "Or I'll have to do your makeup again."

He paid her no attention. Melissa huffed and started bickering with Joy again. They raised their voices at each other and stomped to the side for another round. Eric took this opportunity to make eye contact with me.

"Did you just call me a hussy?"

"It just came out," I said, scowling.

He laughed for a moment, then lowered his voice again. "Is this your idea of being nicer, then?"

"If you keep on tormenting me..."

"How was that tormenting you? I was just asking you a question."

I decidedly looked away from him.

"All right, all right. I'll stop." He smiled. "I'm only trying to distract you, remember?"

Call it whatever you want; I knew it was to torment me. If that really was his way of distracting me from my pain, it worked. But if he kept acting like this, he would end up driven into a wall again. Head-first, this time.

Undeterred as always, Eric tried to tickle me. I landed a sharp slap on his hand.

"Zak, Zak. Look at me."

"No."

"Zak, I've never been called a hussy before. It's a historical moment in my life! You have to look at me."

"I don't."

He stretched in front of the mirror, filling my field of vision whether I wanted it or not. "In any case, thank you. I was feeling nervous and now I'm so much better."

This time, I glanced up. Eric had finally managed to say something sensible; *that* was a historical moment. His chin propped in his hand, he was gazing at me.

So he was nervous after all. And today wasn't even a kissing scene.

I was about to offer some comforting words, but in the reflection of the mirror, I caught Joy looking up from her phone to flash him a smile, which he returned in kind.

Caught in the act!

"Why are you flirting with Joy?" I said through gritted teeth.

He laughed and shrugged at the same time. "I'm not. I'm just smiling back."

"Humph."

"That's the polite thing to do when someone smiles at you. You should try it." He scrunched up his face. "Especially after promising to be nice to me!"

"You don't think Elodie would mind?" I spoke harshly.

He became serious, considered it a moment. "Mm. I guess she would, maybe a little."

"A little? They're best friends!"

He frowned. "But that's her problem, right? Not mine, not really?"

I was shocked at his indifference. Obviously, we were not the same sort of people, and we didn't move around in the same circles. But still. How could he be so inconsiderate about such things, when he was so attentive to people in general? It's like he was two different people at once.

"Why are you so bothered by this?" he said. "It's not like—"

Surprising both of us this time, I slammed my fist on the table, sending one makeup brush rolling off the table. Eric caught it without even breaking eye contact with me.

"Forget it!" I took a deep breath. "I don't want to fight before our scene."

But I could see in his eyes that he was burning to fight some more. He even licked his lips.

"Cut it out. We're shooting in a few minutes." I sat properly and smoothed the lapels of my livery. "I told Camille I would deliver my best work. I can't focus if you're fooling around."

I thought he would deny fooling around at all, but all he did was tug at my sleeve.

"I'm committed too, you know!"

I shook him off. In truth, I myself couldn't understand why my fist moved on its own when he asked me a simple question. But I knew for sure I didn't want to fight with him, either today or tomorrow, and I felt our conversation would go nowhere satisfactory at all. He was wrong in his actions. He was wrong, and I didn't want to have to be the one to tell him. I threw him a haughty look.

"When you hear *Action*, you can take the lead, be my lord and master all you want, but outside, I'm the one in charge. So when I say cut it out, you cut it out."

Eric whistled out a long breath. "Yes, sir." Then he added, with a pout, "You're so scary."

Just as I was losing control of my lips and they began curling up against my will, I caught sight of something and froze. Alberto was standing right next to me, looking like a breath of cool wind. He was so quiet I hadn't heard him come near at all. My stomach contracted painfully. He retrieved something from a dark duffle bag set against the makeup table, turned it in his hands, looking unsure of himself. To my surprise, he spoke to me.

"Big scene, today."

Alberto really was talking to me. My mouth opened, but no sound came out. His own face contorted, his lips twisted, his brow furrowed. Then he jerked his thumb over his shoulder.

"Better get going, then."

I nodded. He revealed a clipped smile and stalked away toward Arthur.

I turned to Eric. "Did you see that? Did you—"

Eric, his eyes screwed shut, was muttering to himself, looking anxious. He looked like he was praying. With a smile, I left him to it.

When Joy and Melissa were done with my hair and makeup, I joined the others in front of Arthur's camera. I expected Duvo to look anxious, but I was surprised to find Michael less relaxed than his usual self. Still, when he sought my eyes, I looked away. Then I heard Eric's voice behind me.

"You're gonna have to talk to him eventually, you know. Look at him, he's so cute when he's miserable."

"He's miserable?"

Eric grabbed both my arms, twirled me around so I could look at Michael. He did appear more focused, but not exactly miserable. Meanwhile, Alberto definitely looked off, standing behind Michael with an awkward air about him.

A part of me wanted to run to Alberto, hurl my arms around his neck, and tell him I forgave him. On the other hand, the mere sight of him now made me feel uneasy. I felt thoroughly confused. But perhaps these new sensations were a good thing; they might help me move on. In the meantime, even if I knew I'd have to talk to Michael sooner or later, I felt like letting him suffer another couple of hours, for good measure.

Just as I was congratulating myself on being a petty little rascal, Michael looked up and our eyes met. I flushed terribly and turned around, straight into Eric's arms. "Shit, he saw us!"

Eric chuckled. "I love it when you swear."

This time, he was too fast. His hands were pinching my waist before I could wriggle out of his grasp.

"Mind the clothes!" Duvo shouted at us from the back. "They're expensive!"

We parted at once. I even took an extra step back as a precaution.

"They're nice," Eric said, admiring himself in a mirror. "What do you think? Do you like it?"

"It's… fine," I muttered.

I wished we would start shooting. It was getting hot under the livery. But of course, Eric wasn't happy with my lukewarm compliments, so he advanced on me again.

"Fine? You're not at all nicer than before. I'd say you're worse."

I tugged at my collar. "You look great. There. Happy?"

"Well, thank you kindly, my good sir."

The inexplicable Southern drawl was back, surprising me into laughter. Immediately, Duvo charged toward us, his glasses askew.

"No Southern accent!"

Eric was frightened enough to back into one of the studio lights. "I was just j—"

"No!" Duvo poked him hard in the chest. "I swear to God, if I hear anything resembling that accent, I'm firing you on the spot!"

Eric clung to the studio light with terror in his eyes. Michael approached him and put a hand on his shoulder.

"Calm down," he said, with a pointed look at Duvo. "No one's gonna fire anyone." I glared at him until he removed his hand from Eric's shoulder. He gave a little cough. "Can you both please take your positions?"

Eric and I stood on our marks at the opposite sides of the set, and Joy came to check our complexions. This time, Eric kept his eyes on his shoes. Melissa approached him with the comb again, and again he refused her, but as Duvo said nothing, she came to me instead. She checked that not one of my hairs was out of place and gave me a warm smile.

Behind the camera, Arthur looked confident, a broad smile on his face. Standing by him, Michael and Alberto stood, serious as ever. Awkwardly lifting the boom pole, Sander almost stuck it into Duvo's eye.

"What the hell are you doing?"

Sander half-bowed to him. "Sorry!"

Even if the scene wasn't too difficult, consisting mostly of stolen glances and not much else, I felt a mounting tension, and a thin layer of sweat was forming on my palms. On the other side of the room, Eric was unusually quiet.

"You'll be fine," I said, loud enough for him to hear me.

"Silence!" Duvo said.

Eric's face split into a smile. "You think I can do it, then?"

I took on a haughty air. "Yeah, yeah of course you can do it."

"Silence!" Duvo shouted.

"Shh!" Michael said, putting his finger on Duvo's mouth.

Duvo stared at him in wonder. "W-what?"

"Chemistry," Michael said. "There. We have it."

"… Thick as thieves," Duvo was saying, looking smug.

Binta was shaking her head. "Damn… I wish I'd seen it."

"I couldn't believe it myself. Chemistry's off the charts. This movie's gonna be good. No, great."

A faint smile on my lips, I was waiting for Duvo to give me leave after wrapping up our last scene for the day. Eric, unbearably proud with himself, had already rushed to the changing rooms to remove his stuffy suit.

We were so good that filming was over shortly after lunchtime. Duvo had summoned me to his side for a few words but had forgotten all about me when Binta came out of the kitchen with flour on her cheek.

"Michael was right in the end," she said. "About them needing some alone time."

"Yes, yes I guess," Duvo said in a resentful tone.

"Cough, cough," I tried to get their attention. "Ahem."

"You have to stop being jealous of twenty-year-olds."

"I'll never stop being jealous of twenty-year-olds. Little shits. They're twenty. They can deal with it."

"Ahem!"

"Oh!" Duvo removed his hands from Binta's waist. "You're still here."

I tossed him a condescending look. "Can I go?"

"Yeah, yeah." He waved me away.

"The afternoon is all yours," Binta said with a smile.

I wasn't even out the door when he had already put his hands around her again, seeking her lips.

Binta was a smart woman. Everyone knew that. What did she like about him? Some people made for the strangest pairings. Like Michael and Louis, for instance. Yasmine said Louis was the opposite of Michael in everything.

Alberto and Michael had a lot in common. And Alberto fancied Michael. Then why weren't they together already? Even if I thought it was gross at first, after thinking about it, it's not that the age difference between them was shocking. And if Duvo could do something like seducing Binta on what was technically a school trip, then why wouldn't Michael be able to seduce Alberto between two takes? For all I knew, it had already happened.

If Alberto was throwing himself at me, I wouldn't be able to resist. And if Michael wanted to throw himself at Alberto, Alberto would let him. Gosh… Must be nice to be Michael. I wouldn't have minded being him for a few days.

But Michael looked like he wished to be somebody else. Or that's the impression I got when I stepped outside after changing back into my usual clothes, and found him on the terrace, hunched over the railing. He looked miserable, as Eric said, twirling a little object between his fingers, staring at the grove stretching beyond. With horror, I saw that he was smoking a cigarette.

"Michael! What are you doing?"

Michael glanced at me, then his cigarette, then back at me and sighed. "Don't tell my boyfriend."

I approached him, cautious, and still a little mad. "Who's your boyfriend anyway?"

Michael's eyebrows rose. "Really?"

After a noncommittal shrug, I joined him and we bathed in silence for a moment. The ruthless sun was hanging high in the sky; I felt naked in its light. But when the words came out, my voice was steady.

"I'm in love with Alberto."

A light twang of pain reverberated through my chest. At the same time, I felt a mild confusion again.

Michael gave an almost imperceptible nod. "I know."

"But…" My shoulders sank. "I think he's in love with you."

Michael took a sharp breath, but he didn't reply. It didn't seem like he wanted to talk to me, so I stepped back, ready to leave. But he took a long drag of his cigarette and spoke in a tired voice. "I think Louis's cheating on me with some stupid rockstar."

I turned around, my mouth hanging open. Michael had leaned low onto the railing and was frowning at the trees. I returned to his side, too stunned to say anything. When he looked at me again and realised who he was talking to, a flash of alarm passed in his eyes.

"I'm sorry, I don't know why I told you that."

"That's okay," I said tentatively. "You can tell me things."

Perhaps it would be good for both of us to empty our bags here and now. The problem was, I wasn't particularly skilled at this sort of conversation. I tried to think of what my sister would say. "Are you sure?"

"No."

"Then what makes you think he's cheating on you? Isn't he like, crazy about you? Bordering on insane, according to Yasmine."

"He's supposed to be!" Michael spoke angrily, completely out of character. "But now he's on tour across England, and I have such a hard time getting him on the phone. It's never a good time. If I call during the day, he's asleep. If I call during the night, he… he seems to always be partying and he can't talk to me."

"But isn't he working?"

"Yes. But this new band he's representing… I don't like it. The singer's some hot guy who tries to seduce everything that moves. They're together every night. Drinking, probably. It drives me mad."

"Don't you trust him?"

Michael bit his lip, hard. "I'm supposed to, but I'm having a hard time at the moment. He's so aloof on the phone, like he doesn't want to speak to me." He hung his head. "Seriously. It's like I can't even go one week apart from him without freaking out like a high school kid."

Ouch, thank you very much. I was that close to baring my fangs, but watching him so miserable, I didn't feel like biting his head off, even if I was shocked at how thick he was.

"The solution is pretty simple. You have to call him, now."

"He's sleeping at this time."

"Fuck that. Call him. *Now*. Yasmine would kill you if she saw you moping around like that. She would tell you to drag this loser out of bed and get the truth out of him by any means necessary."

Michael managed a small smile. "Yeah, she would definitely say that."

"Honestly…"

"It's not always so simple, though. I'm afraid of his answer. If he tells me he's messing around with that guy, what am I going to do?"

"Break up," I said, with all the confidence of someone who's never been in this situation, ever.

"But I don't want to." His voice broke a little.

Hearing this, I couldn't help but let out a little breath of relief. "You promise?"

Michael finally smiled and gently bumped his arm against mine. "I know it's going to come as a shock to you, Zak… But I'm not interested in Alberto."

Of all the things Michael could do to rile me up, this was the one I was the keenest to forgive. So, I too, bumped my arm against his.

"He can be quite scary," Michael added. "Truly, I haven't been chased around so intensely since that time Louis had convinced himself I was hiding something. He followed me around film school all day wearing an old trench coat and dark sunglasses, terrorising everyone who came across him."

I turned away from him to hide my disgust. "We should talk about how insane your boyfriend is one day… To a professional. A cop, perhaps?"

"Mmh, sure," Michael said absently. He seemed to be relishing in the memory.

"Anyway!"

My voice brought him back to reality. He patted my hand. "I'm sorry Alberto doesn't realise how great you are, Zak. Trust me, we've all been there. But there are other people who—"

"Don't start! This doesn't work on me."

He looked amused. "If you say so."

I bounced on the balls of my feet, trying to find the right words. "I guess I should be happy with you telling me that. But I saw how uncomfortable he was this morning and… I don't want that for him either."

"I think he's already moved on, honestly. If not today, then tomorrow."

"But—"

"He's not even that into me."

"You mean he's straight after all?" I banged my head against the railing. "I'm so confused!"

Michael laughed. "Some people obsess over the things they can't have, and… Alberto doesn't seem the type to obsess for a long time." He read my expression and put a hand on my shoulder. "But never mind him. You did really well today. Isn't that good news?"

"It was easier than I thought," I said truthfully. "It felt…"

"Effortless?"

"Don't you start."

Michael graced me with a dimpled smile. His green eyes sparkled with mischief. "Mind you… I was right about Eric."

I clenched the railing with both hands. "What… what about Eric?"

"Nothing! I'm just saying… I was right!"

I stomped my foot. "Start by calling your psychopath of a boyfriend first, then congratulate yourself later."

Michael nodded and put out his cigarette in the ashtray with a smile. "You are so like your sister, it's incredible. You could be twins."

"Thank you, I appreciate that."

We exchanged a laugh. Little by little, some of the tension I didn't even realise I had, lifted off my shoulders and I let out a relaxed sigh.

A strange, pleasant feeling came over me, a feeling that all was well in the world at this precise moment. That the loss of Alberto wasn't so painful, that there was still hope, and that Longchamps had more to teach me than I ever dreamed it could.

"Thank you," I said to nothing and no one in particular.

17

MY DISTRACTION

On the other side of the house, the others were having a little gathering of their own. Michael and I walked together to the pool and found the girls stretching on the lounge chairs in their best swimwear. Xavier and Kayvin, kneeling by Joy and Melissa's chairs, were getting sunscreen slathered onto their tanned skin. Eric was throwing around his tennis ball, his face scrunched up in concentration. I felt a sudden urge to take his ball and throw it as far as I could to see if he would fetch it for me.

"Zak!" Camille called out to me.

It pleased me to see her. Michael gave my shoulder a friendly squeeze and pushed me toward her. From the corner of my eye, I noticed Eric was looking at us, a satisfied little smirk plastered on his face.

As I approached Camille's chair, I heard my mom's playlist playing through a set of portable speakers. I looked around in shock.

"H-How!" In vain I searched my pockets for the missing iPod.

"Oh yes, I took that," Camille said.

I gave her a helpless look. "I can see that!"

"We love it, it's very retro," Melissa said.

Joy agreed. "Please don't touch the music."

"My father loves this old stuff," Xavier said. "But he usually prefers classical music, you know. He's a bar—"

"Baronet, yes." Joy put her bare foot on his shoulder. "We know, babes."

Eric turned to me. "Have you come to hang out?"

"I guess."

He bounced on his feet. Joy saw that and let out a crystalline laugh.

"You wanna play badminton?" he asked.

"Hmm…" I pretended to think about it. "Over my dead body."

"Are you sure?" His eyes were full of mischief already.

"Don't you start."

Melissa and Joy started chanting my name, urging me to play. I immediately shut down.

"Enough, enough." Eric was laughing as he approached me. "Zak's my boy, leave him alone."

I pursed my lips. "Don't call me your boy."

"Sorry. Zak's my man, leave him alone."

Inwardly, I slapped my forehead. Grinning, Eric swung his arm around my neck, pulling me closer. But two could play that game. With a sudden urge to tease him right back, I enveloped him with my own arm, resting my hand on his hip. He twitched, but his smile stayed put.

Immediately, Joy summoned him over.

"Come here."

"Why?" he asked, but he came trotting anyway.

Fetch.

"Come here!" Joy cooed. "I'll apply sunscreen for you."

There you go. I tried not to glare at her too hard, but I couldn't see myself after all. To my surprise, Eric stopped in his tracks.

"I'm good, thanks."

Take that! Interiorly, I pointed my finger at her and laughed. But she insisted.

"You'll bake if you don't protect yourself. Come on."

"I'm good." Eric returned to his ball. "I'm already wearing sunscreen."

"Really?"

He stopped, turned, and grinned. "My mom's not a baronet, she's a redhead. And I inherited her pale skin."

Kayvin perked up when he heard him. "Your mom's hot."

Eric's smile froze, but he said nothing, and no one else seemed to notice.

Camille took my hand, pulling me to the lounge chair next to hers.

Meanwhile, Kayvin and Xavier were exchanging odd looks. Kayvin looked torn, but Xavier less so. He called Michael's name, and Michael, who was busy staring at Kayvin with eyes as wide as saucers, looked back in surprise.

"Will you play with us?" Xavier said. "Charles-Henry usually makes our fourth, but he's baking a cake with Nadia."

Kayvin sniggered. "Yeah, right."

Michael hesitated, then probably decided playing with the guys was better than following my advice and calling Louis. "Sure. Why not."

Just wait until I tell my sister about that, I thought mercilessly.

Kayvin began to walk toward Eric, but he was stopped with a simple gesture.

"No. Michael, you come with me."

"What? Why?" Kayvin looked crestfallen. "We always team up together!"

Eric smiled, but his tone was firm. "Not this time."

"Come on!" Kayvin almost bared his teeth.

"What? You're afraid you can't beat us?"

Something about Eric's countenance seemed to have an irresistible hold over Kayvin. He didn't dare talk back. Michael, who had not one ounce of competitiveness inside him, walked over to Eric's side with a slightly worried expression.

After Eric dumped his tennis ball and the contents of his absurd shorts' pockets on a side table before everyone's dumbfounded gaze, they started their game of badminton. The rest of us watched with more or less interest. Joy and Melissa were talking about their favourite drama which I'd never heard of. Joy would interrupt their conversation occasionally to cheer Eric with great enthusiasm. My eyes couldn't help darting toward her every time she went a little overboard with her encouragements. She was getting on my nerves. Turning to Camille, I spoke through gritted teeth so that Joy couldn't hear me.

"When will she stop flirting with him?"

Camille laughed. "What's happening to you all of a sudden?"

"It's disrespectful."

"How so?"

"She's Elodie's best friend."

"Ah." Camille pondered for a while. "You have a point. But it's Eric's choice, after all."

Eric's choice. Of course, it was Eric's choice. But I thought he was better than this.

"It's dirty. Cheating on your girlfriend with her best friend. I seriously hope he's not gonna do it. For his sake, I mean."

"But…" Camille leaned forward. "They're not together anymore."

"They're… not?" I stiffened all over.

But just as my mouth opened to demand more information, Alberto appeared on the steps. The mere sight of him was enough to turn my mind blank at once. My insides twisted and churned as though they weren't sure whether I should feel elated or anxious. Alberto traipsed toward the row of lounge chairs, sunglasses perched on the tip of his nose, a book in his hand. I caught a glimpse of the cover. It was a Sartre.

He sat on the other end of the rows of chairs, next to Melissa, and shook his beautiful hair away from his face. Joy and Melissa looked at him, then me, then each other. When I met their gaze, they pretended to be absorbed by something else. Seeing I wasn't saying a word, Joy gained confidence and turned to Alberto.

"Huh, Alberto?" She sounded a tad nervous. "Do you want some sunscreen?"

"No, thank you."

"But you'll burn out here."

We waited a long time for his answer, and I thought perhaps he had fallen asleep.

"Fine," he said.

Joy got up with a grin and approached Alberto. Evidently, she shared with Eric that irrepressible need to get her hands on people. But to everybody's surprise, as soon as he saw her approach, he jerked aside as if she were an infectious rat.

Joy had no idea how to react. "You said—"

"I said fine, I'll burn, then." His expression was unreadable behind his sunglasses.

Joy returned to her seat with a startled expression. She hesitated, then extended the bottle toward me. "Zak, do you want some?"

Alberto's head flicked in my direction, but I couldn't see his eyes. I shook my head in silence, and she didn't insist.

Oblivious to all that, Eric and the others were focused on their game. Eric raised the racket over his head and his short sleeve slid down to his shoulder, revealing his toned and now golden arm. He hit the shuttlecock and moved away from the net, bouncing on his feet. Our eyes met; he flashed me a playful wink.

I suddenly felt dizzy and screwed my eyes shut. "I think the sun's hitting me pretty hard."

"Take these!" Camille said, pushing a pair of huge sunglasses up my nose. "I always carry several because I never know which one I'll want."

"Thanks," I said, grateful at the instant relief. "I have a pair upstairs and I never use them."

"Boy, oh boy," Camille said, staring at my face.

"What?"

"You look like a movie star."

I shook my head. "… Nonsense."

But when she reached out to stroke my hair, I didn't protest. It felt really nice. For a while, I let her pet me like a domesticated cat, watching the game contentedly, focused on the shuttlecock's trajectory, and nothing else.

Eric was really fit and didn't show any signs of fatigue, proving once and for all that exercising every morning at ungodly hours did have amazing effects on one's body. When, mocking Xavier's terrible shot, he burst out laughing and his child-like mirth filled the air around us, I suddenly remembered something and grabbed Camille's wrist.

"Did you just say Eric's not dating Elodie anymore?"

Camille's eyebrows rose to her hairline. "Yes, ten minutes ago."

"Is that true?"

"I'm not sure, it's just something I heard. He didn't say a word to me."

"Is he or is he not?"

Not that it would change things, of course. But if that were the case, I wouldn't be able to object if he wanted to date Joy. And seriously, why would I? It's just that Eric was my friend, and I didn't want him to be a loose, cheating kind of person. I just wanted to be reassured, that's all.

Joy appeared to be sleeping, but we all knew she was staring at the guys. Camille put her hand on her chair to get her attention.

"Joy."

"Hm?"

"Is Eric still with Elodie?"

Joy and Melissa shared a long look.

"No, he's not, actually."

My pulse quickened. Why on earth didn't he tell me? He was

always chattering about bees and insignificant stuff like that, so why would he omit to say something like that? Unless…

"Since when?" Camille asked, as though she read my mind.

Joy turned once again to Melissa before answering. "I've just found out about it." She sounded cold. "I get why you're asking, Camille, but don't even think about it."

Camille removed her sunglasses and gave her a surprised look. "What did you say?"

Joy's tone softened, but she also removed her sunglasses, revealing a resolute expression. "I've got dibs. Been fancying this guy since last year. It was *my* number I asked Elodie to give him. But she snatched him from me."

Camille stared at Joy blankly as though at a loss for words.

I wasn't at a loss for words. There was a lot *I* could say. But no one asked me, so I just sat there, scowling.

"I like you, Camille, really," Joy said in a tone that settled the matter. "But Eric's mine."

"Presumptuous," I muttered without thinking.

Joy heard me and laughed as she slid her sunglasses up her nose. "You're right, I know. It's a bit crazy. But Eric has always liked me!"

"Eric likes everyone," Camille spoke in a chilly voice, clearly vexed by Joy's rudeness.

It worked. Joy's face looked tense behind her sunglasses. Then she attacked again.

"See? You like him!"

"No, I don't. Not like that anyway. I'm just saying, he likes everyone."

That was a fact. There was nobody in this group that Eric hadn't made feel as though they were amazing, charming, and important to him. It was maddening. But it was also part of his charm.

The strange dizziness returned, making my ears ring. I pinched the bridge of my nose.

"Yeah, right," Joy was saying.

"Really, I don't want to date him," Camille insisted.

Joy sniggered. "Are you seriously telling me that if Eric went down on his knees and said he was desperately in love with you, you would reject him? *Him*?"

I blinked fast, trying not to imagine the scene.

"I wouldn't want anybody to get down on their knees for me," Camille said, her face set.

Yes, yes, Camille. *That* was the right answer. My girl!

Joy had a sigh of impatience. "Just answer the question."

Camille had gone silent, probably thinking not answering would be the best way to upset Joy some more. Joy opened her mouth to add something, but Melissa gripped her arm.

"Oh look, Kayvin has taken his shirt off."

"Finally!"

The conversation was dropped on the spot.

I watched the girls through strained eyes. Hussies, the lot of them. As for me, I was a hypocrite.

My mother always said that when you don't like someone, you simply have to make an effort and force yourself to find one thing you can like about them. One. Surely, there must be one thing about this person that you like. Thinking of her words, I had to admit Kayvin took great care of his body and looked quite impressive. If only he weren't a terrifying beast posing as a human being, he could have been just as popular as Eric.

Xavier couldn't be behind his bestie for too long, and his shirt went off as well. He glanced in our direction and I snorted, amused. Camille had lowered her shades a moment, but she preferred to lie back on her chair and listen to the music playing softly through the speakers.

We all baked in the sun for a while, until the game turned sour.

Michael and Eric were close to a victory against Kayvin and Xavier. After a particularly good shot from Michael, Eric, naturally, couldn't resist pulling him into a hug. Kayvin's eyes narrowed darkly, and he pushed Xavier away, telling him to get a grip. Xavier threw another sheepish look toward the row of lounge chairs and the girls sitting on them. Too distracted, he missed. Game over.

Eric, footballer style, jumped straight into Michael's arms, who was so surprised he fell backwards, and they both tumbled in a tangle of limbs. The girls sighed in unison.

"I would watch that film," Melissa said.

"I'd pay double for it," Joy added.

My whole face tensed. Eric's glee was practically indecent. Without any thought about how they looked, he untangled himself from disoriented Michael. Pulling him to his feet, he slapped his back and shook him as though he were nothing but a rag doll. A harsh ray of sunlight fell over him like a spotlight. His hair appeared a golden crown, his whole face was alight, his eyes so bright they seemed to glow as he raised his fist in victory.

How handsome he was…

How could I have not noticed this before?

Embarrassed by my own thoughts, I tore my gaze away, only to freeze on the spot.

Alberto's head was turned toward me. Was he looking at me? It seemed that way. Who could say, with our sunglasses masking half our faces? I immediately felt a violent flush creep up my neck. Alberto quickly dipped his head, plunging back into his book, and hid his face in his hand.

On the side, Kayvin was angry. He had lost the game, and Michael had taken his spot. For some reason, Arthur's arrival with a pitcher of iced tea made him even angrier.

"Oh great. All we needed was another fag."

There was a silence. Arthur's movements froze; he looked at Camille and me helplessly.

"Am… I? Are you talking about me?"

Kayvin's face was turning red now that everyone was watching him.

"Don't listen to him," Camille said, eyes flashing. "He's just being a big bully as usual."

"Excuse me, who are you?" Kayvin retorted.

Xavier scratched his head. "What's going on?"

For once, I felt just as confused as him. We were just relaxing and watching a silly game. But all of a sudden, the tension was so thick we could almost see it with our own eyes. Michael rolled his eyes to the sky, as though he had encountered many similar situations and couldn't be bothered anymore. Personally, it was the first time I was going through this. Kayvin had never liked me, but now I could understand the root of the problem, even before Eric approached Kayvin.

"What's up with you?"

Kayvin looked like he was having a massive headache. His voice sounded broken when he spoke. "Why are you hanging out so much with them!" He was gesturing at me and Michael.

"Because they're cool. What's the problem?"

"You know what the problem is!"

"No, I don't." Eric genuinely looked like he didn't see the problem. He was either moronic or pretending to be.

"People are gonna think you're one of them!"

"One what?"

"Fag!"

Michael put his head in his hand; Joy's mouth opened in shock; most people looked completely bewildered. I merely watched, biting my tongue. But Eric burst out laughing.

"Watch yourself, then. Aren't you sharing a room with Alberto?"

Xavier gasped. "Alberto's gay?"

He turned to Alberto, who was yawning, stretched on the lounge chair, his hair falling into his eyes. He waved his hand lazily.

"Please leave me out of this."

"That's not the same!" Kayvin had turned a dark shade of plum.

Eric gave his friend a half-stern, half-concerned look. "Why are you so worried about what people think anyway?"

Kayvin looked anguished. "Why don't you care!"

Eric never stopped smiling. "Who cares what people say or think? When you know something's not true, why worry so much about it?" He patted his friend's shoulder.

Camille rose from her seat with fire in her eyes. "And even so… even if Eric were the gayest man on the planet, it still wouldn't give you the right to be an asshole about it."

Looking just as furious, Joy got up and pulled Michael in a possessive hug. They both nodded in unison. Eric threw a helpless look at Camille and tightened his lips shut.

"Wait." Joy nestled in Michael's chest and smirked. "Maybe you're the one in love with him." She laughed, which only enraged Kayvin some more. Eric sighed, but Kayvin was snarling.

"Fuck you, I'm not a fag!"

Michael raised his hand. "Enough! Don't speak to her like that."

I agreed with Michael. He could be an asshole to us if he wanted. But to speak to a girl like that? Joy was his friend, too.

"You might not like dicks," I said flatly. "But you sure act like one."

Camille snorted, but Eric's childish laughter sent Kayvin over the edge. With a terrifying smile, he reached out to grab me. Arthur interposed himself between us, screaming:

"Don't touch him, you f…" but he lost spirit when Kayvin pulled him by the front of his shirt instead, "… ancy jellybean?"

"Fancy what?" Joy looked nonplussed.

"That's what I thought." Kayvin looked both angry and awed. "Another fag."

"Let him go!" Camille shouted, her eyes blazing.

He didn't even spare her a look. But Eric approached him

cautiously and put a hand on his back and another on the arm that held a gulping Arthur.

"Come on, man." His voice was soothing. "Let him go."

Kayvin was like a wild dog, but he still respected the authority of his pack leader, so he reluctantly let go. Eric patted him on the back. "Good. All good."

And then he pressed his palm on Kayvin's chest and sent him flying into the pool with a simple push.

Kayvin splashed into the water with a curse. The girls screeched in shock; I jumped back, my hands on my mouth; Arthur hid behind me; Xavier, his mouth opened, turned to Camille.

"Hey, you..."

With a roar, she promptly shoved him into the water as well.

"Let's scram!" Grabbing her bag, Camille ran, limbs flailing, toward the front of the house.

She didn't have to tell me twice. Pulling Arthur by the wrist, I bolted after her. I threw looks over my shoulder as I ran and saw Joy and Melissa laughing behind their fists and Michael looking toward the heavens as though he wished he were back home instead of dealing with little shits like us. His book covering his face, Alberto appeared to be sleeping.

I slowed down, letting Arthur overtake me, when I realised I'd left something... or someone behind. Eric was still by the pool. Michael was giving his hand to Kayvin to help him out of the water, and Eric was telling him not to. And he was right; that was a stupid mistake to make because Kayvin simply pulled Michael into the water.

"Oh God," I whispered.

I started running again. The sound of more splashes reached us as Arthur and I met up with Camille and her billowing skirt in front of the house.

"I don't know where I'm goiiiing!"

She plunged into the grove. Just then, Eric appeared on my right. He had raced from the edge of the pool to Camille in less time than it took me to blink.

"Through here!" He took the lead. I knew where we were going: To the lake-slash-pond. To our place. But I didn't feel uncomfortable about it. I felt thrilled, and a little drunk. After a wild race across the grove amidst the sounds of Eric and Camille's laughter, we all emerged panting into the clearing.

"Boy, did that feel good!"

"You're both insane!" I said.

Camille pointed a finger at Arthur. "*You fancy jellybean*?"

Arthur was bending over to catch his breath. "I just said the first thing that came into mind. Try thinking of something better when Kayvin's about to punch you in the face."

"I like it," Eric said. "Fancy jellybean it is."

"Eric!" Arthur slapped a hand over his mouth. "Did you just leave them there?"

Eric didn't even break a sweat. "The moment Michael got in there, I thought to myself: She's right, let's scram."

"You could have helped him!" I said, but I was laughing too.

"The girls went in like warriors to help Michael. They seemed to be having a good time."

I wasn't so sure Michael liked being hurled into pools against his will by people who thought of him as a fag, but Michael knew how to take care of himself. And if he didn't, I'd ask Yasmine to avenge him.

"Won't Kayvin try to find us and beat the shit out of us?" Arthur asked anxiously.

"Kayvin's not stupid enough to ditch a pool party with two hot girls just to get back at me."

"You don't sound afraid of him."

Eric yawned and stretched under the sun. "Why should I be afraid of him?" In all his splendour, he looked at our worried expressions and laughed. "He knew I'd get him the moment he flapped his gums about my mom. I'm sure he's fine. And besides, I'm not the one who called him a dick!"

I lifted my fingers to my mouth. "That's me. I did! Does that mean he's gonna kill me? I feel he's going to kill me. I should have never said that. I don't know what came over me. I swear to God, I heard my sister's voice in my head. And she spoke right through me."

Eric, still laughing, threw his arm around my neck and ruffled my hair.

"Hey!" I tried to break free. "Let go."

"Don't worry, he's not gonna kill you," Eric said, tightening his grip. "He's probably embarrassed that you stood up to him and he will leave you alone from now on."

"Okay but let go."

"Let's hope so," Arthur said, his face ashen. "He really seems to hate Zak for some reason."

Eric finally released me. Glaring at him, I took a gulp of fresh air.

Camille didn't mind Kayvin so much. Her eyes full of wonder, she walked over to the edge of the shimmering lake.

"This place is wonderful!" She began twirling alongside the bank among wildflowers and butterflies, her skirt flowing around her, exposing her underwear once again. Eric slapped his hand over his eyes.

"I can really feel the inspiration!" she said. "Can't you?"

Eric muttered something incoherent.

"Don't fall into it," I said in a warning tone.

She stuck out her tongue. "I hope I do, just so you realise it's not a big deal!"

"I'll watch over her." Arthur walked over to her with his fists clenched.

My mouth felt sore. I realised I was smiling from ear to ear. I turned around and found Eric staring at me, a glint in his eye.

"So… is that enough distraction for you, or… do you want more?"

I felt myself flushing for no reason. "Pff. As if you did all of that for my benefit."

"What if—Hello! Are you blushing?"

Was he a dog or a hawk? Damn him!

"I'm not."

"You are!" Eric approached with springy steps. "Do it again." Before he could grab me, I jumped out of his way. His nose wrinkled. "I'll make you do it again."

"You can die trying."

"So snarky!" He licked his lips. "I love your snark. You're such a meanie."

Before I could slam my foot in his kneecap, he leapt aside, laughing. Camille returned, leaving Arthur inexplicably shaking by the bank, and dropped to her knees.

"My dog would love it here. He would chase after all the pretty butterflies."

"You have a dog?" Eric beamed as if this day couldn't possibly get any better. He sat down next to Camille with glittering eyes.

"'Course I do. His name is Gilbert. Do you want to see a picture?"

Camille plunged headfirst into her bag, searching for her phone. I sat down beside Eric. He looked at me and mouthed the word: *Gilbert?*

I put a finger in front of my lips, smiling. He tried to seize it, so I sent him rolling with a kick in the shoulder.

"He's a good boy!" Camille said, showing off a picture.

Unlike *this one*, I thought.

"He's perfect!" Eric agreed after one quick look.

"I have a dog too, you know…" Great. I sounded like a jealous ten-year-old.

"You do?" Eric said. "Do you have a picture?"

I patted my pockets automatically, hoping to find my phone in there. But I usually didn't carry my phone around in my pockets, nor did I have pictures of Rufus. He had a tendency to swallow anything that was pointed at him. Besides keeping creeps away from my sister's skirts, that dog had never rendered me a service in all his five years of existence.

"No," I said with regret. "But I have a rabbit."

Eric giggled. "A little bunny?"

"His name is Bugs Bunny." I paused. "But my mom always calls him Sir Floppington, and I'm starting to suspect he likes it better."

"Sir Floppington!"

Eric burst out laughing, dragging Camille along. These two children appeared to enjoy that name very much, reminding me again that my mom, twenty years my elder, was cooler than myself, the old fart. That thought brought a smile to my lips. I suddenly felt like seeing her and holding her in my arms.

With their attention focused on pictures of Eric's peers, I left him and Camille and went to check on Arthur.

"Zak, this place is awesome." His eyes were full of stars.

"Yeah, it's not bad."

"We could get a boat! Row to the centre. You know, the four of us."

The four of us. How great that sounded. I smiled and patted Arthur's shoulder. "Come sit with us."

The others were still pining over Camille's dog.

"So cute!" Eric's face was practically glowing. "I want to make him mixtapes!"

"Mixtapes!" Camille roared with laughter. "You're crazy." When she saw us, she tossed the phone away.

We sat in a circle, Camille and Eric in the harsh sunlight and Arthur and me under the protection of a large tree. A warm breeze gently caused the leaves to twitch and shiver like timid maids. In the nearby expanse of wild grass, the cicadas were unrelenting. I felt like lying on my back on the warm ground and closing my eyes.

"Who found this place?" Camille asked, pulling my sleeve. "And how?"

"Eric found the lake." I noticed he was holding a wildflower by its stem and was about to tickle my ankle with it. I slapped his hand away. "But he never said how."

Eric rubbed his hand absently. "There's nothing to it. I was just walking around, and I found it."

"But why? What were you looking for?"

The petals of the flower he held brushed against my ankle. I hissed until Eric withdrew his hand, laughing. Camille stared at the surface of the water for a long time, a thoughtful look on her face. Then she turned to us.

"Isn't it more of a pond, though?"

Eric slammed his hands on his knees, startling us all. "Thank you!"

Poor Arthur, who was finally beginning to relax after the whole scene with Kayvin, cursed in fright. Camille rubbed his back to soothe him.

"Zak is convinced it's a lake, but it's a pond," Eric said.

"No." I didn't even bother looking at him. "It's a lake."

The stem re-entered my field of vision, floating dangerously close to the hem of my shorts. This time, I ground Eric's hand under my foot. Instead of yelping or crying out, he snorted.

"Mmmh…" Camille said. "More of a pond."

"It's a lake!"

"Arthur, you must choose," Eric said.

Arthur looked around our circle with anxious eyes. "I'm sorry, Eric, you're my hero, but I have to go with Zak here. It's a lake."

"There you go!" I gave Eric a haughty look. "Who's your lord and master?"

Before he could retort, Camille pulled out her phone. "Why don't we look it up?"

"No!" Eric lunged at her, surprising us. "I don't want to have the answer. I'd rather leave it."

Camille shrugged and put the phone back in her bag. The four of us lay on our backs. We watched the clouds pass and indulged in daydreaming. My thoughts eventually diverted back to Alberto. I recalled his reaction — or lack thereof — when Xavier asked if he was gay. Alberto was so mysterious, no one seemed to know anything about him.

Eric was lying next to me with his eyes closed. I wondered who or what he was thinking about. Perhaps Joy; perhaps nothing at all; perhaps he was completely asleep. After a while, Camille sat up, rummaged in her bag, and started taking notes in a notebook. She smiled at me through a strand of hair. Her open, pretty face made me feel irrepressibly close to her.

"Do you hold the truth of the universe in your notebook?" I asked, my voice sleepy.

"Not yet. I'm only sixteen."

I laughed quietly.

"But you're wise, for your age," Arthur said, sitting up.

"Only because I hang out with old people."

While I was laughing, Eric had propped himself on an elbow and had stuck the flower stem into my shoe. I removed it and stuck it in behind his ear, where it stayed.

"Eric, why is Kayvin so blatantly homophobic?" Camille asked, her pen hovering over her notebook.

Eric's eyes widened. "You don't bother with easy questions, do you?"

She ignored his shock and pressed on. "Is it possible that he's in love with you? He seems jealous, after all."

"He's not." Eric's expression darkened. "He's just like that. He hates everyone."

"He doesn't hate you," Arthur said.

"Okay, almost everyone. I know he thinks he's watching out for me, but he's not. And it's best not to bring up this subject around him ever again. You see how riled up he becomes."

Arthur let out a giggle. "However, did you see Xavier's face when he found out Alberto was gay?"

We all laughed as we remembered.

"Xavier's always the last one to pick up on things," Eric said, lying down. "But I don't think Alberto has a chance with him."

"More like Xavier doesn't have a chance with Alberto," I muttered.

My answer seemed to rub Arthur the wrong way. For a moment, he seemed to be thinking hard about something. Then he looked like he couldn't take it anymore.

"I'm sorry, but I need to ask." We all looked at him. "Zak, why do you like Alberto so much?"

There was a silence. I could see from the eager look on their faces how they were all wondering the same thing.

"Are you seriously asking me this?"

"Yes."

"Why?"

Arthur's shoulders sank. "Because I told you! I'm in his class, I see him almost every day."

"And…"

"Do you know what people say about him? It's the running joke since the first semester."

"No, I don't, and I don't care."

"I'll tell you anyway. People say he has no soul."

My eyebrows drew together. Actually, it wasn't the first time I'd heard that. Just the other night, Joy and Melissa were talking about it around the fire. And before that, I'd heard it from Nadia herself.

"Why?"

"Because… there's nothing to him! He has no conversation, no passions, no interests in anything whatsoever…"

"Or perhaps you just don't share the same interests."

Alberto liked fine arts and going to exhibitions. That's what he said when he introduced himself to the Drama Club.

"I'm just telling you what people say: That he's dead inside. Unless he's different with you, then I don't understand."

It was difficult for me to answer that since we'd never spent time together. Our longest conversation ended with him telling me he couldn't throw himself away to a loser like me. Not the greatest feeling ever. Perhaps it took someone soulless to say something like that… or perhaps…

"Perhaps he's just too pretty," Camille said, with a gentle pat on my knee.

Eric, quiet until then, gave a tired groan. Arthur straightened up, a grin spreading across his face.

"What, Eric, too good for Alberto?"

"It's Alberto who's not good enough."

"Ouch!" Camille said, smacking his knee.

I was too stunned to protest. His words were harsh. Then why did they make me feel sort of… happy? Meanwhile, Arthur pretended to innocently pluck flowers but was glancing furtively at Eric.

"Go ahead, ask," Eric said, laughing.

Arthur beamed. "Then who would be your type of man?"

"You, of course, Arthur," he said, suddenly lunging at Arthur to mess with his hair.

Of course, he wasn't serious. He was never serious. And while I was looking away, he had stuck two more flowers into my shoe.

"That's probably the best compliment anyone has ever given me." Arthur's hair was a mess after Eric was done with him.

"Nooooo!" Camille reached out to pet Arthur's head.

Eric glanced at me then and winked. Did he really think that being an unstoppable coquette was endearing him in the eyes of everyone? A compliment here, a compliment there? Did it really work that way in this world of his?

"Yes!" Arthur's cheeks were flushed with pride. "How would you feel if the most popular guy at school told you he had a crush on you!"

Eric stretched his neck. "Wouldn't know, since apparently, I'm the most popular guy at school."

"Show off," I said, smiling.

He glanced down at my feet. I followed his gaze. A whole bunch of flowers were sticking out of my sneaker now. Eric looked away, the picture of innocence.

A distraction.

18

OUT OF HAND

D ays later, I woke up with a start.
Bright, blurry shapes lingered in the back of my mind. The more I tried to catch remnants of the dream, the more it faded into nothingness.

I lay quietly for a while, until eventually, I was conscious even of Arthur's light snoring. My gaze drifted toward Eric's bed in the opposite corner of the room. Empty.

With a gasp, I lunged at my phone to check the time.

Seven.

This time, I would catch him!

Sniggering under my breath, I put on my clothes feverishly, and in the absolute silence of the corridor, slunk into the bathroom.

Our little movie was going great. I was reconciled with Michael, and Kayvin hadn't killed us — or Michael, for that matter. Since that time at the pool, when Kayvin pulled Michael into the water and inadvertently drowned his phone, they had been on much better terms. Michael dragged Kayvin for a long conversation during a campfire, and Kayvin emerged calmer, and kinder somehow. He even lent his own phone to Michael anytime he needed it. Additionally, the fact that Kayvin and Xavier ended up flirting and *undisclosed details* with Joy and Melissa in the pool probably played in our favour.

If Charles-Henry and Nadia had made their relationship official pretty much since the party, Duvo and Binta still thought they were fooling us all by pretending they were only co-workers. Camille and Arthur spent much of their time talking about "the movie" huddled together around the fire at night, and I, well… I was sort of enjoying myself at Longchamps, most of the time.

Only when I was not being relentlessly harassed by my friend Eric, the new official member of the Not-A-Loser club, and the most infuriating person ever born.

With a movie to shoot, two friends, and an untrained puppy to deal with, I didn't have much energy left for reading or for nurturing the other thoughts which used to occupy my mind constantly before.

Today, we were shooting a difficult scene, called *Confession*. Adam confesses his feelings to his footman and he's rejected. This intense moment in the movie was one Eric and I still couldn't agree on. He thought they should kiss. I thought Adam was lucky enough to leave the scene with his balls intact. For days we negotiated between takes, during lunch breaks, around the campfire. And for days he also tormented me so much that I was looking for a way to pay him right back.

Since I woke early for once, I thought I'd bring him breakfast, appear like a nice guy. In truth, I wanted to sneak up on him and give him a fright. The offerings were simply an apology for the heart attack I intended to give him.

When I left the house, my hair still damp, a bag of fresh fruits given to me by Old Rich's wife Janine swinging in my hand, I felt giddy, full of adrenaline, knowing I was that close to solving an old mystery that had been gnawing at me for a while. Just what was Eric up to so early in the morning? What did his training consist of? Would I catch him doing push-ups, and if yes, would I really interrupt him or would I flatten myself to the ground and spy on him shamelessly?

Now that I had noticed Eric was attractive, I hadn't been able to push the thought away. And it was fine. He wanted to distract me; how far I actually took him up on this offer was my business. He didn't need to know. But in truth, I owed Eric much. Because looking at him, joking with him, and acting with him had allowed me to slowly move on from Alberto.

A memory of Joy leaning over our table suddenly flashed behind my eyelids, completely unwelcome. With an annoyed groan, I pushed it out of my mind.

After looking around the grounds for signs of Eric, I hesitated to walk to the village. He could be returning from his morning run. I might meet him on his way back, panting, his shirt clinging to his chest... or he could already be back home. I trotted in the direction of the lake, blaming a restless night for my spinning thoughts.

I made sure to be extra quiet as I trudged through the grove, hiding behind the apple trees, ignoring the loud concerto of horny birds overhead, focused on my target. The clearing finally appeared to me through the branches. The morning sun fell softly on the patches of wildflowers and the twinkling surface of the water, bathing the place with a romantic feel. I scanned the bank once, twice.

My heart stopped when I saw him.

Eric wasn't doing push-ups or jumping jacks or whatever else I expected. He stood shirtless in the lake, water up to his waist, his face turned up, muttering to himself.

My heart swelled in my chest. I couldn't believe my luck!

In his state, Eric didn't notice me at all, and an urge to giggle seized me. Unfortunately, I couldn't hear a word of his and assumed he might be humming or singing to himself. With slow movements, he turned around, water gently rippling around him, until he had his back to me. How peaceful he looked then... Such an image of innocent bliss. Squatting behind a tree, I wondered: what would be the best way to destroy it?

I thought crawling amongst the wild grass and then blowing an air horn once closest to him would be an effective way to teach him a lesson. But the only person I knew who carried that sort of object around was the headmaster of Colette, and mercifully, he wasn't here with us. So clearly, I'd have to go another way, sneak up on him and hope that simply showing my face when he least expected it would give him a fright.

With Eric still facing away, I stalked out of the cover of the trees and tiptoed to the edge of the bank, then carefully squatted where the grass was tallest. The blades teased my bare calves to the point of agony, but it was worth it. Even from here, I couldn't hear what he was muttering about. I began shaking in anticipation, just as he slowly revolved back toward me. When he was facing me, I filled my lungs with air and rose from my hiding spot.

"Busted!"

Oh, I did give him a fright. Eric gulped and jerked back with flailing arms, sending water splashing everywhere. With a vengeful "Ah!" I stood, a mocking finger pointed at him.

Frozen in the middle of the lake with his hand clutched to his chest,

Eric looked like he was about to cry. I looked down on him, triumphant. Finally, he muttered something. I put my hand behind my ear.

"What did you say?"

"… What time is it?" His voice sounded so hoarse it was hard not to laugh.

"I don't know. Half-past seven maybe? Early enough that I caught you."

Eric drew his fists to his chest, his wide eyes fixed on me. He made no motion to get out of the water and looked so vulnerable, I couldn't believe how well my prank had turned out.

"Anyway…" I wiped my brow. "What were you doing in here? Meditating?"

To my surprise, he said nothing.

"Then what were you muttering about?"

No answer.

My confidence began to dwindle.

"You… I… Did I get you or what?"

"You got me."

All right. He looked terrified. It was my first attempt at teasing someone as relentless as him, and it turned out he couldn't take it, and now I'd have to spend my savings on a PTSD counsellor to have him fixed. Hell. It was almost disappointing.

"Look," I said shaking my bag of goodies. "I brought you breakfast!"

"Thank you." His tone was polite, but he remained frozen to the spot.

"Care to join me, then?" I smirked. "Or do you want me to pelt you with fresh fruits? I don't mind."

Eric looked away, the tips of his ears flushed. "Could you turn around first?"

"Hang on…" When I finally understood what was going on there, I let out a loud gasp. "Are you naked in there?"

This changed everything. It was like trying not to think of a pink elephant. My thoughts converged to one thing and one thing only, my gaze immediately sweeping down to his lower body.

Eric quickly plunged his hands into the water to hide his private parts. For all his usual confidence, he looked really small right now. His helpless features tugged at my heart so much that my whole face began

244

to tingle. But I couldn't back down; I had to crush him if I wanted to claim victory.

"Pff!" I threw my head back. "Don't worry. I can't see a thing. But what's with the sudden modesty? Aren't your football friends used to seeing you naked?"

His answer was to pull both hands out of the water to slap them over his face. Instead of giving him space, I took another step forward with a wide grin and saw what he was trying to hide. I gave a cry of delight.

"Why are you so red?" The sight of his flushed face had more of an effect on me than five cups of Xavier's punch. "Why are you so red?" I clapped my hands, feeling very wicked.

Eric sobbed behind his hands. "Why are you so mean?!"

"Serves you right for the way you've been tormenting me."

He stilled and sniffed behind his hands.

"Did you learn your lesson?" I said, jubilant. "Will you be good from now on?"

He parted his fingers, revealing an eye so blue I momentarily lost the power of speech.

"What—" He cleared his throat. "What's good?"

"I... huh..." Ah, why did he have to sound so cute and miserable! Now wasn't the time to lose face. Not when he was within my grasp. I crossed my arms and stuck my chest out. "Let me think... No more tickling, pinching, putting me in a headlock, ruffling my hair, hiding around corners to jump me, uncovering my feet when you leave the bedroom in the morning — yes, I've noticed — and then..." I took a long breath as he dropped his arms to the side and watched me, slack-jawed. "... No more bee talk, no more sticking flowers in my shoes or anywhere else for that matter — I've noticed that one as well — no more smelling my hair, no more calling 'Zak, Zak' repeatedly until I drop everything to listen to your nonsense, no more comments about my a—"

"Enough, enough!" His hands flew back to his face. "I get it!"

I quirked a dubitative eyebrow. "Do you? Really?"

"I'll try, I promise! I'll be good."

"Perfect."

I waited. He seemed to be waiting too. Eventually, his hands slid down his face again, revealing a frown.

"Will you turn around now or do you really want to see me naked?"

And he began rising from the water!

I immediately whipped around, my heart pounding. I didn't want him to get the chance to turn the situation on its head. I was the tormentor this morning; he was the victim. But his words were already bouncing around in my head. Did I want to see Eric naked? No? Yes? A little bit, maybe? If I did, was it wrong of me? Yes, yes it was. Because… Because I still loved Alberto, and Eric was my friend.

If Eric was my friend, then, why was he so embarrassed right now? Because I was gay? Deep inside, were straight guys worried about being molested by the likes of us? Did women think the same about their lesbian friends? How did it work? How did anything work?

While my heart was racing and my brain was doing unnecessary little cartwheels on its own, Eric had gotten dressed, and smelling an opportunity for mischief, had already drawn uncomfortably close to me.

"Food's gonna get cold," I said, tossing the bag at him.

"What?" He took on an innocent air.

"Don't get close!"

"You didn't say I wasn't allowed to stand next to you."

"You were standing right behind me."

"Sill, you didn't say."

"You agreed to be good!"

His eyes squinted in silent reproach, but he eventually sat down and opened the bag. Taking a look at the fruits inside, he gave me a small smile. I observed him carefully: After his fright, he looked more tired than usual. I knelt by his side. "What's wrong?"

"Nothing."

"You look nervous. Did I spook you?"

Seeing my expression, his smile deepened, but he didn't answer. I poked his shoulder.

"Did you run to the village this morning?"

He pulled a banana from the bag and nodded. "I just got back… and I… I needed to cool down."

He sounded like he was having trouble catching his breath. I couldn't help flashing him a devilish smile.

"Did I frighten you that much?"

He shut his eyes, the tips of his ears still glowing.

"Oh-oh," I said, too proud of myself. "I really did a number on you."

For the first time ever, Eric glared at me. It only increased my fun, but I didn't want him to become mad at me before shooting an important scene either. "Look, I didn't know you were such a scaredy-cat. You're the one always jumping me. If you can't take it, don't do it."

Hearing the gentler tone of my voice, Eric finally seemed to relax. He stretched, a pout on his face. "I wouldn't persecute you so early in the morning."

"If you call that persecuting, what would you call what you're doing to me?"

He glanced up. "Is it torture?"

My eyes narrowed.

"Oh, well!" Eric sat more comfortably and shoved the whole banana into his mouth and began chewing happily. He had returned to his normal self at last. When he'd finally swallowed, he added: "We should have a timeframe. How about setting up office hours? Torture allowed from eight to five, or something."

I waved my hand in his face. "You'd never be able to stick to it. From eight to five. You must be joking. At midnight last night, you were literally pulling my leg."

"I wanted to stop you from going upstairs!"

"So you had to cling to my leg for that? On a staircase? My knees and elbows are still bruised!"

Eric shrugged. "Alberto helped you up."

"That's the only reason you're still alive. Everything that happened to you this morning was karma. Deal with it."

Still, I peeled a second banana for him. He went for it roughly, his fingers slamming against mine. A sharp tingling sensation ran through my spine. I clenched my fists on my knees.

"I can't believe you brought me breakfast." Eric reached out to ruffle my hair. "Sorry," he added, giggling at the results.

"Did you… Did you…"

He looked at me, his mouth full. "Oops! Sorry, I forgot."

Was it a lack of memory or neurons? Could he really be that… Mmph! Before he could fully return to his bad ways, I would slam another nail in his coffin.

"Tell me…" I made an effort to sound almost innocent. "Do you always end up in the lake naked, or was today special?"

In an instant, his whole face was glowing again. He tried to act cool, but even his laughter sounded a little forced. "I did today."

"What were the odds of me showing up to see it!"

More forced laughter. "You said it!"

Who would have known… Eric could be modest after all. Preposterous.

Adorable.

Joy's face, so close to Eric's, flashed once again in my mind. I felt as though I'd been stabbed with a poisonous needle. I decided to change the subject.

"Do you know we have less than a week left?"

"Yeah," he said, now biting into a bright red apple. "Six days, actually, counting this one."

There was a silence. So he was counting too. But why? I used to count the days that separated me from coming home. Now I was counting the days that would separate me from…

I stilled myself with a careful breath. "I'm looking forward to seeing my sister."

Eric answered with a smile and took another bite of his apple.

"Do you have brothers and sisters?" I asked, curious.

"A brother."

"Are you close?"

Eric shook his head. "Not really."

Though I knew few relatives could enjoy the sort of close relationship I had with my sister, I was still surprised to hear these words.

"What do you mean?"

"We're very different. He lives in the U.S. with my dad. He *is* basically my dad. Sports nut, bold, confident, all that."

I snorted. "And you're… what?"

Eric pulled a face. "You won't find my brother doing castings and playing parts. Gay parts, at that."

"So, you haven't told them?"

"I haven't said anything to them." I must have looked really surprised because he glanced at me and laughed. "Wait 'til my dad hears what I've been doing this summer. He'll try to kidnap me and send me over to the Marines."

"No! No way."

"I'm kidding." Eric gently bumped his sneaker against mine. "He's not that bad. But he won't get it. Neither will my brother for that matter."

"What did you tell them before you came here?"

"The truth. Or something like that." His smile was somewhat sheepish. "I'm here because I screwed up and I've been punished. I never told them I would crash the casting! So I didn't tell them I got the part."

"Will you tell them?"

"It depends, doesn't it? You know... On the outcome."

I nodded. "I get it. No need to burden yourself unnecessarily if the movie turns out crap and no one ever sees it."

"Precisely," Eric said, getting up. "Now let's shoot that scene and make sure this movie isn't complete crap." He held his hand out for me. "At least for your resume, and for Camille and Arthur."

"And for Michael."

I took his hand without a thought. Eric pulled me up as though I weighed a whole bag of nothing and brushed a twig off my shoulder.

"I'm happy you're not mad at him anymore."

"I wasn't really mad at him." I looked down at my hand. "I was defeated."

"And you're not anymore?"

"The movie is what matters the most. My broken heart can m—" With a deep frown, I interrupted myself. I was about to say *mend*. It was true that I'd been thinking less about Alberto lately. I had been so busy. And he had made himself scarce.

"Can what?" Eric asked.

"Nothing."

On the way back to the house, I was still lost in thought. While I was trying to make sense of my current feelings for Alberto, I came to a stop in front of a large apple tree. I reached out to pluck a fruit, but Eric caught my hand.

"Not yet."

"They'll ripe just as we leave this place," I muttered. "Then it will be too late."

Eric released my hand. "Take a bite now then."

"No." I stepped away from the tree. "You're right. I might get sick from it."

Eric observed me quietly from the corner of his eye the whole rest of the way. His fingers linked behind his head as he walked, he suddenly blurted out, "Should we kiss, then?"

I tripped on my own foot. "What?"

My mind had jumped straight back to the image of him bathing in the lake, sending my heart thrashing around my ribcage.

Eric looked unfazed. "Confession scene."

"Oh, that! Yes, of course."

"Of course, we should kiss?"

I looked at him. His eyes had returned to their normal state, bright with a flash of mirth. It had taken him less than half an hour to find something to torment me with that wasn't on my list.

"No, no kissing," I said, with a pang of regret. My eyes bulged. *With regret?* What the hell was happening to me? "We… We…" I stammered. Shit, it was like I couldn't think straight anymore. "We agreed with Camille that Thomas isn't ready. So don't mention it anymore."

"I won't mention it anymore," Eric said, and he accelerated toward the house.

Alberto was standing behind Michael, looking at me without seeing me. He appeared to be in a world of his own, despite Duvo screaming into Michael's indifferent ear at his side. Alberto, in a navy blue shirt and linen shorts, his hair tousled as though he'd just woken up.

Alberto, Alberto, Alberto… I had almost forgotten.

I turned away from him reluctantly and blinked. Eric was looking at me. He laughed at my bashful face.

How…

They were so different.

Was it even possible to like them both? Was that what was happening to me?

No, no. Eric was only a distraction. Alberto had haunted my dreams for close to a year now. He wouldn't be dethroned so easily, by someone… by someone like that. Hearing Joy's crystalline laughter in my mind, I shook my head, my fists clenched.

Duvo was done screaming. Michael gazed at him patiently. "Of course, everything is ready, Laurent. You're the one who's ten minutes late."

Duvo looked around the set, panting. "Binta had misplaced her— she required my assistance. Stop prying! But all the same… Thank you for holding the fort."

Michael bit his lip, and seeing me, waggled his eyebrows. Someone was in a good mood today. Good to know; I needed some of his chill to counteract my own stress. Just like poor Thomas, I felt like a rubber band about to snap. *Confession* was an important scene, during which Adam was so intense that my character could barely hang on for dear life. Already, it was stifling inside my livery.

"We're shooting in ten minutes," Michael said, while Duvo moved on to torment Arthur behind the camera.

"So, you still think you can handle this?" I asked him, nodding toward Duvo.

Michael let his arms drop to the sides. "The thing is, the one I have at home likes me, at least! When he gets hyper I know which buttons to push to calm him down. This one won't respond to the same touch, I imagine."

"Eww."

Michael laughed. "Yeah... Try to forget I said that."

I turned back to Eric. He was stretching and jumping in place, as though filming a scene and running across a football field for ninety minutes were exactly the same thing.

"Zak, Zak."

I ignored him.

"Zak."

"Hm." Slowly, I shook my sleeve to take a close look at my watch.

"Zak!"

"It took you exactly eighty-two minutes," I said flatly.

"What? To do what?"

"To break your promise."

"Ah!" He paused, his finger on his chin. "In that case...!"

He lunged at me, no doubt to grab my neck and ruffle my hair. I threw my hands in front of my face and leapt aside.

"You promised!"

"Only that I'd try!" He charged again, but Joy and Melissa screamed in unison.

"Don't touch him!" Duvo barked.

Eric froze mid-movement. I looked over my shoulder at Duvo and the girls, not daring to move either. Melissa's eyes were burning with fury.

"I have done my best with his hair and his outfit, and you won't mess him up!"

I turned to Eric, jubilant. "See? Don't mess me up. It's not allowed."

Eric gave me a somewhat constipated look and stomped toward the snacks table. There, Joy, who was directly next to him, made a show of turning her back to him. I blinked, unsure that I'd seen right.

Joy was mad at Eric? Could it have anything to do with what happened yesterday? Just thinking about it made my heart sink.

Eric always had his meals together with his other friends and was usually accompanied by Melissa and Joy. But the rest of the time, Eric, Camille, Arthur, and I were pretty much inseparable nowadays. After a long day of shooting, we were finally beat and went together to the dining room to rest before dinner. Those who weren't at the pool hung there as well.

Soon, Camille and Arthur excused themselves to work out details about tomorrow's scene, and I was left alone at the table with Eric. I had my book with me, but Eric had nothing to do, and I could feel him bursting with boredom. He tried for as long as he could to remain quiet while I was reading, but there was only so much a brash pup of his age could take. So I wasn't surprised when I saw him reach out a hand toward me.

"Zak."

"Hm.

"Zak!"

"What, Eric?"

The way he was beaming at me, I felt he was about to say something totally inappropriate, and I frowned in anticipation. But Joy suddenly appeared, and leaning on one hand over the table, she obscured me from Eric's view.

"Hey, Eric."

She smelled of vanilla. So much vanilla.

"Hi, Joy."

I could hear the smile in his voice. I shifted aside to observe his face. His eyes were glinting.

"Isn't it great that your name literally means joy? I think it's great. What do you think, Zak?"

"Hm." I couldn't say much more through gritted teeth.

Joy let out a crystalline laugh. "Do I… bring you joy, Eric?" She was very good. The way she was leaning over the table, offering Eric a full view of her assets. Impressive.

Clearly, she'd had enough of the smiles and the pointless flirting, and she had decided to make her move. She was a radiant butterfly, and he was just a short-sighted and hot-headed flirt. There was no way in hell he would not be seduced.

"Yes, of course, you do," he said pleasantly. His face showed he meant it.

She slid closer to him, bent her fair neck, and whispered some words in his ear as I watched, wide-eyed, growing furious for no reason. Eric's expression turned from curiosity to awe.

"Seriously?"

She nodded and made a come-hither gesture with her finger. Eric's eyes lit up. "Now that would definitely bring me joy!"

Joy's neck turned scarlet. She jumped off the table, Eric pouncing after her.

That's how it was done, then, I thought in silence.

As he walked behind my chair, Eric's hand found my hair, ruffled it mercilessly, and lingered for the briefest moment on my neck. The touch of his fingertips burned my skin. I dug my teeth into my lip, refusing to look at him. When I finally glanced over my shoulder, he was trotting behind Joy in the direction of the kitchen. I could only stare after them, speechless.

Go, then. Go roll in the hay with Joy or whatever. With that look on her face, there's no way she was taking him for a guided tour of the kitchen. In any case, it was nothing to me. I returned to my book.

Soon after, I was flinging the book aside.

I'd had enough of this. Eric was single. Joy was single. They were old enough to do whatever they wanted. If he wanted to roll around in the hay with her, he had every right. Perhaps he would even get off my case once he got off. That wouldn't be a bad thing. Just the opposite. With each passing day, his hands took more and more liberties, and with each passing day, I allowed him to get his way when I absolutely shouldn't.

The way Joy handled him, that sort of thing… It was way beyond my field of expertise. Hell, I wondered what would happen if *I* started whispering dirty things in his ear. Sometimes I thought he would actually take me on, for a laugh. An experiment, whatever. He was a few days without a girlfriend now, so anything would do, right? He had *so much* energy. I bet he needed extra attention in that department as well. For sure, I was no Joy, I couldn't help him there. It would be too offensive to even imagine.

It was best to stay away from his flirtatious ploys to make me blush, even if they were just intended as a joke or a distraction.

When Eric and Joy returned, it was dinner time, and I was in great conversation with Camille and Arthur and I didn't notice them at all. For the rest of the night, and without fully understanding why, I found myself incapable of even glancing at her. Meanwhile, Eric was acting just the same, making me feel both annoyed and good, and at midnight, he was clinging to my leg and refusing to let me go to bed.

Perhaps this episode was the reason I had a somewhat agitated night and woke with a start from a confusing dream. Or more certainly, it was the reason why I couldn't get Joy out of my head, nor the feeling of uneasiness that pervaded me when thinking of Eric trotting away alongside her. But now, she was standing in front of us, almost bearing her fangs while looking at him, and immediately my heart went thrashing against my ribcage.

Innocently slurping my iced tea, I glided toward Eric. He was holding a plastic-wrapped brownie with a puzzled look on his face.

"Do you have pockets in that thing?"

"Why is Joy angry with you?" A vicious part of me hoped that perhaps he couldn't get it up, and Joy was angry and vexed about it. I read that these things could happen. Granted, I didn't want it to happen to Eric, because… he was my friend. But I was fine with anything which would drive a wedge between them. Joy was all right, I guess. But I'd prefer if she stayed away from him.

"She's not angry with me." Eric sounded surprised.

"I think she is."

Eric looked over my shoulder and noticing the swirling dark clouds hanging over Joy's head, let out a small gasp. "Oh! I guess you're right. She's mad. I hadn't noticed."

"Why?"

Eric's flirty smile came back with a vengeance. He tossed the brownie aside and advanced on me until my back hit the wall.

"Why do you want to know?"

Holding his gaze, I waved my watch in front of his face. "Eighty-five minutes."

"Stop counting, I know I'm hopeless. Why are you asking?" He got so close he was practically rubbing on me. "Would you like to know what happened?"

Several alarms began ringing in my ears. All of them blaring *Danger! Danger! Please remove yourself to a safe location!*

"… No."

This wasn't the answer Eric was hoping for. With a sigh, he leaned against the wall next to me.

"You're no fun, Zak."

"I never tried to deny it."

"Good one." He chortled. "Soon, you'll find out what happened anyway."

"Why? How?"

He put his finger on my lip. "Shh."

Duvo just happened to be walking by. He stopped dead in his tracks. "Are you two making out between scenes now?"

"Yes!" Eric said, grabbing my hips.

"No," I said, pushing him away with a burning face.

I couldn't believe the fact that scaring him shitless this morning only bought me about eighty minutes of peace. Come on!

"Dedication's one thing, but remember, the costumes are expensive," Duvo said. Throwing us a suspicious look over his shoulder, he walked straight into the camera.

"Zak," Eric said.

I didn't answer, distracted by Michael's reaction to Duvo's clumsiness. He had thrown away his notebook and was sobbing in Arthur's arms.

"Zak!" Eric tugged at my sleeve.

"What?"

"He already thinks we're making out…"

"Get off me, you… beast."

I was that close to filing a complaint for sexual harassment. And yet the moment his hands left my hips, I felt an emptiness I couldn't shake.

I had to get my shit together. What I was feeling was normal. It was summer; Eric was hot; he was my partner on screen. I spent a lot of time with him. He gave me too much attention, which pleased me but drove me crazy at the same time. I spent every minute with him and his stupid jokes. I didn't have a crush on him. It was nothing.

Eric turned around and began to walk away. But then, he looked back and whispered, "Why are you so red?"

"Cut!" Duvo was tearing out his hair. "That. Was. Perfect!"

Michael was nodding, his chin in his hand. "Unexpected, but good."

Eric shook out his hair and dropped into the nearest chair, looking proud of himself. I waited until most people had turned their backs to us to vent my anger at him.

"Warn me next time you want to improvise!"

He stretched his legs out in front of him. "Then it wouldn't be called improvising, would it?"

He looked so chill. How could he look so chill after what he did?

After I had told him countless times Thomas wasn't ready, Eric improvised in the middle of the scene, hurled himself at me, and tried to kiss me. It took every nerve in my body and soul to stay in character, to not ruin the take. Now I wanted to scream at him for putting me through this. And Eric was acting like nothing had happened at all.

"If you don't like it, ask them to reshoot it. I won't do it again."

I bit my tongue. Hard. If Duvo and Michael liked it, going so far as calling it perfect, who I was to judge? What was I afraid of, after all? It was acting. I was Thomas in that scene. It's just… Looking at the footage, would everybody see? How terrified I was that our lips would touch? Would the reason for that terror be palpable as well?

"I told you Thomas wasn't ready…" I sounded feeble all of the sudden.

"I know! That's how I got the idea."

"The idea?"

Eric jumped to his feet. "I knew Thomas would push Adam away, but Adam had to try anyway. You looked so afraid," he added. "The take was perfect."

I opened my mouth to protest, but nothing came out. Eric observed me an instant, his smug features contorting.

"You really are angry at me… You're shaking. I'm sorry. I promise, I would not have kissed you! I'd have stopped before that."

My body was indeed trembling. Trembling and aching. Was it anger? Yes, some of it. But I was less angry at his boldness than at myself for almost being found out.

Eric's lips. Eric's lips approaching my face. I had begun to think of them with more fervour than I was willing to admit. When his hand approached my wrist, I threw him a scathing look.

"I'm gonna go," he said, stepping back. "Let me know when you're not angry anymore."

I watched him dash out of the room like a cartoon character, my forehead throbbing from frowning too much.

"It was really good," a gentle voice said behind me.

Exhaling cautiously, I turned and met Alberto's gaze. The coolness of his grey eyes extinguished at once the fire inside mine.

"Oh…" I was too nonplussed to think clearly. "… Thank you."

We stared at each other a long time, his long eyelashes blinking slowly. Was he going to say anything else? I could only wait. For once, his presence didn't send my heart reeling. It was actually the opposite. So, I waited, frowning but unafraid.

All of a sudden, his features relaxed and he graced me with a faint smile. It completely threw me off, and a wave of longing surged through me. Alberto... I loved Alberto. He was the one...

Why was I losing myself to my own distraction?

"I'm... ahem... I'm glad you liked it."

Alberto didn't respond, and after another brief moment of silent staring, he bent down to remove a piece of marking tape from the floor. Leaving him to his tasks, I went to the snacks table and drank some iced tea to cool down. I thought of pouring the whole jug over my head but abstained at the last second. Seeing how I was stabbing the contents of my cup with my straw, Xavier, who was helping dismantle the lights, gave me a weird smile.

"What?" I said, "Did you spit in it?"

"No."

He was too dumb to look insincere. He opened his mouth to say something, but I turned away and walked toward Michael, who was smiling to himself as he was packing away.

"This Eric really is something, isn't he?" he said when he saw me.

Sucking on my straw with vigour, I looked long and hard into Michael's face, feeling something akin to worry. I was again thinking about how much Louis and Eric had in common.

- Similar height: check
- Blond hair: check
- Blue eyes: check
- Infuriating: check

Eric was *totally* Michael's type. I pulled my bitten straw out of my mouth.

"What do you mean, he's really something?"

Michael straightened up. His smile faded when he saw my face. "... How are you getting on? The both of you?"

"Fine," I said darkly.

Michael laughed. "It's not a trick question, you know."

"What do you want me to say?" I looked away. "He's nice."

I recalled the earnestness in his eyes that time he said, "You want me to be good, don't you?" and shivered all over. Just a few meters away, Alberto was on his knees with his hair falling into his eyes. After a while, I tore my gaze away, my head buzzing.

Michael had obviously been ogling me the whole time. His laughter deepened, as did the scowl on my face.

"What's so funny?"

"Nothing," he said. "Don't mind me. I'm just happy."

He did look happy. It was almost insulting when I was torn between so many conflicting emotions, I couldn't even comprehend myself.

"Why are you so happy anyway?"

Michael flashed me a dimpled smile. "I had sex last night!"

Hearing this made me feel like I'd been sprayed in the face with a pressure washer. I choked on a sip of tea. "Why the hell would you tell me that!"

"I'm sorry, sometimes I forget you're not Yasmine."

I stomped my foot. "Why the hell would you tell my sister that!"

"She's my best friend! Who else would I tell?"

"Nobody!" My voice broke in outrage. "It's private information!"

Michael snorted, looking five years younger, and closed the duffle bag at his feet. I shook my head disapprovingly. Then a question arose. Despite what I'd just said, I found myself too curious not to ask.

"But... Michael..."

"Yes?"

"How did you manage... that?"

"Manage what?"

"Having sex with Louis when he's in England and... You did have sex with him, right, not—"

"Yes, of course with Louis!" Michael clutched his chest, reminding me of Eric and his flushed face at the lake. "We... I... The phone. We used the phone."

A smirk stretched my lips when I thought of what Kayvin would say if he found out what his phone had been used for.

"You made up with that psycho, then?"

Michael beamed. "Yes! I followed your advice and called him every night until he spilt the beans. Guess what? He was distant because he didn't want to admit he hates working with this band. Especially the singer. He didn't want me to think less of him for his lack of profession-alism. But really, he wants to quit."

"Oh. That's bad, I guess."

"No, that's perfect!" Michael's eyes sparkled. "I'm going to set him up with my cousins' band. They're good and they're straight." His expression darkened. "Or they will be after I talk to them…"

I guess there was a little psycho side to Michael after all. Perhaps he and Louis weren't that different. I wondered if I had anything in common with Eric at all… Then I thought I'd better stop asking myself stupid questions.

"Everything okay, Zak?" Michael said as we left the set. "You looked angry after the take."

My head was still buzzing. I was coming down with a serious headache. "I'm fine. It's just… Eric improvised."

"And?"

"I didn't want him to."

"Did you tell him that?"

At least Michael looked concerned every time I spoke to him. I appreciated that.

"I… told him I didn't want Adam and Thomas to kiss. But he felt, in the spur of the moment, that Adam would go for it even if it meant rejection."

"And that made you angry?"

"It makes me angry that… I…"

"Zak?"

I looked away.

What really made me angry was that it happened on set and I had to reject him. That I had to stay true to Thomas. It made me furious that I'd missed such an opportunity to feel his lips against mine.

It was pointless to deny it now. My distraction was getting out of hand. So out of hand, I'd even forgotten I loved Alberto.

19

THE BOAT, THE GAME, THE REWARD

When I left Michael and went to lunch, Eric was already at his table with his gang. From my spot in the corner, I could see him clearly. He never sat with his back to me. He was always there in plain view, a glance, a wink away.

It was clear the little game of teasing I allowed him to play with me was getting out of hand. I had to cut back on all of it. I had much more to lose than Eric in that game. Playing around is one thing, but how would he react if he found out I was beginning to have confusing thoughts about him? He would think me shallow, capable of jumping from one guy to the next in a matter of a week. He would also think it was really sad, considering everyone knew he was straight. Poor little Zak, he would think. I shouldn't have messed around with him so much. But it was so much fun!

It wasn't too late, however. At least, contrary to my thing with Alberto, I wasn't delusional about Eric's feelings about me. Eric liked to play, and I enjoyed his attentions way too much. When I'd ask him to stop playing, he would stop, and I would return to a normal existence.

What was my normal life, though? I thought while stabbing the potatoes on my plate. Pining after Alberto, who wouldn't spare me a glance? But just as I thought that, Alberto met my eyes as he looked up from his table. Surely there was nothing to it. If I could learn one lesson from my time in Aurons, it's that I had a propensity for romantic delusions. I wouldn't be caught at it again.

When Arthur and Camille joined me, there was a spring in Arthur's step that seemed both familiar and strange to me. I wondered if these two didn't have a secret of their own.

"Zak," Camille said, falling with all her weight on the chair. "This morning, you were so good. How could you have acted with such shock, fear, and misery at once?"

"Don't forget the glint of desire in the eye," Arthur said. "Like he really wanted to give in, but he couldn't."

The piece of potato I'd stabbed with my fork fell back onto my plate with a thud.

I hesitated to tell Camille Eric had improvised the whole thing. Something told me she knew this already. I glanced resentfully at Eric on the other side of the room; he was talking to a moody Joy, using all his charms. What was he up to this time? I could, in theory, approach their table under the pretext of picking up a napkin or two from Sander and Alberto's table. The problem was, it was Alberto's table, who would then think I was stalking him. Now that I was *not* stalking Alberto, he was going to think I did. My existence was nothing but a never-ending succession of trials and disappointments these days!

Eric clasped Joy's hand between his own. She dropped her surly act, giggling. My hand moved on its own, stabbing another potato. Next to her, Xavier suddenly looked in my direction. Startled, I knocked over my plate. Arthur gasped in shock.

"Zak, are you all right?"

"Yeah, yeah."

"You weren't listening, were you?"

Eric sprung off his table, his cheeks aglow, and ran straight out. Xavier reached out a hand to stop him, but Eric was already gone. Kayvin stared after him with a dark expression.

"You're right," I said, turning to Arthur. "I wasn't listening."

"We were saying we should go to the village today. Pick up a few souvenirs for our families."

I tried to imagine what Yasmine would do with a few baubles from the convenience store and grimaced. It would still be a viable plan. Anything but staying here and having weird thoughts again.

"I guess, yes."

The other two happily went on talking about what they needed to get from the village. I thought of Eric's lips approaching mine on set. Why did it have to turn out like this? Soon, we'd be filming our most important scene. Unless Camille changed it, we'd have to kiss. If a failed kissing attempt sent me reeling like this morning, what would the real deal do to me? And how would I be able to even rehearse it? I never thought a guy like Eric, of all people, would make me feel so self-conscious. I tried to remember a time I hated him. It felt alien, like something that happened to someone else a long time ago.

I was still lost in confusing thoughts, absently stabbing my potatoes with a murderous expression, when said Eric suddenly plopped into the chair opposite mine.

"Guess what," he said, his whole face bright from unknown delight.

Camille and Arthur waited, a keen look on their faces. I gave him a blank look.

"I've got a surprise for you." Eric was making it hard not to make me feel special from the way his eyes were sparkling as they turned to me. My heart gave a little sigh.

"What is it?"

"I can't tell or it won't be a surprise anymore."

"But…" I said darkly. "You said 'guess what'. And now you —argh!"

He had leaned forward to swat me or perhaps ruffle my hair, so I had to jerk away.

"Sure, let's go, then!" Arthur said.

Camille was already shovelling inhumane forkfuls of salad into her mouth. Eric watched her with round eyes.

"Take it easy, there's time."

"But… Weren't we supposed to go to the village?" I accidentally spoke in a cold tone, which made them all look at me in surprise. But I thought if there was a chance to spend less time around him, wouldn't it be best for the both of us? By that, I meant for me. Only for me.

"Come on, Zak," Camille said. "We can do that tomorrow."

"We need to rehearse our most important scene tomorrow." I sounded even colder. Eric's eyes widened slightly.

"But I'm still working on that one," Camille said. "I want to up the tension until it's unbearable. I want that, when they kiss, even the homophobes stand on their toes and clap and weep and everything!"

"I don't think that's going to happen, sorry. Haven't you done enough work on that scene?"

"Not even you can tell me what to do when it comes to my scenes, Zak. I'll give you the updated version as soon as it's finished. You will be able to rehearse it this weekend. Don't worry so much about it. You'll be fine."

Eric knocked his fist on the table. "It's settled, then, you can come see my surprise."

There were all staring at me with varying degrees of surprise and expectancy. Just as I was about to give in, we were interrupted by Xavier. He stood behind Eric, waiting for someone to notice him. Eric twisted his neck to look at him.

"What's up?"

Xavier looked even more confused than usual. He wouldn't answer Eric's questions with simple words, so Eric got up and stepped aside for a second. Arthur, Camille, and I exchanged glances, and after less than a minute, Eric sat back down.

"What was that about?" Arthur asked.

Eric hesitated. "I'm actually not sure… and it wouldn't be fair to draw conclusions," he added, with a quirked eyebrow at me.

I clenched my fists. "Now I want to know!"

Eric leaned back in his chair. "Then you have to check out my surprise." He turned to Camille. "Hurry! We don't have all day!"

Camille began shovelling food into her mouth again with bulging eyes until he pulled her to him and apologised for being an ass.

Eric was giddy on the way to the lake, his cheeks pink, with Arthur and Camille bounding at his side. Only I was dragging my feet, throwing longing looks over my shoulder, wondering if I would be able to get away quickly or if I'd have to be subjected to Eric's torment for much longer.

"It's such a nice day again." Camille stretched out her hands as if she wanted to hug the sun.

"It's getting hotter every day," I said, feeling an urge to complain.

"Look at Eric's tan. Sun's really got to him."

I briefly glanced at Eric's golden nape, then forced my thoughts back to Alberto's diaphanous skin. Fortunately, I was distracted by our arrival at the lake.

Camille immediately let out a cry of joy. Tethered to the bank, a small rowboat, barely big enough for the four of us, was glinting in the sunlight, as though winking at us. Arthur made a sound like a shriek and ran toward the boat. Camille turned to Eric with teary eyes and shook him mercilessly. "This is perfect!"

Eric let her shake him a few more times then gently set her aside.

"Seriously," she said, "how did you manage this?"

Eric glanced at me, full of mischief.

"Let me guess," I ventured. "Old Rich."

"Who?" Arthur asked.

Eric explained his little black market deals with the old maintenance guy. "This time, I had to pay in brownies. They were harder to get because your lot seems to eat them by the dozen."

"You've been saving brownies?"

"For about a week now!" We stopped in front of the boat. Arthur was already climbing inside. "The moment I saw this boat in the barn. But I only got the last brownie today. It was a hard one to get, but I managed."

"What did you do?"

"Literally snatched it from someone's hand."

Suddenly, the scene I had witnessed earlier, with Eric putting his hand in Joy's, made more sense. I felt the corner of my mouth stretch into a smile and looked down to hide my face, only to blush furiously when Eric's sneakers entered my field of vision.

"So? What do you think of that?"

I glanced up at his smiling face. "You are an awfully good planner, you know that?"

He made no answer, only extended his hand to help me into the boat. Everyone seemed so happy with the surprise, I didn't feel like ruining the mood by saying I wanted to return home. And I sure couldn't hurt Eric's feelings like that. I could only hope he'd keep the teasing to a minimum. And since he'd helped Camille on board first, I didn't see the problem with taking his hand.

Once inside, Eric took hold of both oars, and we slowly made our way across the lake.

"It's perfectly safe," Eric whispered to me. He had been staring at me and had clearly misread my expression. It was the fact that our legs were so close together that made me look like I was under duress. His fault. He should have never improvised this morning.

"The light is perfect," Arthur commented. "We should have shot something here."

"We still could," Camille said.

"Wouldn't it be romantic?"

Eric and I exchanged a glance and smiled. Arthur was such a hopeless romantic. But when Camille nodded with fervour, he immediately looked away. It was clear Arthur felt something for Camille. Did she return his feelings? How could it be so simple for some and so complicated for others?

With a sigh, I plunged a hand into the water. Its coolness soothed me.

"Oh," Camille said. "I've got the perfect thing."

She pulled my iPod and the portable speakers from her backpack. A few seconds later, my mom's now infamous playlist was playing over the ceaseless chatter of birds and cicadas.

"Will I ever get this thing back?" I asked.

She patted my head. "Only when you deserve it."

Arthur lay down as comfortably as he could at the front of the boat. His eyes widened when Camille put her feet on top of his legs. I glanced sideways at Eric, but of course, he probably thought two people entwining their limbs meant nothing special at all, since his expression didn't change. He carefully set the oars back into the boat. Soon after, the surface of the water was so still, it was like we'd never disturbed it at all.

"That's too bad you gave all the brownies to Old Rich, Eric," Camille said after a sigh. "It would have been nice to have a brownie here and now."

Arthur hummed his approval. Eric gave us a sneaky smile. I drew my knees to my chest, worried he might do something silly.

"I do have one brownie left," he said.

"You do?" Camille abruptly pulled her legs up, accidentally kicking Arthur in the kneecap in the process. His eyes welled up but he didn't utter a word.

From his monstrous shorts pocket, Eric pulled a little package wrapped in aluminium paper. He carefully opened it to reveal a generously sized brownie. Arthur and Camille went *Ooooh,* and Eric grinned, his eyes soft.

"How did you get such a beautiful specimen!" Arthur said. "They're usually those small things wrapped in plastic."

"This one has been made by Charles-Henry and Nadia, it's not store-bought."

"Its value has increased ten-fold," Camille said.

"Yeah, Charles-Henry is really good at this."

"That's not what you took from—" I stopped myself before I said too much. Thankfully, Eric didn't notice I almost slipped up.

"Xavier gave it to me earlier."

"Why would Xavier give you this?" Arthur asked.

Eric, once again, hesitated. "He'd just heard I was collecting brownies. When he gave it to me, I had already sealed the deal with Old Rich. But he really insisted on giving it to me, so I took it."

Eric began removing all sorts of things from his pockets. His crumpled script made Camille's eyes bulge. She picked it up gingerly between two fingers before setting it aside with a grimace.

"Who cares why Xavier gave you this treasure?" she said. "What matters is when we're going to eat it."

"Right now, I guess." Eric finally found what he was looking for: a small set of plastic cutlery. He wrenched open the wrapping and took out the knife.

To our surprise, Eric was an absolute maniac when it came to portion control. With the tip of his tongue out and a focused frown on his face, he cut the brownie in perfect little squares of equal size. Arthur tried hard not to laugh and ended up coughing in his fist. I was too awed to say anything. Once done, Eric distributed the portions to each of us, but when it came to his own portion, it laid untouched on the aluminium wrap. So when we were done eating, Camille eyed the last piece of brownie with a bright and alert eye until Eric playfully shoved it right under her nose.

"You should have it."

"No," she said, though she clearly looked thoughtful about it.

"Come on, you're our fearless leader."

"Fearless leader?"

"Yeah, we're all here because of you."

I muttered my approval. "You wrote the film, Camille. Have the brownie."

"No. But I'll play you for it."

"Play?"

Eric, clearly not interested in brownies as much as games, perked up and sat up straight. I instantly was reminded of Rufus and hid my smile behind my hand.

"I mean, we should play for it. Just like in *Notting Hill*."

"I don't know this game."

"You've never seen *Notting Hill*?" Camille looked at him, shocked. "With Hugh Grant and Julia Roberts?"

Eric, to my surprise, shook his head. "Nope."

"Oh my God!" Camille said, pulling at her hair. "You suck! You actually suck!"

"Oh," Eric said, looking disappointed.

Seeing his little face, she lunged forward to hug him, forgetting I was between the two of them. I gently pushed her away just before her knee shattered my tibia.

"Sorry!" she said. "I didn't mean you actually suck. It doesn't matter if you don't know, Eric, I'll explain."

His expression cleared at once. It was like, for a moment, he thought he wouldn't be able to participate in the game.

How cute. How unhelpful.

"In the movie," Camille said with a serious expression, "the group of friends decide the one with the saddest act will get the brownie. We're the self-proclaimed loser club. So, the biggest loser of our club will get the brownie."

Eric looked confused. "I thought we were the Not-A-Loser club."

"It was an attempt to feel better about ourselves! In truth, we're totally lame."

"Got it." His sly grin curled his lip. "Let's play, then. But let me tell you one thing: you'll never get it." He pointed to the last piece of brownie.

"Don't say that. I created the loser club."

Eric sat cross-legged to make himself comfortable. His knee brushed against mine, sending a chill down my spine.

"Sure," he said, "sure."

"I'll go first, then," Camille said.

We all waited in silence while the birds sang mysterious songs overhead.

"Where to begin?" Camille's voice became serious. "I don't have many friends, as you have all noticed. I haven't much in common with popular girls like Joy and Melissa. People call me *Miss Know-It-All* at school, which sucks. *Anyway*." She waved her hand dismissively. "I've been mostly hanging out with old people like my mom and her friends. My dad has left us, so he doesn't count, and he doesn't care. The girls at school I could have called my friends actually resent me since I got this prize for my play, so I'm pretty sure I'll be friendless when I get back to Colette after the summer. And the worst part is… I don't even care." She took a deep, resounding breath and smiled. "There! That's how far I'll go with this one."

"You'll have to do better than that," Eric said kindly. "It's like you're not even trying."

She smiled. "Are you serious?"

He nodded. "You're still so cool!"

I had to agree with him on that one. Camille seemed to me like the

267

coolest person. I secretly approved of her not being like Joy and Melissa and approved even more of the fact she didn't care for surrounding herself with fake people. In my book, Camille was the opposite of a loser.

"That's all you'll get from me today."

"Then you definitely are a loser." Eric wiggled his eyebrows playfully. "I can't believe I didn't see it before."

Clicking my tongue, I almost shoved him, but thought better of it. I would not put my hands on him anymore or let him put his hands on me. It had become too dangerous.

"Just wait your turn," Camille said through narrowed eyes.

Eric had registered my reaction but did not say a word. He turned to Arthur instead. "Arthur?"

Camille poked Arthur's foot with her own, which seemed to wake him from his reverie.

"Yes!"

"What's your loser story?"

Arthur turned his head to the clear blue sky overhead to gather his thoughts.

"First, my name is Arthur, and I don't like it. Second, I'm Flemish. No one knows or cares about Flanders, so that defines me pretty well, I think. No one seems to see me either. When they do, it's to make fun of me to my face, so I prefer to be ignored somehow. My parents are also pretty good at ignoring me. They enrolled me at Colette because no one speaks Flemish in France, of course, but they never ask me how it's going, if I like it or anything. They're too busy with their own lives." He had spoken really fast, without so much as glancing at us. Seeing we were listening so quietly, he took a breath and resumed at a slower pace. "I had friends in Flanders, but moving away made it impossible to see each other often, so they've moved on. It made me feel invisible again. Do you know that I've been Kayvin's neighbour for years, we've been attending the same schools for years, attending some of the same parties, but he still doesn't know my name? No one ever takes me seriously. Until… until Duvo. Duvo looked at my amateur work and said it would be great if I were to be the DOP for this project. That was the first time I was really acknowledged by someone. It truly felt amazing."

There was a silence. When I thought about how I also didn't pay much attention to Arthur all those times he was trying to get closer during Drama Club, I felt a twang of shame. How could I have been so self-centred? I'd never let him feel that way again, that's for sure. I'd sit

with him during every Drama Club session, and hopefully, I'd participate in every one of his projects.

"That's almost a decent story, Arthur." Eric broke the silence in a
light tone. "But now you're a respected DOP, Camille's legs are on
your own, and you and I are secret lovers. Isn't that a good ending?"
His eyes were full of compassion. Immediately, Arthur's face
brightened.

"It is! To be honest, I don't feel like a loser at all at the moment.
This is the best summer of my life. After all... my secret lover is the
captain of the football team."

Eric linked his hands behind his head and sighed. "You said it
beautifully, baby."

"Oh God, spare me," I muttered.

"Look at him grumbling over there," Arthur said. "He's jealous of
our love."

No. I was just tired of Eric's incessant flirting with everyone. His
actions had consequences. Why couldn't anyone agree with me on this?
Camille laid a gentle hand on my shoulder.

"Zak, stop frowning, it makes you look murderous. Tell us your
loser story instead."

I had to laugh.

"What?" Camille asked.

"Do you even need to ask?"

"I don't understand."

I gestured at my face. "Hello, I'm an Arab?"

My words had the effect of a slap. Eric swallowed noisily, Camille's
face contorted in a painful grimace, and Arthur, now beetroot red,
went into another fit of coughing.

"Are you okay?" I said, concerned he might choke.

"I don't... I didn't... You're not white, really? I didn't—"

"Shh-shh," Camille said softly, patting his shoulder so he would
stop hyperventilating. "It's okay."

I couldn't help laughing. "Yeah, don't pretend you haven't noticed.
I'm an Arab in a country where people won't admit they have a racism
problem. So the cookie's mine." I made a gesture toward it. "For all the
prejudice and misconceptions I'll have to contend with for the rest of
my life."

Eric's hand clamped around my wrist, stopping me. "Not so fast,
young man."

"What? You're gonna tell me you hadn't noticed either so—"

His grip tightened. "I've noticed." We locked eyes, both unwilling to surrender. "But you'll have to do better than that."

"Better than systemic racism?" I tried to break free of his grip.

"Zakaria." His tone was gentle and yet authoritative. My stomach did a weird cartwheel. "The mere fact that you're calling this brownie a cookie only proves that you don't deserve it. Come on. Do better."

"Really?"

Eric let go of my wrist but not of his notion. "I'm not trying to diss your experience or anyone else's, but Camille and Arthur both told us something really personal."

"And?" I was trying to sound like it wasn't my problem.

"And…" He wrinkled his nose a bit. "We wanna know something personal about you."

He sounded a tad meek as he spoke the last sentence, cute as hell for a wild dog. Arthur and Camille nodded in agreement, so I admitted defeat.

"Fine, but you better confess to some serious shit when it's your turn."

"Don't stall." He knocked our kneecaps together, sending another surge of current through my spine. I squeezed my eyes shut, trying to think of something personal. Something personal…

"Oh…" I got it. "I got rejected by Alberto."

Camille kicked her feet in the air. "So did everyone else!"

"Damn you. Good point." I put a finger on my chin. "Then… I'm short. And I'm too skinny."

Arthur snorted noisily. "Bastard. Do you have any idea how handsome you are?"

"No." I looked at him, serious. "I really think I'm too short and too skinny."

Camille shook her head. "You'll never get the brownie using your physical appearance, Zak. You're way too cute."

"I don't believe you."

"You should!"

I knew better than to ask Eric and get teased as an answer, and pointedly avoided looking at his face.

"But you never had a crush on me," I told Camille.

"I'm sorry." Her mouth twisted. "From the moment we met, I thought you were gay."

"Okay, then, I got rejected by Alberto in front of everyone. Isn't that a loser thing? But oh, wait… No one seemed to give a damn, so that's a plus."

"Silver lining spirit," Arthur said. "Such maturity. And as such, you cannot have the prize."

"Hang on!" I clasped my hands together. "I'm a loser! I can feel it!"

"You're not!" Arthur protested. "You are top of your class in everything. Even in drama, where there are no grades."

I clicked my fingers together. "Typical sign of a loser!"

"Wait." Camille held up a finger. "Losers would take Ancient Greek. Do you take Ancient Greek?"

I began nodding enthusiastically, then paused. "Actually, I dropped Ancient Greek. It was clashing with the Drama Club. But I still take Spanish, Italian, and advanced mathematics."

"Okay…" Arthur said, his eyes wide.

Camille gasped. "But you must be swamped with work!"

"It's not like I have so many things distracting me. I go to school, and I go home."

"You never do anything for fun?"

"Of course I do, but it doesn't involve leaving my home. Oh, and I have a library pass. What else do you need, really?"

Eric chimed in. "Friends."

"See?" Without thinking, I pinched Eric's shin. "I have no friends! I should have started with that. I'm officially the wo—aah!"

Touching Eric was a mistake. As if he'd been holding himself back for too long, he immediately threw himself at me to retaliate. Clenching my ribs and gritting my teeth, I could only wait for the tickling storm to pass. Camille had to use one of the oars to get him off me.

"Stop! Leave him alone. You'll overturn the boat! Good boy. Now sit."

With the flat edge of the oar digging into his chest, Eric obediently returned to his seat. Panting, I tried to fix my hair to the best of my abilities, my whole body itching and aching from his touch. I must have looked a proper mess.

"Do I get the brownie by default after getting molested or—" I paused. Eric's face had turned a bright shade of pink.

"Okay, so Zak's a friendless loser," Camille said, indifferent to our shenanigans. "Except he has us now. So, completely disqualified." She tossed me a haughty look. "Loser."

"Then…" Arthur was thinking aloud. "Then the brownie goes to me, doesn't it?"

"Eric, aren't you going to try for the brownie?" Camille asked.

"I wanted to!" Eric said, his face still pink. "But it seems I'm not allowed."

"He's the Anna Scott of the game," Arthur said. "You're, by definition, the least likely to get the brownie."

"But I didn't even have the chance to say anything!"

"You're right. Go ahead, then."

Eric rubbed his hands together. I thought for a moment he was struggling to dig out something interesting, but then I realised he looked more like he didn't know where to start.

"I'm not like all of you," he said.

"Clearly," Arthur said with a teasing smile.

Eric gave a little laugh. "I meant I'm not very good at school. Not very good at all. I think I failed my exams last month. I'll never get an award for writing a play, that's for sure. And I'll never be top of the class either."

Arthur lifted his hands. "Yeah, but how many football games have you won! And trophies? And your career is just beginning, right?"

Eric gave him a look that seemed almost fearful. "Yes, I have football. My life is all about football. Mornings are for football, evenings are for football, and my weekends? Guess: Football! It's been like this for so long, I can't remember a time where it wasn't. But my dad is very proud, he wants me to get into Harvard straight out of Colette."

"Harvard?!" Arthur and Camille said together.

"Harvard, yes." Lifting his blue gaze toward the matching sky, Eric let out a sigh. "But I don't like school. I can never focus on anything. Teachers hate dealing with guys like me, so I always end up at the back of the class, doodling. Of course, I'd never get into Harvard. So he wants me to get a scholarship through football."

Arthur grimaced. "I didn't even know Harvard had a football team. I mean, soccer. I mean—You know what I mean."

"I wish I could tell you the same, but my dad's been going on about that for years now. Oh, and spoiler alert: I don't even want to go to Harvard. I like being here. I like my life as it is. I know my father sees me becoming some kind of champion, but I just wanted to play football because it was fun, and now it's become this whole thing where I'm being asked to choose between a club or a scholarship, living with my mom or my dad, choosing France or the U.S.... I'm beginning to feel tired."

"But you can't let your father choose for you," Arthur said gently.

Eric pursed his lips. "I'm used to listening to him. He always says if you're good at something, then pursue it seriously, that sort of thing. And I have. I've worked hard, I got into a good club, I've done what I was asked because I really thought it was going to be my future for a long time... But then..."

Camille leaned forward, her eyes bright. "Then what?"

"Something happened. I changed."

Too far to nudge Eric, she shook me instead. "Explain, or no prize."

He rubbed his face with his hand. "I can't explain exactly... One day I woke up, and everything felt different. As if I'd been struck by lightning. So many little things I didn't notice before started to feel like huge burdens. My whole life was about football. My friends... they were also part of this world. I saw my life for what it was... Imagine waking up and realising Kayvin's your best friend... Even though I knew he would gladly stab me in the back to get my girlfriend, and he wouldn't stop there either. He would take over my whole life if he could... and sometimes I feel like letting him have it. I don't know."

I had never seen Eric like this before. His head hung low, his gaze was lost into a tiny crack at the bottom of the boat. None of us dared say anything, even to comfort him.

"Once I started having these thoughts," he went on, "I couldn't stop them, couldn't stop wanting other things. And not just other things... But *everything*. What if I want all of it? What if I don't want to choose? I want to be French and I want to be American, I want Paris and I want New York, I want to play football and do a million other things. Is that wrong of me? Or am I just making life difficult for those around me? I don't want to be difficult. I just want to be happy."

The streak of red in his eyes as he glanced around the boat made my fingers twitch. I wish I'd been a confident person like him or Camille so that I could have reached out to him. But I wasn't like that. I could only stare, wide-eyed, as his expression turned from vulnerable back to carefree in a few seconds.

"You're the opposite of a loser," I said in a forcefully teasing tone. "You'll never get this prize."

His gaze fell on me. "No, I don't think I will."

Camille crawled over me to pat his knee. "You're a nice person, Eric—"

"Thanks!" He forced out a laugh. "You're an even nicer person, Cam!"

"— but you are not the biggest loser. Not this time."

Arthur nodded. "You're too sweet, and funny, and sexy, and everyone loves you, as they should, and—"

"All right!" I said. "Get a room, you two!"

But Eric smacked his lips at Arthur on the other side of the boat, even going as far as winking.

"Should we share the brownie, then?" Arthur offered, a little red in the face. We all agreed. And Eric ate his portion this time.

Minutes after eating, I began feeling really sluggish and sleepy. Recalling I didn't get more than two hours of sleep last night, it made sense to me. But after a short while, something else occurred to me. My thoughts were just as mellow as my body. I felt strangely relaxed and dumb at the same time. It was totally unfamiliar.

"What is happening?" Arthur muttered out of the blue.

I felt Eric move next to me. His face got really close to mine, but I was too slow to react. In his eyes, I could see every detail of his irises, from the clear shade of blue that made up most of it to the specks of white forming a bright ring around his pupil. I had never seen anything so enthralling in my entire life.

When Eric moved his face away, I felt like whimpering.

"Guys?" His voice was calm. "I don't want to upset you… but I think there was weed in that brownie."

Arthur tried to sit up. "What?"

"Yes!" Camille laughed. "That's why we feel so good."

"And hungry…"

Eric slammed his forehead. "Fucking Xavier."

"Don't be too mad at him," Camille said. "He gave you his last piece. He didn't mean anything bad by it."

"I know." Eric looked at me. "But still."

Camille waved her hand. "Anyway, it's done. Nothing we can do about it. Let's just chill."

I wanted to protest, but I couldn't even be bothered. I wasn't annoyed, for once. I wasn't feeling nervous. Not even when Eric changed position and lay down next to me. I felt quite warm, with my legs dangling out of the boat, enjoying how peaceful everything was and the feeling of Eric's arm against mine. My thoughts drifted away to the sound of Bardot's voice, and my heavy eyelids gave up and fluttered shut.

Then, something brushed against my cheek. I opened my eyes.

It was sometime later. The sun had already dipped behind the trees, and a breeze tickled the bare skin of my shins. I couldn't recall where I was at first. My face felt warm and comfy. I raised my head a little, blinking… and sat bolt upright, horrified.

My head had been laying on Eric's arm!

He was asleep, his face turned to the side, his arms outstretched. And apparently, I had taken advantage and used him as a human pillow.

With a jolt, I scrambled to the other side of the boat. Camille and Arthur were gone, and we were much closer to the bank. Did we row back at some point and I had slept through it all? Why didn't they wake me? Did they see me sleep in this awkward position? It was so embarrassing!

Eric moved, the arm I had been using twitching lightly.

All right. Stay calm. He might not have noticed anything. I pinched my cheeks, decided to lie my way through it, not tell him anything. But when Eric opened his eyes, he looked at me and smiled.

"Oh, you're awake."

"I'm awake."

Rubbing his eyes in an adorable sort of manner, he sat up too.

"Where are the others?" My voice sounded raspy.

"They left some time ago."

"I didn't… I didn't hear anything."

"You were sleeping so soundly, no one wanted to wake you." He grinned. "Tell me. Is my arm comfortable?"

I jerked my head, mortified. Not only did he know, but Camille and Arthur probably saw it as well. Could I blame it all on evil brownies? I had to say something before he thought I had a crush on him or something.

"I'm sorry I did that."

"What?" He looked surprised. "Who cares? It's totally fine."

"But I didn't want to…"

"To what?"

"I didn't even want to do that."

Cringing from embarrassment, I dipped my hands into the water, using them as oars to get close enough to the bank so that I could jump off and make my escape. But unhelpful as always, Eric got up and slammed his foot on the edge of the boat, freezing me to the spot.

"Zakaria, don't hurt my feelings. I exercise every day. You must say you like my arm, or I'll be very sad."

Oh no. He had switched back to teasing mode, and I was in no condition to fight him off right now. I realised we were at the lake, the perfect spot to exact his revenge for what I did this morning. But if he had to torment me, then I wouldn't go down without a fight.

"Be sad, then," I said, trying to sound as aloof as possible. We were almost at the bank now. "Who cares about your arms? I don't."

"That's it, baby. Give me some snark."

My cheeks grew hot. "Shut up."

"Are you embarrassed?"

"Who says I'm embarrassed?"

"Your face, and the fact that you're obviously trying to escape."

"I'm just sick of your face, that's all."

With a giggle, Eric removed his foot. "Zak…" He lowered his voice. "Why are you so embarrassed? It's not like you woke up on my—"

"Stop!" I pointed my finger at him. "Not another word. I will throw you overboard."

Eric paused, clearly weighing his options. But just as I extended my fingers to reach for the roots growing on the side of the bank, he screamed.

"Look! There!"

With a start, I followed the direction of his finger. There was nothing there. "Idiot! What are you scaring me for!"

"Here! Here!" He looked maniacal, jumping in place in the boat. "Bee!"

Just as I caught a glimpse of a buzzing insect, Eric lost balance and fell backwards into the water.

With a shriek, I lurched forward, stretching out my hand, before letting out a sigh of relief. The water wasn't deep at that level.

Eric came out dripping. He only had water up to his waist. A frozen smile on his face, he pushed his hair back with one hand and lifted the other to his mouth. There was only so much I could take at this point. I forgot to look worried and, hiding behind my hands, I began shaking with laughter.

"That's what I get for almost breaking my neck?" Eric feigned shock. "You're laughing at me?"

"So much for balance," I said through tears. "How did you even make it to the football team?"

He pouted, sending me into another fit of sniggering. It's like he was destined to end up in the water no matter what. Poor puppy. The way he looked, dripping wet... his hair pulled back, his shirt sticking to his torso, the warm light of the sunset bathing his face in golden light, the blue eyes fixed on me... My laughter slowly died in my throat.

"What?"

"We... We're gonna be late for dinner."

After a pause, Eric nodded. Pulling the boat with me inside, he trudged back to the bank. The sight of his wet shorts clinging to his backside made my heart thump.

"Why did you freak out when you saw that bee?" I asked, in an effort to distract myself from unwanted thoughts.

"I wanted to show it to you! It was really furry."

"That was worth breaking your neck indeed."

"That one was so furry, it would have proven you wrong." Eric turned around to shoot me a glare. "If only you'd looked when I told you."

"Oh, believe me, I looked!"

I didn't miss a thing, I thought, my eyes glued to his drenched shorts.

When we reached the bank, Eric extended his arm for me. His hand was hot, his hold firm, and I was back on dry land in no time. Eric secured the boat, and we slowly made our way back to the house. At some point, he patted his pockets, gave a little "Hm", and shrugged before picking up the pace. Inwardly, I gave a million thanks to the sweet little bee that distracted Eric from the subject of me waking up with my head on his arm.

The worst part was that I had no recollection of doing it. It must have happened while I was asleep. And since I was asleep, I couldn't remember how it felt to have my cheek against his bare skin...

What a missed opportunity. There wouldn't be another like that, for sure. I should not have sat up so roughly. I should have stayed put a moment longer, I should have brushed my finger against his—

"What are you thinking about?" Eric's voice tore me from my thoughts. "The best way to tell the others about this?"

"I... hum..." I gave him a quick look. He was grinning as usual. "Do you want me to tell them?"

"Not necessarily. I was just curious about what you wanted to do."

I didn't answer straight away. I waited until he glanced back at me curiously.

"I'll do whatever you want," I said.

I sounded defeated.

20

DOGS MUST BE KEPT ON A LEASH AT ALL TIMES

"Am I boring you or something?"

My fight against a yawn concluded in defeat and was heard by my sister on the other side of the phone.

"No!" I said, rubbing my eyes. "Of course not."

"Are you sure you're okay? You haven't said anything remotely interesting."

I cursed my sister's sixth sense under my breath. "That's because a lot has happened, but nothing... important."

"Hm... Right."

On Sunday morning, my cheek was still burning from waking up on Eric's arm, despite no incidents recorded yesterday. We spent most of Saturday apart, which helped. Camille worked hard on her climactic scene, Arthur and Michael spent the afternoon watching dailies with Duvo, and Eric played around all day with his friends. And I got to breathe a little easier, from my hiding spot in the utility closet, my gaze drifting from Alberto's white silhouette to Eric's golden one.

Calling Yasmine was proving more difficult every time, but today especially. Talking about Eric in mild terms had become near impossible. And I was just thinking about this when Eric barged into the bedroom, drenched in sweat, and found me huddled under the covers, my phone to my ear. We both stared at each other with round eyes and spoke at the same time.

"You're late!"

"You're still in bed?"

"I'm what?" Yasmine said on the other side of the line.

I held up my phone for Eric to see. "Hang on a second, Yas." I muted the call. "It's almost nine! You're usually done much earlier than that."

Eric walked over to his bed and picked up some clean clothes from his suitcase. "I went for a run last night, so I slept a little longer this morning."

"Why did you go for a run last night?"

Walking toward the door, Eric laughed and didn't answer. Just as he was leaving the room, he turned abruptly and said, "Finish your phone call, I'll bring you breakfast this time."

The situation, the offer, his smile... For a split second, I forgot who we were and where I was, and like an affectionate wife, I returned his smile and without thinking... blew him a kiss.

I didn't know if he saw it, because he was gone when I dared to look up. My face burning, I promptly slid under the covers and silently wept tears of shame until Yasmine began screaming that she would break my neck if I didn't unmute the call immediately.

A while later, just as I hung up, a stampede mixed with high-pitched screams alerted me of the girls' arrival into the corridor, and shortly after, Eric, Arthur, and Charles-Henry came charging into the room.

"Catch!"

Eric hurled a red brick at me. It bounced off my forehead, destroying half my brain cells, and fell flatly on my sheets. I looked down; it wasn't a brick, but an apple. Furious, I ignored Eric's apologetic grimace and threw the apple right back at him, missed by a long shot, and watched it tear through Charles-Henry's stuff on the nightstand.

"Guess what!!" Arthur threw himself onto my bed, landing on my feet. "We're going to the beach!"

With a pat on the stunned C.H.'s shoulder, Eric retrieved the apple and stuck it in his pocket. I rubbed my forehead, trying to make sense of what just happened.

"We are?"

Gripping his elbow, Eric effortlessly peeled Arthur off the bed and sat down in his place. "We are. Binta just announced it. Hurry up, get ready."

"But how? When? What—"

Eric shook his head. "Oh no, little Thomas. No thinking."

The way he said little Thomas made my stomach twitch strangely. Arthur and Charles-Henry started for their things, bumping into each other as they gathered sunscreen, towels, and sunglasses. Eric tried to pull the covers to force me out of bed. I pulled them back to me.

"Leave me alone!"

"Yeah, like that'll ever happen."

He was like a dog with a toy, and I believed him. Just as he stood up to exert more strength, Xavier knocked on the door, saving me. With a sigh, Eric dragged himself to his suitcase, picked something up, and walked over to Xavier to give it to him. Xavier looked excited and left.

Eric saw my surprised expression when he returned to his spot on my bed.

"What was that about?"

He casually picked up the covers, forcing me again to pull against him with all my strength. "He wanted my shampoo."

"Why would he want your shampoo?" I gritted my teeth, straining against his pull.

"I don't know. To smell like me, I guess."

"But why? Spit it out, or I'm telling everyone about how you fell off the boat."

"Traitor." Eric suddenly loosened his grip. With nothing to strain against, my fists flew straight to my chin.

"Ouch! Fuck!"

"Nice one!" Eric patted my feet over the covers. "Xavier overheard Camille when she said she loved my shampoo. I think he likes her."

"He... He what?"

Eric waited until Arthur and Charles-Henry were out of ear range, then leaned closer, and his breath tickled my ear. "I said I think he likes Camille."

"Yeah, I heard you the first time," I said, turning away. This sort of proximity wouldn't make my case any better. "Why didn't you say so before?"

"He didn't want anyone to know. He thinks she doesn't like him."

"He's right." My eyes narrowed. "And now he's gonna smell like you. Another guy she doesn't want to date."

"Don't say it like that! You'll hurt my feelings."

"Your feelings..."

I spat on his feelings. No, worse, I doubted their existence. Did he really not notice I was on the verge of exploding from his mindless flirt-

281

ing? Just to prove my point, Eric took advantage of my distraction and began pulling at the covers again.

"You haven't seen my tennis ball, have you?"

"No."

"I haven't seen it in days."

"Good. Good riddance."

Eric's eyes took on a wild glint. He tugged at the covers ruthlessly. "Come out of there."

"No way." I gritted my teeth. "You'll tickle me, I can see it on your face."

"No, I'll be good."

He looked innocently into my eyes, but I knew better. I jerked my legs under the covers in an attempt to kick him off the bed.

"Don't you start! It's Sunday."

"Exactly. Aren't we supposed to kiss today?" Eric pinned my feet with one hand while the other tugged at the covers. "And look, how convenient, you're already in bed."

A bucket of water over my head would have had less effect. That dog was right; we were supposed to rehearse our kissing scene today. But after starting off the day like this, there was no way I could act like a pro. I became completely limp as though I was surrendering. With a look of triumph, Eric crawled up the bed, preparing, no doubt, to tickle me. I felt under my pillow for my copy of *The Ladies' Paradise* and slammed it on his face. He clutched his nose and yelped in pain.

"What was that!"

"Serves you right for acting like an animal."

"Come on, Thomas," Eric pleaded, rolling around in my sheets. "I just wanted to tickle you! Don't be like this."

"Get lost, Adam."

My skin was already itching the moment he took Arthur's place on my bed. All the progress from yesterday had gone out the window. If he put his hands on me today, I honestly didn't know how I would react. Looking at him lying flat on my bed and bawling was difficult enough. It took me a lot of willpower as well as Arthur and C.H.'s presence not to straddle him and teach him a lesson.

That was it. I was slowly degenerating into a beast myself.

His fake tears dried, Eric climbed out of bed just as fast as he had jumped in, his finger on his chin. "I like the way you said 'Get lost'. Let's tell Camille to add that line. I believe it will make the movie better."

282

The movie. The damn movie. Camille had delivered her final draft. Each new version of the kiss she wrote over the past few days saw it becoming more and more passionate. Even though there was nothing more I wanted to do all day, there was no way I could rehearse it in my present state.

Thirty minutes later, I found myself packed like a sardine in Janine's car, with Michael at the wheel and Eric in the passenger seat, while I was sandwiched between Arthur and Camille, her lithe legs kicking excitedly into my shins.

The beach was half an hour away. Michael was trying to follow Binta and Duvo, both at the wheel of Old Rich's ancient van and Duvo's aunt's car, packed with the rest of us. Michael's decision to drive us, the losers, was quite the scene, because his fangirls were determined to have him. But in the end, Joy, Melissa, and Nadia crammed themselves in the back of Binta's ride and Charles-Henry, who couldn't believe his luck, from time to time waved at us from the passenger seat.

Michael wasn't a very confident driver. At first, I thought it was because of the state of the road or the fact that he was driving on the opposite side compared to what he was accustomed to. Then I attributed it to Charles-Henry's distracting waves and thumbs-ups, before I finally understood.

He simply wasn't used to driving around with a hyperactive puppy on the passenger seat.

Hunched over the wheel and holding on for dear life, Michael regularly threw anxious glances at Eric, attempting to convince him to quiet down, but Eric was too excited. He wouldn't stop drumming his hands on the dashboard and was determined to sing aloud *Viens Changer Ma Vie* by Renée Martel, his favourite on *my mom's* playlist.

"Do you know any other song?" Michael asked with tears in his eyes after the fifteen-minute mark.

"It's our song," Eric said, outstretching his arm and flexing his hand toward the three of us crammed in the back seat. I blankly stared at the annoying hand opening and closing before my eyes, unaware of what to do. Camille eventually fist-bumped the hand, and Eric withdrew it from my sight.

"That's lovely." Michael used a placating voice. "But you don't have to sing it three times in a row, do you?"

"Fine… Fine."

Eric succeeded in staying silent for exactly twenty-two seconds, all the while glancing at Michael. Then he couldn't take it anymore. "Do *you* know any songs?" he barked, startling Michael.

"Of course, I do."

"With lyrics in them," Eric added slyly.

Michael shook his head. "You're stressing me so much that all I can think of are songs you shouldn't sing aloud in cars."

"Oh, do tell!" Eric shouted in his southern drawl, gripping Michael's shoulder.

Michael let out a yelp. "Fuck! Eric, did you do drugs this morning?"

Eric turned around, beaming. "Michael said the *F* word."

"You're all a bunch of prudes, I swear!" Camille roared, her hair whipping my face.

"I'm on your side, Michael," I said breathlessly.

Eric turned around sharply. "Which side is that?"

"The side that wants to arrive there in one piece."

Michael saluted my reflection in his mirror, and after a hefty tut-tutting, Eric filled his lungs with air and resumed his massacre of Renée Martel.

"God, help me." Michael bumped his forehead against the wheel and hit the klaxon.

Eric laughed. "Are you always so edgy on the road?"

Even I had never seen Eric so ecstatic. I took it for a sign he was extremely fond of the beach. After all, all the dogs are.

"*Excuse* me." Michael gave a bitter laugh. "Are you always like this on the road?"

"YES!"

I leaned forward innocently. "Stick his head out the window so he can wag his tongue and cool off."

"Seriously?" Michael sounded panicked. "Do I need to do that?"

Camille, Arthur, and I snorted in unison. Eric shook his head, his lips pursed.

"Don't listen to them, Michael, listen to me!"

Eric resumed singing, and Michael drew a shaky breath. Eventually, he reached out and patted Eric's forehead. Eric's eyes widened, but he didn't stop singing.

"You don't have a fever," Michael said, sending Camille into a fit of laughter. "How about when you're driving to your games? How does your coach bear it?"

"I'm the captain. I can do whatever I want." Eric gave a loud sigh. "You should see what I get away with in the showers."

Arthur let out a nervous laugh. He gave me a pointed look and started fanning himself. Refusing to acknowledge any of this, I squeezed my hands around my kneecaps and pretended not to be bothered by the hammering in my chest.

Meanwhile, Camille had flipped open her notebook. "Details, please, Eric."

Michael sighed. "Please don't say another word."

After stopping the car on the beach's parking lot, Michael jumped out so fast that he may have accidentally broken a Guinness record. Kayvin and Xavier also ran out of Duvo's car looking worse for wear. Perhaps because they were trapped in the back of Old Rich's van with Sander, who was just an inch smaller than a mountain.

Alberto emerged without a wrinkle on his linen shirt. I swallowed a lump when he slid down his sunglasses and peered haughtily at the sun, the beach, and by accident, me. I didn't know what to do, trapped under his gaze. But he did something strange and unexpected: he rose his hand to his hair and sort of flattened it, in a self-conscious kind of way.

"Zak, are you coming?"

Eric swung his arm over my shoulder and tore me away from Alberto. Michael was already streaking across the beach, halfway to the shore, surrounded by his girls. Xavier and Kayvin finally seemed to have learned a valuable lesson, which was to follow Michael wherever he went, because he was the ticket to the girls. With a shriek of laughter, Melissa hopped on Michael's back. Duvo squealed behind us.

"Oh, come on!"

"Laurent." Binta shook her head as she laughed. "Let them have fun."

"Put her down!" Duvo yelled, making me flinch. "That's a lawsuit waiting to happen."

Duvo overtook us and, pulling Binta by the hand, ran after Michael. Binta followed half-heartedly, pressing her giant hat on top of her head.

"You believe this guy?" Eric said.

The sweet, candy-like scent of his breath wafted into my nose. I realised his arm was still around my shoulder and I pushed him away.

"Yeah. How dare he worry about us, am I right?"

"We're not kids anymore," Eric said with a smile. "And we're not made of glass."

I wasn't so sure about this, so I said nothing. I sure was feeling pretty brittle, especially when Eric stood so close.

It was a beautiful day, and many people had the same idea as us. Rows of mismatched beach towels blanketed the expanse of brown sand, the seaside wind flapping countless beach hats and umbrellas. You could find all sorts of people: from groups of friends sitting together around rudimentary picnics, to dads swimming with shrieking toddlers and mothers tanning with a book over their nose.

Camille and Arthur were already in the water, jumping over the frothy waves with the others. Eric and I walked over to the spot where they had ditched their personal belongings. He removed his shirt and stood before me in his swimming trunks. Though they were not so different from any of his pairs of shorts, they were better fitted, and I didn't know where to look.

"Go play," I said in a firm tone. "I'll be here for a while."

"Sure?"

"Sure."

He left to join the others. From behind the safety of my sunglasses, I stared after him. He was so fit. It was annoying how the mere sight of him, which left me indifferent less than a week ago, was now enough to blind me. At some point, he stopped and threw a look over his shoulder. I thought he might come back, and my lips tightened. But after a smile, he went into the water and immediately was assailed by Joy. Evidently, she had forgiven him for what had transpired the other day.

What did transpire the other day? I never got the chance to ask. Not that it was any more my business now than it was days ago. Eric said I would find out eventually, but all I had were theories and no conclusive information.

With a sigh, I unfolded a towel and sat with my chin on my knees. It seemed she hadn't given up on him. She tried to hop on his back just as Melissa had done with Michael. He turned to her, laughing, and a bitter taste filled my mouth. Then, coming out of nowhere, Camille threw herself at him and claimed the spot on his back. Eric left with her to where Arthur was standing, Joy turned green, and the corner of my lip curled up.

After a while alone, I was relaxed enough to remove my clothes and lay in my own swimming trunks, my gaze wandering toward the far-away boats on the horizon. Dealing with the heat was easier near the sea. I drew in a deep breath of briny air and let out a contented sigh. It reminded me of my childhood summers in Tunis; of my mother's long hair brushing my cheek as she held me close. That song she was singing… That same song that was playing on the boat the other day… Eric's arm soft and warm under my cheek...

Slamming both hands on my cheeks, I gave a groan of despair.

Standing a safe distance away from the others, Alberto had dipped his toes in the water. His faithful Sander was talking animatedly to him, but Alberto was silent as he stared into the distance, the wind dancing through his hair, conferring him an elusive aura.

I picked up *The Ladies' Paradise* and plunged right back into the story where I left it. I was near the end now, where after much suffering, things were looking up for poor Denise, aside from the fact that her sexy boss was after her, and she had a hard time resisting his advances. I was so enthralled by her trials that I didn't notice that it had started raining at first, until drops of water fell onto the page I was reading. Surprised, I looked up.

It wasn't raining. It was just Eric standing behind me, his head bent down. Droplets of water dripped down from his hair onto my face. I shielded myself with my hand. "Can I… help you with something?"

Apart from tilting his head, he didn't move an inch, and more droplets came splashing on the back of my hand. "Zak…"

"… What."

"Do you want to put sunscreen on me?"

"Nope." I pushed my palm against his leg, and he went staggering back. "Definitely not." I used my book to shield my face when I felt my cheeks grow hot.

"Come on…" Eric coaxed.

"Not gonna happen."

I knew he'd be difficult as soon as he heard my refusal. I was expecting it. Of course, I was right. He jumped in place like a spoiled child.

"Would it hurt you to help out a friend for once?"

Curse him!

I took a deep breath. "It would, especially when he's asking like that."

Eric whined and stomped his feet, but I didn't give in. In truth, nothing would hurt as much as every nerve in my body if I had to put my hands on him. To say nothing of the comments we would get. What was happening to him today? He usually kept the worst of his teasing to moments when we were alone, but now he couldn't even be bothered anymore. Well, at least, this time, I chased him away.

But it was wrong of me to assume that. Eric took out his towel and began unfolding it carefully next to mine. Immediately, I reached for my T-shirt. He paused.

"What are you doing?"

"Guess. I don't feel safe being half-naked in front of you."

"Smart choice, Zakaria." He grinned. "Everyone knows I'm not to be trusted around helpless young m——"

"Don't call me helpless."

Glaring, I threw my T-shirt over my head. Eric watched me get dressed without blinking. He had been single for almost a week now and was acting increasingly slutty. Perhaps he needed flirting and teasing, like a zombie needed brains to survive. He didn't take it seriously, so he couldn't possibly understand he had me tipping over the edge. When he spoke again, I was on my guard, so his words surprised me.

"Look at them together."

He was pointing at Camille and Arthur. They had separated from the others. She was screaming in laughter at something Arthur said, and he was red to his ears.

"They're cute." Looking at them made me feel strangely envious. I dipped my nose into my book. "They... they should date."

"You think so?" Eric beamed. "Me too! We think alike!"

I doubted that. If he knew my thoughts right now, he wouldn't think that *at all*.

"They're a good match," I admitted. "I don't know why it hasn't happened yet. I think they kissed at the party."

"I think they did more than kiss at the party."

I glanced up, smirking. "Look at you, gossiping like an old woman."

To my surprise, he looked at me with eyes glinting with pride. I turned my face away, confused by his weird behaviour. Abandoning his towel, Eric scrambled to his feet.

"Do you wanna rehearse or what?"

"Here? Now?"

We couldn't rehearse here. Not in front of everybody, with Kayvin and everyone so close. I'd never be able to relax, and they would get the wrong idea. They might think we're fooling around — because that's exactly what it would be, on my part.

All I could think about was that damn kiss.

Eric didn't have Alberto's lips. In truth, probably no one did. But the more I thought about how his lips might feel under my own, the more my head swam. I coughed in my fist.

"I can't. I'm reading."

"Seriously?" Eric groaned and squatted behind me. "You know this thing by heart. Can't you read it some other time?"

And lose this perfect excuse to watch him run around half-naked all day? No sir.

"I'm afraid I can't," I said, congratulating myself for sounding like a snob.

"What's it about anyway?"

"It's about..." He suddenly put his chin on my shoulder, cutting off my breath. "... Many... ahem... things." I scrambled around in my brain for the plot of my favourite book. "But... but my favourite thing is that Denise, the poor employee of the store, is devastatingly in love with her employer, Mr Mouret, who's completely out of her league."

"Why is he out of her league?" Each of Eric's words reverberated through my neck, making my scalp tingle.

"He's..." I heard how small my voice sounded and cleared my throat. I wouldn't fall apart. I wouldn't. No matter what. I focused hard on the plot of my book. "He's her boss. He's rich. He strolls around the store, and he's surrounded by powerful women. Denise's a poor shop girl with nice hair. She doesn't even think he knows her."

"What does she do to get him, then? Does she get him, at least?"

"Yes, of course, or I would've thrown this book away immediately."

He chuckled. The chin was removed, and his hand ruffled through my hair, then his heat disappeared and left me wanting more. He sat beside me instead.

"How did she get him?"

"By being awesome."

"Just that?" He frowned. "Nothing else?"

I tried not to blush at his interest in my book, but the fact that my cheeks were prickling told me I failed.

"No," I said, collecting myself. "She was just being awesome, hard-working, keeping her head down, and she was refusing him as well... She was refusing to be his mistress because that was disrespectful."

"Oh! So he just wanted to po—to sleep with her?"

I nodded. "He thought it might alleviate his obsession with her. I don't know. Men are stupid sometimes."

He said nothing, probably because he knew full well it was true.

"She never gave in," I said. "Eventually, he proposed to her. Because, she didn't know, but he was obsessed with her too. He would lose everything without her. So, in the end, she won everything, and she didn't have to become a person she didn't want to become. It's the perfect ending."

"It's good," Eric said.

His admission drew a smile on my face, which in return enlarged his, and we sat there beaming until, self-conscious of my throbbing pulse, I averted my gaze.

"You should read it one day."

"But now I know how it ends!"

"You can still enjoy it."

Eric didn't get to say more. He was summoned to a game of beach volley with his friends and the girls. I was very aware that whether he was close or walking away from me, my body reacted in the strangest ways, as though some new parts I didn't know of were coming to life. If I didn't find a way to deal with this soon, it would become frightening. Perhaps rehearsing the kiss was the best plan of action after all. Or perhaps it was a mistake.

Shortly after, Camille and Arthur took Eric's place, and what was once a peaceful spot became a mess of sand, towels, laughter, and sandwiches. Considering the only food I had encountered this morning had left a bump on my forehead, I accepted the sandwich Camille gave me gratefully.

"Isn't this great?" Camille said, her mouth full. "The beach, the sun, the seagulls?"

"It's all right," I said.

Arthur didn't say anything. He was looking over at the beach volley game, his mouth agape. Camille followed his gaze.

"I thought you said you didn't want to play!" She spat a bit of ham. "Oops. Go if you want."

"I'm fine…" Arthur seemed distracted.

"What is it?" Camille poked him with her foot.

Arthur gave a sigh. "Eric is so fit, God damn it!"

I choked on a bit of chicken sandwich. Camille hurried over to rub my back, her lip curled up into an amused smile.

"Well, well… What do we have here?"

Arthur tore his gaze away from his crush and shrugged. "Nothing. I'm just saying."

Before I could stop myself, I had adopted my teasing tone — that was Eric's fault; all my bad habits were. "If I had a euro every time you lusted after Eric…"

"I'm not lusting!" Arthur said. "I'm… envying. He's really handsome, that's all."

"He is," Camille said dreamily.

"Yes, yes, he's okay." I wiped the sweat on my forehead.

"Zak, be serious."

"Zak prefers guys like Alberto," Camille said, patting my ankle.

I nodded.

Shameless liar said the little voice in my head.

Arthur snorted. "Eric's hotter."

After craving a guy for almost a year, some reactions become instinctive. I removed my sunglasses just to shoot Arthur a venomous glare. He threw up his hands.

"Okay, I'll admit it! Alberto looks very nice."

"Thank you."

"But Eric is insane! He rises every morning at six, whether it's a weekday or the weekends, and…"

There would be no stopping Arthur. He was Eric's biggest fan after all. His man-crush might have even exceeded mine, and I was nurturing naughty thoughts about his lips. I could only listen with a churning stomach as Arthur listed all the things he loved about him.

"… And then he runs seven kilometres to the village and back! And then, after his run, he does push-ups and lunges, and squats, and all sorts of things! And after that—"

"He swims naked in the lake!" I chortled.

Camille and Arthur's heads both snapped toward me. Camille even dropped her sandwich.

"He what?"

"It's true. After he's done, he cools down in the lake. Naked."

I loved the effect my words had on them. Arthur's eyes had gotten as round as frisbees.

"You saw him?"

I nodded slowly. "I caught him once. He was in the middle of the water, muttering to himself. It was weird."

It was adorable. But they didn't need to know that.

"Muttering?" Camille said pensively. "He was muttering?"

"Yes!" I turned to Arthur. "Your hopeless crush was talking to himself in the lake."

"That's just his lines," Arthur said, biting into his sandwich. "He's always muttering his lines."

I paused, surprised. "His lines?"

"I heard him a few times. It's the lines from the movie. He told me he has a bad memory. So he's always practising."

"But... but he never does that in front of me."

Arthur shrugged. "He's intimidated by you, I guess. It seems you read something once and you know it by heart." Camille and Arthur exchanged a knowing look.

My heart swelled at the thought of Eric, anxious about his lines, learning them by heart every minute of the day to deliver his best work.

It was so cute!

No. It wasn't a good time to think about these things. Or the heat would get to me again.

"Do you want me to ask him out for you, Arthur?" I mused, trying to regain control of my emotions through sarcasm.

"I love it," Camille said in an unusually soft, cooing voice. "I love a straight guy who admits to having a guy crush."

Arthur looked at her. "You... you do?"

"Hell yeah."

Laughing light-heartedly, Camille tossed her hair back and returned her gaze to the sea. Arthur's expression merged into something akin to devotion. I looked at them in wonder. If these two were not dating by the end of this trip, then there was no chance for the rest of us.

Half an hour later, the beach volley game was over. Kayvin was carrying Joy on his shoulders, looking jubilant. Eric returned to us, an angry-looking sunburn stretching over his shoulders. Camille gasped in shock.

"Eric, you're burning!"

"That's because no one wants to help me!" Eric said with a glare directed at me.

I jerked my head haughtily. I'd take it. Better this than collapsing from a heart attack the moment my fingers grazed his skin.

"I can do it if you want." Arthur seized the bottle.

Eric eyed him briefly. What was he going to say? "Camille will help me."

"As you wish," Camille said with an air of surprise.

She went to work. We discovered something about her right then: As skilled as she was with words, she was hopeless with her hands. She squeezed half the amount of the bottle onto Eric's skin. I noticed his discomfort when she did, but it was wiped off his face a blink later. Camille immediately understood her mistake and glanced at me with the most adorable grimace of disgust and started patting at Eric's back. It couldn't be agreeable for either of them. I would have done a better job... if I'd only accepted to do it. Camille had no idea how to rub her hands over the smooth muscles of his arms or the hard lines of his back. It was almost insulting.

"Have you two rehearsed your last scene?" Camille said, suddenly all business.

Eric was playing with the sand like a toddler. "No. Zak refuses to kiss me."

"Lies!" I cried, before Camille could bite my head off. "I'm not the one who said he was nervous to kiss another guy."

"That's not true!" Eric said in a panic. I knew he didn't want to lose face in front of Camille. "I'm not nervous."

"Liar."

"The nerve on this one! I've been trying to kiss him for days, and he's the one who's all..." he looked down at his skin, "... slippery."

"Excuse me?"

But Eric was laughing. He once again got the upper hand of the conversation, leaving me feeling at a loss.

"You can practice on Arthur if you want," Camille said, teasing. "He was just re-confessing his impossible man-crush on you."

"Is that so?" Eric immediately turned sly.

"You are my secret lover after all," Arthur said with a nod.

"Let's do it now!" Eric shook himself off and planted both feet in the ground. "Here's your chance. Come to papa."

Camille laughed and Arthur blushed. I thought Eric had taken my snark a little too strongly and was desperate to show us he wasn't afraid at all. And of course, it was me it would slap in the face. If I had to watch him make out with another guy, I swear...

"Come-on-come-on-come-on-come-on!" Eric was dancing in place.

"Really?" Arthur said, now not really sure he was into it. "You were serious?"

"Sure I was! Some people are implying I'm afraid to kiss a guy, so…"

Camille was looking from Arthur to Eric to me and back with her mouth open. "I'm not sure what's going on," she said, "but I sure won't interrupt you."

"Come here." Eric extended both arms toward Arthur. "I promise I won't put it in if you don't want me to."

Hearing this, my insides collapsed onto themselves.

"I'm out!" Arthur said suddenly. "I thought I never wanted anything else, but I was wrong. I'm not worthy."

"Eric, you… were… talking about your tongue, right?" Camille asked in a weak voice.

Eric pulled Arthur into a rib-shattering hug. "Hush, hush, it's all right."

"I'm sorry…" Arthur pretended to sob. "I'm too straight."

"That's okay. I knew you couldn't be perfect."

"This is ending up in my next film," Camille said.

"Really?" Eric shoved Arthur aside. "You're writing a new film?"

"I am now!"

Camille recovered Arthur who still looked shaken by the events, or just aptly pretended to be so he could nestle in her arms. He was sticky with sunscreen from Eric's hug, but she didn't seem to mind. Meanwhile, my heart wouldn't stop hammering inside my chest. Eric was so lewd and inappropriate; I should have been disgusted. But of course, there was something wrong with me. My body seemed to react the opposite way.

Eric licked his lips and turned to me. "You? You're game?"

"Certainly not." I turned away, offended to be his second choice. "Anyway… with our luck, everyone will see us, and then we'd have some explaining to do."

"Oh! I know!" Eric slapped his forehead. "We could tell them we're rehearsing a scene for a movie!"

"Ha-ha. Hold the snark. I don't want to rehearse here." I saw him approach with a grin and jumped aside. "And I don't want to play your games."

"Fine!" Eric said, looking miffed.

After taking a long, critical look at us, Camille dragged Arthur for a walk along the beach. I expected Eric to go with them or back to his friends, but he stubbornly glued his sculpted ass to the towel next to mine.

"I said I didn't want to play your games."

I was still trying to understand what was happening to my body every time he got too close or said something really inappropriate. It wasn't anything like I was used to. It was violent; terrifying, and also… intoxicating. I was beginning to feel concerned.

"Why are you mad all of a sudden?"

"Who's mad?"

"You are. You don't want to play anymore."

Because… you silly flirt. We had gone too far with the games. My skin was burning; only the most violent shock would break the spell. I wondered if there was a haunted house nearby. Still, I put on a brave face and spouted some nonsense.

"That's your fault. You broke my skull and my jaw earlier with your stupidities."

Eric drew closer. "Which one hurts the most? Your skull or your jaw?"

"Huh…"

I hesitated. In fact, neither of them hurt at all anymore. I was merely pulling his leg to hide how flustered I was.

"Fine." Eric drew out a breath. "Let's say your jaw, then."

Without warning, he bent his head down and pressed his lips to my chin. My blood went from boiling to completely frozen.

"W-what the hell are you doing?"

I wouldn't need a haunted house after all. After that shock, I'm pretty sure my face was white.

"What?" Eric mercilessly ruffled my hair. "I made it better."

I looked around for witnesses, but no one seemed to have noticed anything. People around us were going about their business, oblivious to Eric's slyness. He had gotten away with it.

"I told you to stop playing around!" I said in a murderous voice.

"Don't be like that!" He pouted. "I owed you one anyway."

"What?"

"You blew me a kiss earlier, didn't you?"

My shoulders sagged. "Oh." So, he had seen *that*. "I… I was distracted. I was thinking of my sister."

Eric furrowed his brow, then laughed. "Anyway, I told you I wasn't scared to kiss a guy."

Oh, that's what it was about. Of course, it was. Still, he had gotten his revenge; the spot where his lips touched my skin was sizzling.

"Now it's your turn," he said.

"My turn?"

"You hurt my nose earlier. With that!" He pointed at my book.

You dog. Just wait to see who you were messing with. The shock from your kiss only helped me collect myself. Your loss.

"Yeah… I did," I said, biting my lip. "Do you want me to make it better?"

He nodded with fervour.

Ah! As if I'd let that happen. I leaned forward. His face split into a triumphant grin, but at the last moment, it's my book that I pressed on the tip of his nose instead of my lips.

"What the...?"

"See? All better."

Eric wrinkled his nose. "No." His hand seized one end of the book. "I wanted you to make it better, not the book."

"Tough luck," I said, tugging at the other end.

Using his muscles, he pulled harshly. The book ended up in his hand, and I almost slammed into his chest. Naturally, I scrambled up to my feet in fear.

I had always considered myself a pretty reasonable person, a cold-blooded pragmatist. Today I was the opposite, a mere thread away from turning into a criminal. I looked down at Eric in agony. His eyes had gone strangely dark.

"Why must you always torment me?" I wiped my brow with the back of my hand.

"Why must you speak like an old guy wearing a monocle and a top hat?"

"Why?" I asked again, snarling.

"Because…" Eric tilted his head. "It's fun."

"I get it, but why me?" I picked up my book. "Can't you play with someone else?"

"Don't want to." He turned momentarily serious. "We're gonna have to rehearse that scene, whether you want it or not."

"I know!" But if we did that now in the state I was in, it would become a mess. "Later, okay? You should enjoy your time at the beach." I used my hands to shake the sand off my swimming trunks.

"I am," Eric said.

"Good."

"Zak, I like your swimming trunks."

"Okay."

"Zak."

"What now?"

"You have such a great ass."

Eric dropped this anvil on my virgin skull without warning, and I staggered back in shock. Eric didn't see my shock, because his eyes were on my ass.

I was used to his teasing, but now his eyes were searing. I saw with horror that he actually *meant it*. The sun had finally gotten to him, burnt a hole straight through his head. Unexpectedly, Eric flung his hand toward my butt.

"Can I touch it?"

"What??" I jumped back with an unseemly yelp. "No!"

Eric fell flat on his stomach, his hand still stretched out. "Let me touch it!"

I looked at him, bewildered. "You are so slutty!"

"I never tried to deny it!" he sobbed, flexing his hand helplessly. "Please! I've been alone for so long!"

"It's only been a week!"

He pounded the floor twice with his fist, his eyes red.

I clenched my own fists and drew a sharp breath. "I'm going for a walk."

"Hey, wait!"

"Get lost!"

I ran away from him before my body betrayed me and he could see my burning cheeks. In vain, I rubbed my face raw. Tears of embarrassment gathered at the corners of my eyes.

If only we had been alone…

I would have let him do it.

I would have succumbed to his unbearable teasing. That was the cold-hearted truth. I had wanted to feel his hands on me just as I had begun to crave his lips. I sure knew how to make a fool of myself. I thought I had experienced it all with Alberto, but I had no idea I could feel this way, as though my insides were being stirred around with a cruel ladle.

Kicking the sand beneath my feet only made me more frustrated, the voice in my head asking annoying, relentless questions. What would happen if you let him touch you? Just once… What if you say yes the next time he teases you? Then what?

Was this weird feeling in my loins worth losing the best friend I'd gotten in years? Was I really a hopeless guy who was attracted to everyone? Or was it just a spur-of-the-moment crush induced by summer and Eric's games? What would it take to find out?

For all our sakes, I decided it would be best to rehearse this kissing scene after all.

21

KISS ME LIKE YOU MEAN IT

The return home was silent.

Camille and Arthur were cuddling in the back of the car, with myself pressed against the window to give them space, staring at Eric's neck seated in front of me.

"I guess you ran out of energy, then," Michael said.

Eric didn't answer.

"Don't want to sing anymore?" Michael glanced over his shoulder at us. "Anyone?" Seeing my face, he smiled and turned on the radio.

Everyone was tired after a day at the beach, but Eric was acting completely different since I'd left him. This was making it difficult to ask him to rehearse after dinner, but it also was a relief to have my thoughts to myself for once. And what thoughts they were.

When I left Eric, I didn't walk that far. From my spot in the distance, I saw him get up to join Camille and Arthur in the water. I didn't want to return yet, so I stood there motionlessly, and that's when I saw Alberto walking over to me, alone. I didn't think he was seeking me. More likely, he was returning from his own stroll, and seeing me alone, hesitated to stop by me or not. I knew he wouldn't. After so many months throwing myself in his way, he'd never given me a second look. But today, his steps were unsure as he was making his decision. Eventually, he decided and came to a stop at my side, with the wind ruffling through his shirt and his hair. He held his sunglasses in his graceful hands, and in the bright sunlight, I could see how cool his eyes were.

Alberto's silence was really surprising after two weeks of Eric's banter and childish laughter. Though I could appreciate it, having him near me and not sharing words seemed absurd and a little frightening. So, I decided to do something I truly hated, and engaged in small talk.

"You're not with the others?"

And that's why I usually never bothered.

Alberto's lip twitched. "No."

Good answer.

After that botched attempt, I expected him to leave, but he stayed put. With one hand, he attempted to discipline his hair, but with that seaside breeze, it was a lost cause.

God, he was beautiful. Glowing in the sunlight. A living, breathing piece of art.

"I saw you were reading earlier."

Alberto nodded and showed me his book. *No Exit*, by Sartre. "I saw you reading too."

He did? He was looking at me, then? Despite my best intentions, my heart skipped a beat. Stay calm, I told myself. Alberto is just chatting with you. Nothing to lose your cool over. I turned my head toward the spot where Eric, Camille, and Arthur were swimming. They seemed to be talking. I wondered if their conversation went easier than mine. Probably.

"Do you like it?" I asked to get Alberto going a little.

"I'm only at the beginning."

"Oh."

Alberto was reading the same book while lounging at the pool days ago. He hadn't made any progress since. However, I shouldn't be too surprised. We were all particularly busy here.

I showed him my book. He only glanced briefly at the cover.

"We had to read that back in September."

"I know. It just became my favourite book."

"I found the endless description of women's clothing really annoying." Alberto's tone was neutral, and yet there was an edge of coolness to it.

Well, we didn't have to agree on everything. And perhaps he was right. There was a lot of *that* in the book. I had a tendency to skip over them to get to the good parts — but that was my fifth reading this year alone.

"Which one's your favourite?"

Alberto cocked an eyebrow. "My favourite book?"

"Yes."

He thought about it for a moment. Then when it seemed that he found it, he merely shrugged. "I don't know."

There wasn't much to say after that. But he didn't look like he wanted to leave. His eyelids fluttered shut. After a moment, I wondered if he hadn't fallen asleep while standing.

While I stood, immobile, watching him, I came to a strange realisation: After the rollercoaster my nerves were subjected to earlier when I was near the hotheaded Eric, being around Alberto was like stepping into a refreshing pool of spring water.

"You have such a calming presence, Alberto." His head snapped toward me, his eyes wide with surprise. I had never seen him that way, and inadvertently revealed a smile. "I mean it too."

Alberto blinked while staring at the spot where Camille was now screaming with laughter. "I have something to tell you."

My heart thumped. I forced myself to sound normal. "What is it?"

Alberto sucked lightly on the tip of his sunglasses' temples; my eyes were drawn to the sight. After a while, he spoke, "I said Michael and his guy were having problems. But it seems I was wrong."

"Oh…" Not that I was expecting anything, but still, I didn't expect that. "You weren't that wrong. They were having communication problems. They sorted it, however."

"Yes." Alberto's face relaxed, his gaze turned absent. With a flick of his wrist, he unfolded his sunglasses and pushed them up his nose. "I'll see you later, then." His Italian accent lingered on every syllable, turning them irresistible.

Alberto, why! He was such a mystery, and soulless or not, it was impossible for me not to be drawn to him. Walking away into the distance, his linen shirt flapping with the wind, the sunglasses giving him an air of a perfume advertising model. It seemed that, to me, Alberto would always be Alberto.

When I returned to our group, Binta and Duvo were rounding us up to depart. Everyone looked tired and contented, but no one looked more spent than Eric, who acted like he was coming down hard from a sugar rush. Without a word, he got dressed and gathered his stuff and was so limp Michael had to help him to the car.

When we arrived home, I thought to ask him about rehearsing our

301

last scene, but he stuck to Michael like a shadow, and the two disappeared inside the house.

"What's wrong with him?" I asked Arthur as we followed.

Arthur yawned at length before answering. "I guess even Eric gets tired sometimes."

Eric remained that way all through dinner, not responding to anything, his chin in his hand, not even sparing one glance at our table. A feeling of dread filled me gradually. Was it me? Was it because I told him to get lost when he tried to touch me?

In theory, I had every right to be mad at him. Eric was slutty, but he also probably knew he crossed a line. He had no idea I was attracted to him, so he *should* be assuming I was the one who was mad at him. Perhaps he really was simply tired, as Arthur suggested. I'd have to ask him at campfire after dinner, then.

Eager to speak to him as everyone settled around the fire, I was disappointed not to find him. Kayvin and Xavier were there, so where was he? Annoyed, I took a seat at random and was shortly after joined by Camille, Arthur, Nadia, and Charles-Henry.

It was merry around the fire, with the girls singing songs to pass the time, and Xavier struggling to plug his own iPod into the portable speakers. My gaze kept returning to the doors, anxious to see Eric again. Then I felt someone sliding next to me. Relieved, I turned around and my smile froze: It was Alberto. Apparently, there was no other space to sit. Sander was sandwiched between Melissa and Joy and seemed like he had no intention of moving.

Still, to have Alberto so close and so still next to me was what you could call a surprise. Of course, he didn't speak. He was absently listening to the girls' performance while watching Xavier struggle with his iPod. Typing on his phone, Kayvin did nothing to help. Eventually, Alberto let out a sigh and, feeling my eyes on him, abruptly turned his head. His face in the dusky light was a thing of beauty. The flames reflected in his cold pupils gave them such intensity, he almost looked demon-like. I stared blankly, at a loss for words, then said out of nowhere, "have you seen Eric?"

Twice, he blinked. "I saw him in the kitchen with Michael."

"With Michael?"

"They were doing the dishes."

"They what?"

The first notes of a popular pop song coming from the speakers informed me that Xavier had successfully plugged in his iPod, commanding our attention. Joy, Melissa, and Nadia rose from their seats and began performing the song while dancing, and the campfire was suddenly transformed into a show.

Alberto watched the girls' efforts without interest. Camille and Arthur scrambled to their feet and abandoned me, saying they were going for a little midnight stroll. I envied them; it seemed easy enough for them to flirt and fool around and steal kisses in the middle of the night. Meanwhile, I had one definite crush on my left and a potential other doing dishes in the kitchen, and no idea what to do about any of them.

When the song was over, some clapped, some cheered, and Joy walked over to us to grab a bottle of water. "So? Did you like it?" she asked with a glowing smile.

Alberto stifled a yawn. "You got the lyrics wrong."

"No way." Her smile faded. "Did we?"

Alberto nodded. "You said *Boy, you really got me bad.*"

"And?"

"It's not *Boy*, it's *Girl*."

"That's it?" Joy's expression was full of contempt. "I guess you really like this song."

"I don't. I'm just correcting your mistake."

Joy looked like she wanted to correct the mistake that was Alberto, but her face transformed when she spotted something over our heads.

"Eric! Eric!" She bounced on her feet. "Did you like it?"

"It was great!" Eric, beaming, almost trampled Alberto to get to Joy. "I love this song!"

"I know!" She squeezed his wrists. "You sing it all the time. That's why I chose it. But apparently, you got the lyrics wrong."

Eric gently moved her aside. "Why did you do that when I was doing dishes in the kitchen?" He looked crestfallen. "I've only seen the end. It sucks!"

"It was only a rehearsal. We'll do it again tomorrow — *with* the right lyrics, this time," she hissed at Alberto. He merely shrugged, and Eric plopped down beside me.

The whole time, I had been watching this exchange with a thumping heart. Now that Eric was by my side, I exhaled a shaky breath: I was sandwiched between Alberto and Eric. It was almost like the romantic plot of a cheesy movie. But at least Eric was by my side again.

"Speaking of..." he whispered.

"Yes?"

"Rehearsal, now."

"Now?"

Eric's eyes were glinting in the firelight. "If not now, then when?"

His words made my limbs turn soft. I bit my tongue to recollect myself. "You're right. We're almost out of time."

We could perhaps slip out unnoticed and rehearse once or twice before everybody went to bed. I looked around the fire for Duvo and Binta.

"Don't look for them." Eric had read my mind. "I passed them on the way out. They were going to the back to look for board games."

I spoke in a cautious tone. "I don't think they're actually looking for board games."

Eric's eyes widened. "Zak! You're starting to get it! What happened to your innocence?"

"You," I mumbled.

He snorted, and my heart swelled. So relieved was I to see him smile again and feel the heat of his arm as it brushed against mine, that I didn't care who saw, who heard, or who noticed what. When I left the comfort of the fire to follow Eric into the darkness, I didn't hesitate, pausing only once to throw a tentative look over my shoulder at a yawning Alberto. I was moving in automatic mode, following only an odd, deep-seated instinct which told me to be around Eric at any cost. The house, the grounds, everything looked different, almost mystical in the dark. It filled me with a thrill. I felt strange, ecstatic, in love with the place, the moon smiling over our heads, the trees standing tall and strong like benevolent guardians, the vigilant owls watching us soundlessly.

"It's beautiful," I said breathlessly.

The sleepy lake's surface reflected the moon and the expanse of stars overhead. The cool, fragrant scent of wild grass filled the air. I turned to Eric when he didn't answer. I guess he wasn't too good at effusions of the sort. He just stood there, looking at me.

I didn't want to speak first. He was so quiet, it was intimidating. The last time we spoke, I told him to get lost. Now we were here, back on our familiar turf, and I was wringing my hands, wondering how I really felt about him.

"Are you still upset?" he asked.

"Me?"

He was so very serious. I took a few steps away toward the bank. He didn't follow me.

"I was just playing around, you know…"

Oh. He was talking about his flirting earlier. He did assume that I was mad after all. If only he knew… But this was a good opportunity to settle that problem once and for all. I had come here to rehearse and use this as an excuse to get a kiss from him so I could move on and get my shit together. Without his constant teasing, it would be easier for me to keep my cool and my feelings in check and perform my role normally for our final scene tomorrow. After this, it didn't matter what would happen; after this, I could go home and rest. I wouldn't have to see so much of him. He was only a distraction. I'd be fine again in no time.

"You were unrelenting," I said, not looking at him. "I got tired of it."

I heard him sigh. "I'm so sorry. I thought you were having fun."

"I wasn't, not really." My heel dug into the grass.

"I'll stop." He sounded anxious.

"It's best if you do, honestly."

"I totally, totally understand."

No, you don't understand, I thought. But it was all the same. It was done.

"Okay," I said, turning to him and forcing a smile. "Let's do this."

Eric looked completely wretched, his fingers digging into my arms.

"I like you… and then I don't. You make me ache for something I didn't know existed until now. At times I don't want it, I admit it. Other times I feel thrilled and alive. All thanks to you."

My knees weakened. The words were too much. I had to sit, or kneel, or slump on the ground entirely. Either way, my body urged me to give up and give in. But I stayed true and standing. The despair in Eric's eyes was like a spear plunging through my chest, shattering my ribs and bursting open my heart. I opened my mouth…

"And then they kiss," I said, breaking the scene. With a tired groan, I collapsed on the grass.

We were done.

"Then they kiss," Eric repeated, looking down at his messy scribbled-over script. "And then——"

"Would you have kissed him?" I asked suddenly.

Eric blinked. "What?"

"Arthur, earlier. Would you have kissed him?"

Eric's eyebrows drew together as he attempted to recall that thing he did a million years ago — from his point of view.

"Ah, that! A peck, maybe. Nothing further than that." It looked like he wanted to add something, but he didn't. From the corner of my eye, I watched him sit with a straight back at a respectful distance from me, and I felt a sharp twang of annoyance.

Twice we repeated the scene, and not once did he take the initiative of throwing himself at me as the script suggested. Now that he was feeling awful about what happened at the beach, he didn't want to touch me at all? I felt wronged.

I felt really wronged!

What was I supposed to do? Since when did he listen to me when I ordered him to stop messing around? It was infuriating. He looked like a contest-winning dog, all good and obedient, sitting a safe distance from me, while I was almost panting with my tongue out, internally screaming: Kiss me, kiss me, kiss me!

I couldn't take the initiative; since my character did not in the scene. So how could I get him to kiss me without sounding desperate? Now that our roles were reversed, I couldn't imagine myself lunging at him to tickle his ribs or ruffle his hair. So out of character.

I'd have to do it my way. With *words*.

After a little cough, I said in a cautious tone, "We didn't do it."

Eric's eyebrows knitted together. "Do what?"

"The kiss."

"Ah." He flashed me a nervous smile. "I didn't feel like… I didn't see the need for that."

Oh, suddenly he didn't see the need for that! The moment I was desperate for him to unleash his inner slut, he went all virginal on me. It was going all wrong. *Do something!* my own newly inflamed shameless voice hissed in my head. *You're both here, alone, under the moonlight, at the edge of a sleepy lake. The setting is so romantic that if you don't do it, your heroine Denise will rise from her fictional hero's grave to pound you with her fists.*

I pushed the slutty voice into a dark corner of my mind and slammed the door in its face. "We already kissed," I said in an offhanded tone.

"That was a peck." Eric sounded tired. "Your aunt probably gave you better kisses."

I glanced at him. "Hum... Is there something you want to tell me about your aunt?"

"What? No!" He dipped his head, and I assumed he was laughing quietly into his knees. "I'm just saying, this sort of kiss won't get you *Best Actor*, that's for sure."

It was my first kiss, show some respect! But that wasn't the point right now.

"But listen, we talked about th—"

"Are you really not nervous?" Eric cut me off, pulling chunks of grass with his bare hands. "I'm joking about it, but I'm nervous, you know." He looked up. "You... you..."

His admission only triggered a wave of affection for him. Of course, he was nervous to kiss a guy. He was straight after all. And I was nervous too, for very different reasons. It was perfect for me. I didn't even have to lie.

"Of course, I am," I admitted. "It has to be perfect."

His gaze turned earnest. "Yeah, that's the thing!"

"The movie—"

"The movie—"

"Has to be—"

"Perfect! Clearly!"

... Clearly.

For a long time, we stared at each other in silence. It's like he was waiting for me to make a decision, as the veteran actor of the two. And on my side, I was pretending to think about it, while in fact, I already knew I would be kissing this guy tonight.

"It's decided, then!" I sounded pro enough. "We have to do it." I stole back a glance. His hand had flown to his neck and was rubbing it furiously.

"... I guess so." Getting up, Eric inexplicably began stretching and jumping in place. "So, how do we do that?"

"I assumed with our lips," I said drily. "What are you doing? Preparing for penalties?"

I expected him to snort, but Eric answered with a grunt and dropped down on his knees opposite me. I assumed the same position. Suddenly each of our movements seemed difficult and clunky, as though our bodies had grown tenfold in size.

Why was this so difficult? He seemed to be asking himself the same question, from the way he was frowning at me.

"But..." he began. "I..."

"What is it?" I snapped, impatient to get to the kissing part.

Eric wrinkled his nose. "Do you even find me attractive?"

My shoulders sank. What was he getting at? This wasn't the time to be fishing for compliments. It took a lot of self-control not to shout *No!* just to punish him for the magnitude of confusing emotions I was feeling for him. It took an equal amount of control not to admit I had grown to find him impossibly handsome.

So I glared. I was really good at glaring. If I glared hard enough, he wouldn't notice my flushed cheeks. "We're actors. What difference does it make?"

He blinked. "God, you are brutal at times."

"Thank you."

"Why are you assuming I'm complimenting you?" Eric's face was still scrunched-up, afflicting him with a serious case of cuteness which only made everything more difficult.

"I don't know!" I shouted in a broken voice.

Why are you talking so much! I was on the brink of despair, hating every second spent without his lips on mine, and he was blabbering on and on!

But he wasn't supposed to know that. If I didn't pull myself together, he would know I was attracted to him. If that happened, I was screwed.

"Come on," I spoke, more gently, "let's get it over with, okay?"

I hoped my words would convince him that I wasn't as desperate as I felt. It seemed to work. After a loose shrug, Eric drew closer. I'm pretty sure I shivered. I didn't know where to put my hands, so I pressed them to the ground and looked severely at him.

"Don't move," Eric said, his voice low.

Since he was technically the expert, and because I loved the authority in his voice, I obeyed. Our eyes met, and I read nothing but determination in his. I tried to match his look, lest he could feel the turmoil inside me. His face approached mine; I fought the urge to laugh hysterically. He stopped inches from my lips.

"Kiss me like you mean it."

I threw my head back in protest. "I will. I'm an actor."

He smiled. "I'm not."

Then he kissed me.

Fear, suspense, thrill, a little bit of wonder. As my heart pounded in my ears, a lot of things went on in my head at the same time. But mostly, and annoyingly, Alberto.

And just as I was sweeping him out of my head, it was over. Eric was already leaning away, smacking his lips as though it was business as usual to kiss people at midnight on the edge of a lake. I sat there, numb, feeling cruelly disenchanted.

That… That was it?

How… boring!

After such suspense and expectation… How disappointing really, barely any better than the peck he gave me at the party. In fact, it had been so short and so chaste that I didn't even get to enjoy myself. And I blurted it out. "It was… chaste."

"Chaste?" Eric sat at a healthy distance, his hands neatly folded on his knees, a picture of innocence. Where was the wild animal who made a pass at my ass mere hours ago? I kept pressing the bell, but no one was answering. Hello, can we get some service over here??

"Yes, probably too chaste." I picked up the script. "The script clearly says the word *passion*. There was no passion at all."

"Oh, right." Eric gave a thoughtful nod. "No passion."

I tossed the script over my shoulder. "That's not going to cut it. We can definitely do better." After a pause, I added, "… I think."

There was a silence. I pretended to cough to conceal the loudest heartbeats ever recorded in history. Could he feel it? That I was leading him on? I waited with bated breath.

"Okay. Let's do better," he said eventually.

Eric rubbed the back of his skull with both hands and began crawling toward me. I dared not move but watched his movements closely, straining my eyes. When he got near enough, he put his hand on my waist, removed it, replaced it with a frown, and looked up at me.

"Yes, that's fine," I encouraged him.

He straightened, shook his hair back, cleared his throat. "It will probably be less awkward during the shoot."

I nodded while thinking: We can only hope so. This time, I met him halfway. Open lips met open lips. Our breaths intertwined.

Bumpy. It was bumpy. I closed my eyes, tried to relax. This time I had a better grasp of how soft his lips were, how carefully they brushed against mine, the faint scent of the strawberries we had for dessert on his breath. Something flickered in my chest, sparks flared across different parts of my body, igniting a trail of lights along my tingling spine. I began to feel strangely hot, and before long, my breathing was accelerating. I didn't think it was normal. Afraid of what he might think of me, I broke away first.

Eric leaned back in silence. Despite my fear that he could read my flushed face like an open book, I couldn't help raising my head. His eyes were darker than the night.

"Better," he said.

"Better." I nodded. "Much better."

Eric sighed and lay on his back, looking done and happy with it. I dipped my head to catch my breath in silence.

That was it, then. Enough. I got what I wanted, and I knew what to expect tomorrow at least. I could relax a little; I knew what he tasted like now. I just hoped I would keep my cool when he would kiss me after uttering Camille's heartbreaking words.

With time, I had become more and more amazed at how collected Thomas, my character, was throughout the film. How he did not beg Adam to kiss him senseless right there in the drawing room was becoming more and more baffling to me. In the past, Alberto naturally drew some physical reactions from me. But when it came to Eric... I found that it was like I didn't know my own body after all. Why else did I abandon all reason and lured Eric into kissing me by pretending to rehearse? It was done. That's what it felt like to be kissed, really kissed. We had done it.

My spine was still tingling. I swiped my tongue over my lip in an attempt to retain a hint of strawberry. It was already gone. I pushed my disappointment down. Another kiss would have been too much. Ridiculous, even. We didn't need — *I* didn't need another kiss.

But then Eric's voice rang in the night, and my whole body sprang to attention.

"But, hum…"

"Yes?"

Eric propped himself on his elbow. "I don't know, you tell me."

His face was serious. None of the usual teasing, the sly grin, the mockery with which he usually drove me insane. Whatever spoke using my voice was not me.

"It was a bit lacking, wasn't it?" I was possessed. This was the only explanation.

"I guess you could say there was something…"

"Something was definitely missing." And it kept talking, apparently. Unchecked. I threw a nonchalant look at the script I had tossed aside earlier. "The scene clearly is all about longing and despair… that's what I read when I see the word *passion*."

"More passion, then?" He hesitated. "I mean… It wouldn't hurt to try."

"Yes, yes, I agree. We can try."

Eric returned to his initial position on his knees. On the outside, I appeared perfectly composed. On the inside, I was throwing a triumphant fist in the air, thanking Eric for his unwavering professionalism when it came to rehearsing.

One last kiss, then. It wouldn't be hard at all. Looking at Eric, I didn't need any inspiration to brew a little passion.

I stretched out my hands; they were feeling stiff. He rubbed his own against his folded thighs. Then he returned his palm to my waist.

"Here goes," he said.

But he didn't move, just gazed at me with a startled expression. I waited, and waited, and waited…

Then I clicked my tongue.

"Do you always pause like that before you shoot, or—hmph!"

I never had the chance to finish. Eric's hand flew around my neck and yanked me to him. Our lips collided. I lost balance and fell flat on my back. Eric collapsed on top of me, his lips seemingly glued to mine. The sudden weight of his body cut off my breath. Seeking something to hold, I found the front of his shirt and twisted it in my fist.

Eric's kiss turned more assertive. One of his hands moved to my shoulder and pressed it down. But I had no intention of going anywhere. I followed his lead, my lips dancing against his own. My grip over his shirt slowly relaxed, while my other hand clutched a handful of grass. A shard of sky was visible from the corner of my eye; a sea of stars shimmered over my head; soft grass tickled my exposed flesh. I shivered when Eric's thumb grazed the bare skin of my waist. My legs gradually parted on their own.

Eric's breathing intensified. He increased the pressure on my nape and pulled me closer. My hand released his shirt and snaked around his neck. All the tension in my body left me, and I turned soft and loose. The feeling of a burning tongue, slowly skimming along my lips, then nudging itself inside, elicited from me a sound of surprise. With clumsiness and avidity, I lapped at this soft intrusion. Eric gave a small sigh; his fingers dug into the flesh of my waist. The onslaught of sensations robbed me of every sensible thought, making my spine sizzle, quickly turning me into a panting, gasping wreck. Only one vague notion remained: I had to stop this before I did something I'd regret. But I was paralysed, filled with the certitude that nothing in the world could feel better than this.

Then his hips moved.

A frail whimpering sound like that of a wounded animal escaped my mouth. Something shifted in the dark. The grass trapped in my fist ripped with a crunching sound.

In an instant, the spell was broken.

Tearing myself from my trance, I gathered what was left of my strength in my hands and pushed against Eric's chest with all my might. He fell on his backside.

I sat up. My legs were too weak to stand. It felt like all my muscles had turned to jelly, in contrast to a certain part of myself that had become unmentionably stiff. I could only turn away from him and work on regulating my breath, incoherent thoughts swirling around my head, making me dizzy.

What just happened? Did he feel that? Seeing how my hands were shaking, I hugged my knees to hide them.

"Zak?" Eric's voice was hoarse.

I decided not to meet his eyes. Possibly forever.

"Did I hurt you?" He sounded worried.

"No."

But also, yes. A little. There, inside my chest.

"Are you sure?"

"I'm fine!" I snapped.

But I wasn't. My lips were swollen and numb. My skin was burning, seething at me for putting an end to this. It felt so good. Why did it feel so good? I had spent days mocking Eric for acting slutty, when the real problem here was me all along. Launching myself at a straight guy this time. How could I be that stupid twice in a row? I really had a knack for falling for unavailable men.

Eric waited in silence while I pulled myself together. I couldn't look at him, so I had no idea what he could be thinking. Just how much of this kiss was rehearsing and how much of it was him enjoying himself? I couldn't tell and I couldn't ask. I could only assume it was a little bit of both. He said it himself; he had been single for too long.

As of now, he stood in silence like a good boy. He wasn't teasing or making fun of me. That meant he hadn't noticed anything alarming while we were kissing. Our friendship was still safe, then. With a sigh of relief, I rubbed my hands over my face. I could still fix this. I just had to act indifferent. I casually returned the conversation to the movie.

"We can't do that during the scene tomorrow." I sounded serious. "We're not making *Brokeback Mountain*."

"What's that?"

What's…? I could strangle him, I swear. "Do you even watch movies?!"

Eric threw up his hands. "All right! Chaste, then."

I stared at these hands in disbelief. A minute ago they were touching me, leaving burning handprints over my waist and shoulder. I forced myself to draw a long breath. I was an aspiring actor. I could pretend my way out of this mess.

"No," I said. "But probably something in between."

Eric made a salute sign. "Noted." His face scrunched up again. "Are you sure you're all right? You look—"

"Let's just go."

I slammed my hands down and pushed myself up. Eric rose after me. From the corner of my eye, I could see he looked concerned. Perhaps he was wondering if I would tell people, alert the authorities about how he ended up on top of me. After all, he'd already begged to touch my butt earlier today. With that thought, I couldn't stop the corner of my lip from curling up.

It looked like we both made interesting discoveries tonight. Despite his claims to be nervous about kissing guys, once he got going, Eric had no qualms about pinning them under him to get to business. As for me, I really enjoyed being held down by him, and who knows what I would have allowed him to get away with if I'd known him to actually like me. He made the word *passionate* seem stale in comparison to how I felt when his tongue brushed against mine. I had to shake my head ruthlessly to smother the memory.

Eric rubbed the back of his neck again, a nervous grin spoiling his handsome face. "I'm sorry, Zak, really…"

"Why?" My brow furrowed. "I told you I was fine."

"Earlier, you…" He snuck a glance at me. "Anyway… You know me, I always get carried away."

There was no need for him to scramble up for needless words. I knew he was the kind to get carried away; I liked that about him. I liked a lot of things about him. Too many. Except for one thing.

He liked girls more than he liked me.

Staring at his face all twisted with worry, I gave a long sigh. "At least tomorrow, it will be over."

I was thinking about my turmoil, but when I saw Eric's eyes widen,

I noticed I'd spoken out loud. It would have been suspicious to try to justify myself now, so I said nothing. We stared at each other for what seemed to be an infinite time. Finally, Eric broke our stalemate and the silence with a scrunched up expression.

"I'm tired."

I heard a rustling sound nearby. Above our heads, an owl took flight. With a twinge in my heart, I made a silent prayer for its unlucky prey.

22

THE FINAL TAKE

There was a special atmosphere in the house the next morning. Excitement filled the air. Everybody was a little on edge.

The final take, at last.

For some of us, the final kiss.

Duvo expected it to take all day to get right. Michael agreed, but only because he had to reshoot everything Duvo did himself.

To my surprise, Eric was sitting at our table when I came down, facing Camille and Arthur, a focused look on his face. I wondered if this was his pre-football game expression and smiled. When he licked his lips, I bit mine harshly before I became swamped with memories from last night. I wanted to be kissed by him, and it happened. Now I needed to move on if I didn't want to find myself friendless again.

"So, what did you two end up doing last night?" Camille asked, pouring milk over her cereals. "We saw you leave together."

"We finally kissed," Eric said, his chin in his hand.

I spat a bit of milk back into my spoon and swallowed noisily. Arthur wasn't so good: Milk sprayed out of his mouth sprinkler-style, splattering Eric's cheek, hair, and T-shirt. Eric picked up a napkin and dabbed himself.

"Baby, learn to control yourself."

Arthur grinned stupidly. "Look who's talking."

"You were rehearsing, I assume?" Camille said innocently enough.

"Of course!" I snapped, since no one seemed to pay attention to me. "Why else would we be kissing!" I stabbed my cereal with my spoon, furious at Eric for using such a casual tone when describing my life-shattering experience from last night.

"Heartbreaker," Eric said, kicking my leg under the table.

My fist tightened around my spoon. "That's enough."

"Anyway, Camille. It's done. We kissed, and Zak was no prude."

"Eric," I spoke in a warning tone.

Arthur began cackling like an old witch. I silenced him with a glare.

"Not gonna lie," Camille said, her cheeks pink, "I was kind of worried. Duvo is worse. He's counting on you to fall apart. It's sad."

I huffed haughtily. "Don't know why you all assume I'm some sort of delicate flower or that I can't do my job. I'll kiss you as many times as the director demands it," I added with an angry side glance at Eric. "You can count on that."

Eric whistled. "Fair enough."

"Don't you make him angry before the take," Arthur said, his mouth full.

"You're right, sorry." Camille cleared her throat. "I'm very happy to hear you were kissing yesterday." She spoke slowly, as though addressing some two-year-olds. "How was he, Eric?"

Eric shrugged, hurling a ten-foot spear straight into my fragile ego. But of course, he had had countless experiences. Meanwhile, it was technically my first kiss. Or one of them. It slowly dawned on me that Eric was somehow responsible for each of my firsts:

1) First peck
2) First (very) proper, closed lips kiss
3) First open lips kiss
4) First French kiss

Bonus: First mind-blowing bodily reaction which occurred when — *Hush*. It was a secret.

And… we were not even dating.

That was it! I truly felt pathetic.

First item on my to-do list for September was to get myself a proper gay boyfriend to kiss at any hour to remove the lingering humiliation. *And to get more of that tingly spiny sensation...* said the slutty voice in my head.

It wasn't even 9 a.m., I really needed a boyfriend.

Eric annoyingly put his banana peel into my empty bowl before rising from the table. "I've got to get ready. See you soon."

He walked off, his gaze absent, reminding me of Alberto. Staring after him, Arthur gave an evil snigger. "Eric's so out of it this morning."

"What do you mean?" Camille said.

"He's all nervous, isn't he?" Arthur's eyes glinted. "And earlier I found him in the bathroom, his head in the clouds and his toothpaste falling off his toothbrush. Five times, I called him. I had to shake my hand in front of his face to get his attention."

"Perhaps he didn't get enough sleep," Camille said.

I jerked back in horror. "Not my fault!"

"…" Camille blinked. "No one said that."

I felt myself blushing for no reason.

"I'm also going to make sure my set-up is ready," Arthur said. "Wouldn't want to fuck up this scene. Must be perfect." His gaze lingered on Camille, who was busy eating spoonfuls of cereal with a happy look on her face.

"You two should date," I said when he was out of earshot.

She raised her eyebrows. "That came out of nowhere."

"Sorry. It's just a thing I felt I had to say."

With my failures in love, defined by my fruitless obsessions towards Alberto and Eric, Arthur had no choice but to become my Denise, and Camille my Mr Mouret. Considering how well they were matched, how obvious it was they liked each other, and that their bloody sexuality was compatible, then for all of our sakes, they had to end up together and bring a happy ending to this absolute mess of a summer trip.

Camille smiled. "Why do you think that?"

"It's obvious you have awesome chemistry." I drummed my finger along the table. "Also, he's a great admirer of your work. That's like… the best compliment you can possibly get."

Camille stared dreamily after Arthur, who could be seen in the corridor squeezing Eric's biceps in plain view of everyone. "He's rather nice. And funny. And sweet." She turned her gaze back to me, a teasing smile on her face. "And what about you?"

"W-what about me?"

Her unexpected question made me break out in a cold sweat. Camille had the air of someone who knew a valuable secret.

"Don't think we didn't notice yesterday…"

"Notice what?"

"We all saw Alberto talking to you at the beach."

"Oh!" Relief flooded through me. They didn't see Eric kiss my chin or make a grab at my ass. Success! "It was nothing. Just a few words."

Camille looked thoughtful. "Alberto never spares the energy of a few words for no reason. Or so I heard."

"I'm sure it's nothing."

And I meant it, too. I was done with my disillusions. Alberto, or Eric, they were both fantasies after all.

There were people like Eric who were made to pollinate the world, going from flower to flower. And there were people like me who should never get involved with other people. Too intense to have fun, too shallow to not be swept away by looks, too awkward to get to know people even on the surface.

At least I had chosen the perfect career. I'd live the life of countless lovers without having to become one. In the end, wasn't that enough?

～

When I arrived on the set, I almost tripped over a light, earning myself a glare from Xavier, who had, in the end, discovered he cared about our little gay movie.

I then almost bumped into Eric, who apologised, so I apologised, and we both went to stand at opposite sides of the snacks table, where Nadia had kindly left a gallon of iced tea. I began frantically pouring myself cup after cup, barely careful not to slosh it all over my livery.

Despite my best hopes that it wouldn't, something seemed to have changed between Eric and me. Neither dared to look at the other in the eye. I guess that's what happens when you share a sweltering kiss with another guy. It's bound to feel a little awkward. With any luck, he might have a revelation about this sexuality and decide to date me.

…

…

…

And just when I woke up promising myself not to fall into delusions ever again. If anyone noticed, or worse, asked, I could surely attribute it to our nerves before the great scene. And my nerves, my nerves… They tingled and ached when I thought of what transpired last night.

Duvo was of course yelling at Michael, who had some time ago lost his qualms about pretending he wasn't the real director of the movie. Whether it was the camera angle or our acting directions, it had never been a smooth ride between those two. Of course, today, confronted with the importance of the scene, Duvo was losing his cool, and Michael was too invested now to let him play around and ruin the take.

"Just step aside, Laurent!" He sounded exasperated. "I know what I'm doing!"

"Why are you always acting like you're better qualified than me?"

Michael was biting his lip and looking like the next word that would come out of his mouth would either destroy his relationship with Duvo or the movie. Guess what he chose.

"Laurent," he said seriously. "I'm gay and you're not. Of course, I'm better qualified than you for this."

Duvo stepped back. "But... that's not... how it... works?"

But Camille was shaking her head. "So insensitive, sir."

"Seriously, Laurent..." Binta looked disappointed.

"Oh, for *censored* sake." Duvo threw up his hands. "Have it your way."

Duvo stomped toward the snacks table, and Binta had to stop him from stuffing an entire brownie into his mouth out of spite. I tiptoed toward Michael before he took notice of me.

"Michael... Did you just throw your gay card at Duvo?"

With a blinding smile, Michael bent over to look into the camera. "I did. You should learn that sort of skill, Zak. Might come in handy."

"Have you no shame?"

He chuckled. "Not when it comes to this movie."

Lifting my head, I saw Eric smiling teasingly at me. My heart stopped. I whirled around in a panic and landed straight into Alberto's arms.

"Ouch, sorry."

Alberto watched me pounce aside with a complicated look. "Good luck."

"Thanks, Alberto."

Camille's words came rushing back in my mind. It wasn't the time for this; I had to focus on the scene. I shook them away and stood on my mark. Eric stood on his. He looked stuffed in his fancy outfit.

"Nervous?" I asked, my heart pounding.

He exhaled a loud breath. Yeah. He was nervous.

"Don't forget to kiss me."

"I won't!" I protested. "But, wait. Aren't *you* supposed to kiss me?"

"Right." Eric frowned. His tongue darted out to lick the corner of his lip. "So, you think so? It's not very clear. It says 'Passion—"

"— overtakes them'. But it's him. It's him who started it… in the script."

"You're right. I got it." The tongue retreated, and I could breathe again.

Michael and Camille walked over to us, leaving behind a stunned Duvo to be comforted by Binta.

"I need to ask," Michael said. "Are you still comfortable with this? Both of you?"

I nodded, of course — too enthusiastically even — before Eric could do better and make me look like a fragile snowflake. So I was surprised when Eric spoke up.

"Actually… Could you get everyone out? Everyone who's not needed?" He scanned around the room. "Like Xavier, Kayvin, Joy, or… everyone?"

"No problem," Michael said gently, turning to Alberto.

"Get him out too," Eric said.

Michael hesitated. Alberto gave him a nod, then left the set without a word or a look back.

"Do you need me to leave as well?" Camille said. "Would that make you more comfortable?"

"No, no." Eric took her hands. "You stay. I'm doing this for you at this point." He gave a nervous laugh.

Watching him in that state was bemusing. To my surprise, in the face of Eric's agitation, I felt amazingly collected. Eric noticed and pursed his lips.

"How can you be so calm?"

"How can you not?" I flaunted my confidence now, in vengeance for how he made me lose my mind — and the feelings in my legs — last night. "We've been over this a million times."

I couldn't tell him the truth. That it was definitely the best idea to get the kissing out of the way yesterday. Neither of us died, and I could finally see things clearly — sort of — for once. That's how I could stay so calm.

"You're right." He laughed. "It's just…"

"What?"

"It's the last t—the last one."

"Aww." I gave him a sympathetic smile. "You'll shoot other scenes, you know."

Eric didn't have time to answer. Michael asked everyone left to be ready. I turned one last time to the camera, saw the comforting presence of Arthur hunched behind it. He gave me a thumbs-up.

"We're all here for you, guys."

Eric's nervous smile turned into a grimace, then slowly vanished from his face. His brow furrowed, his jaw clenched, his demeanour took on another dimension. Eric was gone, and I was staring at Adam. This was our break-up scene, where Thomas, afraid, attempts to sever the bond between them, only to finally surrender to his desire to Adam.

"We're too different, it will never work," I muttered to myself.

My lines. How appropriate.

Then I'd turn away from him and attempt to leave. He would run after me, despair in his eyes.

"You would leave without saying goodbye? Am I nothing to you?"

"Nothing to me? Nothing to me?" I would slowly fall apart. *"I've become obsessed with you. While you... Oh yes, you like me now. But in two days, two weeks, two months? What will happen to me when you tire of me?"*

"We can get away together. Leave this world, it's nothing to me, we could—"

And so on for a while. Despair would increase, then passion would overtake us, and we would kiss. I looked at the furniture around the room, realising with some shame I was hoping for more or less the kind of messy embrace we shared last night. The little writing desk, happily situated against the wall, would be the perfect spot. If I played my cards right, that's exactly where he would be kissing me.

"Everyone ready?"

Standing behind Arthur, Michael looked serious. Camille had her hands clasped together under her chin. On her left, Duvo was practically shaking to shout *Action*. I filled my lungs with air and exhaled slowly. The soft voice of Michael saying the word was just like a magical incantation, a spell being released. At once, sparks flew, the air on set sizzled with electricity.

～

It was over in a jiffy. Perhaps longer. Or shorter. Impossible to recall. At some point, I was vaguely aware of Eric improvising again, when he charged ahead and his fingers curled around my wrists. My thoughts weren't my thoughts exactly. I wasn't Zak; I was Thomas. The apprehension that battered through me was mixed with shameless excitement and a desire for these hands never to let me go.

"You can dress me up in your fancy clothes, but I'll always be me. I will never change," I said defiantly, returning to the script.

"But I don't want to change you!" Eric said, his eyes full of want and hurt and fire. "You're the one who changed me!"

That line wasn't in the script either; it was completely improvised. But this time, nothing could throw me off. On the contrary, it enthralled me. I felt Adam's desperation in my core, and tears welled up at the corner of my eyes. Eric's grip on my wrists intensified. Passion definitely spilt over, as the scrip intended. I was neither here nor there, my mind turning blank. But when I came to, the edge of the writing desk was digging into my back, my heart was pounding, my skin was boiling, and Duvo had leapt into Michael's arms and was kissing him with streaming eyes.

It was over. And the experience was so mystifying that I couldn't even remember it. I stumbled back when Duvo rushed to Eric and me to throw his arms around our necks. He was laughing and crying at the same time.

"Do you remember that time when I said you two had zero chemistry?"

"No," Eric said coyly.

"Oh, well... Perhaps it didn't happen at all." Duvo let go of me to squeeze Eric's shoulders. "You were both extraordinary. The whole set was bursting with tension. I'd never thought two kids would be able to pull it off."

Eric wrinkled his nose. "I'm not a kid."

"Ah, Eric, but you are." Eric freed himself from Duvo's grip, looking vexed. "Let me tell you. You really should join the Drama Club. You have to challenge Zak, or he'll turn into a diva."

Eric's features relaxed. After watching their exchange with an amused smile, I protested with a grimace. Everyone here seemed to have forgotten Alberto was my official challenger after all — including Alberto himself, who was back on set and staring oddly at me.

Xavier arrived to remove the lights. His eyes bright, he sauntered to Eric. "So did you two kiss? Did you?"

To both our surprise, Eric sighed impatiently and walked toward the exit. Pleased by people's compliments about our obvious chemistry on screen, I felt naughtier than my usual self and turned to Xavier on my way out.

"More than once," I said, enjoying his shocked expression.

The problem was, I didn't see in front of me and crashed straight into Kayvin. Mortified, I held up my hands. "Sorry!"

"As you should be," Kayvin said darkly, but none of this shit hurt me anymore. I beamed at him. He stared back, in shock, and I even caught a glimpse of accidental softening behind his frown.

I was feeling elated, full of energy. I knew I had delivered excellent work. Everything felt just right. At this instant, I could want for nothing more.

I ate back those words the instant I found Eric half-undressed in the changing room. His dimpled back, first revealed to me at the beach, would haunt many of my dreams for years to come.

"It's me," I said, though he could very well see me in the mirror.

Eric didn't react and continued to remove his clothes with his eyes down. He usually didn't give a shit about his modesty, but I did, so I went to remove my clothes behind the screen on the side. After a while, I began to think something was wrong. Why was he so silent? My excitement waned. Speaking from behind the screen, I forced my voice to sound teasing.

"So... you improvised again."

"I had to," his voice answered.

I stretched myself on my toes to catch a glimpse of him. He was hurriedly throwing a T-shirt over his head.

"Are you going to miss it?" I said to his reflection.

"Miss what?"

"Looking like a lord."

Eric looked at himself wearing his usual T-shirt and shorts and shook his head. "Not really. They must have been really uncomfortable most of the time." He abruptly turned on his heel to face me. "You should hurry."

"Why?"

"Just hurry!" His impatient tone startled me. "They're waiting outside."

"Fine, fine."

Like I cared about people waiting outside. I was still drunk on our success — so drunk that I had to fight against the urge to slump into Eric's arms and mess around with him. *Eric, haha, let's kiss again, just for laughs!* This could possibly be my last chance. Of course, I did nothing of the sort. I wasn't that stupid.

Eric seemed hesitant to add something, most likely an apology for rushing me, but he preferred to trot out of the room. I removed the rest of my livery in silence and with darkening thoughts. At least it was over. After all, Eric had only done what I had asked. Actually, he'd always done what I asked, and more. There was only one thing I couldn't ask of him. No matter how much I wanted it, I couldn't make him gay. It was better to accept reality and move on.

After a resolute look at myself in the mirror, I got out of the changing room with my head held high. Outside, Eric was assailed by everyone, and while talking to Camille, his smile returned. But when Joy ran her hand through his hair, advising him on how to go upstairs and wash it properly, he impatiently moved aside.

I observed him in silence. He looked different; agitated, a bit sickly. He kept tugging at his collar, his forehead creased. After everything we'd been through and the compliments we garnered today, I couldn't understand why he wasn't happy. He was Eric. When was he not happy?

I didn't want to add to his troubles by annoying him needlessly. But when he separated from the others and descended the front steps, I couldn't help myself and followed him gingerly.

"Eric?"

When he saw me, there was a glint in his eye. He slammed his hand on my shoulder and yanked me to his side. I exhaled a breath of relief when I felt his hand on me. With great force, he dragged me away down the steps, out of earshot.

"We were awesome, weren't we?" He sounded out of breath.

There was nothing more blinding than his earnest blue eyes. I had to shake my head to recover a bit of sense and answered with a smile.

Eric insisted. "You don't think so?"

This time, I laughed. "It was so intense, I don't even remember filming it." He gave a burst of childish laughter that forced a grin out of me. "Eric, you were great. You were…"

"No, *you* were!"

"We both were."

"We're like… the perfect team." As he spoke, his smile slowly faded, and his gaze turned absent.

I felt like hugging him, but that was probably a bit much. So instead, I decided to tease him. "What's wrong? You look like you're about to shoot another scene. Or maybe, the penalty of your life." I was so proud of myself with my shady football reference. "You know, like at the World Cup." *There, have another. You are so cute, you deserve it.*

324

My reference was so unspeakably pathetic that it tore Eric from his trance. "Sorry. I was just thinking about something."

"Thinking about what?"

"Ah…" Eric smiled at his battered sneakers.

"Tell me!" I couldn't stop myself; I gripped his wrists and shook him. "I insist."

Now laughing, he offered no resistance and became very limp. "I was thinking, maybe we should…" His voice trailed off. He saw something over my head and froze.

"Yes?"

He seemed at a loss for words. "Hum…"

"What? Do I have a halo over my head?"

I turned around, wondering what that was about. All I saw was Alberto, standing atop the front steps with a serious air about him. I blinked at him curiously. Alberto's cold eyes briefly swept over Eric before settling on me.

"Can I speak to you?"

Alberto wanted to speak to me?

"What? Now?" I released Eric's wrists.

Alberto nodded. He looked almost shy. I turned back to Eric, eyes wide, certain to find him just as mind-blown as I was. But Eric was looking down at his hands.

"Sorry," I said. "I'll be right back."

He shook his head. "That's fine."

"I'm just gonna see what he wants, then I'll be back."

Eric gave an energetic nod. "Yeah, yeah, go."

But something felt off. I found it difficult to leave him here alone. "Wait… What were you saying earlier? We were cut off. You said we should do what?"

"Nothing!" Eric waved his hands. "I was just thinking we should…" He coughed. "Go down to the village. To celebrate."

"Oh, sure!"

He didn't need to act so weird about it. He had me worried for nothing. Still, I made no move to leave, as if something was keeping me glued to the steps.

"Are you going or not?" he said with a smile.

I scratched my head. "I don't…"

Eric barked out a laugh that sounded like a release. "What are you waiting for? Go!"

And so, what else was there for me to do? I left him behind and followed Alberto into the house.

23

CATS AND DOGS

He took me to the other side of the house, and we emerged through the back doors to the pool area, near the fire pit. Alberto looked into the fire pit for a long time. There was nothing in there but ashes. I checked my watch, thinking of Eric waiting on the other side.

"What did you want to tell me? Did Michael say something?"

Alberto tore his gaze from the pit. "Michael?"

"Do we need to do some reshoots?" I clutched my chest. "Did they lose the take?"

At last, Alberto understood the meaning of my words. "No. Nothing like that." He looked down at his feet and smiled. Who knew what Alberto was made of? All I knew was that he rarely smiled. So the sight of his curled lip commanded my attention.

"The take is perfect," Alberto said.

"Good, good." I nodded. "Wait! Did Michael show it to you or—"

"I saw it live."

"I thought you were banned!"

He seemed amused at my shocked reaction and brushed his hair back with two long fingers. "I snuck in and watched anyway."

Alberto casting smiles and breaking some rules. *And* asking to speak with me. I may have woken up in an alternative dimension.

"I didn't know you liked to live dangerously." I wanted to sound entertained, but I sounded kind of awed. Which didn't surprise any of us.

"Mm, not really," he said. "Sorry."

"No, it's fine!"

I was getting excited by this unwarranted shyness. He dug his teeth into his bottom lip, gnawed on the poor flesh without mercy. My hand twitched, itching to stop him.

"You were great," Alberto said to the fire pit.

"Wow, thanks." I pinched myself to make sure I wasn't dreaming. "But I only followed Eric's lead—"

"You *are* great." Alberto turned his back to the pit and looked at me. I could only listen, at a loss for words. He didn't seem to mind my silence. "I was wrong when I said those things to you. At the party."

My mouth fell open a little. I pinched my wrist again. Harder, this time.

"Anyway, you weren't the first one to ask me out." Alberto rubbed his eye. "But... you're the first one I like."

After pinching myself twice more, I realised my mouth was open and snapped it shut.

"You like me?" My tone was heavy with disbelief.

This wasn't real. I may have banged my head last night when Eric pushed me down, and everything that happened since was a coma-induced dream where everybody liked me, where I was a great actor, and where the most beautiful guy on earth stood before me and spouted nonsense.

There was no way. Now that I had resigned myself to the fact Alberto never showed me any regard or affection, that my thoughts of a future together had been nothing but a childish fantasy, he was saying this?

"You like me?"

I could only parrot myself at this point.

Alberto fidgeted with his hands. "Yes. I like you. You're nice." He paused. "I'd like to go out with you."

A dry laugh accidentally broke out of my chest. I slapped my hands on my mouth. "Sorry, sorry." I shook my head. "But it was you who said—"

"I know." He waved his hand. "I say a lot of things."

No actually, you don't! You infuriating ascetic angel! You don't! I wished you'd blabber incessantly, that would have saved us some trouble.

"You can understand that I'm really surprised," I said in a thin voice.

"Sure." He didn't look like he understood. His expression was unfathomable, *à la* Alberto. I watched him carefully, incredulity plain on my face.

I wanted to believe him. *He was Alberto.* I had been mad about him for almost a year. I knew I liked him the moment I met him. Now he said he liked me too, which was everything I wanted to hear, so why was it so hard to believe him?

"Alberto, are you an honest person?"

He was distracted by a bird flying overhead. I waited for his answer with a thumping heart.

"I don't know," he said.

"That's… a pretty honest answer."

"Is it?"

We both stared at each other in silence. My heart was racing; my fantasy beloved actually wanted to be *my beloved.* I felt like a deceived donkey who finally got to eat the carrot. And somehow, it felt terrifying.

"A-Are you scared right now?" I blurted out.

Alberto's cat-like eyes narrowed. "No. Why would I be scared?"

"I don't know."

He tilted his head. "Are you scared?"

"A little."

"Why?"

I hid my face in my hands. "I don't know!"

Alberto was shy, or he didn't like talking. Alberto was quiet and peaceful. He was my first love, and naturally, I belonged with him. It was needless to look back at anything else now. Alberto wanted me, he was perfect for me. He admitted his mistake, and we could grow together as human beings.

He liked boys. And he liked me.

I was really lucky.

Still, I tossed several looks over my shoulder. I don't know what I was expecting to see; there was clearly nothing there. Alberto watched me act crazy with patience. Eventually, he smiled.

"What do you say?"

"I don't… know." With these words, I shocked myself. "I need to think about this."

"That's okay. I understand if you're a bit mad at me."

"No, that's not—"

"I'll ask again soon."

Alberto reached out a hand and tucked a strand of hair behind my ear. A hopeless endeavour, but I shivered when his fingertips brushed my skin, cool and soft.

The tables had turned, no, flipped. I felt like a god at this instant, and I didn't feel worthy. So, when Alberto shuffled back into the house, I dropped into a chair and exhaled a breath of relief. What the fuck was going on? If I didn't bang my head, then was this place in an alternate reality?

Alberto asked me out!

Alberto was mine for the taking. It was the chance of a lifetime. And I didn't grab it.

For a moment, I wondered what madness possessed me to not accept him on the spot. And then madness appeared, blond and windswept, in my field of vision. Surrounded by laughing faces, Eric swept a glance outside through the open doors. When our eyes met, he winked.

In the afternoon, we all crammed each other into various cars and drove to Aurons. After a complete failure to entice us to go with them, Binta and Duvo left us to visit a local exhibition. Our group of ruddy teenagers stormed the village like a tornado, uncaring about disturbing the sleepy mid-summer peace, a little like the way Alberto stormed into my life with a confession which left me dumbfounded to the point of numbness.

I spent the afternoon tailing an overexcited Camille and her devoted Arthur, not even paying attention to my surroundings. Neither of them noticed my weird behaviour; between their frantic shopping and the super obvious flirting, they had enough on their hands, and it was perfect for me since I could wallow in my own thoughts in relative peace. As for Eric, he shared his time between us and his friends. Not once did he ask what Alberto and I talked about. Considering the amount of time he spent helping me with my love affairs, I was surprised at first, but at the same time, I felt a little relieved. It was strange to be wanted by Alberto after so much time fantasising about it. To meet his gaze by accident, only to find it lingering on my face. Alberto wanted me. How hard was it to say yes? Only a fool would refuse him. I'd repeated that to myself often enough.

The afternoon dragged on. At some point, we gathered around the village's fountain for a break. Xavier attempted to throw Michael in the fountain, slipped, and ended up in there himself. Michael watched him with round eyes, then turned on his heel muttering, "That's it, I'm going home!" but Joy and Melissa convinced him to stay.

Binta and Duvo returned, looking suspiciously ecstatic after a local exhibition about handmade baskets, but whatever. Since they offered to buy us ice cream, no one thought of giving them a hard time.

Unfortunately, there was no ice cream shop in Aurons. Because of the heat, we were all more or less crestfallen. But after a moment of silence, Eric mentioned that the bakery across the street sold ice cream cones.

"That's great!" Duvo clapped his hands. "Let's go, then."

And just like that, he crossed the village square and pushed open Mona's door, followed by Camille, Arthur, Binta, Michael, Eric, and me. There, a succession of strange things happened, weird enough to force me out of my reverie.

The moment Mona and her daughters spotted Eric, they began screaming and chanting congratulations while throwing confetti. As I stood pretty close to him, his dumbfounded expression didn't escape me. His cheeks turning bright pink, he shook his head and waved his hands so fast that they became blurry.

"Congratulatiooooons…" Mona's voice died in her throat.

There was a big silence. Eric looked as if he was about to die from embarrassment. No one could understand a thing. Michael was the only one who was beaming.

"What are we celebrating?"

Mona and her daughters exchanged a look, then glanced at Eric, who seemed to have slightly recovered.

"The end of filming," he said in a croaky voice.

One of Mona's daughters lifted her hands. "Congratulations!" Her tone was forcefully high-pitched.

"Oh, that's nice!" Duvo said, puffing out his chest. "I'm the director… and…" he pointed at Michael behind him, "so is this one."

Mona's daughters were listening to Duvo politely, but when they saw Michael, their eyes widened in delight. Binta snorted and pulled a defeated Duvo to the side. My attention was focused on Eric, who was communicating with Mona through pointed glances and over-exaggerated blinking. He accidentally saw me looking, and his blush returned.

At this instant, a loud *slam!* made us all jump. Alberto had walked headfirst into the glass door. Binta rushed to open the door for him and pulled him inside, using one of her hands to brush aside his hair and check for a wound. He stared at her blankly.

"Are you okay, Alberto? You didn't see the door?"

Alberto was the only human being on earth who could look dignified after a group of people witnessed him bash his head against a glass door. He shook his hair and gave a light cough.

"I… hum… I wasn't looking… at the door." He gave me a furtive glance. My heart skipped a beat, and without thinking, I flashed him a smile. He turned all shy and looked away.

After buying ice cream cones, we all sat around on the edge of the fountain to eat them. With the sweltering heat plaguing us, they were really welcome. Only Eric had remained behind to chat with the bakers. Joy heard what just happened and was concerned about Alberto's possible concussion. She offered to feel his forehead, but he ran away before she could spring from her seat and didn't return.

The whole incident was quickly forgotten. Duvo and Binta gave us a few minutes to finish our shopping and meet at the cars. Soon, I was the only one left at the fountain, slowly munching on the end of my ice cream cone. My thoughts kept returning to what happened earlier between the bakers and Eric. That was really weird. I was still obsessing about it when Eric came out of the bakery and squatted at my feet, holding an untouched ice cream cone.

"You're supposed to eat it," I said.

"You want it?" Eric lifted it under my nose. "I want yours."

My own ice cream cone was nearly devoured. Only the small crunchy bit filled with chocolate was left.

"You're too late." I frowned. "I've already gotten one. I can't eat both."

Eric rubbed his nape with a hand, his expression somewhat crumpled. But immediately after, he revealed a sly grin. "So? Did Alberto ask you out?"

My mouth fell open. "Are you a mind reader? How does that work? I always wanted to ask."

"So he *did* ask you out."

Feeling strangely nervous, I kicked my feet. "Are you surprised?"

"Yeah, a little. He never showed—"

"Any interest? I know. I'm starting to believe he's weird, like Arthur said." I paused, then added, "But I don't mind. He's Alberto."

I didn't want Eric to think I was so shallow that I would reject Alberto at the first sign of a flaw.

"That's great, though, isn't it?" Eric asked. I didn't answer. He nudged me with his knee. "Are you happy?"

I avoided his gaze. "Yes, of course, I'm happy."

Eric said nothing, as though he was pondering what to say. After a second, he pointed at the remaining bit of my ice cream cone. "Give it to me." His tone was commanding. His eyes bore into mine, earnest and warm.

Fortunately for Eric, I was a sucker for his authoritative ways. They were so rare and yet so enthralling. So my first thought was to shove the little piece right into his grinning mouth. My fingers twitched in anticipation.

As if he could really read my mind, Eric caught my wrist and led my hand to his lips.

Unfortunately, at that exact moment, Alberto appeared around the corner, returning from god knows where. He took one look at Eric on one knee at my feet with his hand around my wrist and froze. I became cold all over as if he'd caught me in the act of cheating.

"You're back!" I forced a smile.

While Alberto and I were locked in a staring contest, Eric tightened his grip on my wrist until I dropped the piece of ice cream cone. He caught it and tossed it in his mouth with a smile. "Thanks." With that, he jumped to his feet and walked away in the direction of the cars. Absolutely shameless.

Meanwhile, my back was soaked in cold sweat. I could only imagine what was going through Alberto's mind at the moment. After all, wasn't I supposed to be madly in love with him? Ask anyone and they'd tell you. So how come, a few days later, I was hand-feeding straight football players while grinning like a toddler?

I hung my head in shame and waited for Alberto to say something. But he only extended his hand and said, "Do you want to hang out with me after dinner?"

My eyes widened. "Sure!"

I took his hand. It was slightly cool — how?? — and so soft. I had been dreaming of this particular hand for a long time; feeling it in my own felt completely surreal. I quickly released it and wiped my sweaty palms on my shorts. When I lifted my head, Alberto was still looking at me.

At this instant, Duvo's shrill voice at the other end of the square urged us to pick up the pace and get our asses into our allocated cars. With a long sigh, Alberto led the way, and I followed feeling inexplicably taut.

After dinner, it became impossible to silence the rumours. When they saw me leave the dining room with Alberto, Camille and Arthur almost choked on their dessert. Feeling slightly uneasy for not telling them he had asked me out, I quickly made a few gestures to indicate I'd explain everything soon, but they both looked even more confused, so I wasn't sure they got the message.

We met Xavier, Kayvin, and Eric on the way outside. Instinctively, my eyes sought Eric's. The smile he cast didn't seem completely genuine. I wasn't too surprised: After all, Eric had never seemed particularly fond of Alberto.

"Come sit with us around the fire!" Xavier slapped his hand on Alberto's arm, leaving a red handprint on it.

Alberto glanced down at his arm with a blank look. "I'm going out front with Zak."

"Zak can come too!" Xavier beamed. "The girls are going to sing!"

"Then I really have to go."

Xavier didn't catch the sarcasm. "See? Excellent."

Kayvin cut this conversation short by slamming his fist on top of Xavier's head. "Don't! You idiot."

For once, I agreed with Kayvin. Neither of us wanted to be in each other's company. We went our way and they went theirs. I tossed a look over my shoulder just as Eric did the same; he laughed at my face before turning away.

Alberto and I stood alone on the front steps. The sun had just dipped behind the trees. A warm and gentle breeze rustled through the leaves, brushed past our ankles, and danced with our hair. Since Alberto didn't seem to want to break the silence, I decided to ask him a few questions, but he surprised me when he spoke first.

"Let's sit down." He pointed at the steps.

I followed him obediently, my gaze roaming over his body from head to toe, trying to reconnect with the feelings the mere sight of him used to spark within me. I did like him; I did fancy him still. But something was holding me back from jumping into his arms.

Music and singing voices reached us from the other side of the house. The girls were performing their song with great enthusiasm. The show was soon followed by claps and cheers, some laughter, then the voices died down. Meanwhile, Alberto and I were sitting in silence on the front steps, with only the whisper of the breeze for company.

"Did you want to ask me something?" I said after five full minutes — I checked my watch. Alberto shook his head, his bottom lip disappearing between his teeth. "Then, would you mind answering a few things for me?"

This time, he nodded and released his poor lip. "Okay."

I went straight to the point. "You're not in love with Michael, are you?"

I had figured out by then what was holding me back was simply a lack of information regarding his intentions. If he'd answer me right, then I'd fall into his arms. As simple as that, right?

Alberto shook his head without hesitation. I felt some tension leave my shoulders. That was it, then. Soon my doubts would clear and I would be able to say *Yes!* without feeling like I might be making a mistake.

"You like me," I said. "Not him."

"No. But..." Alberto yawned. "Sorry. I thought I liked him before."

Honest. He was honest. Aloof and mysterious to a mind-boggling degree, but at least he was honest. We could talk like this. I felt confident.

"Then... What happened?"

Alberto lifted his shoulder in a half-shrug. "Nothing."

Because I trusted Michael's near ridiculous devotion to his psycho boyfriend, I accepted this answer.

"When did you start liking me?"

He tilted his head. "Why does it sound like you're interviewing me for a job?"

His tone was gentle, his expression neutral, but his words hit the spot, and I couldn't help but laugh awkwardly.

"Is that how it sounds like? I'm sorry."

Alberto dug his teeth into his lip again. "Is that a thing people do? Am I missing something?"

"I don't know. I've never dated anyone."

"Same."

How?! That was another question to ask. But now that he made me realise how I sounded, I didn't dare poke my nose any further into his business.

"Just one last thing..."

"Okay."

"Since you like me, why did you say those things to me at the party?"

Alberto considered my question with a thoughtful expression. "That's…"

The sound of two voices approaching interrupted him. Somewhere on the side of the house, Kayvin and Xavier were arguing about something.

"… he promised!" Kayvin sounded furious.

"If he said he'd do it, then he'll do it, don't worry." Xavier was trying to placate him.

They emerged around the corner and saw us sitting on the front steps. Kayvin gritted his teeth and went straight inside, but Xavier cast us a bright smile and walked over to us.

"What are you two doing? Watching the sunset?" He flung his arm around Alberto's shoulder.

Alberto's eyes narrowed. "I'll tell you if you tell me who Kayvin wants to kill and why."

Xavier guffawed and dropped his ass next to Alberto, hugging him tighter in his embrace. I coughed a little, but he didn't notice.

"He's been fighting with Eric again. Doesn't matter."

Alberto and I exchanged a glance. My curiosity piqued, I put on an innocent air. "What are they fighting about?"

Xavier looked at me with his vacant eyes. "Nothing. Girl stuff. Other stuff."

"Girl stuff? What girl stuff?"

Alberto rose an eyebrow at me but didn't comment.

"Joy asked Eric out, and Eric said no."

"I thought Eric never said no," Alberto said.

"Who said that?" I hissed in defence of my friend.

"Eric!" they both said. Xavier was ecstatic that they spoke at the same time and laughed heartily.

The tension in my shoulders returned tenfold. Partly because Eric had been bragging nonsense about himself, and partly because I was angry for not being privy to this conversation. If I'd known he never said no, then I…

… had to stop with the delusions and return to the real world, where Alberto was waiting for me to stop being an ass and date him as any reasonable person would.

"Anyway, Kayvin's angry now." Xavier absently dug his fingers into Alberto's shoulder as he spoke.

"What the hell does that have to do with him?" I muttered. "Or… Does Kayvin like Joy?"

Xavier shook his head. "Kayvin likes Elodie."

"I don't get it."

"I'm like you, Zak-Zak! I don't get it." Xavier sighed. "Joy! Elodie! And this Drama Club thing. It's dragging. Really boring, if you wanna know what I think."

"Drama Club thing?"

Xavier let out an impatient sigh. "I mean, Kayvin's right to be mad! Eric asked us to do it, and we all got punished, but Eric got to have fun with you" — Xavier tossed me a pointed look — "and Kayvin was okay with it at first, because Elodie ditched him, so his heart was broken—"

As I listened to him, my mouth gradually fell open. "Wait, wait, wait." I waved my hands to stop him. "Eric asked you to do what?"

"Break into the Drama Club. That was his idea."

Alberto lifted his index finger. "Oh yeah, I knew that."

Xavier's empty eyes betrayed no deceit. He was telling the truth. Eric was the one who instigated the destruction of our club? And he never felt the need to tell me?

"Wait… What?"

Xavier pursed his lips. "I… I don't think I was supposed to tell you. I think he specifically asked me not to tell you. But it doesn't matter, does it? Don't tell him I told you, or Kayvin's gonna say I'm an idiot."

"You are an idiot," Alberto said softly.

I sat there on the steps, my blood pounding in my ears. "I can't believe it…" I whispered. "Why would he do something like that?"

"Because it's fun!" Xavier laughed. "It was, too. Except when we got caught. My father was a bit upset that the headmaster wanted to punish me. My father, who's a baro—"

"Why didn't you tell me?" I turned to Alberto.

He answered in a flat voice. "Was I supposed to tell you?"

Xavier was oblivious to my dismay. He held Alberto close, squeezing his shoulder affectionately. "So? What are you two doing all alone? You said you'd tell me."

Alberto's face showed no emotion. "We're dating now."

Xavier and I both looked at him with bulging eyes.

"Oh! Right! You're gay!" Xavier released Alberto and scrambled to his feet with an awkward smile. "Doing gay stuff. Good for you, good for you!"

With that, he inexplicably ran into the house, leaving the two of us alone on the front steps, probably afraid of turning gay by association. Despite a vague need to ask Alberto what exactly his relationship with Xavier was, I let silence fall around us.

"What you told Xavier," I said after a minute. "I don't think… We're not dating, are we?"

Alberto tilted his head. "Yet."

The look he gave me made my heart thump; I hid my agitation behind a frown. Seductive Alberto frightened me a little. I wanted him to make a move on me just as I wanted to run away in the opposite direction. My scowling face seemed to amuse him. He tried again to tuck a strand of hair behind my ear, just as he did earlier today, and admired the result with unreadable eyes.

"You look angry." His voice was like a whisper.

"I'm sorry. That's not your fault. I'm thinking of something else."

Eric, that damn liar. I swear to God, in the future I'd ask everyone I meet to take a polygraph before even thinking of introducing them to my sister's dog.

Why would he hide this from me? What else was he hiding?

"You know… about us…" Alberto's voice was languid and soft in the twilight.

"Huh…?"

"I feel it's pointless to ask you again."

Alberto, the gay Vitruvian man, was struggling to get my attention. If I weren't so pissed off at Eric, I would have shed tears of shame.

"No, I'm sorry!" I rubbed my face with my hands. "I'm really sorry. I've been really distracted all day, but I'm really thinking about it, you know! I'm just…"

"You're what?"

Alberto didn't look mad. He watched my face carefully, as if trying to read my mind. I dipped my head.

"I'm… confused. I'm really not sure any of this is real." A dry laugh escaped my lips. "You must be used to people asking you out and such, but I'm not. I feel, from now on, if people can't find a way to prove to me they like me, I just won't believe it. I won't believe anything at all."

"That's fine."

Alberto didn't mind that I sounded so emo. He reached out and took my hand. I lifted my head, surprised. I don't know if he pulled me, or if I just slumped forward, but the next instant, my lips were pressed against his.

My eyes widened in shock.

Before I blinked, it was already over. I wondered for a split second if that, too, was a figment of my imagination. But it wasn't. Alberto was still so close I felt his minty breath on my face.

"I guess I'm asking again," he murmured.

His lips were like chains wrapping around my heart. The words they spoke were casting spells. I hungrily tried to capture them again but was met with soft laughter.

In a daze, I leaned away from Alberto, scrambling to regain some sort of focus. Words came tumbling out of my mouth, unrestrained and nonsensical. "I... I need to talk to Eric."

Alberto's lips parted in surprise. With an apologetic smile, I brushed away the dirt on my clothes and headed back inside. With my luck, I entered right at the moment Joy was storming in from the other side of the house with bloodshot eyes. She charged straight into my shoulder, sending me spinning like a top, and didn't bother to apologise. When I came to my senses, I noticed my back was resting against someone's chest.

"Oh," I said upon seeing who it was. "I was looking for you."

Eric gave me a warm smile. "You were?" One look at my face and his smile was wiped off. "Oh. You were. It's just that you're the second person who seems to want to murder me tonight. Scratch that..." He gestured at the staircase where Joy was last seen. "... The third, and I'm not used to all this hostility."

"Then stop messing around with people, perhaps they'll like you better."

Eric's eyes betrayed his surprise. "Wait. Are you really angry?"

My lack of reaction spurned him into action. He took my elbow and pulled me toward the drawing room. He made sure we were alone and closed the door behind him. "Don't be angry at me, Zak. I mean, really angry. I like it more when you're fake-angry. It's more fun."

"*Fun.* So much *fun.*" I sounded more dejected than angry, to be honest. He seemed to agree and scratched his neck with a worried expression.

I didn't want to be angry at Eric. I liked him very much. I was hurt that he tried to destroy our club, and even more hurt that he tried to hide it and said nothing when I accused Kayvin of instigating it. I didn't want to be mad; I wanted to understand. So I dropped my arms to my sides and attempted to make him talk.

"Is there anything you want to tell me?"

"No. Why?" He looked panicked now. "Is there anything *you* want to tell me?"

"Like what?"

"I don't know…"

My head started to buzz unpleasantly. I pinched the bridge of my nose. "You're responsible for breaking into our Drama Club, and you never even thought about telling me?"

Hearing this, Eric bounced on the balls of his feet with the guilty expression of a puppy caught wrecking the living room. With his lack of poker face, how could he manage with all these lies?

"So you found out."

"Yep."

"How?"

I bared my teeth. "Is that really what matters here?"

"I guess that's why you're angry."

"Yeah, a little. Mostly disappointed, though. Why would you do such a thing?"

Eric didn't answer at first, but he soon flinched under my glare. "Look, I could tell you, but I have a feeling it would make you angry… er."

"Angrier than 'I did it for fun'?"

His hands lifted defensively in front of his chest, and he backtracked into an armchair. "Oh… well… when you say it like that…"

So it was true? He really did it for fun? I was so surprised by how dumb he was that I momentarily forgot that I was angry.

"Why… Why did you hide it from me?"

Eric heaved a breath of relief. "Technically, I didn't hide it. It's just that I didn't mention it."

Seeing how he tried to smile, my anger returned. My spearing glare wiped his grin off his face. "Makes me wonder what else you're hiding."

His silence was like salt in my wound. Anger or pain, I didn't know which one twisted my stomach the most.

"What?" he said helplessly. "You've never hidden things from anyone?"

It's like he didn't want to talk about anything seriously. His face, the way he averted my eyes, the half-amused tone of his voice, I couldn't stand it anymore. My fingers digging in my temples, I screwed my eyes shut.

"I just want you to admit it!"

"Admit what!"

"That you…" I felt unsure all of a sudden. "That you… lied to me and you… you sacked my club."

He spread out his hands. "But you won't even see the difference when you return to school. It was nothing!"

"It's not nothing to me, you don't get it!"

At this point, I wasn't sure I was talking about the club anymore, but Eric couldn't possibly understand that. I felt like crying. Eric approached with a helpless expression.

"Why are you so upset?"

"I'm not upset."

"You are." Eric gripped my wrist. "Tell me why!"

Like hell. So that I could embarrass myself in his eyes forever, possibly turn into a joke for him and his friends? He'd have to torture me to death before I admitted my crush on him.

"I have nothing to tell you. I'm going back upstairs."

"Are you gonna date Alberto?"

I paused. "What's it to you?"

Eric let out a laugh. "After all the time and effort I invested in bringing you together, you're not even gonna tell me?"

He was right. I owed him that, at least. But I looked down at my feet, not knowing what to say. Technically, I didn't accept. But we also kissed.

"What do you think?" My words came out in a timid mumbling, pretty pathetic.

Even angry, I still had the nerve to ask him for advice.

"Oh, okay." Eric took a step back. "I mean, that's good. That's great. I think he's… he's…" His eyebrows drew together. "… lucky to have you."

I sighed. "You never liked him, did you?"

His face darkened. "He's a fucking idiot."

A silence stretched between us. I didn't know what to say after hearing that, and he looked like he was surprised at his own outburst. He pursed his lips and dipped his head.

"There, the truth comes out at last," I said softly.

Eric's expression crumpled. He hurried toward me and tried to grab my wrist again. I jumped aside with a warning look.

"Zak, I'm sorry! I know you like him. I shouldn't have said that."

Trying to ignore the sinking feeling in my chest, I shook my head. "I'm going upstairs."

Eric stood in front of the door, blocking my way. His whole face was flushed. "Please, I'm sorry. I didn't mean it."

I glanced at him. "You didn't?"

He hesitated. "No, I… I did!" I pushed him aside to open the door. He clung to my sleeve. "But that doesn't mean I think *you're* an idiot for liking him."

With a sigh, I let my arms drop to my sides. I clearly had no idea what feelings I was experiencing at this moment. Between him and Alberto, I felt like there hadn't been that much space for me to think, to breathe, these past two weeks.

"Is that… Is that all you wanted to say?"

"Hum… Yeah. Unless there's something else you wanted to say."

Eric's eyes still looked the same. Clear, blue, and earnest, just like the first time I had looked into them. He hadn't changed at all since that time. It was all me. It was always me.

It was time to let go.

"No. I'm good."

Eric gave a small nod. "Then I'm good too."

But he caught me again the moment I left.

"Hey, hey. We're still friends, aren't we? I know I lied. I lie, sometimes. But they're just little lies. The club, it looks fine, I promise."

I pulled my wrist free. It wasn't about the club. It wasn't about the club! Just like Joy a few minutes ago, I stomped toward the staircase and began climbing the stairs with a knotted stomach. Eric called out after me, his expression anxious.

"Why do you care so much about that little thing?"

From the top of the stairs, I stared into his face, feeling tired. "Why do you care about nothing?"

24

WE'LL ALWAYS HAVE LONGCHAMPS

E ventually, all good things come to an end. Personal items and piles of clothing were returned to their suitcases; heaps of sheets and pillowcases were removed and tossed on the floor to await laundry, and the bustle in the kitchen died down. Our steps would no longer clatter on the black and white tiles, Joy's tinkling laughter wouldn't bounce off the halls, Xavier's guffaws wouldn't frighten the birds, and the wildflowers would remain safe from Eric's itchy hands and would never stick out of my shoes to tickle my ankles again. It was time to depart Longchamps and return to Paris, to our lives.

While everybody busied themselves and ran to every corner of the house to gather misplaced belongings, I stood outside, long packed and ready. The bus that had brought us to Longchamps waited in the driveway to take us back. Only Kayvin was ready before me, and so ecstatic that he even offered to carry people's luggage and store them away into the bus for everyone.

My steps instinctively took me to the grove for one last look, to the apple trees under which I stood, lamenting the fruits weren't ripe yet, and to the clearing where our lake, our pond, our haven had witnessed the blossoming of a beautiful friendship. "It doesn't matter whether you were a lake or a pond," I muttered to the indifferent body of water, standing amidst the swaying reeds. "In the end, I'm grateful for you."

The nearby sound of footsteps and rustling leaves forced me to turn around. Eric emerged from the grove, his eyes narrowed against the bright rays of sunlight, and he stopped upon seeing me. We looked at each other without saying a word.

Last night, I went upstairs without any desire to continue our conversation. I slowly and mechanically started packing up my things, lost in my thoughts. After my little outburst, I didn't feel mad anymore, only strangely worn out. Despite the confusion, I wanted to impress on myself that everything would be all right. Eric and I were just friends to start with. Whatever happened that muddled our relationship, it was all on me, really. A distraction turned into a silly crush. Nothing terrible had happened. We may have kissed, but I had a bulletproof excuse for that: The movie. Now that it was done with, I had nothing to worry about. Once I'd remove Eric from my sight, he'd be forgotten. Only the warmest memories of him would linger, just like Longchamps itself.

And as for Alberto… I was going to Tunis next week, and he was off to the south of France with his family. That morning, we agreed to go on a date on our return. He gave me his number on a piece of paper, and I typed mine on the keyboard of his phone with trembling fingertips.

Alberto would always be Alberto.

"The apples didn't ripen in time," I said dumbly, staring at Eric's feet to avoid losing myself in his blue eyes.

He kicked the dirt with the tip of his sneaker. "Someone else will get to eat them."

"That's a consolation, I guess."

Eric walked over to me with slow steps. In his hand, I saw a bunch of wildflowers.

"Are you planning to propose to someone?" I said in jest.

He gave a loud snort. "I wanted to keep them, show them to my mom."

"They'll fall apart by the time you get home."

"Doesn't matter."

With such an opening for teasing, I couldn't help myself. "Look at you. It appears you, too, have a romantic streak."

Eric rubbed the back of his neck. "I should have told you before. That I can be romantic." He saw me frown and quickly added, "I mean, if I'd told you, maybe you wouldn't be making fun of me right now, that's all."

While he laughed, I approached and cocked my head. "You can't expect me not to snigger. A football superstar picking up wildflowers and... Actually, I should have known there was something off the moment you went on and on about furry bees."

Eric pursed his lips. "Still unconvinced?"

"I still don't want to take the risk of getting stung."

"That's because you're confusing bees..." He reached out his hand, and his finger poked my nose. "... with wasps."

Just like the first time we hung out here, I had a hard time meeting his eyes. This time, the reason was different. This inoffensive gesture felt like the last time Eric would ever put his hands on me. Sadness spread through my chest like a dull ache; I turned away. This wasn't the time to be overly sensitive.

"Did you come to say goodbye?" Eric's voice sounded soft behind me.

"I guess."

I heard him ground his sneaker into the dirt. "Me too. We had some pretty good times here."

My eyes closed for a moment.

We met, we fought, we met again, we became friends.

We cuddled on a boat; you fell into the water.

We rolled around in the grass and tasted each other.

"Yeah. Some."

Eric drew closer, close enough that the scent of his peachy shampoo wafted into my nostrils, artificial but also sweet.

"I'm sorry about last night," he said. "And about not telling you about the Drama Club thing, I guess. I didn't know how to tell you. I didn't want you to think I was... insane or something."

I turned around to face him. "I know, I know. I'm pretty scary sometimes. I get why you didn't want to tell me. You didn't want to get scolded."

Eric's eyes never left me. "And about Alberto too. You know I'm happy if you're happy, right?"

"Right."

"I'm really, really happy for you if that's what you want."

Eric's earnest eyes or his peachy shampoo. Which one was the most dangerous? I really couldn't say.

"Yes," I said absently.

"I'll always be your friend."

"Okay."

"We'll always have Longchamps."

What was with those words? Tears began to prick the corner of my eyes. What an idiot. Couldn't even leave a place without bawling like a kid.

"You're not… You're not gonna sign up for the Drama Club in September?"

"Don't think I'll have time. With football, and all."

"But isn't it what you wanted?"

"I got a taste of it this summer. I consider myself happy already." Seeing me all serious, he added, "I'll try if I can. *If* I can. Okay?"

With that, he revealed another gleaming smile, which begged the earlier question to be asked again: Eyes, smile, or peachy scent? Which one was the deadliest?

"That's good enough," I said. "Camille has plenty of gay movie ideas, and I'll need a partner on screen."

Eric's eyebrows rose. "Why does it have to be a gay movie?"

I flinched. "I don't know why I said that."

The way he cocked his head made me believe he would jump headfirst into that opening. "That's all right, Zak. I know you couldn't help it because you want to kiss me again." Seeing my scowl, he chuckled mercilessly. "Come on, come on, don't make that face. I know you're my biggest fan."

My face had probably turned green by then. Possibly, possibly, I was his biggest fan. Definitely, definitely, I wanted to kiss him again.

Damn, why was I so predictable? As Camille said once, how often do people lose themselves to a pretty face? And in that case, a pretty, pretty cool specimen of a human being.

Before I could betray and embarrass myself, I started toward the grove in quick steps. "Let's go back, or they'll leave without us."

Eric followed after me, overtaking me in seconds. "Like hell, they would. And if they did…" He turned around with a last sly grin. "… I wouldn't mind at all."

I refused to be beaten by him and picked up the pace. "Oh really, what would you do? Move into the mansion or with Old Rich and Janine?"

"I'd build us a cabin right here in the trees."

"Sure. And we'd live a life of domestic bliss. Raising bees and eating bad apples. Cooking mud pies and washing up in the lake."

"Sounds good. I'm in."

"Let's just… hurry back, okay?"

Eric snorted. I stopped adding fuel to his nonsense, and the journey back to Longchamps was finished in a somewhat awkward silence.

Back at the mansion, we found everyone gathered outside. Alberto was dozing off against the bus. Eric opened his mouth when he saw him, but in the end, he didn't speak. He and I parted quickly and abruptly, and Camille and Arthur, seeing me free, rushed toward me to take me to the side.

"Is that true, then? You and Alberto?"

I hid my surprise behind a bashful smile. "I may have a date with him in three weeks. How do you know?"

"Guess, duh!" Camille stuck out her tongue. "Eric told us."

"Oh."

But I never told Eric that I had accepted to go on a date with Alberto; I only agreed to it with him an hour ago. But never mind, it was done and so technically, I was dating Alberto, the most beautiful man on the planet.

Was it me or did it still feel too unreal?

Camille shook my sleeve. "Eric also told us about the Drama Club."

"Are you really angry?" Arthur asked, his brow furrowed.

"No, I've moved on, but…" I lowered my voice "I'm still amazed at how dumb he was to do something like that! I've spent more than two weeks in very close quarters with him, and he never struck me as stupid. Okay, a bit silly at times, but that kind of dumb, really—"

"Okay, we get it."

"In his defence," Camille said, "he looked so penitent when he told us, I couldn't help hugging him, and I ended up comforting him like a doting mom."

I clicked my tongue in frustration. "That's great, fall for his tricks. Undo all my training. But don't complain when he starts chewing your shoes or peeing on the floor to get your attention."

Camille and Arthur exchanged a startled look. I felt something poke my shoulder and turned around: Alberto was standing behind me more or less awake, his cool eyes fixed on me.

"Do you mind if I sit with Sander on the way home?"

"No?" I said, taken aback. "Why would I mind?"

"We weren't going to give him to you anyway," Camille said.

"Yeah, he's staying with us," Arthur said.

Alberto nodded absently. "Okay, good night—see you later, I mean."

He shuffled back toward the bus.

"One day, one day, you'll have to explain him to me. You'll have to," Arthur said.

I stared after Alberto's long silhouette as he climbed into the bus. "No promises."

At the front door, Eric was saying goodbye to Janine and Old Rich. Looking at them, one would have thought they were relatives. I wondered with a smile if Mona's daughters back at Aurons would ever recover from losing him.

When the bus departed, crunching the gravel under its wheels, most people threw a longing look back at the old mansion bathed in sunlight. I was one of them.

How much had changed since the day I arrived, alone and anxious to remain so, as opposed to now where I feared never to see my friends again… But I didn't need to worry too much. Today, finding a seat for myself and opening my old book was out of the question. Whether it was the bus or the train ride, Camille and Arthur never left my side.

The dynamics of our little group was forever altered. The football players had lost Charles-Henry to Nadia but had gained Melissa as well as Joy, whose bright personality seemed to have already gotten over getting rejected by Eric last night. Alberto spent the whole way home getting acquainted with the window as he slept, while Sander showed clear signs of resenting him. Michael and Eric sat side by side both on the bus and the train, and for once Kayvin didn't display any signs of jealousy. On the contrary, he seemed to relish being the object of Joy and Melissa's attention, believing Xavier to be no threat to him. As for Duvo and Binta… they fell asleep on the train and had to be awakened by Camille, Arthur, and me because everyone else wanted to leave them on board to teach them a lesson.

The train rolled to a stop at Montparnasse station. A few parents came to pick up their progeny, but I didn't expect anyone to come for me this time. After finding out that Camille lived only a few minutes away from me, we decided to walk home together. There was a clamour as people exchanged last-minute phone numbers and addresses with each other. I collected Camille and Arthur's. Joy and Melissa parted from Michael with teary eyes.

"Where are you going, Michael?" I asked when he walked over to us.

"I'll be staying in Paris for a while. At least until the editing is done," he said with a smile. "A kind old lady is letting me stay at her place."

"Miss Eugénie?" I recalled Louis's eccentric neighbour, whom my mom was fond of. "We're practically neighbours. Do you want to walk with us?"

"Unfortunately, she promised to pick me up in her car. I would invite you to join us, but I worry about your safety."

"Oh, okay."

Something brushed past me; I stepped aside and saw Elodie, aka the most popular girl at school, dash toward the cluster of people surrounding Eric. At first, I thought she came to pick up her best friends Joy and Melissa, but she ran straight into Eric's arms, and his face brightened like the bloody sun.

"That's Elodie!" Camille elbowed me in the ribs.

"I couldn't tell, really," I said, my eyes narrowed. "We just spent a whole year in the same class."

"Sorry, Mr Grumpy."

My hands balled into fists behind my back. "I thought they weren't together anymore."

"They could just be friends," Camille said lightly, before pulling Michael into a fierce embrace, blocking my view.

Oh, right. Because friends hug each other like that.

If I thought Joy was a pretty butterfly, then Elodie was a particularly beautiful one. Naturally blonde hair, naturally rosy cheeks, her face looked fresh and dewy as if she were a newborn baby. Her almond-shaped eyes crinkled at the corners when she smiled, and that smile, by the way, was annoyingly bright and warm and — in short, she looked nothing like me. Plus, she carried an air of authority and charisma that was out of this world, a natural-born leader kind of vibe. The sort of person you absolutely cannot hate, even when you really want to.

After what felt like ten minutes, Eric finally parted from her, and they both left the platform together, tailed by a surly Joy. I stared after him with a heavy heart. There was a time when he didn't want to leave my sight, not even for a second. He was my coach, my friend, my confidant. Now he was going his way, and I was going mine.

I would never know the warmth or brightness of his presence again. He would no longer chase after me like an excited puppy, mutter his lines while standing naked in the lake, or collect brownies to borrow a rowboat.

He wouldn't wait for me at the end of class; he'd be too busy. He wouldn't make plans with the three of us; he'd have his other friends.

He'd never torment me again, with his eyes, with his words, with his hands.

It would be like we never met.

~

For me, life would return to normal only when my new semester at Colette would begin. If my summer with Eric, Camille, and Arthur was over, I still had a full month of holidays left before we returned to class.

My family and I travelled to Tunis where we remained for two weeks. As usual, my grandparents complained about my size, my frame, and my sulky moods. And as usual, I let them do as they pleased with an affectionate heart.

Naturally, they pestered me about my love life, and if I had a girlfriend, and why still no one? *That's because you're so skinny, you don't eat enough, and you're working too hard, poor boy, but we're so proud of you.* The more my grandmother asked, the more I felt like coming out to everybody. Superman-style, I would have torn my straight clothes apart to reveal a gloriously gay but uncannily similar outfit, screaming "You should see who I'm dating right now!" But I succeeded in restraining myself. It would be better to introduce the notion when I'd have secured the heart of my beloved.

During that time, Alberto and I texted somewhat regularly. He was in the South of France with his family, and in his words, "Bored and anxious to come back". Through our text conversations together, I discovered we had chosen the same high school diploma field, Literary, and so there was a chance of us ending up in the same class in September. Alberto and I had similar tastes in everything. It was like he simply was a much, much hotter version of me. When people have so many fields of interest in common, they're bound to be great together.

As I expected, distance played in my favour. Little by little I came to miss Alberto more, and my friend Eric retreated to the background with the others. Contrary to Camille and Arthur, he never bothered to contact me at all, which made the task of forgetting about him all the easier.

And so, a week after my return to Paris, the long-awaited moment finally arrived, and I left my house with a thumping heart to meet Alberto for our first date.

At Luxembourg Park.

At 10 a.m.

On a Sunday.

It was fine, it was fine. Alberto was a little unusual, Arthur warned me, and if his idea of a romantic date implied walking around the park on a Sunday morning and not more standard things like going to the movies or to a restaurant and smooching on the threshold after walking me back, that was fine too. Alberto was more than the fantasies I'd nurtured about him. I needed to get to know him, just as he'd get to know me.

I met him by the main entrance to the park at exactly 10 a.m., my hands shaking a little. "Why here? And why now?" I couldn't help asking the moment I saw him.

A somewhat helpless shrug was his answer.

Fortunately, Alberto looked so dashing, it quickly diverted my attention. It seemed he got even taller in the last three weeks, and perhaps even prettier. I didn't know if it was because I'd just spent two weeks in Tunis ogling hot guys at the beach, or if it was because my hormones were acting up, but I was happy to see him and really impatient to press him up against a tree and finally find out if he was a good kisser. But when I tried to take his hand, he hid it in his pocket.

"I don't hold hands… in public," he said when he saw my face. "I don't want to get beat up."

Oh, I got it. The streets of Paris were filled with self-proclaimed alpha males always on the lookout for women to harass, and they usually had no qualms coming after us too. But there was almost nobody in the park at this hour. It was 10 a.m. in August! Even Parisians were hard to find at this time. I mean, come on!

All the same, I dipped my head and hoped I might be able to touch him later. "I get it," I muttered. "Wouldn't want to mess up that face."

Alberto heard me and revealed a hint of a smile, the rest of his face hidden behind his sunglasses. "Come with me, I know a good hiding spot."

He led me to a secluded spot behind a row of trees, rekindling my hope for clandestine kisses. Alberto checked on all sides before we sat on the grass. "No one will bother us here."

"I believe you," I said, after counting the number of people strolling through the park in the distance. There were eight.

We sat in silence for a long time. My gaze wandered to a patch of daisies while waiting for Alberto to start talking. About *anything*. His holidays perhaps? Maybe not. In his texts, he said he was bored and was longing to go home.

I started fidgeting despite my best intentions. His silence unnerved me. I wanted to talk to him, but I found I had nothing to say. I wanted to touch him, and yet felt like he was made of the most perfect material and touching him would only spoil him.

"I'm excited to go back to school," I said, for the sake of saying something.

Alberto answered with a nod. "Me too."

I asked about his holidays, his projects for the autumn, his photoshoot for a model agency in September — his mom had wanted to get him a contract with them for a long time but said he had resisted thus far — his family plans to go skiing in Switzerland for Christmas, none of which seemed to enchant him. I briefly told him about my plans even though he didn't ask and ended up asking him about the Drama Club.

"Are you going to sign up this year?"

"Depends."

I was a little surprised to hear that. "On what?"

"On the day it's scheduled."

Silence. More silence. Silence which should have made me feel at peace, but I felt like my skin was itching and burning next to him.

I wondered what Eric was doing right now. Football, probably. Would he text me one day? Were we really still friends? A painful feeling gnawed at my chest when I thought he might have forgotten me already.

Camille and Arthur clearly hadn't. In those three weeks, Camille had sent me many pictures from the Spanish coast, and Arthur had texted me a blurry picture of someone allegedly famous he met in his hometown of Flanders. Eric never wrote to me, and on second thought, I had never bothered to give him my number, and he had never bothered asking for it. And why would he have asked for my number anyway? Wouldn't that look weird, a straight guy asking me for my number? I should have asked for his number, but then, wouldn't that look weird as well? But why would it have been so weird? I had no problem asking for Arthur's number. Why couldn't I ask for Eric's number? No. He should have asked for mine. He was the confident, boisterous one after all. But perhaps he didn't want it. Listening to myself rambling on right now, even I wouldn't want to hang out with myself. Couldn't blame Eric for not wanting to stay in touch either.

But back to Alberto.

I lay on my back and watched with tight lips as he settled on his stomach next to me. He took out a new book from his backpack. It was in Italian.

"So did you enjoy *No Exit* in the end?"

He shrugged.

"Are you enjoying this one?"

"It's okay," he said, plucking a daisy and staring at it absently. "I don't think I'll finish it."

I was about to protest vehemently. What? You seriously don't finish books? What is wrong with you, you otherwise perfect creature? But he slid down his sunglasses and swept his feline eyes over me, and all I could utter was a pathetic sound that sounded like an agreement.

I wish I'd taken a book to read too, but like a fool, I expected to make out with my boyfriend the supermodel instead of having so much time to kill.

Alberto had other things on his mind, clearly. Holding his daisy between his long fingers and sucking on the end of the stem, he was absorbed in his new book. I refused to give up and racked my socially-awkward brain for something else to say.

"I like your shirt."

Alberto looked down at his ordinary yellow T-shirt. "Thanks."

"You always dress really well."

"Thank you."

Alberto offered his thanks mechanically and in a flat tone. He was probably used to hearing the same flattering platitudes over and over again. I was just another one in the sea of people who found him irresistible.

My chest tightened. I must have been jealous.

Alberto turned a page from his book, the daisy still stuck between his lips. "So do you."

"So do I what?"

"You dress well."

I blinked. "Do I?"

Alberto almost smiled. "Mm-hm."

"But I always dress more or less the same."

"It's one less decision to make in the morning."

I couldn't help smiling. "Do you worry about what you wear in the morning?"

"I don't really make these decisions."

"You're joking." I almost sat up, but I didn't want to spoil the perfect view I had of him.

He gave me an odd look. "Yes."

Oh, so he had a sense of humour. Albeit a little strange, just like him. I chuckled nervously to acknowledge his joke, and he returned to his book.

"Well, you look really nice."

"Thank you."

Again, thanks were proffered without even skipping a beat, but no other conversation followed up. After this, I started to grow worried, like something was off for a while, and I couldn't put my finger on it, and then it hit me. Did he even like me? I couldn't feel it. I thought I wouldn't mind, that I wasn't needy, that I could get used to his unusual ways. But in the end, I did mind.

"Alberto?"

"Hm?"

"Why did we come here?"

He tilted his head. "I thought it would be convenient."

"No, I mean, why did you invite me here?"

"Because I wanted to see you."

"You did?"

You really did?

Alberto's eyebrows drew together. Even his frowns were elegant. "What's wrong?"

I was being mental, looking for ways to convince myself that Alberto didn't like me. When he *did* like me. He asked me out. He asked me to come here, to this secluded part of the park, hidden behind trees, where no one could see us.

I gathered up my courage. "You... You can kiss me if you want."

Alberto sucked on the flower he had in his mouth, removed it, and with the head of the flower, brushed my nose. "I know."

I waited, hopeful, since it was the perfect setting, and knowing how similar we were in our tastes, he was supposed to have realised it already.

Hello? Paris? Blue sky? Full trees, green grass, patches of daisies? Hell, there was even a family of chirping birds somewhere over our heads. What more could he possibly need? A beret-wearing, old accordionist singing Edith Piaf like in the bad movies?

"There's no one around," I whispered.

"Mm." Alberto had returned to his book.

"No one can see us."

He looked up just in time to see me staring at his lips. "Okay. I see."

I blinked innocently. With slow movements, Alberto bent his head down. His lips, perfect in every way, touched mine. I sighed against their warmth, hoping he would open them so that I would be allowed to taste him. Tasting Alberto, at last. But the lips retreated, and Alberto was soon back into his book, looking very pleased, meaning as pleased as he could ever display himself to be.

I didn't move. My lips still parted, I stared at the blue sky. So clear and blue...

You want me to be good, don't you?

I pinched myself hard to get rid of the image of Eric's irises glinting in the sunlight.

"You're so cute when you look angry," Alberto said.

I started. "Do I look angry now?"

"Very."

"Then kiss me."

"Later." He pushed up his sunglasses and returned to his book.

One thing was certain, not every seventeen-year-old was tormented by their hormones. Alberto was as cool as a mountain stream. But I was tormented by mine, especially as I lay so comfortably next to him after eleven months of pining. If he liked me angry, would he like it if I took charge? Was I capable of it? Had I read too much *yaoi*?

The memory of Eric pressing me down in the grass came rushing back. I screwed up my eyes until I saw stars.

Of course, I didn't move that day. I turned my face away instead, in the hope that it would help me cool off a little.

In the nearby patch of daisies, a fragile-looking flower was swaying under the weight of a buzzing intruder. I stared without interest at first, until the culprit released the flower, and with a flutter of wings, flew right under my nose. With a gasp, I sat bolt upright.

The bee was indeed wearing furry pyjamas.

Part Four

'US'

25

THE LOSERS OF THE GAME

I had lost Alberto to the crowd already. Hundreds of students were amassed past the Colette front gates, some excited to reunite with old friends, some anxious at the thought of starting a new year, some not yet quite operational so early in the morning — like Alberto — and others like me whose neck was painful from stretching in order to find a certain face amidst a sea of strangers.

On this Second of September, heavy white clouds hanging overhead, exactly five weeks after we parted, I finally saw him.

Eric's hair was exactly the same length. His hands were hidden in his ugly shorts' pockets. He wore an equally tasteless football jersey under his backpack, a testimony to his affection for some Spanish team. And naturally, he was laughing. He looked so radiant that it explained why the sun decided to remain hidden behind the clouds this morning.

With a quick glance at Alberto, who was with Sander, towering over the others and easy to find in a crowd, I edged along several clusters of students to get a closer look at him.

Surrounding Eric was the same old crowd, Kayvin, Xavier and Charles-Henry, Joy and Melissa, and several other boys and girls who made a group of at least a dozen. Close to him stood Elodie, in a matching denim dress and headband, looking almost half as good as him in his rags. And here I was, on the first day of school, frozen to the spot, constantly readjusting the strap of my backpack for something to do while waiting for my friend to notice me.

Eric's eyes wandered around the courtyard with nonchalance and eventually fell on me. My heart gave a wild thump; I raised a timid hand. His own remained in his pockets, but he acknowledged me with a faint smile.

A faint smile only? For me?

Just as I forced my lips to curve upwards not to lose face, Eric's smile deepened a little, then turned teasing, and he mouthed words I couldn't hear. With a racing heart, I was about to take a step forward and close the distance between us, when he turned his head to the side, and I realised he was actually talking to Elodie while he was looking at me. Worse, she burst out laughing at his words, and he turned his back to me to nestle into her open arms.

Whenever it was that Eric had decided to get back together with Elodie was none of my business, and it wasn't the source of the deep sadness that spread throughout my chest at that exact moment. They looked perfect for each other, and since he clearly couldn't handle one week of celibacy, I didn't want to imagine how the rest of his summer went. But did he have to ignore me? What happened to "I'll always be your friend", then?

Just as I waited, hoping he'd glance at me again, Alberto found me between two yawns and took me to the side.

"Are you all right?" he asked, rubbing his eyes.

"Yeah, why?"

"There are less people in front of the board now, let's go and see where we ended up."

I knew better than to take Alberto's hand as he led me toward the bulletin board by the building's front doors. I had spent the rest of my summer doing all sorts of activities with him, but none of which involved smooching like raunchy teenagers, and I'd given up on such silly thoughts by then. Alberto's gestures of affection were almost as rare as his desire to strike a conversation.

Oh, but he was gentle, and he was beautiful. Who was I to complain when I was so lucky that he even deigned to look at me?

There were two Literary Baccalaureate classes at Colette. I was in one of them and saw Camille was in the other. That, in itself, made my already thin enthusiasm evaporate altogether. Just as I was trying my best not to feel defeated on my first day, she pushed past the crowd congregating around the board and jumped straight into my arms. Camille wore one of her flowery dresses with gold sneakers and smelled of coconut milk. Behind her, Arthur, his hair shorter, looked the happiest I'd ever seen him. Having them both in front of me made me realise how terribly I'd missed them.

"We're not together, Camille," I said miserably.

Alberto poked me. "But we are. You didn't even notice." The way he ran his finger along my spine made me shiver.

"Sorry," I said. "My head's all over the place this morning." I took his hand but couldn't hold on to it, and it retreated into the pocket of his hoodie. "What about you, Arthur? Are you with anyone you know?"

"Yeah, sort of," Arthur said, with a look at Alberto. "I'm with Sander and Oliver."

"You're lucky," Alberto said, almost with enthusiasm.

Arthur flashed him a tight smile as he took Camille's hand. Contrary to Alberto, Camille gripped Arthur's hand firmly and leaned into his side.

"Wow!" I said, astounded. "When did this happen?"

Arthur giggled and wrapped his hands around her waist. I couldn't help feeling a pang of jealousy when I thought of Alberto standing next to me with his hands buried in his pockets.

"This?" Arthur laughed and kissed Camille full on the lips. She turned beetroot red but didn't push him away.

"Eww." Alberto turned his face away.

"Yeah, this," I said faintly, ignoring my weird boyfriend.

"We're not sure," Camille said with a smile. "It happened gradually."

"But it happened!" Arthur's face was glowing.

I watched them for a few seconds before realising I was gaping at them. Avoiding Alberto's gaze, I coughed in my fist. "Are you, ahem… with Eric, by any chance?"

Arthur frowned. "No. He passed. He's in Terminale[1] now."

"Oh, good, good. I mean, for him. He didn't tell me."

"Really?" Camille looked surprised. "He texted me many times over the past few weeks."

How fucking neat! And to think I was supposed to be his friend. Wonderful.

"I regret going for this class," Arthur said with a grimace. "I wish I'd taken Literary so I could be with you too, Zak."

---

1. Terminale: senior year of high school, during which students will pass their final exams.

"Not with me?" Camille said with laughing eyes.

"Hey! You should try to ask the headmaster to put you into Zak's class! Like this, he won't be alone!"

"Yes, that's a good idea!"

Alberto looked at Arthur coldly. "But I'm in his class too."

Arthur blanched. "Sorry, I forgot."

Alberto rubbed his temple with a sigh and turned his back to us. Camille and Arthur immediately pulled me into a rib-shattering hug. Thank goodness they loved me. After seeing Eric earlier, I'd started to wonder if the whole trip to Aurons had been just a dream.

"We've got to go, let's speak soon!"

Camille pecked my cheek. Arthur's lips left a wet kiss on my other one. "Let's have lunch together?"

"Definitely!"

I watched them enter the building hand in hand and couldn't help feeling frustrated for some reason.

"You're making a cute angry face again," Alberto said in my ear.

"It's my eyebrows," I replied absently. "They're expressive."

Alberto adjusted my backpack strap with his long fingers. "Let's get inside too. Unless there's someone else you want to talk to."

I twisted my neck left and right and caught a glimpse of Eric's golden hair not too far behind us.

"Maybe I…"

But Alberto suddenly pulled me by the elbow and hurried toward the front door. "Let's go."

Tossing a look over my shoulder, I saw a group of giggling girls following after us with pink cheeks. Alberto's fangirls! I had forgotten about them. I used to resent them, but now, they were in a position to resent me! I basked in shameless triumph for half a second and then thought about it, and I couldn't help but let out a bitter laugh.

With the way Alberto treated me, there was no way they would realise we were a couple at this point. Even I wasn't so sure at times.

It took only a week before I gave in. A week of catching glimpses of Eric around corners, observing him going to classes flanked by Kayvin and Xavier; or dressed in his Colette football jersey and talking animatedly with our headmaster, often surrounded by a dozen people, more than half of them pretty girls, and never, never sparing a glance for old Zakaria, that guy he spent two intense weeks with and whom he once pinned to the ground to smooch until his legs gave out.

Pathetic.

One dose of longing, another one of anxiety, and a zest of resentment. Swirl it around and there it was: The perfect recipe for a little acting up.

Drama Club was now on Wednesday evenings, and we had lost Alberto due to scheduling conflicts. So it was alone that I left the building, while Camille and Arthur went to the library to pick up a really important book.

There was no book. I wasn't an innocent anymore. They were having a good time between two aisles, and my exceedingly beautiful boyfriend hadn't kissed me in three days.

Once I got outside the building, I pulled my hoodie over my head to protect my hair from the drizzle that had been falling all day. I accidentally bumped into Joy, Melissa, and Elodie in great conversation and mumbled some parting words. When I looked up, I spotted Eric nearby, standing under a plane tree.

Even though he was alone, I hesitated to go to him. But then I noticed he was wearing the exact same clothes he wore when he fell off that boat after I woke up on his arm. I couldn't resist and stomped toward him with my fists clenched.

Eric saw me approach, but he lowered his head and pretended he didn't, focusing on the small rubber band he was playing with. I stopped in front of him with an artificial smile.

"Hey, Eric!"

"Hey, Zak." He stretched and snapped the rubber band between his fingers.

"How have you been?"

"Pretty good, thanks."

"Good, good." I nervously pulled on the straps of my backpack. "What have you been up to?"

"You know… This and that." He turned his head to the side. "The holidays."

Eric's face used to shine whenever he saw mine; now he couldn't even look at me. Our friendship was over. But why?

Because I was silent, he eventually looked up and saw my frowning face. "How are… how are you?"

I pretended not to be completely choked up by the fact that he no longer cared about me and spoke in a forcefully cheerful tone, "I'm great. I'm happy you passed your exams, by the way."

The rubber band snapped, making me flinch.

"Thanks. It was a close call."

There was a silence. It was getting increasingly uncomfortable, like we suddenly had nothing to say to each other. We'd never had that problem before. I was beginning to feel disappointed in him. I thought he'd have the balls to let me down properly at least. *Okay, Zak, summer's over. You were fun, but you're high maintenance, and I have other friends. Let's just think of our time together fondly and move on, okay?*

Ugh, why did that sound so much like a breakup?

"So, you——"

"How's Alberto?"

We both spoke at the same time. My hand flew to my mouth while his rose to rub the back of his neck.

"He's… fine." I felt annoyed that he couldn't think of anything else to ask me about. "He's… Alberto."

After a pause, Eric pointed at something over his shoulder. "Well, I have practice, so…"

He made to turn away. His eagerness to get away from me was like a knife being twisted into my open wound. Wasn't he the one who sought my friendship in the first place? Pestered me, even? So much for that!

And yet, perhaps it was my fault, that I didn't take better care of him during our times together, and after. Perhaps I should tell him that I missed him? Or at least hint at it, not to sound too desperate? But he was already looking at me with an odd expression, as though I was being a clingy ex-girlfriend. I couldn't let that happen.

"Wait."

His movements paused. "What?"

"I just wanted to say…" I didn't want him to see me as a clingy ex-girlfriend, so I soberly said: "You know you can come and see me anytime."

Eric swallowed, the rubber band digging into the flesh of his finger.

I briefly hesitated before speaking again. "It was nice to be a loser with you all over the summer. Don't you miss it?"

There. That was hint enough.

Eric gave a little laugh. "I can't be a loser anymore. I've got to… I've got to get better grades. And I've got to play football."

"You could still join the Drama Club. It's only for two hours on Wednesdays."

"I can't, no."

"But—"

"Football's what I'm really good at anyways."

His words frustrated me. That he didn't want to hang out anymore was one thing, but it was a shame that he would abandon acting when he was so good at it.

"You're a great actor. You shouldn't give up."

Eric stretched his rubber band once more, his gaze absent. "It was a one-time thing, Zak. It was fun, but football's my thing."

"Eric…" My voice shook a little. "Are we still friends?"

The rubber band snapped and broke between his fingers, but he didn't look at it. He looked into my expectant eyes and lifted his shoulder in a half-shrug. "Sure! I'm just really busy now. Can't just hang out with everyone all the time."

His smile was pleasant enough, felt familiar even. But it wasn't the same as the one he used to reserve just for me. It was a little frozen at the edges, or perhaps his eyes weren't in it, but something was off. The corners of my own lips twitched upwards while my heart sank miserably.

There was a time when I thought myself too good for him. Such arrogance, such stupidity. Now, look at me. And look at him, refusing to meet my eyes and letting me know that summer was really over after all.

"Talk to you soon, hey?" he said just as he stepped backwards. When he saw I wouldn't answer, he briefly raised his hand and trotted away into the drizzle.

And that was that. My friendship with Eric was inexplicably over.

It was my fault; it had to be. My personality contrasted too much with his own. I belonged with the Albertos of this world. Eric didn't need a boring, sulky, scowling grinch clutching his thighs and begging for his attention. There was a reason he was the most popular guy at school, after all. I couldn't understand any of it before, and now I felt it, felt it deep into my bones. He was bright and warm like the sun, and everyone wanted to get close, even if it meant living in his shadow. Whereas now I was in a dark pit, where the sun never shone. Served me right.

As a result of this painfully awkward conversation, I resolved to throw myself deeper into my relationship with Alberto, as deep as he would allow us to be. We already hung out a lot, watched movies in dark theatres where he sometimes held my hand, strolled around museums until I knew the collections by heart, and avoided carbs in elegant bistros where we talked to each other in hushed voices and at times exchanged genuine smiles.

I once lost control of myself after such a dinner, shortly after we scurried out of the bistro when they started playing a football game on TV. Alberto grabbed my hand and pulled me out before I could even put on my jacket. He didn't slow down before we were blocks away from the offending restaurant. He was panting, his cheeks red from exertion. My mind went blank for a moment. I roughly pushed him against the door to number 7 Rue du Pot de Fer, gripped his hair, and pulled him down for a fiery kiss that left us both gasping for air. After that, he briefly held me in the dark alley, even pressing my face to his chest when a group of drunken guys tottered past us, looking for an open bar. That time, I actually felt that he liked me.

Alberto made me feel all sorts of things. Things I had wanted to feel my whole life: recognised, important, validated. One smile from Alberto, and I felt the world could finally see how worthy I was.

Yet when Eric used to smile at me, I felt bursting with life.

Despite his reticence and the passing of time, I was still determined to be loyal to the friend I owed so much to. I still had Camille and Arthur, and, to an extent, Eric was the one responsible for my happily-ever-after with Alberto. So roughly a week later, when Camille slammed a flyer onto our table in the cafeteria, — accidentally knocking over my cup of tea which emptied into Alberto's salad — I knew something of importance was about to happen.

"Eric is playing tonight!"

Camille's face was puffy from running, strands of fine hair sticking to her forehead. Behind her, Arthur was nodding excitedly. Alberto looked down at his plate and pushed it away with a grim face.

"I guess I won't be eating that."

I took the flyer gingerly so as not to expose myself, but upon hearing Camille's words, my heart was already thumping in my chest.

"Who's playing?" I said in a disinterested tone. "Eric's club?"

"No, Colette's team."

I gave her a dubious look. "They actually play games? I thought they just liked to walk around the school in their matching jerseys."

"Of course, they play games! Mostly friendly stuff. But some-times… not so friendly. Anyway, tonight's a big one."

"A big one." Alberto glanced at Camille like she was adorably thick.

Alberto really hated football and I needed to respect that, so I ignored his gloomy face and, mercifully, so did Camille. However, I couldn't pretend not to be invested in whatever was going on with Eric.

"Okay," I said. "Who's the enemy?"

Alberto looked at me in surprise. Camille pointed at the name on the flyer.

"The American High School of Paris. The rivalry between the two schools is real!"

"We can't let them win," Arthur said fiercely.

Considering I'd never even heard of the American High School of Paris, I could only shrug. "Why not?" I asked.

"They're American!"

"So is Eric," Alberto said coldly.

"Never mind that." Camille rapped her fingers on the table. "He was joking. We can't let them win because we're from Colette and Eric's our friend. Of course, we have to support him."

I nodded with fervour, but Alberto only looked at us as if we were out of our minds. Arthur tried to coax him.

"Come on, Alberto, it will be fun! Don't Italians generally love football?"

Alberto didn't bother answering him. I thought he might, with the way his lip twitched. Instead, he briskly got up and banged his knee into the corner of the table. He briefly closed his eyes, probably to endure the pain in his kneecap. "If it's tonight, then you can't have dinner with me."

"I can," I said. "I'll be free before 8 p.m., look."

Alberto glanced down at the flyer. Camille and Arthur gazed up at him, waiting for his reaction. I knew Alberto much better than them and wasn't exactly expecting one.

"I'll see you later." With a weary expression, he walked away carrying his plate full of tea.

Arthur leaned forward the moment he was gone. "So, have you shagged him yet?"

I choked on a piece of bread. Camille punched his shoulder.

"Arthur, what the hell?"

"Sorry. I couldn't help myself. I knew the kind of face you'd make."

"Yeah, sorry." Camille offered an apologetic smile. "He's learned from Eric how to rattle you."

I let out a dry laugh. No, he hadn't. He still had a long way to go.

To learn from Eric how to rattle me, Arthur would have to follow me around, tell me nice things, crack my introvert shell, surprise me with a pity-kiss, spend every minute of his free time with me, allow me to lay my head on his arm on a hot summer afternoon, kiss my chin on a crowded beach, relentlessly tickle my ear with his breath and my waist with his fingertips, press me to the ground while smooching me, and finally, casually abandon me and move on with his life. Then, he would be at the same level as Eric.

There. Just talking about it did, in fact, rattle me.

Concerned by my downcast expression, Arthur patted my hand with a small grimace. "Hey, hey, Zak, I was joking..." He sighed. "... I know full well you're not getting any."

"Will you stop!" Camille barked.

But Arthur's words made me burst into laughter. "That's fine! It's not like he's wrong anyway."

Camille's eyebrows drew together. "You're not... Is everything okay between you two?"

I couldn't expect my writer best friend not to be nosy about my relationship. She was always curious about weird stuff, just like when she annoyingly begged me to describe exactly how I felt when I slammed my toe against the leg of a lounge chair back at Longchamps.

"Oh yes," I said, "we do a lot of things together. I'm feeling my culture expanding by the minute."

"And...?" Arthur asked.

"And what?"

"Did you stick your tongue down his throat at least?"

Camille gasped in horror, but the look on her face showed she was dying to know the answer. I cocked my head and raised my index finger.

"What does that mean?" Arthur frowned. "Wait?"

"Once. Once I managed to stick my tongue down his throat."

"Once?"

I nodded, the memory of the sweltering kiss we shared in the dark alley still vivid in my mind. Arthur clapped and Camille let out a sigh.

"I'm a little relieved. I was starting to wonder if Alberto was capable of it."

"Capable of what?" I said.

"I don't know. Normal human behaviours, I guess."

With a slight frown, I pushed a few breadcrumbs around my plate. "He is weird, not gonna deny it."

After a pause, Camille snorted. "Still. I can't believe you made out more with Eric than with him."

"I did what?"

"Didn't you get some tongue action with Eric at least twice?"

My cheeks immediately started to burn. I tried not to stammer, but my mouth suddenly felt dry.

"I-I only recall the one, during—"

"Filming, yes! But didn't you say you rehearsed it the night before?"

"We… Hang on." I could clearly recall rehearsing by the lake and how it ended up being the hottest moment of my existence, but we went all-in during filming too? "I was so into the scene that I kinda spaced out."

Arthur erupted in laughter while Camille tried to conceal her own merriment behind her hand. "Okay, wait until you watch the film."

"Fuck. So I did get more action from Eric than from my actual boyfriend. How embarrassing is that?"

"Alberto might just need a little bit more time," Camille said wisely.

"Yeah… time, or something…" A defibrillator maybe. But I wasn't willing to go down that road at the moment. Instead, I picked up the flyer. "I can't believe Eric didn't tell us about this."

"He probably didn't want to bother us. He knows football isn't our thing."

"But he is! He's our thing, isn't he?" Upon seeing the look Camille gave me, I quickly added, "He said he wanted to be friends, but in the end…"

"He told me he was really busy." Camille's eyes brightened. "Let's show him we support him even when he doesn't have time for us. That's what friends do."

She was right. I wouldn't be a snob. I would go to the sports centre and watch a football game to support my friend, even if he didn't need it anymore.

Arthur watched me fold the flyer into a tiny rectangle. "Do you even know the rules of the game, Zak?"

"Of course, I know the fucking rules."

My reaction only made him laugh. "Did Alberto teach you how to swear too?"

Nope, that was all Eric. I always felt like swearing a lot where Eric was concerned.

Arthur glanced at his phone and gasped. "I have to go, or the new maths teacher's gonna kill me. Let's meet at the gate after class and we'll go together to the sports centre."

Before he could get up, Camille grabbed his face and proceeded to kiss him in a way only confident people in love do.

"Eww," I said, looking away.

"You even sound like Alberto now," Arthur said as they parted. When I squinted at him, he pointed at me and laughed even louder. "Even look like him too! Methinks a bit of vulgar football will do you some good."

I tossed my teaspoon at him and stuck my head in my hands to hide my smile.

Though I didn't know anything about football, I agreed it would do me a lot of good to see Eric again. Even from afar and without speaking to him. Watching him move, run, kick a ball or whatever. At least I'd know he was fine, living the life he wanted to live. And perhaps he would notice me in the stands and see that we still considered him one of us, and that I still cared for him, even if he had stopped caring about me.

I didn't have to be a football connoisseur to understand by the end of the first half that Eric's team was losing. Arthur blamed it on the annoying rain, and Camille on the team being rusty after the summer. I blamed it on us. The moment we took our seats in the stands, I really felt like an intruder and was worried that our mere presence would ruin everything for Eric.

What also surprised me was that people seemed to want to attend these things. Granted, the sports centre was used for amateur games, training, and small competitions, and so it didn't offer a lot of seats, but a good portion of those was taken. We shared the stands with supporters from the other school and Colette students. Joy, Melissa, Elodie, and Nadia were all there, of course. Weren't we adorable, an entire row of little groupies, pretending to be interested in the sport itself? During the second half, however, Elodie felt my burning eyes on her and threw a dark look over her shoulder, so I had to refocus on what was happening on the pitch.

Honestly, I'd never thought I'd ever become a fan of the game after one attempt to watch one live, but still, the experience would have been better if Eric was winning. But it's like he was only physically present on the pitch. He wasn't even trying. He missed two shots that had Arthur sobbing into Camille's arms, and by the end of the game, Kayvin was so angry with him that he was foaming at the mouth.

When the referee blew his whistle to announce the end, settling the score at 2-1 for A.H.S.P, Eric lazily clapped for the successful team and, ignoring Kayvin, dragged his feet to the side to get a drink. It was surreal to imagine I seemed to have enjoyed the game more than he did.

Camille and Arthur were as surprised as I was, and we didn't know how to act.

"Is it me or does it seem like he didn't even want to play?"

"Perhaps he was dragged into it by Kayvin?" Arthur said.

"Let's not go down that road again," I muttered.

"Should we go and talk to him, then?" Camille got up. "It might cheer him up."

I watched Elodie and the others hurry down the stairs to meet Eric. There was already a crowd forming around him. Some of the students from the American school seemed to know who he was from his club and wanted a piece of his time as well. A bitter taste slowly filled my mouth.

"I don't know. He already has so many others—"

"Who cares?" Camille was already climbing down the stairs to the pitch. "He's our friend."

That was the thing: He was my friend, but apparently, I wasn't his any longer. I was fine offering my support and showing him that I cared, but from a distance. I didn't want to repeat the awkward encounter we'd had last week, especially not in front of my best friends. So I followed with my head down, but in the end, we couldn't get past the cluster of people who didn't seem to care that Eric was in a bad mood and that his team lost the game. An annoying number of girls circled around him, lavishing him with compliments, while football fans were pestering him about his next game with his club. With a clipped smile, he was doing his best to answer questions and pretended to accept invitations to a party tonight while Elodie, standing close to him, was shooting glares at any girl who acted a little too bold for her taste.

Then a tiny girl emerged from between the legs of a particularly relentless fan, and casually brushing a strand of hair away from her face, shoved a voice recorder under Eric's nose and accidentally hit him with it.

"Colette Times," she said with authority. "Are you assailed by bitter regrets after the outcome of this game?"

Eric looked down at the girl in surprise while rubbing his nose. "The what?"

"*The Colette Times*!"

A tall and lanky guy with glasses appeared at the tiny girl's side and snapped a picture of him with his iPhone. Arthur's mouth dropped open, while Camille stood on her toes to get a better look at the person interviewing Eric. Then I felt someone poking my shoulder. I turned around and was shocked to discover Alberto.

"What are you doing here?" I said, blinking to make sure I wasn't dreaming.

"I came to pick you up."

Alberto was carrying a black umbrella. My shock grew even more when the corner of his lip lifted into a small smile. I suddenly felt a burst of affection for him. He'd just appeared out of nowhere, saving me from having to speak to Eric!

"Thank you," I said, leaning against him. "I hope it wasn't too bothersome to come here."

Alberto looked away as he lifted the umbrella over my head. Camille noticed him and waved.

"Are you leaving? Eric should be done soon. He'll want to speak to you."

Alberto didn't give me time to reply. "I'm taking him out for dinner. We'll be late if we don't leave now."

Camille exchanged a look with Arthur, then nodded. "We'll tell him you were here."

I didn't think my presence would do anything to make Eric's defeat less painful, but I returned her smile with a nod before walking away.

The rain was forcing Alberto to stay close to me so we could find shelter together under his umbrella. The promiscuity turned me a little bold, and I even rubbed my shoulder against him. He glanced down at me in surprise.

"Alberto…"

"Hm?"

"Do you know the difference between a lake and a pond?"

The question clearly caught him off guard. His brow slightly furrowed and his lips parted, he stared at me as if I was a little mental after all. "I don't know. At the end of the day, it's just water, isn't it?"

I couldn't help but smile at his logic. "You're right."

Following Alberto diligently, I thought with a hint of regret that I had missed the rest of Eric's promising interview.

~

Alberto and I took the bus back to Boulevard Saint-Germain where he had booked a table for us at Le Mabillon. Like always, he picked a vegetarian salad, and like always in his presence, I chose the fish. Alberto seemed distracted the whole time, more than usual. I knew it because he was playing with his food instead of gazing out the window as he usually did whenever he had the chance.

I nibbled on my food, occasionally glancing up at his face to marvel at the fact that I got to be the one sitting opposite him. Even after a month together, I was still wondering what on earth I was even doing here. Alberto's phone vibrated several times; after he ignored it for the tenth time, I suggested he might take a look before I picked up the thing and threw it in his glass of water. Always mildly amused by my scowling face, Alberto read his messages and sighed.

"Would you like to go to a party?"

"A party?"

Look, at my age, being invited to parties should have been on my mind constantly, or at least more often than passing my exams with success for example. But I was Zak. I was more astounded that my boyfriend had offered to do something people regarded as convention-ally fun, than I was actually excited to attend a party.

Alberto pointed at my face with a long finger. "Your mouth is open, but I can't hear any words."

"Right. Sorry. Where's this party?"

"Invalides," Alberto answered immediately. "It's Xavier's place."

"Xavier?" I put my cutlery down. "Why do you want to go to Xavier's?"

His chin in his hand, Alberto ignored my question. "Do you want to go or not? We won't stay long. And you can see your friends."

"My friends?" I frowned when I thought of Camille and Arthur. "My friends are there?"

"The whole football team is there. So are the girls from this summer."

Oh, those friends. Not really my friends at all. Until I realised what the whole football team meant, and suddenly, my pulse quickened.

"You, huh… You say we won't stay long?"

"An hour at most."

I pretended well that he convinced me, all the while hating myself for being a hypocrite, and also excited to see Eric again in a different setting. But the fact is, I couldn't resist. He would be in the same flat, perhaps in the same room. How could I possibly turn that chance down?

Again, I should have bitten my tongue instead of agreeing to go to this hellish place. The moment we passed the threshold, I knew I had no business being here. The music was so loud it was a miracle that the whole place wasn't surrounded by police uniforms. A scantily dressed senior girl with pouty red lips and half-closed lids threw herself at Alberto the moment we came in. I marvelled at the way he leapt aside and watched her tumble into the coat racks without an ounce of concern. However, he didn't get that lucky with the second person who launched himself into his arms.

"Alberto! You came! You actually came!"

Xavier had never seemed so happy. I stood there, trying to understand my own feelings as I watched him nuzzle his face affectionally against Alberto's shoulder, but I was having a hard time feeling anything. Alberto's lack of reaction at being cuddled by a drunk acquaintance didn't strike me as unusual, and even forced a smile out of me. But then, it started to lose its charm and became just plain odd. Xavier grabbed Alberto by the arm and told him to follow him, and Alberto simply told me to, I quote, "Wait here, I'll only be a minute" and let Xavier lead him into the corridor, leaving me alone in a strange place surrounded by drunk people.

Xavier lived in a huge Haussmannian flat with high ceilings, polished chevron parquet and eccentric furniture, not unexpected of the son of a baronet. I followed a group of giggling girls to where the music was its loudest and the people their drunkest.

A large group of students were dancing with abandon in the dark living room. Watching with wide eyes beer spilling out of cups, beads of sweat flying into the air, and intoxicated bodies rubbing against each other to the beat of some electronic music, I couldn't help but check my watch. It wasn't even 11 p.m. and most people appeared severely intoxicated. But to my infinite shock, no one was drunker than Eric, whom I spotted drenched in sweat in the middle of the crowd, bouncing on his feet with his eyes closed while wanton creatures clutched at him and hugged him with misty eyes.

Just as I was about to step forward, Elodie came charging into the crowd, holding a glass of water, and tried to force him to drink from it. He refused categorically and emptied another beer instead. I was shocked; I'd never seen Eric in such a state. A million miles away from the smiling, head-on-his-shoulders person I'd come to know. Joy had once vaunted the merits of drunk Eric, but I'm not sure it was what she had in mind then; right now, he just looked a proper mess.

Time slowly went by during which I got to observe a lot of people get increasingly wasted. At some point, Xavier emerged from the other side of the room with Alberto and about half a dozen pretty girls. Alberto seemed to make conversation with Xavier and answer his questions, which I found annoying, and they weren't paying me any attention.

During one song, Eric threw himself at his Elodie, and they swung around the dance floor together. Elodie seemed used to the envious looks she was getting from the other girls. At least her presence was keeping their claws away from him. Eric's head was buried in her shoulder, and it would have almost looked cute if she weren't looking at Alberto standing on the side with interest. What a hussy. On the other side of the room, Joy stole a few vicious glances here and there while emptying Jell-O shots and stroking Melissa's hair, who was lying passed out by the kitchen door. Kayvin was also watching Elodie with his fist tightly closed around his beer. Or perhaps it was Eric he was staring at. His pale eyes were burning with anger.

And what the fuck was up with Alberto, seriously? I saw him looking at me several times, but he didn't bother to reunite with me. I was that close to stomping across the room and going all soap-opera-jealous-boyfriend on him, but he nonchalantly turned around and disappeared around the corner with Xavier in tow.

Parties sucked. They really did. Why did people do this to themselves? How drunk was Eric exactly, and what would it take to stop him? I wish he could see himself right now and realise he was better than that.

All of a sudden, the drunk girl with pouty lips from earlier bumped aggressively into me. "Hey, you!" She missed her next step, and I had to help her back to her feet. "You... You always stand on the side watching people dance like that? It's creepy." She had trouble articulating, and I doubted she'd remember me tomorrow.

"Yes," I said, arching my eyebrow. "Yes, that's exactly what I do."

"Really?"

I nodded. "I've got a permit."

Her eyes narrowed suspiciously. "You what?"

"Yes, he does," someone said behind her.

Alberto had returned, his tall and handsome appearance a relief that washed away my annoyance. Awestruck, the girl tried to hug him again.

"I-I've missed you!"

Alberto expertly moved away from her to stand by my side. "I don't know this person."

Her expression changed, turning into pure fury. "Shit, man, you're awful!"

"Thank you."

He was looking through her as though she was completely transparent. It really seemed like he didn't know her. The girl hissed at him and slunk away somewhere else. I couldn't imagine a life where, everywhere I went, people wanted to throw themselves at me. I was perfectly content to be Zak in that instant. Not Alberto, and not Eric, whose eyes I met when I returned my attention to the dancing crowd.

Elodie was gone. Drunk-dog Eric came stumbling toward me, unaware or unbothered by the number of hands trying to hold him back as he trudged through. With his blond hair sticking to his red face, he wasn't looking good. I stepped backwards in fear he would vomit all over me, but to my shock, he stopped in front of Alberto.

Alberto did not move a muscle when Eric threw his arms around him and pulled him into a ferocious embrace. Eric took his face between his hands and lowered it until their foreheads almost touched. The whites of his eyes were bloodshot, contrasting sharply with his blue irises.

"Alberto, you're such a great guy," Eric slurred. "Such a great guy!"

"You're sweaty."

Alberto removed Eric's hands with an indifferent expression, but Eric glared at him as if he'd just slapped him in the face. Suddenly, the bouncy Elodie appeared at his side, a large smile splitting her face.

"*Heyyy*, what's going on here? Are you making friends?"

Eric grunted in response, looking close to barfing all over her dress. Elodie didn't seem to mind; with a furtive smile at Alberto, which I didn't miss, she carefully turned his body around, resting his head on her shoulder, and attempted to drag him away, perhaps toward a bathroom. But Eric suddenly broke free and charged headfirst into the crowd where he was welcomed with cheers.

"One hour," Alberto said after a quick glance at his phone. "I'm gonna go home."

"Me too." I couldn't watch anymore. This place was a booze-fuelled nightmare.

I didn't know what was worse: Alberto's mysterious relationship with Xavier or having to witness everyone's barely concealed desire for him; the way their gazes turned greedy after each extra drink. Or was it perhaps having to watch my badass friend fall apart and turn into a pathetic creature under the influence, because he lost a stupid football game.

Or... Perhaps I should be totally honest with myself and admit that the thing that really, really got to me was that Eric came to us and hugged my boyfriend without even a spare glance at me. Not even one.

All I wanted was to teleport home and shower to remove the stinking feeling this short visit left on me. I wished Alberto would just leave me outside of Xavier's flat, but we were going in the same direction and could only part halfway through. When we did, I let Alberto kiss me goodbye absently, not even caring this time that he brushed me off every time I asked him which station he was getting out at. I vaguely remembered his lips against the corner of my own, but I was annoyed by the fact that he smelled faintly of Eric.

Alberto went his way, and I went mine. For once, I didn't look back in hope he might do the same. I simply didn't look back.

26

MY SUMMER OF LOVE AND WOE

The next Tuesday, the moment the Drama Club had been waiting for finally happened: our movie was finished. And after some magical string-pulling from Binta and our headmaster, we were all invited to the Filmothèque du Quartier Latin for a private screening of:

MY SUMMER OF LOVE AND WOE

WRITTEN BY CAMILLE BERTHELOT

DIRECTED BY LAURENT DUVAUCHEL AND MICHAEL PARKER

As I stood almost teary-eyed outside the cinema, I tried to imagine how hard it must have been for Duvo to write down Michael's name next to his, and it made me snigger under my breath.

The day was beautiful like they can be at this time of year, with summer refusing to concede to fall, blessing us one last time with a gorgeous afternoon of high temperatures and gentle breezes. The sun fell on the whole street and people like me were reluctant to leave its warmth, but Duvo was starting to lose patience, and Binta was gradually raising her voice to entice us to get inside.

Inside the small screening room, it was cool and dark. The entirety of the Drama Club, now twenty strong, was enough to fill almost a third of the seats. I watched Alberto's profile with mixed feelings as he stood motionless with his hands in his pockets, his grey eyes staring through the stream of people coming in.

On one hand, I wanted to feel excited to be here with him. It reminded me of the premieres I used to imagine us attending together. On the other hand, my enthusiasm for this sort of thing had waned with each passing week in his company. It was expected since I was the only one who ever showed any feelings out of us two. Eventually, my passion had dwindled, and I had pretty much given up on thoughts of enjoying myself entirely. But today, I wanted to make an effort, considering we had been together for almost exactly a month. I tugged on his sleeve with a smile.

"Excited?"

His cool eyes fell on me. "About?"

"The movie."

"Sure," he said without conviction.

The sudden arrival of Michael put a stop to our conversation. He looked particularly amazing in a black leather jacket and a pair of awesome sunglasses that made him look like a rockstar. I waved at him excitedly.

"Hey, Michael!"

I was no fool; I registered the tension in Alberto's shoulders as soon as Michael drew nearer. I lifted my head to whisper in his ear. "Why is it so awkward between you two?"

Alberto lightly rested his hand on my waist. "Don't worry about it."

Removing his sunglasses, Michael stopped in front of us with a smile that brightened the whole room. "How are you, guys?"

"Great," I said automatically, at the same time as Alberto.

It almost caused him to smile. "We spoke at the same time."

That was easy. I knew what he would say before he did, because one of Alberto's favourite words was *Great*.

How are you? Great. *How's life?* Great. *Your summer?* Fucking great. *Your sex life?* Well… maybe not this one. But yeah. Everything was just great.

I returned my focus to Michael. "Where's Louis?"

"At work."

"Oh."

That was disappointing. A naughty part of myself wanted Alberto to meet Louis and Louis to meet Alberto. Glares would be exchanged; the tension would be palpable in the air; perhaps they would fight, which would be terribly dramatic *and* romantic, and perhaps in the chaos and violence, Eric would show up to rescue me and we would be best friends again.

"So he doesn't want to see the movie?"

"He's good." Michael grinned. "He's seen it three times already."

"He has?"

"Perks of living with me, I guess."

He accidentally — or not — met Alberto's eyes at that moment, and an uncomfortable silence fell upon us. Embarrassed for Alberto, I put an end to it with a cheerful tone.

"You look different today. I mean, you look good and all, but... different."

Michael snorted and, his cheeks flushing, leaned into me and whispered in a secretive tone, "I'm wearing Louis's clothes."

"Why?" I asked, dumbfounded.

"Clothes swap!" Michael squeezed my shoulders, and, seeing Camille and Arthur by the front row, tore down the stairs to salute them.

Alberto stared after him. "Is he on drugs?"

"No, he's just happy."

Alberto's gaze lingered on the back of Michael for a certain length of time, which would have made any boyfriend worry. But the uncomfortable feeling in my stomach wasn't worry, it was shame. Shame that I knew something was off and I was too dumb or smitten with my own fantasy to do anything about it.

Alberto and I... we were not happy.

I only had to look at the smile on Michael's face the moment I mentioned his boyfriend. Or the way he glowed when he told me he was wearing Louis's clothes. If I made Alberto smile, then he took great pains in hiding it from me. As for myself, I haven't felt the burning desire to smile since I...

All of a sudden, a faint memory reappeared in the back of my mind. Sleepy old me, head in the clouds. My cheek on a warm arm. A rowboat's gentle swaying. Bardot's voice like a caress, humming words about the sun. I was happy then; I just didn't know it.

What the hell was wrong with me! It was my first premiere. Yes, it was only a small project, a short film shot in twenty days by a neurotic teacher and a soft-hearted eye candy. But still, I had been waiting to watch this film for a long time, and I intended to enjoy it. And I wouldn't let *anything* get in the way.

More guests arrived, seniors that I personally didn't know, and some which I recognised as members of the Colette football team, absent

Eric and Kayvin. The latter's presence would have surprised me, but what astounded me more was to find Xavier among the newcomers. Followed by a good-looking girl who was scowling at him, he ran straight to us and slapped his large hand onto Alberto's thin shoulder.

"Alberto!" he said with unusually animated eyes. He glanced at the girl on his left. "That's my buddy Alberto."

His *buddy* gave him an indifferent look that had me wonder again what kind of relationship they could possibly have. The girl stared at Alberto as if he were the only glass of water around on a sweltering day. "*You're* Alberto?"

"Thank you," Alberto said without a glance at her. "Why are you here?"

Xavier squeezed his shoulder, and Alberto broke free with a twitch of his lip, which in my experience, indicated mild — or major, who knew with Alberto — annoyance. I felt like punching Xavier in the throat and realised I had recently developed some underlying anger issues and needed to go see a therapist urgently.

"To see the movie!" Xavier said.

Alberto's eyes narrowed. "But you know what the movie's about. You're gonna see two guys kissing."

The girl giggled. Xavier followed suit. "Yeah, I know. I really want to see it."

"Why?" Alberto asked, with the hint of a frown, which I immediately and correctly interpreted as mild — or major — lassitude.

"I don't know. Same reason people watch horror movies, I suppose."

Now I was the one annoyed. I clicked my tongue, and Alberto surprisingly put his hand on my back. "Suit yourself," he told Xavier in a cold tone.

Xavier was about to reply, but something caught his eye, and he scrambled downstairs to the front row. His date followed confusedly while tossing looks over her shoulder hoping — in vain — Alberto would notice her.

"Once and for all," I said, pinching the bridge of my nose. "Why do you hang out with this guy?"

Alberto gave me one of his odd looks. "But I don't."

I must have looked angry. He brushed his thumb along the side of my face, my anger melting in his touch. Any gesture of tenderness from Alberto was already a rare occurrence, but in public, it was almost never seen. By the time I had recovered from my shock, he was pulling me toward the seats closest to the doors.

"Come on. Let's sit down."

He sat me by the aisle so he could converse with Sander and Oliver. From the top of the room, I could observe everyone below without detection. I quite liked doing that, and glancing over at my boyfriend, I noticed he was doing the same. The warmth I felt at the thought was subtle, but it was there.

Shortly after, I heard a commotion at my back and shivered: I knew instantly what it meant. A group of ruddy boys and laughing girls barged into the screening room like a gust of brutal wind and among them, the childish laughter belonging to a bright star made everyone's head turn.

I didn't need to turn; I knew Eric had arrived, and I knew he came with enough people to fill the leftover seats. The rest of the Colette football team came tumbling down the stairs, followed by a group of fit guys who had to be from his Parisian club. I spotted Joy, Melissa, and Elodie among them as well. Soon enough, every one of these people would see Eric make out with me on a giant screen, and it was like this silly dog had not given it a second thought. Warmth spread throughout my chest, and I couldn't help but smile.

Eric and his friends descended toward the empty rows in great tumult until Duvo started barking at them. Eric ignored him and threw himself into Michael's arms as if the two were best friends finally reunited after some tragedy unfairly separated them.

For the second time today, my tongue clicked in annoyance.

Overly stimulated by the presence of so many people to sniff and bounce around, Eric finally took a seat after Duvo personally got up to force him down. He was sitting right behind Michael and messing up his hair. When he caught sight of Camille, he blew her a kiss.

I remembered the time when it was my hair he was ruffling constantly. Sitting so far away in the top row, he probably couldn't see me, or he would have blown me a kiss too. But why? After the fiasco of our last conversation and the horrible way he ignored me at Xavier's party, I was mad to even imagine he remembered more than my name.

Suddenly, Eric stood up again. He abruptly turned and found me staring. He addressed me with a simple nod that could just as well have been for Alberto. I returned his nod but didn't bother concealing the pain in my eyes. With a longing sigh, I seized Alberto's hand. He let me hold on to it until the lights went out.

Duvo had to hiss at Eric to sit down three more times before silence filled the room at last. A moment later, the film began.

Even after years of acting, seeing oneself on screen can still be considered a strange experience. I never minded, it was always what I wanted. On that screen I wasn't Zak, I was Thomas, and if I was really good at looking threatened by Adam's presence, it was partly because I was not a bad actor, and partly because it had taken me less than a week to fall for Eric's many charms.

I witnessed it all with a little smile no one else could see. Some of my reactions had nothing to do with acting — including in our earliest scenes. Was it possible that he had done something to me from the first moment we spoke? Perhaps even the first moment we gazed into each other's eyes? How long exactly had he been hiding in the deepest part of my heart? My own eyes began filling with tears at the sight of our characters falling in love with each other despite the impossible obstacles of the time. To think there was no inhumane law or class difference to separate us now, and yet we didn't end up together. Not that it mattered. I felt I was a decent actor, but Eric was even better: he was so relaxed around me in his scenes, even if he had to fake his attraction toward men, he appeared gayer than I was.

What a waste.

And he looked so handsome dressed as a lord. Each of his appearances triggered a series of whistles and catcalls from girls and boys alike. Duvo threatened to kick everyone out, so Camille shushed him loudly, and even from the top row, I could hear Michael and Eric failing to repress their laughter. I trembled to observe live what I never got to see on set, how Eric acted when my character had his back turned to him, the particularly sexy swipe of his tongue across his bottom lip. It didn't matter, I repeated to myself over that half-hour; it didn't matter; it was all fictional. It wasn't real. It was a fantasy world where Eric fell maddeningly in love with me. What I had with Alberto was real. It had to be.

When we got to the kissing scene, the whole room erupted. I sat on the edge of my seat with burning cheeks, stunned and a little bit turned on. Thankfully, no one could see my face in the dark screening room. How similar was I to Thomas then, simultaneously excited and terrified, both resisting and surrendering to the fact that it was the last time we'd be together. And how similar he was to Adam, bold, confident, and yet, in his openness, a vision of vulnerability.

Oh, and the way we stumbled back into that desk had to be the hottest scene ever shot.

People whistled and cheered even as Duvo sprayed the seats in front of him with spit as he attempted to silence them. Eric rose from his seat, arms up, and accepted the adoration of the crowd as though he had scored a particularly important goal. Some guy screamed, "Kiss, me, Eric!" and I twisted my neck savagely to find the culprit. It was too dark, however. I didn't catch him.

The rest of the film happened without incident. Camille, Duvo, and Michael went for the bitter ending, with Thomas walking away from the mansion with wet cheeks, and Adam looking on from behind his window, his hands clutched behind his back and tears in his eyes. Though this ending was better, felt right for the times, and was award-worthy, I couldn't help but feel awful, wanting realism to go fuck itself in favour of letting us enjoy a happy ending for once.

I told Alberto just so when the lights turned on, people's clapping drowned by the cheers from the overly excited group formed by Eric's friends.

"You should consider yourself lucky that your characters aren't dead," Alberto said in his flat voice. "Homos usually don't make it alive to the end of the movie."

Alberto, Alberto, Alberto.

I observed his wonderful face with a slight frown. What I had with him… Was it really… real? Sometimes I felt he was like the characters I'd just witnessed on screen: he felt almost loving, almost mine, but he wasn't, not really. And if he was a fantasy too, then our relationship was…

Eric and I made eye contact. The corners of his lips slightly lifted up. My heart stopped; I wanted to grab that sober, almost polite smile of his and force it into the kind of grin he used to flash back at Aurons.

The times at Aurons.

We'll always have Longchamps.

Gosh, I wish we had more than memories. I wish we had time. And wind. And words. And bees.

My heart only resumed beating when Eric turned away. The sadness I'd felt lately came rushing back, so did the words I'd repeated to myself:

I'll be fine. I'll be fine.

We'll always have Longchamps.

And that insane kissing scene which I would probably watch repeat-

384

edly in secret for the next decade. However, a part of me protested and struggled against my own words: No, actually, I wouldn't be fine. And I did miss him terribly, and I needed to tell him that. Even if it was wrong of me to have feelings for my straight friend, I'd rather have him around me and suffer, than not be in his presence ever again.

Camille and Arthur noticed me standing like a fool with a furrowed brow and, to my great relief, walked up to us.

"So? So?" Camille took my hands. "What do you think?"

"It was amazing." I patted her hand. "Really depressing ending, though."

She nodded. "It would have been unrealistic for both of them to make it. I wanted to really take a stab at the societal differences of the 1920s. Those were troubled times."

I heaved a deep sigh. "Times are less troubled now, and it still feels unrealistic to me when people find love."

Camille's lips tightened whereas Arthur's mouth fell open. Only then I realised how my words could be interpreted. The three of us glanced anxiously at Alberto. He took notice of us after a certain time and blinked.

"Sure, I liked it."

Arthur appeared about to say something, but was mercifully interrupted when a trio of kids looking vaguely familiar tore up the stairs with determined expressions. Among them, I recognised the tiny girl who interviewed Eric after his game.

"I need to ask you a few very important questions," she said in a pompous tone. "It's for *The Colette Times*."

"Okay," I said, my smile returning.

"All right?"

Snapping her fingers, she turned to her crew, the lanky guy with glasses taking pictures with his phone and another chubby boy who held a video camera and started filming the conversation. The tiny girl shoved her voice recorder under my nose and fired questions at me with the speed of a machine gun, leaving me no time to think or breathe.

"How was the shooting?

"It was fine."

"Was it incredibly hard?"

"No, it was fine, really—"

"What was your favourite part of it?"

"I'm not sure."

"The end?"

"What? What do you mean?"

"Was going home your favourite part of the trip?"

"No. I don't think so."

"Do you still want to be an actor?"

"Yes."

"Is Eric a good kisser?"

"Very."

I'd spoken abruptly, without thinking. The tiny girl brandished her recorder under my nose with a disapproving look. My cheeks started to heat up. Alberto intervened then, pushing the thing away from my face.

"Don't you have anything better to ask?" His eyes shone with real exasperation. "Why don't you speak to the writer or the director?"

Camille shook her head with a grimace and plunged into the crowd to save herself from *The Colette Times*'s inquiries. Arthur followed suit. Immediately, the little girl turned to her team, her finger pointed at Camille.

"Get her!"

"Wait," I said, in an effort to help my friend. "The director's somewhere around here."

A few rows down, Michael was showing Louis's leather jacket to Joy and Melissa. I pointed at him; after all, he was supposed to be good at these things. But Duvo dashed toward us, even climbing over seats in his haste to reach us.

"I'm here, I'm here!"

"Oh yeah, he's here," I said without enthusiasm.

The Colette Times's undaunted team moved on to Duvo with sniggers. I exhaled a relieved breath and looked around me: almost everyone else had left already. Beside me, Alberto still appeared annoyed.

"No one cares about art," he said grimly.

I shrugged. "At least they're covering it."

"You should be covered by *Variety*, not by this maniac."

"Maybe one day." Alberto's impulse to interrupt the interview had not escaped me, and I felt a little amused. But I also felt treacherously impatient to go outside and see if Eric was still out there. The image of Adam and Thomas's kiss was still burning in my mind. "I wonder where I can get a copy of the film."

Alberto rubbed his eyes. "Ask Camille."

What a good idea. I should be able to get a copy. Knowing the writer had many, many perks. If I had known my own feelings before, I would have coerced her into adding five extra kissing scenes. It wouldn't have been the same movie, for sure. But I was okay with that nowadays.

"Is it the last time we're all together, then?" I asked with a pang of regret as we exited the screening room.

"You see each other every week at the drama club." Alberto yawned. "That's plenty already."

"But—" I stopped talking, realising what I was doing — and that he would know who I was talking about if I insisted. "No, you're right."

I tried to walk out of the cinema with Alberto's hand in mine, but he had exhausted his meagre resources of affection. Outside, he found Sander, and they did what they enjoyed doing most: Standing next to each other in silence while checking their phones.

I knew Alberto wanted to take me to a small art exhibition right after the screening, but I wanted to stick around and hang out with my friends, so I slipped away unnoticed to find Camille and Arthur. While stretching my neck to find them, I caught a glimpse of Eric in Elodie's arms. Her hand curled around his neck; she was kissing his glowing cheek.

It'd been four days since Alberto had last kissed me. If I counted the faint feeling of his lips against the corner of my own as a kiss. A feeling of yearning expanded rapidly in my chest, propagated to my legs, and forced them to move toward Eric. I wanted to separate their embrace, to wrap my own arms around his neck and to shower his cheeks with my own kisses, even though I knew it wouldn't be welcomed and I'd make an ass of myself. Still, I elbowed my way past half the football team and their friends, *The Colette Times*'s unrelenting team surrounding Joy and Melissa, as well as Xavier and his date, until I found myself face to face with Eric and Elodie.

Eric and I both gave a loud and clumsy "Hey!" at the same time.

There was a silence.

Then again, at the same time: "What's up?"

Neither of us dared speak again. Eventually, Elodie cleared her throat, and Eric quickly pushed her toward me.

"This is Elodie."

"We were in the same class!" Elodie and I snapped in unison.

This was starting to become a thing. I wanted to run away and melt into a puddle of embarrassment, but I couldn't let her win either. It was awful. Mercifully, Elodie hated awkwardness more than I did and eventually took a step back, using the excuse of needing to speak to Joy and Melissa. I was glad to see her gone on account of how jealous of her I was for obvious reasons.

"How lame was that?" Eric said between two snorts.

When my expression turned serious, his own smile vanished from his face, and he almost swallowed the piece of gum he was chewing.

"I'll tell you what's lame," I said, staring deep into his eyes. "If I hadn't forced my way through your barrage of people, I would have never gotten the chance to talk to you. Are you avoiding me?"

"No," he said, looking away.

Liar!

That he would avoid me because I wasn't exactly a good friend, that I went too far and developed a crush on him that he may or may not have been aware of and may or may not have made him feel uncomfortable was one thing. But our other friends? They were innocent.

"You're not even talking to Camille and Arthur anymore. I guess you really meant it when you said you were done being a loser."

Eric's smile returned, albeit a little forced. "Don't be like that. I was just about to go talk to them."

"When? When I was gone?"

The tip of his ears turned bright pink.

"See?! You *are* avoiding me."

His expression turned impatient. "I told you I was busy!"

"You also told me you were my friend, and you told me you'd try, and—"

"So what?" He looked surprisingly moody and defensive for someone who pretended to be so innocent.

"You're not too busy for Xavier's parties. Clearly."

My tone was cold. His eyebrows rose in response. "Yeah? And I thought Alberto was too good for parties. Guess not."

"Oh!" I blinked. "Good to know you remember seeing *him* at least."

"I remember seeing you too!" He sneered. "At *Xavier's* party! And I thought you didn't like my friends!"

I was momentarily taken aback. "Really? You saw me? You didn't even spare me one look!"

Eric scrunched up his face. "I remember seeing your *back*!"

My mouth closed. I didn't know what to say. He seemed to be unsure about his wording as well. His expression turned embarrassed.

"As you were leaving…" He sounded resentful. "I saw your back as you were leav—"

"You remember hugging Alberto?"

Eric pursed his lips and turned a shade redder, but defiance was plain in his eyes. "I hugged *everyone* that night."

"That's not even true!"

He didn't hug *me*!

Eric and I stared at each other at length with eyes full of resentment, our jaws clenched and our hands balled into fists. But then, both of our expressions gradually softened and relaxed at the same time. Our lips began curling up, and we ended up smiling at each other. It was incomprehensible, and yet, it made perfect sense.

"I've never seen you in that state," I said once we had calmed down. "You shouldn't get so messed up because of a football game, you know."

He scoffed. "It had nothing to do with the game."

"Oh. What was wr—"

"Just needed to deal with old stuff. All sorted."

Eric suddenly got closer, his sly grin making an appearance. After the past few weeks, I didn't expect that at all. My body reacted instantly and started buzzing with anticipation.

"Anyway, did you come here to fight?" His eyes shone with mischief. He'd reverted back to the friend I'd lost. "Or to tell me how amazing I was? It was to tell me I'm amazing, right?"

I shook my head, but my chest was bursting with affection. "You didn't tell me anything of the sort, why should I?"

Eric gripped my shoulders and squeezed them hard. "Zak, you're amazing. Now, it's my turn. Tell-me-tell-me-tell-me."

His fingers dug into the flesh of my shoulders; it was painful, but it was also the first time he'd touched me in weeks. It took me a lot of self-control not to retaliate by throwing myself into his arms and telling him how much I'd longed to see him and mess with him again.

"You… were… stop shaking meeee… amazing." He released me, and I took a deep breath. "I mean all right. You were all right."

His hand flew to ruffle my hair. Before I could fight back, Binta and Duvo requested a moment of our attention to take pictures of the Longchamps team. Eric immediately seized my arm and dragged me along to the front doors of the cinema.

The old gang clumsily gathered, Duvo and Binta included. Seeing Melissa glued to Michael's chest, Joy attempted to keep Eric close as well, but he dodged her expertly. Naturally, Eric being Adam and I being Thomas, we belonged together in the pictures. Ignoring Joy's disappointed face, Eric slipped next to me and put his arm around me. I immediately and without hesitation retaliated, going as far as squeezing his narrow waist like the inflamed virgin that I was.

"We should hang out again," he whispered as we were being photographed, his own hand now pulling me so tight I was sure to find a handprint on my skin later tonight.

"I agree," I said in a croaky voice, my heart about to explode.

After casting a bright smile at the camera, he shook his head and released me with a serious expression. "But, the thing is, I really can't. I'm too busy."

The elation I'd just felt vanished in a puff of smoke. While the crowd dispersed, I was too stunned to speak. At this moment, Xavier's pretty friend arrived on tiptoes and begged to take a picture with Eric. He obliged with a charming grin and said nothing when she kissed his cheek excitedly. When she was gone, he turned around to find me with my arms crossed over my chest.

"Slut."

Eric's eyes took on a wild glint. "The *S*-word, Zakaria?"

"You deserve it."

He reached out his hand to poke me. "Aww, so mean, and when I have eyes only for you."

My eyebrows rose. "Confirmed."

Eric laughed good-heartedly. Behind him, Joy's expression had turned murderous. Her reaction reminded me of something I'd been dying to know.

"Now that I've got you, there's something I really wanted to ask."

Eric's smile froze a little, but he quickly recovered and cocked his head like a good dog. "I'm all ears."

I refrained from patting his head with difficulty. "Why was Joy so mad at you? I still don't get it."

Eric's expression turned puzzled. "When was Joy mad at me?"

That clueless motherfucker! I knocked my fist on his head. Laughing, he grabbed my hand and pulled me to him. With a pounding heart, I pushed him away, afraid I might lose control.

"Listen, listen," I said seriously. "Joy was mad at you after that time you two left together to do god knows what."

"God knows what," Eric imitated, the corner of his lips curling up. "I. Don't. Know. I don't know!"

"Liar."

"Remind me of what time, then. I want you to say it."

I stepped back to steady myself and threw a look over my shoulder toward Alberto.

"He's not looking," Eric said with a dismissive wave of his hand.

Alberto was indeed in Xavier's clutches. I turned back to Eric with haste. "She said something in your ear, and you made a stupid joke like 'This would definitely bring me joy. *Hahaha*.'" My poor impression of Eric's childish laughter made him giggle, and he reached out to touch either my hair or my face. He earned himself a slap on the hand. "Speak, beast."

"Alright, I'll tell you." Eric drew closer, close enough so that he could whisper in my ear. My whole body became taut in expectation. "She said she would give me dessert... and that the kitchen was clear. So I followed her to the kitchen."

The familiar feeling of his breath tickling my ear turned me into jelly. My eyelids fluttered closed.

"I found the brownies and helped myself," Eric went on. "Then I left. For some reason, she was angry at that. Beats me."

When he leaned away, I took a breath of much-needed air. "Beats you, really?" I sounded sarcastic. That was it, though? That was *it*? His statement made me feel like exploding in laughter and jumping up and down until my heart leapt out of my throat.

"Zak, what are you insinuating?"

I couldn't let him guess my feelings, so I snorted loudly. "Stop playing innocent."

That beast watched my face a long time and scoffed. "Zakaria thinks I slept with everyone there. Between meals... between games, even between takes. I must have been really busy indeed. Is that it?"

Frustrated, I lowered my voice to a mutter. "You didn't sleep with me, that's for sure."

I didn't know how those words escaped my lips. The moment they did, I broke out in a cold sweat. But the ever unfazed Eric pulled me close and buried his hand mercilessly in my hair, the fruity smell of his gum wafting into my nostrils.

"I'd never, Zak. You're so innocent. How could I?"

My heart thumped. For a second, I may have been hoping he'd say he'd sleep with me right here if I wished it. I would have refused and proceeded to mock-beat the shit out of him, of course, but at least he'd have said what I wanted to hear. But I didn't expect him to say *that*.

Everybody saw me as a fragile creature, devoid of human urges and needs, and all I could do was stay planted on my ass right there, sulking in silence, feeling quite humiliated. But his hand was in my hair, annoyingly warm but familiar, the tip of his tongue was sticking out the corner of his mouth, and his blue eyes gazed at the chaos he was wreaking with obvious delight. And I felt my heart both sink and double in size at the same time.

"What?" he asked when he saw my complicated expression. "What did I say this time?"

"I miss you," I blurted out.

I miss you, and moreover, I miss myself when I'm with you. I'm so confused by your behaviour toward me. Do you really care about nothing? Do you really just joke around? Or was our constant bickering and bantering our version of flirting?

If we couldn't be friends, then could we be more?

"You miss me?" Eric withdrew his hand with a frozen expression.

One look at his face and I knew to immediately backpedal to cover my tracks.

"I miss you on stage," I said with a smile. "There's no one to challenge me now." It was best to throw a compliment here and there and excuse myself before I said too much.

"Oh, right." He gave a small nod. "What about Alberto?"

"Alberto has left the club. And in any case…" My shoulders lifted. "He's no match for you."

I meant to compliment him, but I may have spoken too fast: Eric's expression turned even colder. There was no trace of a smile left on his face. I knew I'd said something wrong, but I didn't care to stick around to find out what exactly. At this instant, Alberto came gliding through the crowd, calling my name, saving me from embarrassment once again.

"Let's go. We stayed too long already."

He pulled me away without a look at Eric, and I didn't resist, too grateful to be carried away from here.

When I glanced over my shoulder, Eric was whispering in Elodie's ear, his brow furrowed, and she was looking at me with a startled expression.

27

ALL THE THINGS HE SAID

The following Friday, I almost fell off the edge of my bench when Alberto covered my eyes from behind with his cold hands.

"Guess who?" he asked.

"Alberto."

Alberto.

The word now sounded like a broken record in my mind. I watched my boyfriend walk around the bench with a dubitative frown. "What are you doing here? Weren't you supposed to be with Sander and Oliver?"

Using his hoodie as a blanket, Alberto clumsily sat down at my feet. "Do you want me to leave?"

"No. Of course not. Sorry."

It was just that Alberto had caught me in the middle of some serious soul-searching and a new speciality of mine: Rewinding past conversations to find deeper meanings until my head felt about to explode.

Alberto unfolded his long arm to pluck one of my earphones out and brought it close to his own. "What are you listening to?"

"Nothing," I said, quickly turning off my mom's playlist.

"It sounded like that thing we played all the time during the holidays."

"It isn't."

I tossed the iPod in my backpack. Alberto looked at me with cold eyes; he probably knew something was off. Or maybe he didn't. If he did, why wasn't he doing anything about it? After a full month of being his boyfriend, I felt I still knew nothing about him. It was driving me insane.

Or perhaps I should have admitted the truth to what was really pushing me to the limit these past few days: my last encounter with Eric. His fingers digging into my shoulders, his hand on my waist, his whole attitude which suggested he missed me… and the true culprits. *His words.*

"What are *you* doing here?" Alberto asked, his face turned toward the other side of the playground where the football players usually hung out together. "Class is over. You're not going home?"

"I was just doing homework."

If homework implied re-living my meeting with Eric since it happened three days ago, then I was certainly working my ass off.

Alberto sought my eyes, and I purposely avoided him. My heart was beating too fast when he approached me nowadays, and it wasn't from yearning. Today was even worse: His beautiful face was just the same, and when it turned away, I stared at it with a cold and analytic eye.

Alberto was like one of those statues we admired in museums. I once lost myself gazing at it, marvelling at its beauty, and wanting to possess it. But no matter how exquisite, the original colours had faded long ago. The marble felt cold and insipid. After staring at it for too long, I longed for something else.

Something bold and colourful and full of childish nonsense.

When Eric and I talked after the screening, my state of mind was one of chaos caused by surprise and joy at being finally reunited with him. I couldn't think straight, and I probably missed some of the things he said, in favour of remembering the things he did. But perhaps I'd been wrong all along. Perhaps I should have listened to what he said a tad better each time his cute little lips parted, and perhaps I would have read some things differently.

Or perhaps I had reverted back to delusions and wanted to find meaning where it didn't belong.

And so for all this time, I'd been very careful when mentally debriefing our last conversation. *Oh, he was only joking, he didn't mean it like that. He knows what to say to mess with me and make me blush, he loves to flirt because it makes him look good, he cannot help it, he's always like this…* But at the end of the day, there was that one thing, a sentence so surreal, I didn't immediately pick up on its meaning. A few words spoken in haste which refused to leave my head now, however I tried to make sense out of it: When I made a fool of myself and told him he didn't sleep with me, Eric drew closer, plunged his hand in my hair, and said he would never, because I was too innocent.

At no point in this sentence was there any allusion to the slight complication of me being a boy.

And so, the idea was born, and it lingered, and started growing. I could barely breathe for want of information. Because at my young age and with my inexistent social life, I wasn't really aware of people being attracted to more than one gender, and Eric never said he was.

But he never said he wasn't.

He only said he could never sleep with me because I was innocent. And in the words of childhood pop icon Britney Spears: I'm not that innocent!

I slipped a look at the gorgeous young man sitting at my feet with his eyes closed. Alberto wasn't straight, and he had culture and experience in this world. He probably hung out with tons of people all the time when he wasn't with me. After hesitating a moment and cursing myself at my own shamelessness, I still ended up asking him about it.

"Alberto?"

He slowly opened his eyes, in a sensual way that should have made me fall from the bench, if only my affections were not already engaged elsewhere.

"Yes?"

"Do bisexual people exist?" I couldn't believe my boldness. My heart started thumping in my chest.

Alberto gave me a long look before speaking. "Yes."

"Really? Can people *really* be bisexual?"

After a pause, Alberto's expression turned thoughtful. "I guess. I guess people can be anything, you know."

I watched his face with interest, trying to gain knowledge about him from his answer. I'd heard several things about Alberto's sexuality, all of them sounding both mysterious and ridiculous. It's not like I enjoyed prying, but if he liked men, he clearly didn't like to be physically close to them. Unless I was the problem, and he simply didn't want to touch me. Or he simply preferred women, as I'd heard a few times, and didn't want to backtrack out of our relationship out of misplaced pride.

"Are you, hum… like that?" I asked in a small voice.

Perhaps all he needed to come clean was a direct question. But

Alberto's cat-like gaze fell on me, cold and guarded, and made me regret asking. "What?"

"You're not, then?"

He looked away as an answer. I'd take that as a no, then. But what was he, really?! Was he even human? Or was he really a demi-god like in my childish fantasies? How come he never grabbed my ass or did anything really untoward like Eric was always threatening to do?

Alberto noticed my turmoil and gently poked my ankle. "Are you? Is that why you're asking me these weird questions?"

I dipped my head. "I'm not. I was just thinking, I've never met a bisexual person."

"That you know of."

"Makes sense. It's easier to hide if you play both fields."

But if Eric was bisexual, wouldn't everyone know already? He didn't strike me as someone ashamed of his own desires. And other people already spoke at length of his many, many conquests, none of them identifying as male.

I couldn't make any sense of it.

Alberto nodded sleepily. "My father used to say bisexuals are homos in disguise."

"Really? Do you believe that?"

He shrugged, meaning the conversation was over. I was tempted to ask him about his father, and if he was okay with him being gay, but there was no way Alberto would ever answer me. When I thought of all the things Eric and I shared in comparison even though we weren't together, I felt starved.

Right now, my head was somewhat clearer. With the knowledge that this would be one of my last chances to enjoy it, I drank in the sight of my Alberto sitting quietly on his hoodie and finally noticed that he was holding a crumpled newspaper.

"What's that?"

"Nothing."

I met his gaze. It was empty, expressionless, a dark pit in which I'd fallen once and from where I climbed out little by little by remembering the warmth of the sun on my skin. I started nurturing strange and immature ideas, such as, if he didn't tell me immediately, I'd dump him right here and now.

"Come on, what is it?"

Just at this moment, a group of students walked past sniggering. I clearly saw in their hands something resembling a newspaper.

"Alberto?"

My exasperated expression enticed Alberto to hand over the paper begrudgingly. "It's that stupid paper. I've only read the title and I already know it's garbage."

It was a copy of *The Colette Times*. The *first* copy of *The Colette Times*. And it read, in large black letters:

ERIC T.R. IS A GOOD KISSER

And in smaller letters:

Says partner on-screen when questioned
in front of belligerent escort.

"Belligerent escort?" Alberto tried to snatch away the paper, but I lifted it over my head, out of reach. I couldn't help laughing as I stared at the title, understood its meaning, and imagined Eric's reaction to reading it.

"Belligerent escort?" Alberto repeated, showing signs of helplessness. "I'm your boyfriend!"

My very handsome boy... friend?

Boyfriend sounded too strange, not only on his lips, but on the edge of my mind. Boyfriends kiss and hold hands and sneak around to do all sorts of things. They find excuses to put their hands on each other. Hell, Eric acted more like a boyfriend to me during those magical two and a half weeks than Alberto did in over a month. I still believed most people at school, if asked, would assume Alberto and I were just friends. Which for example explained the group of girls still following Alberto around at all times, or why some of them still came up to us and invited us to parties, and of course, why I felt so lonely even in his company.

But, oh! Eric must have laughed for hours when he read this headline. Or so I hoped. I could clearly imagine him wiping tears of mirth with the back of his hand before stapling this article on his shirt to wear as a badge of honour.

Warm. It felt warm, just thinking of him.

"I don't think she's noticed me at all." Alberto sounded annoyed. "Or she wouldn't have called me an escort."

"Don't be upset. She only mentions me as Eric's partner on screen..." My voice trailed off. "And nothing else."

Under the headline, a picture showed the Longchamps gang gathered together on the front steps of the cinema. Eric and I looked very pro, but I remembered how his hand felt on my waist, how tightly he held me, his words spoken breathlessly.

We should hang out again.

Alberto returned his gaze toward the other side of the playground. Eric's usual spot was still empty at the moment. "Why is everyone so obsessed with that guy?"

I let out a philosophical sigh. "Must be the bees."

"The what?"

"Nothing."

Eric just had a way of making you feel all fuzzy and warm. A contagious love for life. If I weren't already crazy about him, I would definitely be.

Feeling myself blush, I gave a little cough. "Should I read on?"

Alberto sunk back into apathy, his occasional blinking the only sign of cerebral activity in that enigmatic skull of his.

Under paragraphs at length about Eric's figure and toothpaste commercial smile, there was indeed a passionate — if not scathing — review of *My Summer Of Love and Woe*, the "Pathetic tale of two young men desperately falling in love with each other instead of appreciating the value of the many pretty and available young girls in the neighbourhood, who would have been better suited for any of them…"

"Homophobes," Alberto said between yawns. "Now I recognise the Colette touch."

"I think she's got a crush on Eric!" I said excitedly.

Alberto gave me another odd look. I deflected with a smile and read on. The article said nothing about Arthur's skills but bashed his haircut, and Michael was only credited as assistant *to* the director, but after slamming the cowardly Camille for running away from the only free and independent press, it went on to congratulate Monsieur Duvauchel on his real success: his relationship with Binta, the history teacher, covered in more details on page six.

The style of writing was preposterous. My ribs soon became painful from laughing.

"Stop reading this rag," Alberto said, nudging me with his foot. "Let's talk about this weekend. There's an exhibition I want to see about pots from Ancient Rome."

"I don't know, Alberto. I think I'll pass."

After following him around this past month, I was feeling pretty much done with the interminable exhibitions. The thing was, Alberto didn't even seem interested in them. He dragged himself from room to room, struggling not to yawn, looking at the time on his watch. Sometimes he sat in front of a large piece and may have appeared to others like he was deeply moved by it, but he was almost definitely sleeping with his eyes open. There could be no other explanation.

No. Enough of pots, plants, and paintings. I'd much rather keep reading this very entertaining rag which could at least breathe some life into me.

"You don't want to expand your knowledge, then," Alberto said, and I heard an accent of judgment in his tone.

"Something like that," I answered. Then I met his eyes with purpose. "Unless you want to give me a lesson in anatomy."

Alberto looked at me with a blank expression. I held his gaze. My first thought was to rattle him just the way Eric did to me, but now I found myself really curious about what he'd say.

Alberto maintained eye contact for a long time before turning his face away. "Never mind, then."

I guess I had my answer.

With a shake of my head, I dived back into the top-notch journalism from the tiny fifteen-year-old editor-in-chief, Elisa R. When I reached the sports page, I couldn't help myself and snorted all over the ink.

FROM LOVER TO LOSER,
THERE'S ONLY ONE LETTER

Eric T.R.'s pathetic performance during the first football game of the season will live in infamy.

But at least he's cool with it.

"They should call it The Eric Times, not *The Colette Times*," Alberto said.

I pinched the bridge of my nose. "I'm sure you can be in the paper too, Alberto. Just flash your ankle or something, and you'll make the front page of the next edition."

"Do you actually think I care about appearing in this rag?"

"Don't you?"

After all, Alberto was born for front pages. He had a camera-ready face and a menu of cold expressions to choose from every time I pointed my phone at him. Yes, I snapped pictures of us together whenever he allowed me to. Why? Because I wanted to remind myself that I dated a guy like him when… it would be over.

"Give it here." Alberto pried the paper from my clutched hands and began reading out loud in the languid voice I'd always found so sensual. "'Eric was terrible on the pitch last Friday, in a not-so-friendly game between the Colette football team, an amicable club without a coach, and the American High School of Paris, which has more coaches than actual players. The great performance of other players, notably the powerful central-midfielder, Kayvin Figarella, and the amazing new goalkeeper, Mathias Rodin, was not enough to stop the Americans from thrashing us once again. In the stands, their overjoyed hooligan supporters mocked the mostly French team members of the Colette team when they threatened once again to stop eating French fries, a Belgian invention. All because of Eric's inattention on the field.'" Alberto rubbed his eyelids and returned the paper to me. "I literally can't read anymore."

"Haha! Does it make your eyes bleed?"

Alberto didn't answer, but he lay on his back and covered his eyes with his hand. I returned to *The Colette Times* and forced myself to ignore how handsome Eric was in the picture below the article, despite being sweaty and in a dark mood. With trembling fingertips, I shook the newspaper and read aloud:

This exclusive interview shockingly highlights how carefree one of the brightest hopes of Parisian club *** is about things that matter:

"I don't care," Eric Tucker-Régnier, son of fitness centre chain Ventire CEO Stephen Tucker, said when our team interrogated him superbly about how much he sucked.

"But you just lost your first game of the season."

"That's not… This was just a friendly game between two private schools."

"Which you embarrassingly lost."

"2 - 1 isn't that bad," he dared say with a half-smile.

"Indeed, you scored in the second half, but almost by accident. You failed horribly to score TWICE, even though everyone says you're supposed to be great, and the team relied on you—"

"Honestly, that little girl is insane," Alberto said, surprising me. I had assumed he had fallen asleep to the sound of my voice. "She shouldn't be writing like that. She almost makes me feel bad for that guy."

I found her funny, but I didn't want to vex Alberto, so I didn't say anything and read on.

"I'm not the only one on the team…" Eric said, his smile wiped off.

"Poor excuse for a captain, wouldn't you say?" this gifted correspondent asked, showing true journalistic marksmanship. "Don't you think you would have performed better if you hadn't wasted your time pretending to be an actor last summer?"

Last year's choice of Most Promising Handsome Boy *for the* Unofficial Colette Candy Guide, *Eric T.R., wrinkled his conventionally attractive nose, which testified to his shame. He knew the talented journalist was right.*

"It was just a friendly game," he repeated dumbly.

It was clear his head was still reeling from a mild concussion which occurred when the handsome central-midfielder, Kayvin Figarella, slammed into him by accident in the second half. One could say this was reason enough for Eric to miss his next shot, but a professional player such as Eric should have scored despite such a minor injury.

"What was so friendly about being wiped out by some American kids? This was technically an act of war," said our correspondent, yours truly. "Don't you have any regrets about this embarrassment which will taint our reputation for the next decade?"

The young loser gave our team a helpless look. "What?"

He was clearly unsettled by our amazing line of questioning. We decided to cut this interview short to interview more worthy candidates.

"Answer me this simple question, Eric. Do you have any regrets?"

"No." His gaze lost itself somewhere in the distance, and his lips parted. He was undoubtedly contemplating the importance of this brilliant journalist's words. Then he woke from his daze with misty eyes. "No regrets. I played and I lost. It comes with the territory."

He then left the pitch with his head down, shaken from the terrible remorse which plagued his soul. His number two and best friend, the handsome hunk Kayvin Figarella, finished the interview with us.

"Kayvin's not his best friend," I said angrily, crumpling the paper between my hands. "And he's not a handsome hunk!"

Alberto returned to a sitting position with a mocking laugh. "Not anymore, that's for sure. Not after last night anyway."

"What? His best friend, or a handsome hunk?"

"Both."

"Hang on." Curious, I set the paper aside. "What happened last night?"

"You don't know?"

"How would I know? I'm not best friends with Xavier."

My tone was pretty venomous, but it would take more to annoy Alberto. "They fought," he said in with the hint of a smirk.

"Let me guess. Xavier told you?"

Alberto stretched his long limbs. "He's got his uses."

"Like what, exactly?"

"Like knowing exactly what happened between Kayvin and Eric." Alberto's eyes narrowed. "As if you're not dying to know."

Snorting, I plunged my face right back into the newspaper. For a good twenty seconds, I pretended well not to want to know. Then I gave up with a sigh.

"All right. I want to know."

Alberto perked up. The rare times I saw animation in his eyes were usually when we were talking about other people's misfortunes. "Last night after practice, they fought right here." He gestured at their spot.

I noticed that the team and their entourage had arrived, but Eric was notably absent. I wanted to see Kayvin's face, but his back was turned.

"But why?"

"Because of some girl. Odile or something."

My tongue clicked. "Elodie."

"Yes, maybe."

I pushed aside the uneasy feeling in my stomach at the mention of her name. "What happened?"

"Apparently, Kayvin is really into this girl. Remember the last night before we left Longchamps?"

I gave a nod. Of course, I remembered. That night, Alberto kissed my lips for the first time, and I had an equally nerve-wracking fight with Eric.

"Kayvin was furious about something when we saw him," Alberto said. "In fact, Eric told Kayvin and the others that Elodie ditched him. At first, he seemed heartbroken, but then he let Kayvin believe that he'd help him get with Elodie. He even promised to speak to Elodie on his behalf if Kayvin kept his mouth shut about the booze at the party. You know, to protect Duvo and Binta's jobs."

"Oh. I vaguely remember that."

"But it seemed Eric didn't help Kayvin get with this girl at all. Apparently, he even lied about their break-up, so Kayvin got really mad."

My heart slowly sank. "So it was true, then." He never broke up with her. Not entirely anyway. Suddenly, all the warm thoughts I'd been nurturing about Eric turned cold in my chest.

Alberto didn't see the pain on my face and rested his head on his knees with a half-smile. "Kayvin confronted Eric last night. He thought he'd set him straight, but Eric got mad and told him this Elodie would never date an asshole like him."

"That's intense," I said in a drained voice.

"There's more." Alberto's eyes glinted. "Kayvin punched Eric in the face."

"He what?" I perched myself on the edge of my seat.

"Eric fought back. I'm not sure how it went. Xavier's useless at retelling stories, and fights in real life are never as cool as in the movies. But I saw Kayvin's face this morning, and his lip was busted." Chewing on his bottom lip with a thoughtful look, Alberto took some time before resuming. "Xavier said it was a long time coming. Eric hasn't been himself for a while. He fucked up his exams, then he had this weird idea of breaking into the Drama Club. Xavier said they did what he asked because he was depressed. But then Eric decided to be in the movie and stopped hanging out with them. Kayvin's done with him." Alberto suddenly lifted his finger. "Look, he's here."

I followed the direction he pointed in. Eric was crossing the playground with his chin up and didn't even spare a glance at Kayvin who stared resentfully after him. Three girls detached themselves from Kayvin's group to join Eric: I instantly recognised Joy, Melissa, and Elodie.

Eric's girl.

"Anything for true love," I said sadly. Alberto raised an eyebrow; I waved my hand dismissively. "Don't mind me. I was just thinking out loud. Losing a friend sucks, but if Eric and Elodie are truly in love…"

Alberto looked at me as if I was a clueless child. "But they're not. That's the whole point."

"The whole… point?" Nothing he was saying made any sense! I rubbed my face with my hands. "Excuse me for being confused."

Alberto's gaze softened, but I had the feeling he thought me a little too thick for his taste. "They're not together, that's why Kayvin's angry."

I stretched my hands toward him and spoke in a helpless voice. "Can you not hear how confusing that sounds?!!"

Alberto took a deep breath to imply he was about to explain life to me as if I were five years old. "Kayvin's angry because Eric told him Elodie broke up with him."

"Right."

"That was a lie. *He* broke up with *her*."

My stomach dropped with a loud clunk. "He what?"

Alberto glanced down at his nails, then at me, as if he were pondering whether to tell me more or not. Evidently, he elected to go on. "Since he was using this fake break-up as an excuse to act weird, Kayvin lost his mind. He thinks he's a victim in this affair. It's possible that Eric really did talk to Odile, but she rejected Kayvin anyway. That's it. *The end*." Alberto smirked, satisfied, then went through a series of yawns.

"So Eric was never with Elodie?"

Alberto shrugged. "He was, I guess, but not since the end of last term. But he never told anyone, or Joy would have made a move a long time ago. She's really obsessed with him."

"Yeah, I know."

Alberto and I exchanged a look. It's like he knew what I wanted to ask next and dared me to say it.

Are they together now? That's the question I wanted to ask. But I couldn't do that to him. So, I uncrumpled the newspaper, spread it over my knees, and pretended to read for a few minutes, feeling his eyes on me.

There were so many questions in my head: Was he still with her? Why did he conceal from everyone that he was single until after the party at Aurons? And why did he lie about being dumped? All of this stood in the way of him getting hitched to another girl as soon as possible, which was his trademark. And I knew Eric was a good actor, but I spent a lot of time with him, and he never appeared heartbroken. And I should know, because what sort of unusual behaviour did he display when he was feeling low? He did dumb things like getting drunk and ignoring his real friends. But back then, he acted so normally that I really thought he was in a relationship with Elodie, even when he wasn't.

And perhaps today he still wasn't. And perhaps he concealed his celibacy because he didn't want another girl to throw herself at him, like Joy for example. And perhaps the reason he even told everyone he was free had something to do with a pity kiss given to a drunk fool.

And finally, perhaps, perhaps, the reason why he was heartbroken and refusing to speak to me was...

Because he liked me.

In that instant, the playground, the trees, the clouds overhead, and the living piece of art at my feet called Alberto all turned black and white, and only the small figure of Eric standing on the other side retained its colours.

I chose wrong. I chose so wrong.

Did I pursue a fantasy when I already had something real? I should have known the difference, but how could I? No amount of books and movies can teach you about the real thing. How it feels to truly be wanted and appreciated for who you are. The feeling of missing someone's company terribly, so terribly your blood itself aches in his absence and boils at the sight of him.

Fantasies can only sustain you for a while. Eventually, we all come to crave the real thing.

In all of this, I hadn't been fair to Alberto, Eric, or even to myself. When I hesitated to accept Alberto's offer, I should have dug deeper and tried to understand the real reasons behind my reluctance. Now I knew that having things in common with your perfect crush didn't necessarily mean you'd be a good match. Because someone had already shown me how it felt to be with the one you really like. How good you feel around them, and not just anxious. Without the need to constantly perform for them, the only thing for you to do is to simply let go.

Eric had transformed me and allowed me to discover who I really was. And the best part of this journey was to realise that I was more like him than I initially thought. I missed his stupid games, and I missed scooter rides and doing things spontaneously. I missed his way of wanting something and immediately reaching out for it, whether it was snatching little brownies or burying his hand in a guy's hair, planting flowers into his shoes, kissing his chin to make it all better.

I wanted to be more like him. And I wanted to be with him. All. The. Time.

Because he was the one for me.

My blood pounding in my ears, I sprung up from my seat, almost ready to tear across the playground and launch myself straight into

Eric's arms. But the sight of Alberto gazing at me with his feline eyes was enough to douse my burning passion.

Swallowing the lump in my throat with difficulty, I fell back on the bench. His perfect lips curled slightly up.

"Alberto..."

"Mm?"

I hesitated. Once I did this, there was a ninety-five per cent chance this beautiful but impregnable fortress would never speak to me again. I'd better try my best to do it gently — and respectfully. By using truthful words. But all I could do was blurt out, "You're *so* beautiful."

"Thank you."

"No, really…" I studied his face in excruciating detail as the words rolled off my chest. "You are the most beautiful man I've ever seen." He watched me in silence, a strand of hair falling into his eye. I forced down the guilt constricting my throat. "You're gonna break so many hearts over the course of your life… But you're not gonna break mine. For that, I want to say thank you."

A muscle twitched in his jaw.

"You're great, really… You're great. But… I need to break up with you."

Alberto didn't make a move, not even to open his lips. He just looked at me.

"I'm really sorry." My final words came out in a whisper.

I would never forget how cold his eyes were as they bore into mine. A terrible sight which still haunted me years later.

"I really thought we would work well together, you know?" I said, wiping my hands on my jeans. "But honestly, do you think we did?"

Alberto remained still for a long time, then shivered slightly as if he'd awoken from a dream. His eyes were no longer cold.

"Can you go now?" he simply said.

"I…" My breath caught in my throat. It was my first relationship, and my first breakup. And all this time I was certain that if anything should happen, Alberto would have been the one doing the dumping. So I was a little bit surprised to find myself the offender, and I rose from the bench feeling awful. "I'll see you around, I hope."

I had not walked three steps when I heard him mumble under his breath. "Waste of my time, that was."

My movements stopped. I looked at him over my shoulder. "I heard you."

Alberto met my eyes with a shrug. It was like he was saying "What more can I say?" and he was right. What more was there to say? He didn't protest, didn't scream, didn't shed tears. He didn't even try to change my mind and convince me to stay. The month we'd spent together had felt strange, and this week was even worse. I didn't know Alberto very well, but I'd still be willing to bet that he was just as relieved as me to be freed from this relationship.

Still, I cast him a wan smile before I turned my back to him. Alberto was more than a pretty face, I used to say, and I still believed that to be the truth. As for his true face, as uninteresting or terrifying as it might be, one day someone else would be worthy of seeing it. But personally, my Alberto days were now over. I promised myself never to cry for him again, and I was quite certain he would never bother spilling tears for me.

Despite the intensity of my feelings for Eric, I kept my head down not to be tempted by his sight and walked directly home. Now wasn't the time to attempt a reunion. I wouldn't do anything rashly. If Eric had secrets, he might tell me one day, but I wouldn't make crazy assumptions anymore. I'd decided it was safer to do a bit of an investigation before exposing him to my feelings for him.

When I arrived home, my sister called me over. Her bedroom door was open, and I entered with quiet steps. Yasmine sat at her desk amongst piles of clutter with dark circles under her eyes. The way her tired face brightened when she saw me reminded me of someone, and I inexplicably burst into tears in the middle of her cramped bedroom. An unstoppable stream of salty tears came flowing down my cheeks. In vain, Yasmine took me into her arms, pressed me against her heart, and threatened *the bastard*'s life. When I finally looked up, my face was covered in snot, but she didn't seem too repulsed.

"Are you in the pit?" she asked with concern, offering me a tissue.

With a nod, I wiped my nose. "Big time."

"Should I send Rufus to bite his shins?"

"No no, don't hurt him." I gave a loud sniffle. "He really needs his legs, you know."

Yasmine slid me a confused look but didn't insist. I returned to my sister's arms and lay there a while, long after the hiccups of sorrow had stopped shaking me. Outside her window, the sky was blue again.

28

WE NEED TO TALK ABOUT ERIC

W as there a chance, as insignificant as it was, that Eric had feelings for me? That was the only thing on my mind when I woke up the following day.

Until recently, it had never really occurred to me that Eric could be attracted to guys. With a reputation like his and the way he obviously enjoyed interacting with girls, how could I have thought otherwise? But he also had a history of concealing the truth when convenient, and if he weren't straight, wouldn't that be a truth to conceal?

Yesterday I assumed he would never be ashamed, but after last night, I wasn't so sure. How popular would he still be if it came out that he played both sides? As wonderful as Eric was, he was also just a young puppy with his own aspirations, his own pride, someone who delighted in people's attention. Assuming he was bisexual, he was most likely worried about being bullied for this reason.

So, could I make up the difference between my wishful thinking and reality? After tossing and turning all morning in bed, I struggled the whole weekend with my homework, constantly bothered by the same questions. I couldn't know for sure. There are times I felt certain he liked me, and others where I wondered if I wasn't insane and reading way too much into simple acts of kindness.

By breakfast on Sunday morning, I came to the conclusion that I would get nowhere on my own; I needed help. People who knew me, knew him, and had seen us interact together. Level-headed people, but with enough creativity to imagine an Eric who could fall in love with me.

It's not like I had a long list of friends to reach out to in case of need. After skipping Alberto's name on my phone with a grimace, I texted Camille and Arthur and asked them to come directly to my place this afternoon to discuss a subject of the utmost importance.

What would happen if they concluded that I'd fallen into another delusion and there was no way in hell that Eric fancied me? Nothing, probably. I'd admire him from a distance until I moved on, just like countless others had done before me. But my heart was set. I'd rather have a truthful rejection from Eric than a fake relationship with Alberto.

When Camille answered — with a fair share of exclamation marks — that they'd be here at 2 p.m., I informed my mother that my friends were coming for a visit. I would have gotten the same reaction if I'd announced I was getting married.

Camille and Arthur arrived at my place — on time and with grinning faces — but couldn't get their feet in with my mom fussing over them. She spent eons complimenting Arthur's clothes, Camille's hair, and asking a million questions. How did we meet, what was their favourite drink, which teacher did they hate most, etc., until I had to threaten to lock her inside her art studio. Only then, and with a scrunched-up face not unlike Eric's, did she allow us to barricade ourselves in my room while she prepared refreshments.

"Have you seen the paper?" Camille said the moment Mom had closed the door. "I need to get myself hired by them. It's the only good press around here."

Arthur nodded while perusing my music collection. "It's totally punk-rock."

I snorted into my hands. "Didn't they call you a coward?"

"And they were right!" Camille twirled around in the middle of my room, laughing. "I felt threatened by Elisa's authority. But I got over it. Man, your room is so tidy!" She bent her knees to look at my rabbit. "And Lord Floppington's cage is so fancy I almost expected him to wear a tuxedo."

"It's *Sir* Floppington," I corrected, then I added with a slap on my own forehead. "Actually no, it's Bugs Bunny."

"Sir Floppington's just better."

I had to concede. I always felt my rabbit liked my mom's choice for a name better anyway. There were countless Bugs Bunnies out there; perhaps he preferred being a Floppington with a title instead.

Arthur hooked his finger to entice Camille to come to his side. She beamed, and they started messing around with my iPod.

"Do you think Eric has read it?" I asked in an innocent tone. "The paper."

Camille gave a sound of delight when my mom's playlist started playing through my speakers. "Dunno. Why?"

"No reason."

"Elisa destroyed him with that post-game interview," Arthur said.

In truth, I was thinking of the great kisser headline when I mentioned this. I had totally forgotten about the football thing.

Arthur walked over to the office whiteboard I used to brainstorm and outline my presentations. "Dude, are you serious?"

"I like to be prepared," I said meekly.

Camille picked up a cushion and sat on the rug in the centre of my room. "Yeah, that was brutal. It sounded like Elisa had something against him."

"I have a theory." I cocked my head. "I think she loves him."

Camille slid Arthur a dubitative look. He said, "Excuse me if I don't take your word for it, mate, but you're pretty clueless when it comes to these things."

Ignoring the 'mate' coming out of nowhere, I blinked several times. "I'm clueless, you say?"

Arthur nodded as he dropped another cushion next to Camille. "We started making jokes about it behind your back."

"Wait…" I sat down as well. "Who?"

"Camille and I…"

"Don't take it badly, Zak," Camille said with a dark look at Arthur. "They're harmless jokes. Only losers allowed."

"Losers? So that includes Eric."

"Don't worry." Camille waved her hand. "Eric doesn't joke about you."

Arthur gave another nod. "He doesn't even speak about you."

"Really?"

That was off to a great fucking start.

"We barely see him anyway these days. When we spoke after his game, it was only for a minute. He kept saying he was too busy with—"

"Football, school, and stuff," Arthur said. "His words."

"Stuff?" I said. "Like Elodie?"

Camille frowned. "Don't know anything about that."

"I might not be as clueless as you think," I said in an enigmatic tone.

"Oh, do tell!"

They spoke at the same time and in a perfect impression of Eric's Southern drawl.

"Alberto told me a few things that might be of interest..." I produced a small shrug to ramp up their curiosity.

"Alberto told you some dirty gossip?" Arthur clapped his hands. "So there are interesting sides to him after all..." He realised his mistake, and his face drained of colour. "Oops. Sorry, Zak, I keep forgetting you're together..."

"Yeah. About that..."

My guilty expression made Camille lift her finger to stop Arthur who was about to speak. "Are you..."

"I may have broken up with Alberto a little bit."

Camille gasped. "You? You broke up with Alberto?"

"It just wasn't working!" I sounded defensive. "It just wasn't. You all think I'm a prude, but you should see Alberto. I had to practically beg him for kisses."

"But at least you got him!" Arthur punched the air with a resolute expression.

Camille watched him with her mouth hanging open. "What he meant," she said, "was that you did accomplish the feat of being the first to date him. Congratulations on that. But I'm glad you got out. You looked bored out of your mind with him. I guess he wasn't all that."

"Dating Alberto..." I said with a sigh. "Dating Alberto is like... Imagine someone dangling the sweetest-looking cake in front of you but never letting you take a bite."

While Camille pondered my words with a thoughtful expression, Arthur patted my knee with a large smile. "So that's why you texted us? You said you had problems of the heart and you needed your consigliere."

"Your counsel!" I shook my head helplessly. "Learn to read. I'm not head of a mafia family yet."

"But I thought that was a reference to Alberto!"

"No!" I stopped myself from saying more. "No. It was something else."

They looked at me with incredulous faces, wondering what I was up to this time. I didn't know how to tell them without sounding like an idiot. After weeks of filling their ears with praises of Alberto, they were gonna think me an absolute airhead.

"Spit it out, Zak." Camille seemed to have read my mind. "We're on your side no matter what."

With a groan of relief, I leaned forward to take her hands. Arthur went as far as scooting over to hug me from behind.

"All right," I said, trying not to cringe. "The thing is… and you're gonna think I'm an idiot… but all the same…" I squeezed my eyes shut. "I think I'm in love with Eric."

At that exact moment, my dear mom barged in with a giant tray full of snacks and beverages, her giant smile freezing at the sight of the three of us locked in an awkward embrace.

"T-tea?" Mom asked in a croaky voice. "… Cookies?" She hesitated, then added with much effort, "Con… doms?"

Arthur yelped and jumped to his feet to stand behind Camille. She released my hands and revealed a reassuring smile.

"Just a friendly hug, Mrs K."

Mom put the tray on the floor between us with unsteady hands. "No judgement," she muttered. "… As long as you aren't in a cult."

Camille immediately helped herself to a plump cookie. "That's not a bad idea!" One look from my mother prompted her to add, "For a story! A story only."

This slightly awkward episode at least had the benefit of making my mom feel extra conspicuous in the middle of my bedroom. After a quick comment about our awesome choice of music, she hurriedly slunk outside and closed the door tightly behind her.

"So…" I began, unsure of where to pick up. "I was saying…"

Camille bit her lip. "You love Eric."

"I support you!" Arthur spoke too loudly, flashing me a thumbs-up.

Neither of them looked remotely shocked at all. The overly-dramatic part of me found it almost disappointing.

"Okay. Not the reaction I was expecting at all. You don't look at all surprised."

Camille forced a smile. "The thing is—"

Arthur cut in. "We had some—"

"Doubts?"

"Or should I say, suspicions."

"And not only that you liked Eric, but that he, you know…"

My heart lurched hopefully. "Yes?"

"That he... may..." Camille started making weird finger gestures.

"That he wanted to exchange more than lines with you," Arthur said in an almost creepy tone. "Or, wait. That he was a fan of more than your work. Hang on. That he wanted to be more than your partner on scr—"

"We got it, darling, we got it." Camille urged him to sit down and stuffed a cookie in his mouth.

Meanwhile, I had slowly started to turn into a puddle in the middle of the room, a stupid smile pulling the corners of my lips.

"Do you really think so?" That was exactly what I wanted to hear... And for this reason, it sounded too good to be true. I immediately returned to solid form, my face set. "Look. Here's the thing. Sometimes I think he likes me, sometimes I don't. His behaviour is too cryptic. In the end, I don't know anything at all! And you both just said I was clueless."

"Okay, but we're not specialists either, we just..."

"We just saw what we saw... and heard what we heard..."

I resisted the temptation to beg them to tell me immediately all that they saw and heard, electing to be pragmatic instead.

"Consider this," I said. "As far as you know, Eric is straight, isn't he?"

Camille kept her lips firmly shut, while Arthur's face turned serious. "He is. He's got exes everywhere, dating as far as primary school."

I felt the light in my eyes dim and put my head in my hands.

"But," Camille added, "that doesn't mean he doesn't like you. He must have given you signs. Have you interpreted them?"

I dug my hands into my hair. "The signs, the fucking signs... They're all contradictory. I was just thinking that I saw him and Elodie glued to each other at the screening. You were there."

Camille looked about to concede, but Arthur shook his finger in my face.

"I saw Eric glued to half the school, and that was in the course of *this* month."

"And there's that." I gave a solemn nod. "His sluttiness is standing in the way of my answers, that's a fact."

Camille suddenly invoked a time-out by putting her hands up. "Hang on. Do you seriously think Eric is a slut?"

I couldn't help laughing. "Cam. If I seriously thought he was a slut, would I be so hopelessly trying to convince myself he's attracted to me right now?"

"So is slut the way you use it a term of endearment—"

"Yes, yes! And only between men. I'd never call a woman a slut."

"Okay, I was just checking. You may continue." Since we were both looking at her with surprise, she added with a dry laugh, "I was about to ram my foot into your side if you exhibited any late signs of misogyny."

"Right. I'm deeply grateful you asked me first."

"No problem."

"But here's the thing," I said with a pointed look which begged not to be interrupted again. "I thought Eric and Elodie were together when I met him at Aurons. I just discovered that I was wrong. It's possible they're not together at the moment either."

I explained to them what Xavier told Alberto.

"That's all very well, but we need to be sensible about this," Arthur said seriously. "We can't barge into Eric's life like this with our assumptions."

"Are we making assumptions?" Camille said.

"Yes! We're trying to determine if Eric is into… that sort of thing."

"Me. Into me!" I said earnestly.

"No, listen," Arthur said. "Because we might do a lot of damage if we make assumptions and they're false. Now don't get me wrong, Zak, I also thought he had a bit of a weird crush on you. Am I the only one who noticed the way he was all over you?" Camille, her lips pinched, shook her head. "But as far as we know, Eric is straight. That, and we also saw him act ambiguously with other guys for fun. For example, with Michael."

I punched my fist against the rug. "Damn this Michael."

"And with me!" Arthur pointed at his own chest.

"Damn you too, then!"

"Hear, hear!" Camille said, filling her hands with cookies.

"My point is…" Arthur got up. "We're going to need to make a list of every time Eric made it seem like he was into you. We're gonna compare that to the evidence of his boring, boring straightness, and then we'll draw conclusions. Therefore!" He walked over to my whiteboard and picked up the eraser. "I'm requesting the use of this relic."

Before I could protest, he'd already removed all traces of the *Sense and Sensibility* book report outline I needed to submit in English Literature for Mrs Paquin.

"Can I erase this?" Arthur asked after a thought.

I flashed him a fake smile. "What do you think?"

Thankfully, I had already copied it into a physical notebook and typed it on my computer.

"First things first!" Arthur said, taking charge. The delight in Camille's eyes when he raised his voice didn't escape me. "Let's talk about Exhibit 1. The kiss."

"The kiss!" Camille roared. "Be honest now. How was it?"

"Oh, right." I tried to tone down the smugness in my voice. "Which kiss are we talking about?"

"Ah-ha!" Arthur pointed a triumphant finger at me. "Because, of course, there were several. Three, in fact, if I'm not wrong. Two, if I was too drunk and saw incorrectly."

"There were indeed three, detective," I said with awe.

Camille blinked. "Wait, what?"

"I wasn't sure whether or not I was supposed to have seen that," Arthur said. "Also, I really wasn't sure if I imagined the whole thing."

"What happened?"

I took over. "Eric kissed me during the party. But it was really silly. He only gave me a little peck because he heard me whine that I'd never be kissed in my entire life or something dumb like that. I always assumed he did it out of pity. He told me afterwards he thought it would cheer me up, and I believe him. I can safely say that, from my point of view, Eric never seemed into me before the party."

Camille looked pensive. "He didn't?"

"The kiss!" Arthur interrupted. "How was that kiss?"

"One out of five on the steamometer. But a five out of five on the surprise scale."

"Yeah, let's keep that," Camille said quickly. "But to be realistic here, this exhibit is inconclusive. Could be a sign he fancied you or just Eric being a nice guy. Next kiss, please."

"Wait. Imma do this right." Arthur created two columns on the whiteboard. One bore the male symbol, the other the female one. "That's code, in case your mom comes back in. The male symbol means you're the one he wants to—"

"We get it," Camille said with a warning look. "I want to know more about the kisses." She put her hand on her notebook.

"No notes!" I used a pleading tone. "Please, no notes. I'll let you use me as a living study if I ever get together with him. Deal?"

"Deal."

The memory of our little midnight tumble by the lake made me bite my lip with a quivering heart.

"The second kiss was actually a series of three attempts when we rehearsed together. But only the third one matters because it clearly got out of hand. Personally, I wasn't even rehearsing anymore. But I don't know about him. Anyway, if it got out of hand, it's probably my fault."

"Because…?" Arthur raised an eyebrow.

"Because I was being kissed by Eric, God damn it! Who in their right mind wouldn't enjoy that!"

Camille chuckled. "What happened to 'he's a thug and we'll never get along'?"

I rested my chin in my hands with starry eyes. "Oh, but he is a thug."

"Slut!" Arthur excitedly pointed his finger at me. "Did I use it right?"

"Perfectly."

"Okay, I get it!" He dodged the stuffed bear I threw at him with impressive skill. "But what did he do during that kiss, do you remember?"

"Do I remember?" I felt myself blush up to my ears. "He pressed me down. I couldn't move at all. He, ahem… he was really good. Definitely a five out of five on the steamometer. Afterwards, he apologised for always getting carried away. It made sense to me at the time."

"It made sense to you?" Arthur gave me a bewildered look.

"Yes, of course! Earlier he'd asked me if he could touch my ass. Actually, he begged. He said he'd been single for too long… which sounded like rubbish at the time but now appeared to be true."

"Okay, maybe we should have started with that?" Camille snapped her fingers repeatedly until Arthur got the message and wrote *Begged to touch ass* on the whiteboard under the words *Hot kiss by lake*.

My lip curled into a smirk. "I guess you ran out of code ideas."

"I could draw a fruit, but I'm not good at it."

"Forget it." A quick look at the board reminded me of something. "I should also add that he kissed my chin on the beach. In front of everyone."

"Girls, this boy is thirsty!" Arthur said, writing down *Kiss on the chin* in the ♂ column.

"What was his excuse for this one?" Camille asked, looking increasingly puzzled.

"He made me hurt myself earlier by accident. He said he wanted to make it better."

"That's flirting, right?" Arthur asked Camille, hesitating as he stared at the words on the board. "That's flirting, it's got to be."

"How should I know! I once saw him give Joy a hand massage just so that he could take the brownie she was holding."

"Then let's talk about the brownies, by all means!" Arthur shouted in an authoritative voice. Camille and I listened with round eyes. "Days of petty theft, and for what? A friendly excursion on a boat between friends, or… a romantic escapade between two lovebirds?"

"Well, we definitely did the friendly excursion thingy," I said without enthusiasm.

While Arthur was noting everything down, Camille looked thoughtful. "However," she said after a minute. "When we offered to return to the house together, Eric categorically refused because he didn't want to wake you."

"A friendly gesture," I said.

"A friendly gesture indeed," Arthur repeated under his breath. "But didn't he have me row back on my own because he didn't want to disturb the little Zak sleeping against him? A position which Zak occupied only because Eric himself slipped his arm under his head when he was asleep!"

"Wait… What??" I almost choked on the words. "Eric did—Eric put his arm under my head?"

"Oh yes, he did. The—aah!" Attempting to lean against the side of the whiteboard, Arthur almost went rolling into the wall. "What was I saying? Ah! The moment you made a teeny-tiny sound of discomfort, he rushed to the rescue with his bicep, therefore forcing me to row the whole way back even though my own muscles have never known a *single* day of exercise in their entire life."

"Definitely," Camille pointed at the board, her mouth full of chocolate-chip cookies, "Exhibit 6."

"That bastard," I said through clenched teeth. "Letting me believe I was the one who used him as a pillow."

"Oh, really?" Arthur put his hands on his hips. "We can write 'in denial' maybe. So where does that go?"

"Wait, wait." Remembering something, I put my hands up. "Weren't we all high that time?"

Camille bounced excitedly on her cushion. "Eric wasn't! He ate the tiniest portion of brownie, remember?" She turned to Arthur. "I stand convinced. Exhibit 6: Eric wanted Zak to sleep in his arms. Case closed!"

"No, no." Arthur approached Camille and put his hand on her shoulder. "The enthusiasm is appreciated, but we need more clues. What else do we have, Zak? What else?"

I tried to remember other little instances of Eric doing flirty things with me, but between excitement and apprehension, I couldn't recall anything of note.

"I've got something," Camille said, her eyes sparkling. "After all, *I* first started to suspect Eric the day we pushed the guys into the pool. Remember? Eric took us to the pond, and later, we looked at pictures of Gilbert."

"Right, your dog."

"Yes, except that I swiped too far and we came across a picture of you I took on set. I remember saying something like 'Look! he's so adorable!'" Camille laughed at my cringing face. "Forgive me, but it was a good picture. Anyway, Eric seized my phone and looked at your face for a certain length of time."

"Inadmissible," Arthur said. "He just looked at a picture? Come on, you can do better."

"Okay, okay, so what about this? He gave me the phone back and said that you, Zak, were so cute and old-fashioned, he wanted to make you mixtapes."

Arthur snorted. "What the hell—"

I recalled that thing!

"That was about me? I thought he was talking about your dog!"

Camille's eyebrows flew to her hairline. "Why would he want to make my dog mixtapes?"

"I don't know. Eric can be a little weird sometimes. In a good way."

Arthur, sniggering, wrote *Adorable/mixtape* on the board under my symbol. "A mixtape has a romantic connotation, doesn't it?"

"Yes, yes, so it's a clue." Camille looked adamant.

"Anything else, Camille?" I asked with imploring eyes.

I'm not gonna lie, my chest was increasingly swelling with hope and images of a romantic reunion with Eric by the edge of the lake, with him offering his mixtape and with bees carrying little confetti as we exchanged our confessions.

Camille shifted in her seat and picked up a cup of tea. "That's when I really started to notice the little looks he gave you, and how he reacted when he thought I caught his eye, always laughing it off. And Arthur is right: he was always all over you. However, he never did anything that really convinced me. He's nice and goofy with everyone.

Also, he never tried to ditch Arthur and me to be alone with you. On the contrary, he was always inviting us to join you, even when he had the chance to have you for himself."

"That's true," I said softly. "Can't deny that."

"And he was just as flirty with Arthur, if not more, so I was torn. I even began thinking that he was into some sort of method acting crap, that he was trying to play gay to... well, play gay."

"Makes sense," Arthur mumbled, looking disappointed.

There was a small silence during which Camille drank noisily a whole cup of tea while Arthur patted my shoulder as a gesture of comfort.

"But now," Camille said after clearing her throat. "I can't help remembering the self-control comment."

"Explain yourself, girl!" Arthur wrote down *Self-control* on the board, then he turned. "I mean please, my most beloved Camille."

She beamed and only stopped when she noticed me shaking with impatience. "Arthur, do you remember that time when you sighed and you said 'I wish somebody would look at me with the same intensity Eric looks at the pool' and we laughed and then we—"

"Oh, yes. I definitely remember what we did next."

I coughed in my fist.

"Okay," Camille went on, "but just after that, when you ran away to your room to, ahem... get something."

Arthur blushed and I pretended not to notice anything.

"You left me with Eric," Camille said. "He seemed lost in thought and all. I was always amazed at his self-control when it comes to food or other nasty stuff, so I just plain told him how easy he made it look and that I admired his self-control, and he flinched as if I had poked him with a fire iron. He told me it wasn't as easy as it looked, that some days were harder than others. I assumed he meant food, or even alcohol. But then he just ran from the table, so I took his seat to check what could have spooked him. All I saw was Zak sitting on the edge of the pool listening to his iPod, doing nothing special at all."

"... So?" Arthur spread out his arms with a dubitative look.

"So? Babies, he was saying he was struggling with self-control *as* he was staring at Zak!"

"That's not game-changing," I murmured. "Sorry, Camille."

But Arthur silenced me by raising his hand. "He wasn't staring at the pool, then, but at Zak?"

"Yeah."

"Okay, that's gay."

I shook my head. "But inconclusive!"

"Why?"

"Because! Who says that I was sitting at the pool at this exact time? I could have arrived later. For all we know, it was Joy or Melissa sitting at the pool. I remember seeing them on the lounge chairs that time."

"Fine. Scrap that one too if you like." Camille gave a haughty shrug while pouring herself more tea. "I didn't even get to the beach yet."

"Oooh," Arthur acquiesced with a nod. "The beach. The first time I began to suspect Eric myself."

I straightened up with a racing heart. "What happened at the beach?"

"Apart from the fact that he kissed you behind our back—"

"And *begged* you to let him touch your ass?"

"Yeah…" I said in a faint voice. "Apart from that."

Camille flashed me a smile. "Eric is one of the happiest creatures on the planet. He was having a great time at the beach until we left him alone with you. Then you went somewhere, and when he returned to us, he looked different. I thought you two had a fight. He kept looking in your direction as if he was worried about you."

"That's right." I nodded. "I ran away when he begged to touch my… you know. I was afraid I would lose control back then."

Arthur seemed surprised. "Oh, so your feelings for him are not new at all."

"No." I snorted. "They're not. They're so ancient I don't even know myself when they started."

"We were right!" Arthur approached Camille, and they high-fived each other. "You liked him! You were just too thick to realise it."

"Not that thick… Hey!" I glared at Arthur in protest. "For my defence, I realised I liked Eric way before the beach… But I didn't know how much exactly. Alberto was still in my heart, and…"

"Alberto, of course."

"Oh, yes," Arthur said thoughtfully. "It all comes down to Alberto."

"That's right!" I nodded. "When I left Eric alone, I met Alberto on the beach. He wanted to tell me something. I can't even remember what now. Oh, never mind. I was really surprised he wanted to speak to me, but at the time, I didn't make too much of it."

"But that's just it," Camille said. "The moment Eric saw you together, he deflated like an old balloon. He didn't want to play with us anymore. He got out of the water and spent the rest of his time stuck to Michael."

"But…" And I took my time to think about all the instances Eric came to my aid. "Eric offered to help me get with Alberto. He wasn't jealous at all or anything. He really rooted for me. I'm sure of it!"

"Perhaps he did before the party. But kissing you made him realise he liked boys after all! Case closed!" Arthur punched the air.

This time, Camille stopped him.

"I do have one final clue. Again, thanks to Alberto."

"Best not to ever tell him that."

"When he showed up after the final take and dragged you inside…" Camille sighed as she recalled the event. "You and Eric were talking together on the front steps. The look on both your faces! At that time, I thought you were really cute together. You seemed to drink in his words, and the way he was looking at you was really adorable."

"I was really excited," I said in a quiet voice, replaying the moment in my head. "Eric pushed me to give my best. I'd never been so proud of knowing him but in that moment."

"Also, you had a massive crush on him." Arthur arched an eyebrow. "Cam and I were thinking, shit! Is he into him or what?"

"I was so into him. I remember thinking that I wanted to kiss him in the changing room."

"I was there when you followed Alberto inside." Camille's expression turned grim. "I saw how it affected Eric. He stayed rooted to the front steps with a frozen smile, his jaw so clenched I thought he'd smash his teeth. Then he started laughing and muttering to himself. He tried to look normal when he saw me staring at him, but I wasn't duped."

"And you never thought of telling me this?" I asked in disbelief.

"Not really. Fine, I found it weird, but for all the reasons we talked about before, I never had more than suspicions about Eric having a little crush on you. One clumsy word and he could have taken it badly. We all knew he really didn't like Alberto since the party, but now that I think about it, he's never been nice to him. So I just convinced myself Eric looked like that because he didn't want you to end up with a guy he hated. Remember that time at the pool when Kayvin freaked out? I think Eric pretty much told us he was straight. And after all, Eric never told me directly that he fancied you. On the contrary, ever since we left Aurons, he's never mentioned you at all."

I wasn't mad at Camille for not telling me about all this. Even if she had, I'm not sure it would have changed anything. Even now, after an hour of gathering clues, I wasn't convinced he had feelings for me at all.

"Come to think of it," Arthur said pensively, "I should have noticed how weird it was that Eric wouldn't even talk about you. You were clearly his favourite in our group, and then... radio silence."

"When I went to talk to him at school," I said, "he was different. It was clear he didn't want me around. I just thought he didn't want to be my friend anymore."

"Or he followed the old adage," Camille said. "*Loin des yeux, loin du coeur*. Out of sight, out of mind."

"And then there's this weird moment... You know, after the football game, Alberto took me to a party at Xavier's."

"What?" Camille's jaw fell open. "You? To the baronet's mansion?"

"Yeah, it's a flat — and no comment. Anyway, Eric was there with Elodie. He was completely smashed. Drunk out of his mind."

"But why?" Arthur raised his marker but stopped himself from writing. "Because he lost a game?"

"He told me at the screening that it had nothing to do with the game."

"Then it could be you!" Camille clapped her hands. "Exhibit, exhibit!"

"Or it could be any other reason," Arthur said with a sigh. "Like family, or just stress?"

"Agreed," I said. "At the end of the day, looking at this list of clues, what do you think?"

The column with my symbol was filled with Arthur's terms and various poor drawings of fruits. But the other column was equally filled with counterarguments. To me, everything ambiguous Eric did with me could have been because he was a nice person and an impossible flirt. Arthur and Camille disagreed: To them, the steamy kiss by the lake and the boat episode were clear signs of a particular attachment.

"Jokes aside," Arthur said, "no one loses themselves in the middle of a kiss unless they're really into it."

I shook my head in protest. "Unless they're really rehearsing a passionate kiss which was part of the script. Remember how dedicated Eric was to the film? He practically begged you to cast him."

"Fine, fine! It's like you're trying to find arguments against yourself."

"Let's focus on the other side of the whiteboard, then," Camille said with a resolute expression. "What do we know about Eric that's a clue that he's not into Zak?"

"I'll help you there," Arthur said. "If Eric's gay, somebody better tell him soon, because he's dated many girls, and enthusiastically, if you get my meaning." He flashed us a couple of winks which had me grimace in horror.

"Arthur," Camille warned him.

"What, everybody knows it! I know he's a good actor, but no one's that good an actor."

I watched him write *(Very) attracted to girls* into the other column.

"That's a fact, my kittens. Eric likes girls, we all know it."

"That doesn't mean he ever got intimate with them, though," Camille said soothingly.

Arthur's face flushed bright red. "He did, though. He told me."

I looked at him and suppressed a sob. It's not like the news came as a surprise. My time with Eric had taught me many things, and one of the first I noticed about him was that he couldn't keep his hands off people. I didn't need to rack my brain to imagine what those hands wanted to do to those he dated.

"Not helping!" Camille snapped. "Also, how did you and Eric end up talking about—"

"That is confidential," Arthur said solemnly.

I got up and began pacing around the room like a beast in a cage. "Then why are we even having this conversation!" I tore at my hair. "We know it now. It was all in my head, once again. And not just in my head. In your head too, Camille."

Arthur tapped the marker on the surface of the board. "Unless he's bisexual."

"Right. Right!" His words forced me out of my mental cage. "Bisexuals! Even Alberto believes they exist."

"Well, yeah..." Camille said with a frown. "They're bisexuals, not unicorns. Their existence has been documented, you know."

"Yes. All right. I apologise to all bisexuals for doubting their existence. But Eric being one. Do we have any proof of that?"

Arthur dropped his arms to the sides with a grimace. "I've never heard of him getting it on with a guy."

"I was his first kiss!" I said, remembering his words. "With a boy. He told me that. He even told me he was nervous about kissing another guy."

Arthur rubbed his brow with a sigh. "The clues tend to show that he was living a pretty straight life. At least until he kissed you at the party."

"He told us on the boat that he wasn't happy with his life, remember?" Camille said. "Could that be linked?"

"Right!" I slapped my hands on my knees. "He almost failed his exams. He broke up with Elodie, and he decided not to tell anyone. He trashed the Drama Club and got himself punished. Then he decided to audition for the movie. He was totally acting up. That's why everything I read in this column could also be the actions of someone who's bored and wants some adventure in his life. Do you understand my predicament?"

Camille and Arthur were silent for a moment. Arthur turned back to the board with a focused expression.

"Then… Then explain what changed!" he suddenly said. "Explain why we're here today. He must have done or said something which made you think—"

"One of his stupid jokes!" Excited, I cut him off. "It made me realise he had never told me he was straight. He never told me he liked guys either. All he said was a whole lot of nothing that could be interpreted both ways."

"What was the joke?"

"He said he'd never sleep with me because I was too innocent."

Camille flicked her wrist. "Arthur."

"Okay." Arthur wrote the exact quote in my column. "Eric likes his stupid jokes, but that one is clearly suspicious. I think we should stop here and ask him straight to his face." He turned to face us. "Got it, straight to his—"

"If he liked me," I cut Arthur off with a glare, "then why didn't he just say it? You imagine Eric not saying what goes through his mind?"

"Huh, yeah!" Camille said with fervour. "On the boat, he hinted he's worried about causing problems, right? He's just like everyone else, he has secrets. And if he realised he liked boys, or in that case, that he liked you, it could have scared him. Maybe he didn't want to say anything before he was sure you liked him."

"But you were hung up on Alberto," Arthur said. "If I were him, I'd have kept quiet too."

Arthur dropped the marker and went to squat between Camille and me. The whiteboard was a complete mess, just like my head before they arrived. But now my two best friends looked just as confused as myself.

"We did it," Arthur said in a serious tone. "We gathered all the clues we could think of, and most of them show Eric flirting outrageously with Zak. On the other end, we have a straight guy who's never been in a same-sex relationship, had never kissed a guy before Zak, and has a reputation of being really good in b—"

I raised my hand. "Don't say it."

"My point was, there are enough clues on this board to move forward to the next stage."

I almost flinched under his determined expression. "The next stage?"

"I agree," Camille said. "There is enough evidence. Now be a man and ask another man if he's into other men."

"Ask... him? Directly?"

The idea was enticing, yet absolutely terrifying.

"Yes, pop the question!" Arthur furrowed his brow and imitated my voice. "Hey, Eric, you wouldn't happen to have a crush on me, would you?"

"I thought of asking him once..." Camille said. "If he didn't fancy you a little bit."

"Why didn't you?" I asked.

"Because I already knew how he would answer. With a truth that sounds like a lie or something like that." She took a deep breath before launching herself into an impression of Eric. "Of course, I have a crush on Zak. Hahaha! I'm so comfortable in my own skin, I don't mind telling the world I'm gay. Haha! Because I'm not. Or... am I?" She mimed an explosion with her hands. "Mind blown."

I had to admit, her impression was bang on. Arthur seemed to agree as well. For a moment, we all looked at each other, a little stupefied by our discoveries.

"So you... so you think he's bisexual, then?" I broke the silence.

Camille tilted her head. "He might well be and has no reason to scream it from the rooftops."

"What I think," Arthur said with a grin. "Is that Eric is more like 'Oh yeah, my name's Eric, I usually do girls but for this one, I'll make an exception.'"

"So romantic," Camille said with a fake smile.

But I had already scrambled up to my feet, a bright fire roaring in my chest.

"Fuck it, fuck romance! If he wants to make an exception for me, I'll take it." My two friends stared at me as though I had turned into a different person. I ignored them as I struggled to put on my sweater.

"I'm not as innocent as you all think I am, really. I was once called wicked, even." I cleared my throat. "By Eric himself."

Camille, too, got to her feet — with more elegance — and grabbed her bag. "I guess we're going, then."

With a last look at the board, Arthur took a handful of cookies from the tray and with a resolute face, shoved me out of my own bedroom.

29

THE FINISH LINE

I followed Camille and Arthur down the steps leading to my front door with a madly beating heart. Camille took a moment to straighten my sweater and attempted to fix my hair.

"Where can we find Eric on a Sunday afternoon?"

"Football," I said without hesitation.

Arthur leaned against the wall with a smile. "Oh, so you're familiar with his schedule? Is that another exhibit?"

"No, it's a simple deduction. He told us football is all he ever does. But... he also mentioned something about using one day of the weekend to do his homework."

"Problem," Camille said with a frown. "We don't know where his club trains."

"I wouldn't bother him where he works. Let's try his home instead."

Excited, we made for the door. But Arthur caught my hand the moment I touched the doorknob.

"Wait. Does anyone here know where he lives?"

We exchanged helpless glances, neither of us having access to that information. At the same moment, my sister Yasmine, clad in her running clothes, returned from her walk with Rufus. The dog, already excited by an hour of terrorising pedestrians, immediately stuck his head between Arthur's legs.

"What do we have here?" Yasmine asked with round eyes.

Arthur snapped his legs shut with a pathetic little squeal. Yasmine immediately whistled, and Rufus came to sit at her feet like an obedient pup.

I quickly introduced everyone. Camille didn't bother hiding her enthusiasm at meeting Yasmine, but to my surprise, Yas' seemed just as glad. She even apologised to Arthur for Rufus, explaining he usually treated every guy as a potential threat against her.

"What are you up to?" she asked. "You all look like you only have one minute left to save the world and no idea how to do it."

Arthur took a step forward. "We're looking for Eric!"

I stomped on his foot, but it was too late. My sister's dark eyes had narrowed to slits, and they were pointed right at me.

"Eric... The football player?"

"Yes, ma'am," Arthur said sheepishly.

I turned my face away to avoid my sister's sharp gaze. Of course, I hadn't told her everything about Eric. She probably still thought he was my former nemesis turned summer buddy. She had no idea my heart was beating for him nowadays.

Yasmine approached me and forced me to look at her. "Are we talking about the same Eric with whom you spent two and a half weeks in the middle of nowhere, the same one you wouldn't stop talking about on the phone and accused of driving you mad?"

Camille looked away and started whistling. Arthur began to smirk, but Rufus licked his jowls, and his face turned ashen.

"Yeah, okay." I glared at them all with pride. "I like him. I can't help it. I want to see him right now and tell him how much I like him. Sue me! I don't care how much you think me ridiculous."

Yasmine tut-tutted me smugly. "Brother mine, you seem to forget who my best friend is."

I hesitated. "Sacha?"

"No. The other one."

"I... huh... François?"

Yasmine slapped her own forehead. "Michael, for fuck's sake! He was there too, remember? He suspected you had a bit of a crush on the little striker."

"He's really not little," I said, pouting.

Arthur snorted and Camille elbowed him.

"Well, might as well go for it," Yasmine said, gripping my shoulders. "I saw his picture in *The Colette Times* and oh, boy. They don't make blondies like this except in fiction."

"Yeah, he's really dreamy," Arthur said.

"You read *The Colette Times*?" Camille asked with interest.

"It's my new favourite paper. Beats *Le Monde* any day." Yasmine pulled a wrinkled copy from the pocket of her jacket. "It's pretty fierce. I would have liked to have that in my time."

Camille took the paper from my sister's hands and read the headline again. "Yasmine, did Michael ever suspect Eric to have a crush on Zak, by any chance?"

Yasmine cocked her head with a satisfied smirk. "Michael refused to tell me anything."

"Oh," Arthur and I spoke at the same time, sounding equally disappointed.

"Which can only mean…" Yasmine added with a pointed look at me, "there was something to tell."

That was enough to send me over the edge.

"We need to go! Now!" I fumbled with the lock of the door. "I could be making out with him right now! In the next hour, I'll either be smooching him or sobbing into a giant jar of ice cream, but I can't take this anymore. I haven't felt his hands on me in… days!"

"There was some touching, I knew it," Arthur mumbled.

"Yes, dummy, they were lovers on screen." Camille pinched his cheek. "You filmed it."

"I see you have found perfect friends," Yasmine said. "Come on, I'll give you a ride to your lover's place."

Out of nowhere, Camille let out a frightening gasp. "Nadia!"

"No, it's Yasmine." My sister glared at her. "I take back what I just said."

"No, no! Nadia! She can find out where Eric lives! She can ask Charles-Henry."

It took a few minutes and a small white lie about sending a case of copies of the film to Eric's address before the four of us and Rufus could storm outside the flat to cram ourselves into my sister's car, direction Raspail.

～

Some fifteen minutes later, my fingertip hovered over the doorbell to Eric's place. The whole gang was waiting anxiously behind me — including Rufus, who was watching me with curious eyes.

"We should have texted," I muttered under my breath. "We should have just texted to make sure he was home."

Camille walked over to me and whispered in my ear. "It's more romantic this way."

"Right."

She gripped my wrist and forced my fingertip to press the doorbell. Time passed and no sign of life came from inside. When we finally heard someone playing with the lock, we all gasped like idiots.

The woman who opened the door was in her forties, had magnificent strawberry-blonde hair, pale green eyes, and even paler skin. She opened the door in yoga clothes, her hair pulled back with a bright blue ribbon.

Eric's mom looked a little surprised to see four young people and a panting Malinois staring wide-eyed at her as if she were the guardian to the doors of heaven.

"Are you... selling... calendars?" she asked in French.

The gentleness in her eyes spurred some of us into action. Camille pushed me aside in her excitement. "Can we speak to Eric?"

Eric's mom looked at Camille's flushed face. "You're friends of Eric?"

"Yes!" Arthur said.

"Oh." Her pale eyes fell on me. "Then come in, come in."

She opened the door for us, and we barged in, speaking excitedly in hushed whispers.

"Shoes off, please?" Eric's mom said, watching us with an amused expression.

We obeyed. Yasmine even helped Rufus wipe his paws on the doormat. I left my shoes under a set of framed baby pictures.

"Look, baby Eric!" Camille beamed. "He's so cute!"

"No," Eric's mom said. "That one's his brother Andrew. They used to look alike, but not anymore."

Andrew also appeared to be shorter and stockier from what we could gather from more recent pictures.

I helped Yasmine find a place for her sneakers. When I looked up, I was met with a framed copy of *The Colette Times*, first of its kind, which said:

ERIC T.R. IS A GOOD KISSER

*Says partner on screen when questioned
in front of belligerent escort.*

And under it, the group picture showing Eric and me staring

proudly at the objective with our hands around each other's waists. I stared at it in disbelief.

"Why did you frame that?"

"That paper?" Eric's mom let out a childish laugh which sounded familiar. "Eric wanted it framed!"

"Is it the first time he's in the papers?" Arthur asked, squinting at the passage in the article that mentioned the DOP's crazy hair.

"Oh no, Eric's been in the papers since he was a little kid."

"But not for being a good kisser, I assume," Yasmine said with a smirk.

"No. But he plays a bit of football."

She sounded very modest for the mother of someone who may one day be selected to participate in the World Cup.

"Any idea why he wanted this one framed especially?" Camille asked with an innocent expression.

"Who knows?" Eric's mom smiled. "I think he was proud of this one. He wanted it put up immediately, so I had to frame it over his contract with his football club."

She led us through the corridor to an elegant living room. I stepped on the chevron parquet with trepidation. Eric's living room. It was modern, airy, and bright with a cathedral ceiling not unlike my own. A whole side of the flat was made of large windows stretching to the ceiling, bathing the entire surface in daylight. The furniture was sparse and inconspicuous, leaving the abundance of plants to be the stars of the show. From the slightly opened double doors nestled among the windows, I caught a glimpse of a garden overflowing with vegetation.

Arthur bumped into a classy suitcase leaning against the wall and apologised. Eric's mother waved away his apology and offered us to sit on her tidy little sofas, but no one dared. We stood awkwardly in the middle of the room instead. Even Rufus lay quietly between my sister's legs and didn't make a sound.

"So, kids, you said you were friends of Eric." After hearing us whispering in English in her hallway, Eric's mother switched to it. "But something about you tells me you're not from the football team."

"No, we're not," I said.

"Are you from Colette, then?" She put her delicate hand on her chest. "I'm Constance, by the way. Eric's mother."

"Camille," Camille said. "This is Arthur and Yasmine." She pointed at me. "That's Zak. He just needs to speak to Eric real quick."

Before I could retort, Eric's mother's expression changed. She approached me with a strange glint in her eyes.

"You're Zak?"

"Huh…. Yeah. That's me."

After a while, she whispered, "I see."

"See what?" I asked, barely able to restrain myself to add: Did your son mention anything about wanting to touch my ass?

"Wait, guys," Camille said suddenly. "Have you seen this?"

Standing by the tall and narrow library, Camille pulled something out of the pile of papers gathered on one shelf. She walked over to us and brandished a battered copy of *My Summer of Love and Woe*. It was only the cover, but it was decorated with humongous hearts and flowers drawn with a pink highlighter until almost no white remained. It was really garish.

"That's my script!" Camille squealed. She shook the piece of paper with blazing eyes. "But there's only the front page. Covered in hearts and flowers."

"I would hide that too if I were him," Yasmine said with a solemn expression.

Camille, Arthur, and I all turned to Constance.

"He was never good at arts and crafts," she said sheepishly. "But still… It seems he's gotten worse with time."

Camille pushed the cover of her script into my hands with a triumphant smile, then leaned into me to whisper in my ear, "Forgive me for being so vulgar and blunt, but there's no way this guy is straight."

My mind was already racing. He wasn't straight! Hurray! But he also was a really poor artist. Hurray…

"Where is Eric?" I asked in a small voice.

Just then, we heard the front door on the other side of the wall open. Immediately, Rufus got up and began to bark like a wild beast until Yasmine whistled again.

A voice rang from the hallway. "Mom!"

My heart stopped in my chest. Footsteps announced the arrival of my beloved. We all looked at the door with expectant faces until a young man who looked like an older, darker, and moodier version of Eric entered the room with a frown on his face.

"Oh," Arthur said, not bothering to hide his disappointment.

"Mom! Why is there a do——" The young man froze when he noticed us all in the middle of the room. "Who's that?"

Constance gave him a meaningful look. "That's Zak."

Andrew's expression slowly darkened. His eyes instinctively moved toward the garish cover of *My Summer of Love and Woe* in my hands then snapped up at my burning face. His mother slowly approached him, but Andrew suddenly turned around, cupped his mouth, and shouted "Dad!" as loud as he could.

Yasmine took my arm and pulled me to her. Between her legs, Rufus sat down, his eyes bright. We heard more footsteps, then Eric's father rushed into the living room.

"Andy, what did I tell you about screa... ming." Eric's dad's voice trailed off when he saw us.

Eric's brother Andrew pointed at me. His dad briefly gazed at our group, finishing with the dog between my sister's legs. He seemed to be in his mid-fifties, with sharp eyes the same colour as Eric's, elegant salt and pepper hair, and a handsome face. From the way his muscles stretched his shirt taut, it was clear he was athletic as hell.

Behind me, my sister hummed a little too appreciatively, so I kicked her in the tibia. She huffed but didn't complain.

"What's going on?" he said to his son. "Are you afraid of dogs now?"

Andrew poked his dad in the shoulder with a complicated expression. "That's Zak."

What the hell was going on with that?

It was weird to see eyes so similar to Eric's staring at me so coldly. The man wrinkled his nose just like his son too.

"That's Zak?"

I waved feebly. "Hello?"

"Oh, hell no!" Eric's dad shook his head.

If I had no clue what was going on, Constance seemed to have understood the meaning of Eric's father's words and pursed her delicate lips in disapproval.

"Personally, I can see it…" she said softly.

"Will someone tell me what's going on?" I pleaded with her using my eyes.

"No," the father said firmly. "Not gonna happen."

Yasmine put herself between us and spoke with authority. "What's going on here? Zak insists on speaking to Eric."

Eric's father crossed his arms. "Well, he can't."

Yasmine was easily provoked by this sort of thing; she instantly reacted.

"Who the hell do you think you are to say who can and cannot speak to him?"

"I'm his father. Who the hell are you?"

"I'm Zak's sister!"

Andrew jumped in. "And I'm Eric's brother, and I don't want him to speak to Eric either."

"But why?" I rose my voice, hoping Eric might hear us from the depths of his flat.

"What do you mean, why?" Eric's dad suddenly looked uncomfortable, but he quickly recovered. "It's better this way."

"I don't get it. I give up." Arthur sunk down on one of the sofas.

"You all seem to know Zak," Camille asked. "But why?"

Eric's mom looked pleased to be able to answer that one, and she began talking excitedly.

"It's simple! Eric came home one day. He was all miserable and he kept sighing, so I asked, 'How are you today?' and he said to me, 'Oh, you know… A little gay', so I asked, 'A little gay? Do you mean happy?' and he said, 'A little gay. As, in love with a boy'. I was speechless for a second, as you can imagine, but I got over it quickly, and I said, 'Which boy is so special that you fell in love with him?' Then he stopped looking miserable. He closed his eyes and smiled and said, 'Just a boy.' 'Who? Who?' I asked, because I was too curious now to drop it. And of course, he said, 'Zak.'"

"Oh, Jesus Christ," Yasmine said behind me.

But it was too late; I was already smiling. Even if my heart beat so intensely in my chest that I felt just about to pass out, I knew everything would be just fine from now on.

"It's me, I'm Zak," I said with pride. "He loves me."

"Would that we, would that…" Arthur said, with a grimace. He squeezed his eyes shut. "Would we would… Damn. What's the thing again?"

I patted his shoulder affectionally. "We should have asked Eric's mom directly instead of spending two hours playing detectives in my bedroom."

"Yeah, that."

But nothing could alter the way I felt at this exact moment. After a lifetime spent in books and studies and a thirst for knowledge which never left me, I can safely say that this was the most valuable piece of information I had ever collected.

"He loves me!" I repeated for everyone to hear, feeling my eyes well up.

Camille balled her fists in victory. "Confirmed!"

Constance approached me with open arms, apparently to hug me, but the meaty hand of Eric's dad came between us.

"It's not gonna happen," he said in a choked-up voice. "Eric's got a bright future before him. Don't go about ruining it."

I took a step back. "How am I going to ruin his life? You don't even know me."

"Stephen," Constance said in a soothing voice.

Eric's dad looked furious and uncomfortable at the same time. "No. No."

"Please," I addressed Eric's mother. "Let me talk to him."

"Sorry," she said. "He's not here."

"He's not?" Even his dad sounded surprised.

"Yes. He's… grounded."

"Grounded?" Camille, Arthur, and I spoke in one voice. "For what?"

His father frowned. "Yes, for what?"

"Perhaps he didn't tell you… considering…" Constance said. "He fought with Kayvin. The headmaster is making him work at this charity fair at Montsouris."

Arthur jumped to his feet. Camille bounded toward my sister and whispered something in her ear, to which Yasmine answered with a curt nod before pulling out her phone. Stephen looked crestfallen.

"My son fought with his best friend?"

"They're not really friends anymore. Kayvin's a bit—"

"Hell, no! First, he announces he's quitting football, then he fights with his best friend. And now this…" He pointed his finger at me. "This is all you!"

"He… what?" I asked in shock.

"Stephen." Eric's mother sounded tired now. "Eric never said he's quitting football."

"Oh no? He didn't say he would quit the club if they didn't let him —" He was pointing at me and looked like he was about to choke on something. "What the hell happened on that trip?"

Stephen took a second to catch his breath, his expression full of doubt and concern. Andrew slid me a dirty look here and there, which caused my sister to answer in kind. Once calmed down, Stephen then turned to Eric's mother.

"That's enough. I'm going there right now and I'm removing him from this school. He should have been a pensioner at the club full time. You put these notions into his head… and now his whole life is at risk."

When I heard that, my heart began to pound in my ears. I watched helplessly as Stephen left the room, followed closely by Andrew. A few seconds later, we heard the front door slam shut behind them.

"Is he really going to remove Eric from Colette?" Camille said in a small voice.

Constance shook her head helplessly. I approached her with the question that had been on my mind since she told me Eric confessed his love for me.

"You said he loved me, and now I know he did. But I made a mistake and since then…" My voice died in my throat. "Do you… Do you think he still loves me?"

Her gentle eyes fell on me. "When Stephen found out about this, he returned from New York to speak to Eric about his career. He thought he'd have to fight with him to convince him not to do anything rash. But Eric had no intention of fighting. He appeased Stephen by saying that you didn't love him anyway, that you got together with some Italian… shovel? And that you didn't care much for him anyway. Those were his words."

Wonderful. Eric's mom read my face and took my hands in hers.

"Stephen was reassured, but he still told Eric to train harder so that he could crush the Italian football team whenever he'd face them as retribution."

"That's nice," I said numbly.

"But then Eric said that if you were to change your mind, ditch the shovel and get with him, he wouldn't miss his chance this time, and he'd pluck you right off the ground."

My heart lurched hopefully. "He said that?"

"Only last night." Constance's smile widened when mine slowly returned to my face. "So you see, there's hope for you after all."

I hesitated for a moment, then I turned to my friends and my sister with a confused expression. "His dad thinks I'm gonna ruin Eric's life, how can I fight against that?"

Yasmine was the first to speak. "Eric chose you. He even said he would quit football if he couldn't have you."

"I wouldn't advise him to do that," Constance said faintly.

"He's already made his choice," Yasmine said. "You have to fight for him."

Camille nodded and pointed at the garish cover of her script in my hands. "Imagine being loved like that and doing nothing about it? You would regret it for the rest of your life."

I turned to Arthur with hopeful eyes.

"He's really hot," he said. "I'd fight anyone getting in the way if I were you."

I wasn't sure why I expected wiser words. But the effect was the same: The fire Eric's father had smothered with his threatening behaviour was rekindled with a little help. I finally turned to Eric's mom with a resolute expression.

"Eric's father just wants to protect him, you know." She sighed. "He's a bit like a dog at times, he wouldn't hand him over just like that. You have to throw him a bone."

My brow furrowed. "I hope you're not saying I have to fight him. Because have you seen the size of his shoulders compared to mine?"

She hid a smile behind her hand. "Don't let him bully you, that's all."

"We should get going," Yasmine said. "You must tell Eric you love him before his dad ruins your moment."

We parted from Constance and returned to Yasmine's car in haste. Once inside, Arthur flattened himself against the window to avoid Rufus trying to lick his face from the middle seat.

"Such a shame," Camille sighed. Seated on the other side of Rufus, she rubbed his ears absently. "It mustn't have been easy for Eric to come out to his dad."

Arthur poked my shoulder from behind me. "I hope it will be easier for you."

I didn't hesitate before speaking. "I'm sure it will be nothing. I just never told them because it never came up naturally."

"So what are you going to do now?" Arthur said. "Eric couldn't keep his hands off you when you weren't together. Imagine how he'll be once you get together. You won't be able to pass as just friends."

"You're right, bringing Eric home will probably do the trick." I coughed lightly in my fist. "Because I won't be able to keep my hands off him either."

My sister was struggling with her seatbelt. "Ha! The ancestors have always known about you. They're just pretending so you won't feel awkward about it."

I turned to her in horror. "And you're telling me this now?"

Yasmine shrugged haughtily. "You know Mom reads your boy-love mangas, right?"

"She *what?*"

Camille pulled my sleeve discreetly and whispered. "Can you lend them to me?"

"Yasmine, please!" Arthur clapped his hands to command our attention. "What if Stephen gets there before us?"

"Don't worry, kids." Yasmine turned the key in the ignition. "We'll make it. He's probably going to try to get there through Alésia and will get himself stuck in traffic. I'll take René Coty and cut him off."

"Thank you, Yasmine," Camille said, pushing away Rufus's large head to wrap her arms around my sister. "You're a proper loser, and we won't forget."

Yasmine shot me the most dumbfounded look of her existence, and I replied with the silliest grin of mine.

There was no cloud of smoke, no red light blown, no biting from Rufus. Yet I felt like a criminal on his way to commit the greatest heist. Steal the queen's jewels, rob a bank, tell a boy you love him before his father ruins it for you… What was the difference, really?

∿

Camille, Arthur, and I stormed Parc Montsouris with hearts of iron but without a clue as to how to proceed. We were one member short too: Yasmine was left behind so that she could find a place to park, and as a result, I had no idea if we would ever see her again.

The charity fair was organised by Colette and a few other private schools. A little map was offered by a smiling volunteer at all the entrances. Arthur held it in front of us. Despite my best efforts, I was too excited and couldn't make sense of it at all. Stephen and Andrew might already be spewing nonsense to my sweetheart while I was struggling to interpret the dumbest thing ever written.

When I cried out in frustration, Camille snatched the thing from Arthur's hands and dashed forward. Over our heads, the sun seemed to be torn between remaining safely hidden behind grey clouds and finally making an appearance. Agitated beyond measure, we paid no attention to the food stands, or the attractions lined up on each side. Arthur almost tackled a group of children lining up for churros and was lagging behind to give the parents an apology.

I was looking over my shoulder to check on him when someone

slammed brutally into me from the other side. A familiar, posh sounding voice cried out, "Watch where you're going!"

Stepping back, I immediately recognised Joy, followed by Elodie and Melissa. Elodie and I made eye contact. She held my gaze with a strange expression. Camille immediately returned to my side just as Arthur freed himself from the angry parents.

"What are you doing here?" Camille said, breathless.

"What do you mean?" Joy said smugly. "Colette organised a charity fair. It's only natural that we support it."

"Eric and Kayvin are manning the obstacle race," Melissa said with a shrug. "We just went there to say hello."

That made more sense.

"So you saw him?" Arthur asked with a little too much enthusiasm. "You saw Eric?"

"No, we didn't," Joy said with a dark look at Melissa.

I gripped Melissa's wrist with both hands. She blinked curiously at me.

"Where's the race exactly?"

"Other side," she said, extending her hand to point out the right direction. Joy elbowed her in the ribs. "Ouch! What is wrong with you?"

Camille, Arthur, and I darted toward the other side of the park. I whirled around, my hands cupped together.

"Thanks! See you later!"

Joy's eyes fell to my hands and the now wrinkled cover of Camille's script decorated with pink hearts and flowers I was holding. Her eyes widened.

"Where did you get that? That's mine!" She made a go at it.

"Keep it!" I said, throwing it in her general direction with a beating heart. "Keep it, keep it, keep it!" As long as I kept the man himself, she could have everything else she wanted.

Joy clutched the piece of paper with eyes round with surprise, Melissa looked bored out of her mind, while Elodie stared at me with a little smile.

"Move it, Zak, move it!" Camille bellowed, forcing me to pick up the pace.

I was already panting like a wild beast when we arrived near the obstacle race. Perhaps because of the location of the race, the whole area was deserted, with not one child in sight. Instead, we ran into someone else I would have never expected.

Michael, dressed in his own clothes this time, was standing near the ticket booth. His face split into a delighted smile when he saw us.

"Hey, kids, didn't expect to see you here!"

Behind him, a guy dressed in black and who I assumed was his boyfriend Louis was standing a short distance behind him, his face hidden by a gigantic cotton candy.

"No time… there's no time…" Camille said, out of breath. She put her hands on her knees.

Michael approached her and tapped her on the back. "What's going on? Everything okay?"

"Eric!" I shouted in a hoarse voice. "We're looking for Eric!"

"Eric? He's here," Michael said, pointing at the obstacle course behind him.

Just then, the sound of angry voices forced us all to look around. Yasmine had returned to us, pulling Rufus on a short leash. She was yelling at someone behind her.

"I told you not to follow me!"

She was talking to Stephen and Andrew, who had apparently and cleverly decided to follow Yasmine instead of finding the right place themselves.

"It's only fair that you help us after we helped you find a place to park," Stephen said through gritted teeth.

Andy scoffed. "We didn't help her, she stole our spot right in front of us!"

"All is fair in the game," Yasmine said with a snigger. She jerked aside when she saw her best friend Michael standing there. "The fuck are you doing here?" Then she saw Louis and gasped. "And you let this one out?"

Louis's blue eyes peeked from behind the cotton candy.

"Eric, Eric, Eric!" I shouted, jumping in place. This was not the time for effusions of friendship. "I can't see him. Why can't I see him?"

"He's manning the finish line, so he's on the other side of those trees," Michael explained. "We wanted to see him too, but the headmaster won't let us."

Louis evidently had no desire to see any of us and slowly retraced his steps back to the ticket booth. Unfortunately for him, someone kicked the door open from the inside, sending it flying straight into his face.

"What's the racket for?" a booming voice asked.

Everyone present froze, except for Stephen, Andrew, and my sister.

440

Our headmaster, Mr Van Bergen, had the presence of a Greek god and the temper to match. Tall and handsome, he emerged from the ticket booth in his usual suit trousers and tight shirt, a combination known to flatter both his powerful silhouette and extraordinary ego. With a mildly intrigued glance at all of us, he tossed aside the toothpick he'd been chewing on.

"Sir!" I almost threw myself at him. "I *really really* need to speak to Eric."

Mr Van Bergen gave me a haughty look. "And I *really really* need a cigarette, but you won't see me whining about it."

As I stood there speechless, he looked to the sides for a moment, seemed to realise something was off, and walked back to the ticket booth. He pulled a disoriented Louis from around the corner and dragged him sniffling toward us.

"Why are you hiding over there?" Van Bergen said to him. "'Makes me uncomfortable."

Rubbing his nose, Louis stood by Michael with a wounded expression. Without the cover of the cotton candy, I could finally take a look at him. He still wore long hair, this time bound in a messy bun at the back. His jaw looked sharper now. His blue eyes were unusually bloodshot, but it was probably from getting acquainted with the booth door a minute ago. As handsome as he looked, he was nothing compared to the love of my life standing on the other side of those trees.

"Forget about the little boy," Stephen said, crossing his arms over his chest. "I need to speak to Eric first. He's my son."

The little boy? Was I the little boy? I immediately felt my eyebrows draw together murderously.

"No can do," Van Bergen said, a trace of amusement in his voice. "He's grounded until five. You can wait if you want, but not here, or you'll frighten the children."

I couldn't think of anyone more likely to frighten the children than Van Bergen himself, and when I accidentally met Louis's eyes, we both realised we were thinking exactly the same.

"I'm not gonna wait until five," Stephen said with confidence. "I'm his father."

Van Bergen looked Stephen up and down with a little smirk. "Or..." he said. "You can purchase a ticket and race yourself." His eyes narrowed coyly. "Think about it. For the children."

"I'm not..." Stephen clenched his jaw. "That's it, I'm removing my son from your school."

Van Bergen shrugged. "When you see the amount of paperwork needed to do that, you'll probably change your mind."

Meanwhile, a really stupid idea started to form in my mind.

"Come on." Van Bergen was staring at us with judgmental eyes. "It's true the race was originally intended for children. But since most of you look completely out of shape, that should prove enough of a challenge."

The headmaster whistled. Two guys who were standing in the shadows of a tree approached with hesitating steps. I recognised Xavier and Kayvin.

Stephen looked at Kayvin in surprise. "What are you doing here?"

Van Bergen snorted. "Grounded as well. For insubordination or something."

"For the last time, sir," Kayvin said darkly. "It wasn't for insubordination but for fighting within the school walls."

"My point exactly."

"I'm just keeping him company," Xavier said to no one in particular.

"Why did you fight?" Stephen asked Kayvin with a quick look in my direction. "Was it because of a girl, by any chance?"

Kayvin lowered his head. "Yes."

Eric's father turned to me with a shit-eating grin. I stomped my foot in defiance.

"Oh, it is on," I said, suddenly surrendering to the madness in my heart. "I'll race you, old man. First one to cross the finish line gets to talk to Eric first."

There was a silence. Everyone looked at me in shock, except for the headmaster who was admiring his nails with indifference.

"What did you call me?" Stephen looked more impressed than angry at my outburst. He took a moment to consider my proposition, then flashed me a gleaming smile. "Done."

"Brilliant," Van Bergen said to his nails. "But let's make it more interesting. For some obscure reason, the obstacle race isn't popular, and I'm bored." He looked up, a hint of mischief in his eyes. "You race in teams. Anyone who wins can give their privilege to speak to Eric either to the father or the grumpy little kid."

"Hey!" I protested.

Stephen looked surprised. "You would do that?"

The headmaster shrugged. "All I care about is selling more tickets. You know... For the children." Since no one seemed to believe him, he sighed. "And there are no rules, except one. All contestants must have all of their limbs when crossing the finish line."

We all relaxed and laughed at this stupid rule he made on the spot. Except for Louis, who said, "Isn't that completely out of line for a children's race?"

Stephen gnashed his teeth. "There's no way he's serious."

Louis shook his head as if he didn't believe the headmaster was joking at all.

"I'll sue the hell out of him if he is," Stephen added.

Van Bergen gave a thunderous laugh. "Join the line! My spouse is a lawyer and a fucking shark." With that, he gleefully returned to his booth to collect our tickets.

My heart pounding, I turned to my people. "I know I'm being crazy and ridiculous. I'm well aware of it. But Eric's mine. And I can't let his father bully me, or he'll never respect me. So... Who's with me?"

Camille and Arthur naturally stepped forward, followed by my sister. To my surprise, Michael stepped forward too.

"You finally got it," he said with a smile. "Let's say I'm doing this for Eric as much as for you."

I conveyed my thanks with my eyes.

Stephen grabbed Kayvin and Xavier by the shoulder. "You two, you're with me."

The gesture seemed to awaken all sorts of repressed feelings within Kayvin, because he suddenly looked like a little boy. I almost felt bad for him, until he threw me a murderous glare, and I swallowed a lump.

"Wait," Louis suddenly said in a croaky voice. "What am I going to do?"

Yasmine handed him Rufus's leash. The dog immediately started growling and pulling. "You're gonna keep an eye on my dog while I'm kicking ass."

"Oh no," Louis said, dropping the leash. "Yasmine, please. No." He threw Michael a helpless look, which only caused his boyfriend to smile.

"Don't be afraid. He just wants to be your friend."

Louis didn't seem convinced at all.

"Please, Louis." I joined my hands and pleaded with misty eyes. "If you ever wanted to be my friend, please, please, take the dog."

"Your friend? I don't even know you," he said blankly.

Little bitch.

I was about to order Rufus to deal with him, but Yasmine only had

443

to give Louis a warning look for him to comply. With an exasperated click of his tongue, he seized Rufus's leash.

"You better win," he muttered. Rufus attempted to pounce on him, but my sister forced him to sit down.

"Thanks," she said. "For helping my brother. I'll allow you to call me your friend from now on."

"Friendship is overrated," Louis murmured, staring at the dog with anxious eyes.

Meanwhile, Stephen was counting us while walking to the starting line.

"You may have one more," he said with a smirk, "but none of you look capable."

"Hey!" Yasmine pointed a finger at him. "No need to be rude."

He had a point, however. As far as I knew, none of us were athletes of any kind, aside from my sister who used running as an outlet for her frustrations. She was the only one who'd be able to succeed against any of these guys.

And then there was Michael. Technically, he had a chance because of his really long legs, but I knew nothing of his stamina. As for Arthur, he admitted he'd never exercised a day in his life. I turned to Camille with a panicked look.

"Can you run?"

"I'm not great." She tilted her head. "But I used to play rugby if that helps."

"You did what?"

Before she could tell me more, Van Bergen returned with a bunch of tickets and rubbed his fingers together to ask for money. Stephen attempted to pay for everyone, but my sister slapped another fifty euros notes in the headmaster's hand with a dark look.

"Donation," she growled. "For the children."

"Ah, Yasmine…" Van Bergen patted her head. "You were my best student."

Louis chuckled. "Shit, really?"

The headmaster faced him with a smile. "You were the worst."

"Aww, man."

Michael kissed his boyfriend briefly, and he forgot all about it. Yasmine motioned for us to gather in a circle.

"All right, listen. Logically, they're gonna come after Zak with all they've got to stop him from speaking to Eric first. We need to cheat."

"Yasmine!" I blurted out, shocked.

"What? Van Bergen said no rules."

"I think Kayvin's gonna come for me," Arthur said with fear.

Camille's eyes were burning. "Don't think about it, just run."

"I'm really not a great runner," I said meekly.

"Take your time, let us deal with them. You'll seize your chance whenever you can!" Yasmine turned to Louis. "You. Don't lose my dog or I'll definitely end you."

Louis rolled his eyes. "Yes, ma'am."

We all took our positions along the starting line. Looking excited, the headmaster stood in front of us, unconcerned that Xavier's foot was way over the line or that my sister and Andy were exchanging threatening gestures.

I accidentally locked eyes with Eric's father and saw his eyes glinting. A stream of curses came crashing down on my thoughts; this was the dumbest thing I'd ever done. My chest was tightened, not only by anticipation, but by laughter that I couldn't yet let out.

Van Bergen held up his hands. "The race is simple. Don't break an ankle, that would be embarrassing. It's shaped like a half-oval. You have cones, obstacles to jump, hoops in the turn of the circle, balls that you have to throw into a bucket, but no one's gonna check if you don't because who cares… I know I don't. Then nets, then finish line. It's a straight line, shouldn't be too hard. Oh wait, let me add one last thing: You're not allowed to break the obstacles, I need them until five. Anyone breaking them will be disqualified. God bless."

Then Van Bergen pulled a gun out from the back of his belt and shot it without warning. The blast had us all pounce forward without thinking. I thought I heard Louis scream, "Is that a real gun??" but in that exact moment, I didn't feel it mattered.

30

THE PRIZE

It was chaos the moment it started.

Yasmine was faster than an arrow released from a bow and took the lead. My clever sister didn't bother with the cones and bounded over them like a doe. Right after her, Stephen and Andy looked like they would give her trouble. At my back, crazed barking forced me to look over my shoulder. Louis was struggling to hold Rufus back while the headmaster sniggered at his side.

Right ahead of me, Michael, true to himself, had difficulty cheating and wasted the precious time he would have needed to avoid Kayvin, who slammed straight into him and held him down in the grass. I forced myself to ignore my friend and kept running, blood pounding in my ears, with one focus only, get to that finish line and show that old man what I was capable of.

Xavier and Arthur were neck to neck, followed closely by Camille. Ahead of us, Andy crashed straight into the plastic obstacles like an American football player and took the lead, followed by my sister and Stephen. Seeing how one of the obstacles was bent from the collision, I could assume Andy would be disqualified, but I wouldn't bet my heart on it and pushed the thought out of my mind.

I was already starting to pant miserably when Michael and Kayvin overtook me again, covered in dirt from head to toe. With Van Bergen's rule that the first to arrive could decide who would talk to Eric first, no one was paying me any attention. At least I didn't have to worry about being pinned to the ground by anyone other than my bee-loving boyfriend.

We reached the turn of the circle. Stephen's fancy shoe slipped on a hoop and sent him rolling to the side with a curse. Yasmine didn't spare him a look and charged after his son.

"Again?" Michael screamed helplessly as Kayvin used his confusion to tackle him. They wrestled in the dirt. All I could spare was a quick thought for Joy and Melissa who were missing this.

Close behind him, Xavier was about to do the same to Arthur, but Camille, proving that she indeed used to play rugby, intercepted him so efficiently that his whole body was lifted off the ground.

Arthur and I stopped in the middle of the mess of hoops, too shocked to comprehend.

"Are you okay, Camille?" I asked helplessly.

Using her arms to press Xavier into the ground, Camille glared at us. "Run, you fools!"

"I think—" Xavier coughed a mouthful of mud, and lifting his head feebly, observed Camille with misty eyes. "I think I love you."

Camille stared back at him in horror. Raising her hands to the sky, she bellowed, "Noooooooooooooo!"

Arthur didn't seem to want to leave her behind, but I pulled him by the hand and he followed. We reached the throw-ball trial. My sister, Stephen, and Andy didn't bother with that and plunged headfirst under the following net.

"Go, go!" Arthur said, picking up a few balls. "I'll hold them back." He retraced his steps, his jaw clenched.

He was an amazing shot. He struck Kayvin on the head as he was immobilising Michael and screaming at Xavier to get a grip. But Camille was sitting on Xavier's chest with her arms folded over her chest, and Xavier was frozen to the ground, not daring to move a muscle.

I was forced to leave them all behind and joined the others under the net. Andy, bigger than my sister and I combined, had gotten himself stuck. Stephen wasted time trying to free him before he realised the much slenderer Yasmine was already through and getting to her feet. Following him, I slid with shaking limbs under the net and, crawling on my knees and elbows, soon met Andy's helpless eyes.

"Hey!" I said, a little awkwardly.

"... Hey," he answered, wide-eyed.

447

This was the first time my skinny frame got me a look of admiration from a powerfully built guy.

When I emerged, my confidence boosted by about 200%, I could see the finish line in the distance. When my sister saw me at Stephen's heels, she abruptly stopped, turned around, and charged straight at him. They went tumbling into the dirt, and ahead of me was the finish line, unencumbered. Adrenaline had long replaced fatigue, and I forced my legs to run even faster.

"Watch out!" Yasmine suddenly shouted behind me.

To my shock, Stephen, that machine, had already managed to get rid of her. In a few strides, he overtook me, his face brown with dirt but his eyes blazing. In a broken voice, I uttered a cry of despair.

It was over. I couldn't beat this guy. And I didn't even think of taking a ball or two to throw at his face, Arthur style. There was nothing I could do to stop him. My strength left me, and I was left trotting after Stephen helplessly.

But then, the monstrous and familiar sound of barking filled my ears. Before I could even connect the dots, a huge Malinois overtook me, ears flat and tongue wagging, and happily pounced on Stephen's back.

"What the f—" Poor Stephen's breath was cut off as he toppled over, and I stood once again in sight of the finish line.

Ignoring my boyfriend's father's screams for help, I allowed a grin to spread over my face. *Thank you, old boy, I'll never say you never did me a favour ever again.* My eyes stinging with tears, I gathered the last remnants of my strength to sprint toward my prize.

"Eric," I croaked, completely out of breath.

My heart was about to explode in my chest, but the finish line drew closer and closer. At this instant, the sun broke through the clouds and fell on a familiar crown of golden hair in the distance. The person it belonged to stood past the finish line with his back turned to me. His head bobbing up and down to the sound of music, he was oblivious to all the chaos that had happened because of him.

"Eric!" I called again in a hoarse voice.

Eric turned around and squinted at the dishevelled creature racing toward him. Shock stole across his face when he recognised me. His mouth falling open, he pushed down his headphones.

"Zak?" His arms opened instinctively.

My own hands outstretched, I crossed the last meters separating us, and as I jumped straight into his open arms, blurted out, "Catch!"

Eric scooped me up without effort, twirled me around, and brought our lips together.

"Hi!" His eyes were full of bewilderment and joy. His hands firmly supporting my butt, he brushed his nose against mine. "I hope you came here to confess your undying love, or I'm gonna look like a fucking perv."

I was tempted, I'll admit it, tempted to let the word *perv* come out of my mouth, my need to tease him almost just as consuming as my desire for him. But I squeezed my legs around his waist instead.

"Love," I said against his lips.

His eyes widened even more. "Seriously?!" Without waiting for an answer, he kissed me again. And again. And again. When he finally stopped showering my lips with kisses, he was panting as if he'd just finished the race. His breath was hot against my ear when he whispered, "... Is this real?"

The hope in his eyes made my whole face burn. For once, I had nothing to say, so I pulled him to me for more kisses. I, too, was out of breath, and my body was already aching from the race, but in this moment, I couldn't feel anything besides the warmth of his body against mine, the softness of his blond strands between my fingers, and the sweetness of his lips.

Eric had no intention of putting me down. His embrace was powerful enough to bruise. But with an irrational fear of not being able to kiss him again once his father would arrive, I answered aggressively, prying his lips open with my tongue. My stomach purred when I tasted him. He stumbled backwards and managed the impossible, holding me even tighter against him.

Each second spent glued to Eric was taking a stab at my old fart reputation. Our surroundings fading into nothingness, we made out in the middle of the park like a pair of carefree kids. Between kisses and bouts of laughter, Eric jumped up and down with my ass literally in his hands. He was just in the process of covering my whole face with wet little pecks when something caught his attention, and he jerked away with horror in his eyes.

"D-Dad?"

In his shock, the dog dropped me like a stone.

Stephen had seen better days. His grey suit now technically brown, he stomped toward us, followed by Andrew. Rufus was walking at his side and licking his hand. Right behind him, Yasmine, covered in dirt, looked amazed by her dog's behaviour. Behind them, Camille and

Arthur walked hand in hand, oblivious to their own unkempt appearance.

Eric extended his hand and peeled me off the ground with a confused expression. "What the hell is happening?"

"Nothing." I brushed the dirt off my jeans with a little laugh. "Just getting to know each other."

Stephen said nothing but patted Rufus's head with a troubled expression.

Following Camille and Arthur, Michael and Louis arrived walking shoulder to shoulder. Closing the march was the headmaster in great conversation with the tiny Elisa from *The Colette Times*.

"Well done!" Van Bergen boomed. "To whoever won. Who is it, by the way? I couldn't see from my spot."

"I won," I said in a croaky voice.

"By cheating!" Stephen said, pointing a finger at me.

I should have flinched in fear, but I could see that Eric's father wasn't really angry. Eric rubbed my back, his expression growing more and more dumbfounded.

Meanwhile, the headmaster was giving me an appraising look. "That's funny, I would have never bet on that scrawny thing to make it past *this* guy." He pointed at Stephen.

While I scoffed in protest, Eric's father, vexed, shouted at the head-master, "I would have made it to the finish line if not for that dog—"

The headmaster held up his hand to silence him and pointed to a handwritten sign planted by the finish line which said:

NO RULES EXCEPT
WINNER MUST HAVE ALL LIMBS
WHEN CROSSING FINISH LINE

"I planted that," Eric said in my ear, causing my scalp to tingle. "On his orders."

Andrew let his arms drop to his side, but Stephen glared at the sign helplessly. "This is insane…"

Mr Van Bergen shrugged. "Then complain to the headmaster about it."

"You are the headmaster!"

"And I heard your complaint."

"Wait!" Andy suddenly gasped. "The dog didn't have a ticket!"

With cries of shock, we all turned to Rufus as if expecting him to have an explanation. The dog watched us with sparkling eyes, his tongue lolling out.

"Not true," Van Bergen said. "The only sensible thing Louis Mésange has ever done in his life. He purchased a ticket for charity."

Louis let out an audible sigh but still produced the ticket for all of us to see.

"That's not the only sensible thing I've ever done, by the way," he said, with a side glance at Michael. "And you practically forced me to do it," he added with a dark look at Van Bergen.

The headmaster gave a thunderous laugh, then turned to Elisa with a secretive expression. "Don't put that in the paper."

"You're gonna write about this?" Camille asked her.

"I cover everything related to Colette," Elisa said in a smug tone. "That's my mission."

"Journalism isn't dead," Van Bergen said, slapping his hand over Elisa's shoulder. They exchanged proud smirks.

Guess *she* was his best student now.

"Come, let us see how Xavier and Kayvin are doing," Van Bergen said. "They won't want you to write about their shame, so you can blackmail them into telling you some other stuff."

"Great advice, Headmaster!"

They turned around to leave, but the headmaster paused. "Those who didn't need to speak to Eric should follow me and give them their privacy."

"Wait, headmaster." Eric's eyes filled with hope. "Does that mean my punishment is lifted?"

His words were met with a snigger. "You wish. You're staying until five. No exceptions."

Michael was the first to move. He mouthed to Eric to give him a phone call before pulling his boyfriend by the hand.

"You saved the day by releasing the hound," he told Louis tenderly. "Let's get you a reward."

With a triumphant look, Louis balled his hand into a fist and punched the air. Pausing only to give me a respectful nod, which I returned in kind, he followed Michael. Camille and Arthur next came to us, their muddy faces revealing two bright smiles.

"You managed to get so far," Camille said with the look of a proud mother. "Don't back down now."

We shared a group hug between losers, which my sister broke without ceremony.

"Oy! Do you want me to stay or what? This was awesome, but I'm still studying to become president one day."

"You're a brute," Andy said, his blue eyes flashing. "No one's ever going to elect you. But I'd love your number."

"Wow!" Stephen laughed nervously. "Settle down, son." He whispered something in his son's ear. Andy glanced at me, and his face turned red from embarrassment.

"Never mind. Forget it," he said glumly.

Before I could ask what was the meaning of this, my sister pulled me close and kissed my forehead.

"Good luck. Don't forget to come home tonight."

After rubbing his head against Eric's father a couple more times, Rufus barked out his excitement before following in my sister's shadow. Stephen gazed at Eric and me with a complicated expression. Eric immediately pressed me closer to him.

"Did you guys really race against each other for the right to speak to me?"

"Yes!" I said breathlessly. "And it wasn't easy. Your father's ridiculously fit."

Eric's dad was about to speak when he heard me. He gave me a startled look. "I… thank you. I… ahem… own a chain of fitness centres." He actually pulled a business card out of his shirt pocket and handed it over to me. "I can give you a discount," he said after giving me a once over. "You look like you could u—"

"Dad!" Eric interrupted him. "What's happening? Why did you participate in a kiddie race with my friends?" He paused with a frown. "And their dog."

"A good boy," Stephen said with a last look at Rufus trotting away in the distance. Then he scratched his eyebrow with a sheepish air. "The thing is… Zak came to our home and I…" He seemed at a loss for words. "I panicked."

Eric blinked. "You… panicked?"

Stephen reached out both hands toward his son. "He's a boy, Eric! What do you want me to say!"

"I don't know…" Eric scratched his chin. "Say you're happy for me?" Staring at me, he added with a smile. "He's cute, isn't he?"

While I was trying to put my heart back together after it had melted into a puddle, Stephen forced Eric to divert his gaze from my face to his.

"What about your career? How many gay active football players do you know? I'm only trying to stop you from making a terrible mistake!"

Eric gave a childish shrug. "Like I haven't thought about that."

"Answer me! How many?"

"None."

I looked at him, stunned. "None?"

His expression darker, Eric shook his head.

Stephen glanced at me and sighed. "You seem like a good kid, and I had a great time running around in the mud with you and your dog... and your crazy sister... I'm sure you're great guests at weddings and birthdays... but Eric's embarking on a career where it's not allowed to be gay."

"Yet," Eric said with a stubborn expression. "And I'm not playing in the big leagues yet. I don't have an international career either. Can I think about that when it happens? And *if* it happens? Are you saying that I must choose between football and my love life right now? I'm in high school!"

Stephen rubbed the back of his head. "I just want the best for you."

"Here it is," Eric said, pulling me roughly to him. "Let me worry about the rest when I have to, all right? I'm a big boy." He softened his tone. "Right now, I just want him. I don't care if people judge me for it. It doesn't seem all that important to me."

Stephen pinched his lips together, clearly torn between two schools of thought. What I misinterpreted as classic homophobia may have been more complicated than it appeared. My heart filled with hope.

Seeing his father's resolve falter, Eric pressed forward with gleaming eyes. "I've always done everything for you. So please, let me have this?" He glanced down at me. "If you want me, that is. Do you want me?" I nodded quickly and clung to his sleeve. He squeezed me tighter against him. "He wants me, Dad." His expression turned resolute.

Stephen huffed and waved his hand. "Now he wants you! But what about a week from now? Didn't he dump you for an artichoke or something?"

Blushing, Eric spoke meekly. "A shovel... It was a shovel. And he didn't dump me, he..."

"I dated someone else when I had no clue your son had feelings for me," I said, my tone firm.

Stephen looked at his son in surprise. "You didn't tell him?"

"I did—"

"—he didn't."

We both spoke at the same time. Our eyes met and we laughed. Eric squeezed my shoulder.

"I'll deal with you later."

Yums! I thought shamelessly, just as Eric took a step forward to face his father.

"Dad. Listen to me." Eric waited until his dad locked eyes with him. "Anything for true love."

Stephen's expression morphed into shock. He turned to me, his lip twitching. "You... you're really serious about him?"

"Yes!" I said, glaring at him with the full might of my expressive eyebrows.

I saw with surprise that Eric was already smiling as he watched his father's face slowly relax.

"Anything for true love," Stephen repeated softly. And just like that, he extended his hand to me. "You fought well, anyway, it was annoying to have to refuse you."

I awkwardly accepted the offered hand and gave it a firm shake to re-establish my determination.

Before leaving, Stephen put his hands on his son's shoulders. "Be discreet. Don't mess around. Then you should be fine."

Resigned, his clothes in tatters, Stephen dragged himself away, followed by his eldest son. Andy suddenly whirled around and pointed his finger at me.

"If you fuck this up, I'll be back."

Eric sniggered. "Yeah, to ask for his sister's number."

"Well... yes. That too."

I couldn't be bothered to tell him he didn't stand a chance with her, so I just watched them depart nestled in Eric's arms.

"Are you going to be all right with them?"

Eric reached down to take my wrist. "Yeah, don't worry. Dad will get over it. After all, he always does what my mother wants, even today. And my brother always does exactly like him." He tugged at my wrist and grinned. "And it's five!"

I followed his gaze and read the time on my watch. "It is! What do you want to do?"

"Get out of here, definitely."

His eyes fell on me and didn't leave my face for a long time. As a result, my heart started hammering fiercely. Just looking at him made me want to scream at myself for not having acted before. My fingertips itched to touch his face, his lips, and some other places I should be granted access to from now on.

"Let's go to my place," Eric said breathlessly. "I wanna show you something."

"I'm sixteen!" I said in an outraged tone.

Some nerve, I had.

"Not that!" But he had turned pink, to my delight. "I've got something you might like."

Before the headmaster returned to force Eric to help take down the obstacle course, we slunk away under the cover of the trees and used another exit. Eric being Eric, he immediately took my hand, and we went our way up Avenue René Coty.

I had so many things to ask him, I didn't even know where to start. Nor did I know if he was willing to tell me. So, when we stopped at a red light, I started with something simple.

"Eric."

Just having me say his name seemed too much to bear. He pulled the hand he was holding to his lips to kiss it and didn't let go.

"Calm down, calm down," I said. "Tell me something."

"What?" He kissed my hand again.

"What's the meaning of 'Anything for true love'?"

"Oh, that?" He removed his lips from my hand but didn't release it. "It's a family thing. Believe it or not, twenty years ago, my father wasn't allowed to date my mother either. He had to concoct a plan and make all sorts of sacrifices to come back to France and claim her hand. He taught me pretty early that people should be ready to do anything for true love. I think he momentarily forgot his own rules because he worried about me. Then he remembered." Eric pulled me closer and buried his fingers into my hair. "All thanks to your really amazing eyebrows, that will one day make you a famous award-winning actor. And then you'll leave me for some asshole like Ben Affleck or something."

"Ben Affleck, really?"

"OR SOMETHING."

I squeezed his hand tighter between two giggles. "Won't you leave me to date some supermodel with an angular face and protruding hipbones once you become a football superstar?"

Eric feigned astonishment. "I thought I already was a football superstar!"

"That's a good one." I couldn't help chortling mercilessly. "You couldn't even win an amateur game. *The Colette Times* editor wrecked you." For the first time, I reached out and ruffled his hair. Eric didn't move nor did he complain.

"My heart wasn't in it?" he said in a whiny voice. "Or my head? Or my legs? I was heartbroken *and* Kayvin had asked me to let him shine for once. I'm actually okay when I make an effort." He pulled on my sleeve until I stopped laughing. "I am, I am!"

"Okay, okay. I believe you."

"And try focusing on a stupid interview when you see your crush walking away with his boring boyfriend."

His words made me pause. "You… you saw us?"

"Of course, I saw you." Eric looked away as if the memory was unbearable to him. "Alberto's so freakin' tall, remember? Hard to miss. When I saw you with him, I just blanked out and that little girl went for the kill."

"I'm sorry…" I said. "I didn't expect him to show up that day."

"No need for that. But…" With his pouted lips, Eric looked ten years younger. "I made a fool of myself in front of you. If I'd known you were in the stands, I'd have scored eight fucking times."

"Eric T.R., have you no shame? Showing off like that."

He stuck out his chest. "I owe you a good game. You should come and see me play one day."

"Oh… like a little groupie."

"Yes! Everything you love." He seemed to realise something and added in a hushed voice, "No. Forget it. I know it's not your thing."

I rubbed my cheek against his shoulder. "No, I'll go. If it makes you happy."

"Really?" His face lit up like fireworks.

"Look at you." I let out a contented sigh. "You want me to be proud of you, don't you? Good boy."

"Shut up! Hang on…" His smile slowly turned into a grimace of disbelief. "Since when are you—what happened to you? Doing kiddie races with adults and making me say *Shut up*? How did we get here? It's all backwards!"

I quirked an eyebrow. "Your face looks so cute when you're confused."

"Good. People kiss cute things, you know."

I lifted my head and kissed him on the cheek. He made a little dissatisfied sound.

"You can do better. I know you can."

"Fags!"

Out of nowhere, a guy shouted from the opposite sidewalk. I felt my face heat up, but Eric got excited and bounced on his feet.

"There you go! It's official!" He scooped me up and carried me like that for a while, in full view of everyone. I hid my face in the crook of his neck.

"Only you would be happy about that," I said.

Eric kissed my lips as he lifted me a little higher. "I'm happy, I'm happy!"

"You're not afraid we're gonna get beat up?"

He gave a little laugh. "Honestly?" His eyes seemed to have been lit on fire. "I'm more afraid that I'm actually not awake right now."

I stared into his earnest face with conflicted emotions. "Put me down, okay?" He did so immediately, so I pecked his cheek again. "There are so many things we need to talk about."

Picking up the pace, I clung to his hand possessively so that he wouldn't worry about whatever talks I had in mind. Eric immediately turned quiet, his cheeks taking on a pink tinge, and his eyes filled with something that looked a little like bashfulness.

Cute, cute, cute.

And now he was mine.

31

AN EXPLORATION OF ERIC'S SECRET LIFE

E ric opened the door to his flat with an unsteady hand, helped me out of my shoes with rough movements, and dragged me by the hand along the corridor. We passed the door to the living room and Constance emerged, her hands gathered under her chin.

"Baby!" she called.

Eric reluctantly stopped and turned around. "Mom! I love you, but there's no time right now."

Constance barely had time to affectionately touch my shoulder before Eric pulled me out of her grasp.

"I'm gonna open some Champagne," she muttered to our backs.

His hand gripping mine like a vice, Eric led me into a room at the end of the corridor, pushed me inside, and slammed the door behind him. His bedroom was bright and airy like the living room, with white walls covered in... pictures of men, playing football. Not an unusual sight for a boy's bedroom, but I couldn't help smiling anyway. The furniture was sparse here again, with a desk used as a TV stand, a narrow wardrobe, and a handful of controllers scattered over the bleached wooden floors. The shelves lining the walls were mostly filled with awards Eric must have obtained by playing football, but I also noticed a few books. At the end of the room, a floor-to-ceiling double door offered access to the luxuriant garden I had spotted earlier and bathed the bedroom in the warm light of the approaching sunset.

"I love your room," I said.

Eric walked over to me and pointed at the queen bed in the corner. "There's the bed."

I looked at him in panic.

"I only meant you can sit down!" He laughed in his hands while I hid behind mine. While I made myself comfortable on his neatly made-up bed, he went to search into his desk drawer which looked just as messy as his shorts' pockets. He returned with a small book, which he put on my lap.

"*The Ladies' Paradise*," I said in a whisper.

This French edition was really old. One of the earliest thousand copies. The book was musty and most pages were covered in black spots. My pulse racing, I pressed it to my chest.

"Thank you!" I couldn't believe he would have such a thing in his possession. "When did you get that?"

"Some time ago." Eric knelt in front of me. The tips of his ears were pink. "I went to that Shakespeare bookstore for that. I probably looked like a proper idiot, but they were nice, they helped me anyway."

"That's really lovely," I said. "Thank you."

Months ago, nothing could have made me happier than this book. Today, I could easily put it aside in favour of the guy who gave it to me.

"Why didn't you give it to me *some time ago*, then?"

Eric turned his gaze toward the garden outside. "I didn't know how it would be received."

"As a gesture of friendship?" I ventured.

"Which it wasn't," he said with a clipped smile. "And that's why you're getting it now."

"Well, thank you. I love it."

I love you, I was about to say. But I still had some self-control, so I said nothing.

Hesitantly, Eric put his hands on my knees. "I like the way you're looking at me right now."

My cheeks burned. "Me too."

To my surprise, he swiftly removed his hands and moved away from me, going as far as rolling his desk chair a safe distance from the bed to sit on it.

"Everything okay?" I asked with a little frown.

"All good!" He took a deep breath. "You said you wanted to talk about something?"

"Oh, yes!" I scooted a little closer to him and enjoyed watching his eyelid twitch. "I think I've got you pretty much figured out now, Mister Tucker-Régnier."

He snorted. "You got my name right at least."

"And more than that. But I still have so many questions."

Eric playfully rolled his eyes. "Let's get to it then, because I have some demands too."

"Fair enough." I took a moment to organise the questions in my head until I realised the order wasn't important. "Just now, at the park, when you saw me run toward you, did you know I was coming for you?"

Eric immediately shook his head. "No. But I started to get hopeful after the screening. At first, I thought I'd sorted my shit and could be friends with you again. I tried staying away, but… I realised I would rather try to be your friend than never see you again, you see?"

His words forced my heart to a stop. How could they not? They expressed exactly how I felt at the time…

"But I got my hopes up…" Eric went on. "You told me you missed me and then that Alberto was no match for me. I was completely floored when you said that, but I didn't dare to hope too much. I had to clench my jaw hard because I wanted to scream 'I miss you too! In fact, I'm crazy about you. Please date me!'" He laughed bashfully. "Then I heard you were single, so I was planning to ask you out on Monday morning, at the front gate." Seeing me smile, he dipped his head a little. "Zak, you appeared out of nowhere and literally ran into my arms, what was I supposed to do, drop you?"

"You did drop me!"

He looked confused for a second, then erupted in laughter. "Oh, I did! That was awesome!" He forced himself to appear serious. "So sorry, though."

"Right. You dog." Eric took the insult like a compliment, still laughing quietly behind his fist. I scooted a little closer still. "But how did you learn I was single? It happened on Friday after school!"

He stopped laughing. "Xavier told me. He learned it from Alberto himself."

"How?" With a groan, I spread out my hands. "Someone please tell me what is their relationship exactly!"

Eric shrugged. "Don't know, don't care. Alberto is a plague, and I'm glad he's gone."

There was a silence. I didn't quite know my feelings toward Alberto, but I sure didn't want to be on bad terms with him. It wasn't his fault I had fallen for a fantasy version of him. And it certainly wasn't his fault if we didn't work out.

"You're so mean to him," I said. "Even calling him a shovel."

Eric lowered his head a little and took on a sheepish tone. "His face is shaped like a shovel, I can't help it."

"Please stop calling him a shovel."

Eric tapped the floor with his foot, a stupid grin spreading across his face. "I can call him a garden hoe if you prefer, but something tells me you'd like it even less."

I shook my head at him. "Why do you know so much about gardening tools anyway?"

"They all remind me of Alberto."

I slammed my hand on my forehead. "Shut it."

"I'll shut up if you kiss me."

"No!" I forced my expression to look strict. "You must answer my questions first."

Eric rolled his chair closer to me. "I was! And then you went off track and started talking about Alberto. I don't want to even think about him."

I wasn't about to torment Eric with tales of Alberto after I'd made him suffer for weeks. Instead, I reached out and patted his knee apologetically.

"That's fine. I seem to feel the same about Elodie."

"Elodie?" Eric frowned. "Why Elodie?"

"I thought for a while that you were back together."

Eric revealed a sly little grin. "Were you jealous?"

"Yes. Was that your intention?"

"No. We're just friends now."

"You certainly appear very good friends. Every time I saw you, you were in her arms. Like on the first day of school, when I saw you together, and—" Eric began laughing so hard he had to clutch his ribs. "How is that funny?"

"Yes! Serves you right!" He wiped his eyes. "I usually end up in Elodie's arms when you're around. I wonder why."

"So you *were* trying to make me jealous."

"No! It's not my style."

"But you taught me that trick back at Longchamps."

Eric giggled some more. "Zak, I just wanted an excuse to put my hands on you. I would have said anything."

My mouth dropped open.

"And Elodie's been there for me, that's all," Eric continued. "She's known about my feelings for you for a while."

"Really?"

"Yes. You speak of the first day of school? Listen. I'd spent the whole month of August trying to get you out of my head. I tried everything."

I held up my hands. "No need to hear the details."

"Anyway, I felt pretty confident about myself. Then you show up, and you're looking at me with your big brown eyes, and I remember telling her 'I'm fucked. I am so fucked!' And that's why she hugged me." Eric shrugged as if the memory gave him no pain whatsoever. "Be cool with Elodie. She was the only one I could talk to when... Anyway. She was the only one."

"All right."

I wanted to tell him it was going to be difficult for me to be friends with his ex, whom as far as I knew, had slept with him repeatedly, and worse, probably still harboured feelings for him. But today, I wouldn't be burdening him with my lack of self-esteem. Today, I'd get answers to a few questions before moving on to more agreeable shores.

"So..." I asked with a little smile. "When did you start liking me?"

"The first moment I saw you, of course!"

His words gave me pause. "Really? I thought..."

"What?"

"I thought it started when you kissed me at the party."

His eyes glittering, Eric made a small gesture with his fingers. "A *tiiiny* bit before that."

"So when I was glaring at you for being cast, you were..."

Eric grimaced. "Crushed a little, but whatever."

I let out a horrified gasp. "But whatever?!"

He nodded, his eyes closed. "Boy, you were a challenge."

"I can imagine..."

"My first challenge, actually." Eric reopened his eyes. "I've never had to work so hard for anyone else."

He seemed amused, but I could still discern some pain in his eyes. Reaching out, I attempted to put my hand on his knee again.

"Why didn't you say anything?"

With a laugh, he rolled his chair further away from me. "Why would I tell a guy who hates me that I like him?"

"No, but we became friends pretty quickly."

"Yes, 'cause I'm awesome."

"You are, but don't change the subject. Even after we became close, you—"

"Why would I?" His smile froze a little. "Practically the first time we hung out, you told me you loved Alberto. I wasn't gonna out myself for nothing."

He had rolled too far away for me to touch him. I could only cross my arms over my chest with a frustrated expression.

"And you helped me with him! What's up with that?"

"I thought he would send you packing!" Eric laughed and hid his face in his hands. "I really thought so. And then I'd become your shoulder to cry on. Classic."

"Because that worked out so well."

"Kinda." He removed his hands. "You started liking me, right?"

"But it all got so wrong…"

"Yeah." Eric became serious. "I really didn't think he'd actually start to like you."

"If he ever did at all…" My voice trailed off. "But that's a conversation for another time." Eric rolled his chair a little closer; I observed his face closely before speaking. "So… You're…"

"Hm?"

"The whole time… You were aware that you liked guys?"

"No. Yes. No?" Eric scratched his chin. "Huh, that's funny." He forced his chair to swing in half-circles. "I knew I liked looking at guys, but I just thought everybody did, but that boys were not allowed to talk about it. It would be weird, you know? You always hear girls call each other beautiful and all. I just thought it's normal to find other guys hot. I wasn't too bothered about it. I've always been like that, so why would I question it?"

I chortled. "You thought everybody was attracted to boys, everybody."

"Yes, because, you see, there are tons of things everybody thinks but no one talks about, right?" Eric's innocent expression as he explained was priceless. "It never occurred to me that some people didn't find Cristiano Ronaldo hot. I just… underestimated how hot I found him compared to other guys, that's all." He started laughing. "I honestly never thought much about it. Never saw it as a problem or anything strange at all! Now that I think about it, I should have known earlier, with the way I reacted every time Ronaldo and Benzema hugged on the field. But I guess I was a little slow on the uptake. It took meeting you to realise, okay, I like guys. I like girls, but I like guys."

"How did you feel about it?" I asked tentatively.

"Pretty good, actually. I kept thinking, great! More for me!"

As I snorted all over his logic, he watched me while licking his lip, which sent me into a fit of coughing.

"I didn't want to make a big deal out of it," Eric said when I had recovered. "I knew I wanted to be with you. If you said yes, then I'd be with you. If you said no, no one would have to know that I was... different, and I wouldn't have to have that talk with my dad."

Of course. That made sense. Now his sexuality stood in the way of his career. In 2010. We sure could use some progress in that area.

"Do you want us to hide?" I asked. "I could totally understand if you d—"

"No!" Eric's expression was fierce. "Tomorrow, I'm taking you to school and everyone will know we're together."

"Oh, that's nice..." I hesitated. "But maybe wait a little, out of respect for Alberto."

"No." He shook his head.

My mouth opened in shock. "Eric T.R., you are so petty."

"Where he's concerned, yep." Eric nodded. "I'll be the worst. I can't forgive him."

"Forgive him? For what?"

"Not realising straight away that you're awesome?" When he saw me blush, Eric's ears shone bright pink. "And for getting between you and me when he'd blown his chances. *And* for being such a shit boyfriend that you broke up with him. What a prick."

"O-kay. That about settles it, then. But I hope you can find it in your heart to forgi—"

"What about you?" Really done with the subject of Alberto, Eric rolled his chair closer still. "When did you realise you liked me?"

"I don't know." I rested my chin on my hand thoughtfully. "It happened gradually. You were my funny new friend, and then you were in all my thoughts and... it got so bad that even when I dated Alberto, all I thought about was you."

"Really?" He looked terrifically pleased to hear that. "Then what took you so damn long?"

I shrugged. "I didn't know that you liked me."

Eric's smile vanished. "You... Are you serious?"

I explained to him briefly how Arthur, Camille, and I reached the conclusion that he liked me.

"You're nuts!" Eric buried his hands into his own hair. "You're all nuts! Also, I need to see that board."

"There are a lot of badly drawn fruits on it. And by the way, how am I the mental one? You knew I was gay, I thought you were straight. You should have said something. Instead, I had to analyse the signs!"

"What signs?" Eric said, his expression torn between amazement and hilarity. "I thought it was always clear that I had a crush on you. I mean I literally was all over you for two weeks! I jumped you, kissed you, made a go at your ass... What more could you need? I showed you a million times. With all the occasions put together, we could write a really long book."

I hummed appreciatively. "I wanna read that book."

"Too long. Let's make it a movie!"

"Yes! And play our own roles!"

Eric shook his head. "No. You be Eric, and I'll be you."

"Nah. You don't have the eyebrows."

It seemed to remind him how much he liked them, because he finally jumped off his seat to cover my brow with kisses. When he returned to his chair, my face was burning.

"Get it now?" He smirked. "I like you."

"Yes, now it's clear." I wiped my brow with the back of my hand. "But you should have tried something like that before: 'Zak, I have feelings for you. Do you want to go out with me?'"

He bounced on his seat. "I did! I did!"

"When?!"

"My script!" He got up and jumped in place. "It was covered with little messages addressed to you. One note literally said 'I like you, go out with me!' and you looked at it for twenty minutes and never said anything."

"Eric!" I waved my hands to urge him to sit down. "No one can read your handwriting!"

"Really?" He fell back on his seat. "Oh. But I said them out loud too! Ah!" He pointed a finger at me. "During the final take! 'I'm not the one who changed you... You're the one who changed me.' Nothing? Such a meanie! Took me two days to come up with that. Or just this week when I told you I only had eyes for you? No? You're the worst!"

Unable to meet his eyes, I exhaled a long breath. "I accept your judgment. In my mind, you were either very professional or you were just teasing me."

Eric tugged at his own hair with a cry of despair.

"Just like the day we kissed by the lake," I added.

"Professional?" He erupted in laughter. "There was nothing professional about our kiss. If you weren't so nuts, you'd have noticed I walked back home with a limp."

I watched him without understanding, and he clicked his tongue. "Never mind. You'll get it one day."

"No. No…" I recalled my own reaction during our kiss and felt myself blush. "I got it."

He started laughing sneakily. I punched him in the shoulder, only to get my hand caught and covered in kisses.

"Let's get married," Eric said.

"I'm sixteen!"

For fuck's sake.

Eric admired my scowling face for a minute before speaking again. "I do regret one thing, though," he said, his tone softening. "I should have asked you out earlier. I could never tell if you thought of me just as a friend or not. But after the kiss, I thought… I thought you liked me too."

"I did."

"And I'd planned everything. After the final take, I really was about to ask you out."

My heart stopped in my chest.

"I was terrified," Eric said. "But I had to get my hands on you. After that kiss, I felt like I had a taste and I couldn't stop. I thought I had to say something, it would be too stupid not to try. I really was about to tell you everything. Without the movie, I would run out of excuses to be around you anyway. Screw your evil Alberto and his timing." Eric kicked his leg in frustration. "Oh, do you know how much I blamed myself for not locking the changing room and telling you everything? But I couldn't. After what happened at the beach, I felt like a total pervert. And after what you said later at the pond, I thought if I continued, I might lose your friendship too. So I didn't want you to think I was jumping you in the changing room."

I recalled how impatient he was, telling me to hurry. I thought he was upset with me. He was trying to get me out of there to ask me out. We could have been kissing by the edge of the lake for a whole day before leaving. We could have been…

"I can't believe I missed out on a chance of being jumped by you in the changing room," I said absently.

"It's Alberto's fault! He's a plague."

I looked up. "How is that his fault? It's my fault for choosing wrong."

"No, actually, it's my fault for not speaking up earlier." Eric shifted in his seat. "Listen. Even after he asked you out, I still had some crazy hope. I wanted you to choose me. Over him. To come back to me. Of course, you couldn't choose me if you didn't know I liked you. But from my point of view, you knew, and you made your choice. And I would always lose to Alberto."

"Is that why you avoided me after Aurons?"

Eric nodded slowly. "I thought putting some distance between us would help me forget about you. And with Alberto glued to your ass, there was no way I'd put myself through that torture."

"If it makes you feel any better," I muttered, "Alberto was never glued to my ass."

Eric stomped both his feet. "He's a plague! That time at the fountain, I thought to myself, if Zak gives me his ice cream cone, then he likes me. If he puts it straight into my mouth, then I'll kiss him right here and now and I don't care who's looking. But Alberto showed up and you looked like you were caught with your legs behind your head."

"With my what?"

"… Never mind. You're too innocent. Your innocence is sacred."

"Not that sacred," I mumbled.

All of a sudden, Eric got up from his chair. "Really? So, can I touch you now, or…"

One look at his face and I immediately scooted to the far edge of the bed. "All right, some ground rules here. Because you look like you'll eat me alive if I don't set some rules." He nodded like a puppy, his eyes bright, his lips tight in expectation. "You can, but you have to promise to stay decent."

"What's decent?"

"You can't touch me anywhere… funny. No funny business."

He looked disappointed and pouted.

"You should let me take the lead perhaps," I said. "For instance, if I don't touch you, maybe don't touch me then, I d—"

"Okay, great talk." He was panting. "Can I touch you now?"

With a sigh, I scratched my chin. "All right, then. Just a little."

This mad dog pounced on the bed before I could take one last breath and so efficiently that I thought if football didn't work out, he could probably try the Olympics. I couldn't do much except burst out laughing, and he immediately backed off, awestruck.

"What was that?"

"Me. Laughing."

"That was amazing."

"Thanks, you're so dumb, oh my go-mmph!"

Hard to finish a sentence when being kissed and pressed into the bed.

How long did I last before ending up like that? I had bet for an hour; we didn't make it that far. I knew it the moment we entered the room. And that scoundrel had no respect for my rules, so I pinched him until he cried out in pain and jerked away. He knelt on his bedspread and hid his face in his hands. His miserable sobs struck the right chords. I slowly crawled into his arms and rested my cheek against his chest. The frantic beating of his heart was a coded message, a testimony of his affection for me. And I remember thinking... That was how it felt. Being adored. Being craved. I wanted to plunge my fingers into his chest and pluck out his heart to stick it close to my ear.

Maybe I *was* a little wicked.

I lifted my head. Eric was looking at me with a mixture of elation and worry. My own heart racing, I slithered between his knees. He weakly protested, mumbling something about self-control, but I had already covered his lips with mine. He felt divine. He *was* divine. Ripe peaches and the clinking of ice cubes in my favourite iced tea. He was the sun splitting the clouds. And he was Longchamps. Long afternoons of furtive glances between exchanges of lines. Bardot singing "Le Soleil" in a rocking boat as we slept in each other's arms. Warmth. And peace. But he was also the rush I felt the first time I saw baby Rufus poke his head of out of his cardboard box. He was fast cars, the thrill of a chase in an action movie, a gun drawn out of a purse, all kinds of triggers, pulled.

A weak sound rolled off my chest and was swallowed by him. This time he fell backwards. My hands roamed around a little freely. His clamped around my arms. I looked at him, apologised. His grimace said it all.

"You are not playing fair."

I rubbed our noses together. "But am I winning?"

Eric groaned and briefly hugged me. When he asked me to get away from him, I understood and stood up diligently. He got up after me, enveloped me in his arms, inhaled my scent before shaking his head. Turning me around, he left a chaste kiss on my forehead.

"So much time wasted," I whispered, leaning into his embrace. Eric chuckled. His Adam's apple bobbed right in front of me, so I kissed it.

"Your fault for not noticing me drooling all over you with my tongue hanging out."

We rubbed our cheeks together. I hummed against his touch.

"And your fault for not simply telling me you like me instead of doing all that nonsense."

"I like you," he said breathlessly.

The earnest look in his eyes melted my organs. I had to give a quick look down at myself from my chest to my toes to make sure I wasn't leaking.

"And tell me you're not straight, that would also be helpful."

"I'm not straight."

I paused, tormented by his expression. "Tell me you have—"

"— Feelings for you. I have feelings for you." His hands felt my waist, pulled me closer. His face approached mine, his breath hot against my cheek. "I like you very much, Zakaria. I am so very not straight, I—"

Out of patience, I licked his upper lip. Instantly, his mouth opened to receive me. The needy noise he uttered when we connected made my stomach curl with yearning. After a long kiss, I noticed the hands gripping my waist were trembling.

"Why are you shaking?" I said against his lips.

He sighed. "… I like you."

"Yes, I heard you—"

"I like you."

"… I like you too."

"So what if I'm shaking…" Though his eyes were glazed, they were serious. "I've waited a long time to get you."

His words made me laugh. "You have no patience."

With both hands, he lifted me. "No. You have no idea." Without thinking, I wrapped my legs around him. We fell onto the bed again.

"Bad idea!"

I called for a time out. We sat down like two good boys. For another half-hour anyway. Eric looked drunk; he was in love with me. I felt I was about to burst; I was in love with him. We weren't good boys again for another two minutes — especially him. Then we got ahold of ourselves — especially him.

And so on.
And so on.
And so on.

32

LOVE ENDS WITH AN "E"

A FEW MONTHS LATER

On a freezing January morning, we stood before Cinéma Les 7 Batignolles in the seventeenth district of Paris. Today was the closing ceremony of the short film festival Paris Cours Devant, and *My Summer of Love and Woe* was nominated for several awards, including *Best Scenario* and *Best Actor* both for myself and Eric.

Huddled together against the cold in our best clothes, Eric and I awaited our friends. I had once dreamt of sharing such a moment with Alberto. But now no one could make me happier than Eric, his face red from the cold, his gloved hand enveloping mine, the other clutching my waist possessively.

Tomorrow was my birthday. I couldn't envision anything better than turning seventeen with an award in one hand, my amazing boyfriend in the other. I couldn't stop smiling, and it didn't escape Eric, who nuzzled into my neck to remark on it.

"What makes you so happy?"

"Nothing, nothing." I tried to play it cool. "I'm just excited about the party tonight."

Eric and his mother had put together a celebration at their place after the awards tonight, but knowing both of them, I could expect a birthday cake the size of a building come midnight. Personally, I couldn't wait to unwrap my gift.

Because my gift was Eric.

He knew nothing of my intentions, and if anticipation was making me giddy, trying to imagine his expression when I would seduce him tonight was enough to make me bounce on my feet.

"You're cold," Eric noted, holding me tighter.

I suppressed a sneaky laugh and pretended to be freezing indeed. Just as I was about to kiss his glowing cheek, his phone beeped. He struggled with the thing for a minute, then his face broke into a smile.

"Mona and her daughters are wishing us the best of luck."

I looked at the text with a dumbfounded expression. "You're still in touch with them?"

"Yes! They're my buddies. Let's take a picture for them."

Before I could even react, Eric had raised the phone and snapped a photo of us. He briefly checked it out and sent it.

"Your buddies…" I repeated, with a hint of jealousy. "Come to think of it, you never told me why they gave you that weird nickname."

"They gave me a weird nickname?"

"Do you really have the memory of a goldfish or are you just playing cute most of the time?"

"Both!" he said, trying to kiss me.

"No. No kiss until you answer. Why did they call you Eric Singstar?"

"Because of the video game!"

Of course, my knowledge of video games, besides *Mario* something and, for Alberto-related reasons, *Silent Hill*, was pretty much non-existent, so I could only stare with a blank expression.

Eric arched an eyebrow. "It's a karaoke game on PlayStation."

"Good lord."

He chuckled and kissed the tip of my nose. "I always listen to music when I run. I was listening to a certain song when I came into the bakery, and I was really into it, so I kept singing in the middle of the bakery, shouting 'I don't wanna be frieeeends', and they all stared at me like I was crazy."

I snorted and cupped his face with my mittened hands. "You *are* crazy."

"They loved it! So much that it became a thing. I had to do a different song every day." Eric leaned into my neck and breathed my scent. "Guess what? All the songs were about you." He paused, then grimaced. "Except one. One was about Alberto."

"I don't believe you. Give me an example."

472

"You want me to sing right now? In front of all these people?"

"No… I take it back. Knowing you, you'd pick the dirtiest of the lot just to teach me a lesson."

"You know me well, Zakaria." Eric breathed a puff of hot air straight into my ear, knowing the effect it had on me.

"Eric, wait, focus. I'm not done. You remember that time we all went to the bakery to get ice cream? Why were you all acting so weird?"

Eric snorted all over my face. "You were wondering about that? It's so easy. So remember that time I introduced them to you? Yes? So the next day, I asked them if they liked you, and they were like, 'Oh, yes, he's so sweet', and I was like 'Yeah, right? I love him', and they were like, 'Hahaha, so nice', so I stopped laughing and I said, 'No, seriously, I'm in love with him', okay, so after the initial shock, they started rooting for us like crazy! And I told them I'd ask you out after the final take, and so they thought the next time we'd show up together, we'd be together, you see?"

"So when they started singing 'Congratulations'…"

"It was for us, yeah. Awkward."

Awkward indeed. Thank God, Alberto walked headfirst into the door and distracted us all. Of course, I didn't say that to Eric, not knowing how he would react to hearing that particular name.

Seeing me lost in thought, Eric tried to lick my cheek. I slammed my mitten on top of his head.

"You dog."

"Pleeease!" He wriggled and whined like a puppy. "You won't let me lick anything!"

Knowing what I would let him get away with tonight would forever set him at ease, I had no qualms about tormenting him right now. Just as I was pushing his face away, I spotted Camille and rose my free hand. She and Arthur ran to us, their hair dishevelled by the wind. We all exchanged hugs and messy pecks on the cheeks for fifteen seconds before Camille began squeaking, startling some people waiting nearby.

"I'm in!"

Eric bounced excitedly on his feet. "In what, in what?"

"In your class, Zak! I'll be with you starting next week."

I stared at her, bewildered. "How on earth did you manage that?"

Arthur watched Camille flick her wrist and assume a nonchalant pose with adoration. Knowing the feeling, I gripped Eric's hand without thinking.

"I went to the headmaster," Camille said. "I told him that if I win an award, I'd say I could have never done it without the unwavering support of Colette International, the awesome bilingual high school with a really affordable yearly fee that everyone should attend, and that the headmaster was the most handsome—"

"And he agreed?"

She loved going into these outlandish and lengthy explanations, and Eric always encouraged her. If I hadn't put a stop to it, we'd still be there tomorrow night.

Undeterred, Camille nodded with fervour. "Yes! Though he told me to stop licking his really expensive boots. But wait! He also said I needed to find a student to swap with me. I thought I'd ask Alberto, but surprisingly, he refused."

"Why Alberto?" I asked, a little surprised.

Without a word, Eric slid behind me and wrapped me tightly in his arms.

Camille's expression contorted. "I thought, you know, that if he could choose, he'd prefer to be as far away from you as possible."

"Hm," Eric said in the crook of my neck.

"Why do people assume Alberto hates me?" I said in a mildly hurt tone.

Arthur looked amused. "Because you broke his heart?"

"I broke no such thing," I muttered.

"Hm." Eric dug deeper into my neck.

In all fairness, it might very well be true. Since our breakup, Alberto and I were barely exchanging any words. But I didn't think he hated me. I really hoped he didn't.

"In any case, he said no," Camille said. "Told me his schedule was fine as it was and he didn't want to change it. So I had to find someone else."

"I guess he doesn't have any friends in the other class either," Arthur said.

Sander and Oliver were preparing for another degree and were together in Arthur's class. And since Alberto never talked to me if he could help it, it wasn't unusual to see him alone. He sat alone in class, ate his lunch on his own, and went straight home after class. The only times I ever saw him socialising were when Xavier and Kayvin fell upon him on the playground, and he seemed to enjoy the company just as much as I enjoyed a failing grade.

Since his friends were no longer here to keep him awake, Alberto regularly dozed off in class and got snapped at by the teachers. Some he seduced with an apologetic smile. Others were immune to his charms and regularly kicked him out of class. My own table was right next to his in English Literature, and after close observation, I could safely say he didn't seem to give a crap about any of this mundane stuff. But since I'd vowed to not waste any more time on Alberto, I pushed him out of my thoughts and hugged my friend Camille.

"I have a feeling this is gonna be an awesome year." Glancing up at Eric, I found him nodding absently. "What do you think?"

"Oh, you know." He cleared his throat. "You're so cute. The usual."

Arthur snorted loudly. "You're so gay."

Eric smiled. "Just my good half."

But his smile looked a little wan, so it got my attention. I leaned forward and spoke in a secretive tone. "He's nervous."

"I am!" Eric removed his chin from my shoulder but didn't release me. "You're not? All these nominations…"

"The movie *is* beautiful," Arthur said. "It came out just right."

"Right, right. Michael deserves the award for directing the film *and* directing Duvo. Camille, you deserve best script, goes without saying. And Zak should get all the nominations in the world, but I just can't believe I made it up there as well!"

"No confidence in your acting skills, Eric?" Arthur asked with feigned shock.

"Not really, no." He snorted. "I didn't even think I'd be cast."

"You worked hard enough," Camille said, her lips curled up into a little smile.

Seeing Eric's troubled expression, I thought to tease him a little and let out a deep sigh. "I think we were only nominated because the jury wanted to see how hot you really were."

Eric's cold-bitten face turned even redder.

"Don't hide," Camille said. "Show that cute little face. Might get us some last-minute votes!"

"They've already voted, Camille," someone said behind us.

Duvo and Binta had finally arrived. Binta was dashing in a long plum dress, but Duvo, in an elegant black suit, looked surprisingly good for an old man of thirty.

"Shit, Mr Duvauchel," Arthur said with round eyes, "you clean up nicely."

Duvo opened his mouth, probably to smite him for swearing, but

Binta, tightening Duvo's coat around her shoulders, talked first. "It's all me, thank you. You should have seen the horror he kept in his closet."

Duvo coughed noisily to get our attention away from the subject. "How are you, Eric? I heard you dropped out of the Colette football team."

"Whaaat?" Eric shook his head. "You heard wrong. I'm still playing, I'm just not the captain anymore."

"Why? Was it because of the troubles with Kayvin?"

"You should have told the headmaster," Arthur said. "He would have kicked him off the team for you."

Eric looked reluctant to speak on the subject of Kayvin. "I don't see why he'd do that. But anyway, Kayvin deserves a break once in a while. He likes to boss people around, and I don't care. And I'm better off without having to deal with his dad. So's the headmaster." With a quick glance at me, he added, "I have enough drama at my club, I didn't want to get the same stuff at school. With the amount of training I have, I already barely have time for Zak."

"You do find time," I said gently.

He snorted. "There's never enough time, trust me."

Arthur slipped me a look full of allusions. I kicked him in the shin, but it only deepened his smirk.

In truth, I didn't find it difficult to date an athlete. Of course, most of the hours outside of school were allocated to training or playing football. But it gave me plenty of time to study and find acting work here and there. Even when we could only meet on the playground or on Sunday evenings, we were so happy to see each other that each hour was spent cuddling, teasing each other, and having so much fun we never had the time or a reason to fight.

If I was worried about his future in football, Eric didn't seem to be. He didn't think it anybody's business who he was dating and, so far, no one of importance knew about it, even though Eric didn't keep my existence a secret. At Colette, everyone had seen me get jumped in the middle of the corridors while changing classes. One or two of his best buddies at the club knew, but they kept it to themselves. Eric didn't even think his coach knew, and if he did find out one day, he promised me he would review his options carefully and not make any rash decisions. But the day to think about these things had not come. For now, we had each other and we were perfectly happy.

Camille looked around us. "Should we get inside? It's cold."

Everyone was freezing and no one dared to complain. We shuffled into the hallway, and a smiling hostess took us to the large screening room.

"Follow me to the nominee's seats."

We followed her down a few stairs, the sound of our steps muffled by a dark carpet matching the plush and velvety seats. At the bottom of the stairs, the large screen hung over a black stage. Soon, people would walk that stage to announce the winners of over a dozen awards.

"The nominee's seats." Eric snorted. "I still can't believe it."

Duvo paused in front of his row with a little laugh. "I cannot believe that it all began when you vandalised our club. We might have never ended up here if you hadn't been such a hooligan."

While Camille and Arthur laughed, I glanced up at Eric's face. His somewhat bashful expression made my heart grow twice in size.

"Some things have a really good way of turning out," Binta said philosophically.

Duvo missed the affection in her eyes and turned to Eric, a smirk dancing on his lips.

"Yeah, it ended up pretty well for you, young man. But next time you have a genius idea like this, don't be so dumb as to leave your student card at the crime scene!"

Laughing so loudly he frightened some of the people already seated, Duvo took his seat by Binta. Camille and Arthur exchanged a look, but the hostess motioned for them to follow them a row further down, and us after them.

My eyes didn't leave Eric's face. He managed to look neutral enough until he met my gaze, and his cheeks turned pink.

"You..." With my heart stuck in my throat, the words came out choked. "The first time you saw me..."

"Let's sit down, shall we?" he said, pulling my hand.

My blood pounding in my ears, I followed Camille and Arthur to our allocated seats, Eric right behind me. The moment our asses were down, I pulled his sleeve.

"Eric! When did you—"

"Oh look, Alberto!"

Despite my impatience, I couldn't help but turn my head. When I saw Alberto, the ghost flush of past affection warmed my cheeks. Alberto would always be Alberto. Black suit, black shirt, black tie... Everyone who saw him looked, and he looked at no one. He followed another hostess with a neutral expression, bumped into the edge of one seat and gave it a blank look as though he'd never expected such a thing to be found in a screening room.

On my right, Eric was chewing on his lip as though he was about to say something he wasn't sure he should be saying. The hostess pointed to a seat on my left and I shivered. Alberto would have to pass our seats to get to his.

Along the row of seats, people got up or turned their legs to the side to make way for him. A few girls stared after him, their eyes filled with admiration. Eric, too, was watching him with an intensity I found unusual.

When Alberto reached his seat, Eric made no effort to move his legs, and Alberto found himself stuck.

"Hi, Alberto."

I recognised on Alberto's face the mild annoyance he sometimes revealed when he had to talk to someone he didn't want to.

"Hello, Eric."

They stared at each other briefly. When Alberto glanced down at me, I felt myself flush and clamped my lips shut. Eric still didn't move his legs, and I was close to stomping his foot.

"How's life, buddy?" Eric asked with a smile.

Alberto shrugged, but his pale eyes narrowed. I mean, buddy?

"Great. How's football?"

To my surprise, Eric answered. "Pretty good. How's modelling?"

"Fine," Alberto said without enthusiasm.

"You don't seem excited about it." Eric sighed. "Perhaps you should try football."

Alberto arched a perfect eyebrow with contempt. "Should I?"

"Goalkeeper, maybe. You have the size for it."

Alberto's diaphanous skin turned slightly paler. I didn't care for my usually adorable boyfriend bullying my ex, so I ruthlessly pulled on his sleeve.

"Alberto," Eric said, catching my hand and covering it with his own. "There's a party at my place after the awards. You should really come."

I turned to him in shock. He was inviting Alberto to his party?

"Please come," Eric repeated. "I'm gonna text you the address."

Alberto's lips tightened. Sticking his hands in his pockets, he forcibly bumped into Eric's knee to get through. I immediately made way for him while Eric clutched his kneecap.

"Oh my God, he touched me! Alberto touched me!"

Pretending not to notice the glare Alberto threw our way, I bumped my fist on top of Eric's head.

"What's wrong with you? Can't you just leave him alone?"

Alberto wasn't to blame, in my opinion. He was not a plague, nor a gardening tool, nor a damn cat — I'd heard it all these past few months. Alberto still remained the most gorgeous human being on this planet, and I didn't want my sweet Eric to turn into a dick whenever they were around each other.

Eric saw my discomfort. His expression turned earnest again. "Don't worry! I have forgiven him for not realising how awesome you are. I mean... almost."

"Then why are you bothering him?"

Eric took on an innocent expression. "I'm not! I'm trying to be his friend."

"Funny way to do it."

"So?" He shrugged. "Alberto's a funny guy."

I gave a little laugh. "Now you're taking the piss."

"I'm not! We're gonna be best friends, you'll see."

"Stop it. You're making me nervous."

Eric laughed it off and showered my face with kisses. So much that I couldn't breathe. I pushed him away with both hands. "Shove it!"

"Where?"

Someone above us slammed a magazine on top of Eric's head. It was Duvo.

"Stop this immediately!" I had completely forgotten he was sitting right behind us. "Is this how you act on the football field?"

Eric looked at him through streaming eyes. "We might have a bigger audience if I did."

"Shut up, smart ass. Zak?" To me, Duvo spoke softly. "Where is Michael?"

"Who?" Eric asked.

"Michael. Michael!"

I frowned. "Who?"

"Michael! Are you—"

"Aaah, Michael!"

I repressed a fit of laughter while Eric snorted behind his hands. "Michael went on tour with his boyfriend and his cousins."

Duvo looked crestfallen. "But, but... The awards! He practically directed the movie, for Christ's sake!"

"Practically?" Binta said with a quirked eyebrow.

I recalled the words Michael said to me over the phone.

"He said he was right where he needed to be."

Eric leaned in to whisper in my ear. "I have a mental image about this that I'd like to share with you."

"I know which sort of mental image you have because you only think about one thing."

Laughing, he tried to kiss me again, but I turned my face away, so he pretended to slam his head against the empty seat in front of him in despair.

Eric couldn't always control himself in my presence, and I had no intention of helping him learn that skill. Especially not after tonight. But Eric didn't know that... yet.

Duvo was shaking his head. "So much for awards, if people don't bother picking them up. Well, I guess I'll have to do it. But I won't thank him."

"Yes, you will," Binta said. "And we'll all go down to receive it together if we win."

Duvo was inconsolable, however, and needed to vent. "How could Michael do this to me? Do you believe his shithead of a boyfriend didn't recall who I was? A whole year, I taught him. All for nothing."

Eric graced us with one of his childish giggles.

"He was awful, by the way," Duvo went on. "Didn't care about Molière. Who in their right mind doesn't care about Molière?"

"I don't!" Eric raised his hand.

Duvo attempted to slap his magazine on top of his head again, but Binta stopped him.

"Shh, calm down."

I wasn't really listening. I was looking into Eric's blue eyes fixed on the screen below, and how his teeth were digging into his lip. He was too boisterous, a telltale sign that he was nervous, something I'd picked up on after a few heavenly months in his company. Tonight, he was nervous for his friends, nervous for my sake, nervous for himself, nervous to see us kiss again on the silver screen. Whether we won an award or not didn't matter to me. We were already victorious. My imagination trembled and ran wild, flashing forward a few hours into the night, and my heart started thundering madly.

"What?" Eric asked when he noticed my intense stare.

"Oh, you know."

He flashed me a grin. "I do?"

"You do."

He pressed my hand to his chest, and his beating heart told me all I needed to know. Essentially, we were the same.

When more or less everyone was seated, a classical tune started playing and a handful of people made their way to the centre of the stage. People began clapping politely. Behind me, Duvo sighed with relief, and Binta soothed him with a few words. Farther on my left, Alberto was trying his best not to yawn, and failing. Unnoticed, I dipped my head to hide a little laugh. My first award show and I couldn't wait for the thing to be over so I could be left in a room alone with Eric. If the Zak I was only a year ago knew, he would accuse me of insanity. And he wouldn't be wrong.

There's a little madness in the act of letting go. Of letting oneself love and be loved, of treading the same uncertain path billions have trodden before, hoping they will best its trials, emerge victorious, their love the only one to be undying and true.

Eric took my chin and made me look at him before he kissed me. My earlier question was still on my lips, but in the end, I didn't ask. It didn't matter how or when it started. He would tell me one day. Or he wouldn't. What mattered was how it ended, with my hand in his own.

The speakers must have said something funny. The audience laughed, and I snapped out of my reverie. On the stage below, my life-long dream awaited me. On my right, devouring me with his eyes while kicking his feet, was my golden future.

The hour was not done when, Eric's hand wrapped around mine, we went down to pick up our prize.

To the Erics who took risks to obtain what they wanted.

To the Zaks who let them.

FREE BONUS

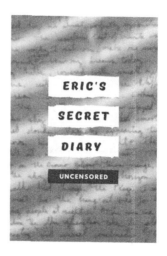

WANT TO TAKE A PEEK INTO ERIC'S MIND?

Claim your copy of *ERIC'S SECRET DIARY* when you sign up for Zelda's Reading Nook, and watch him freak out as he falls in love with the nerdy Zak from a distance.

Members of **The Reading Nook** receive a newsletter every now and then, containing updates about upcoming releases and exciting bonus content featuring their favourite couples. Members also get access to **their own freebies page** where they can find every available art commission, book playlist, exclusive short story — and more.

SCAN THE QR CODE ABOVE TO GAIN ACCESS TO YOUR FREEBIES, OR VISIT:

www.zeldafrench.com

HAVE YOU ENJOYED
YOU'RE THE ONE FOR ME?

If yes, would you please consider leaving a review?

Telling people about a novel you loved is one of the easiest yet best way you can support an independent author. Reviews help convince potential readers to take a chance on books they might have not considered otherwise.

I'm aware that your time is precious, and even a single line, or rating your book a few stars, can truly make a difference.

You can scan this QR code to leave a review on Amazon.

GETTING IN TOUCH

ZELDA FRENCH (THEY/THEM) LIVES IN LONDON, LIKES CATS, SWEARING, GOOD WINE AND ROCK MUSIC, AND REALLY ENJOYS ANGSTY STORIES WITH HAPPY ENDINGS.

YOU CAN GET MORE INFORMATION AT:
WWW.ZELDAFRENCH.COM

instagram.com/zelda_french

tiktok.com/@zeldafrench

amazon.com/author/zeldafrench

goodreads.com/zeldafrench

bookbub.com/authors/zelda-french

IN THE SAME SERIES

I Want To Kiss You In Public
Louis thought he had it all figured out.
He couldn't have been more wrong.

You're The One For Me
One of them has a plan. The other is clueless.
Together they will discover what love really is about.

He Looks So Fine: Part One
Be not inhospitable to – handsome – demons,
lest they be angels in disguise.

He Looks So Fine: Part Two
Is love even enough?

NEXT IN THE SERIES

HE LOOKS SO FINE

"A complex parable that hurts as much as it heals."

— *K. ANCRUM, AUTHOR OF THE WICKER KING AND ICARUS.*

Both mourning from a tragic loss, two high school students find solace in each other's arms, but the secrets they keep threaten the fragile understanding between them.

∽

He Looks So Fine: Colette International Book 3 & 4 is a seven-part story about two young men's rediscovery of empowerment, communication and trust, about the lasting damages of trauma and the healing virtues of friendship. *Part One* contains arcs 1 to 3. The following *Part Two* contains arcs 4 to 7 and concludes their story.

Content Warning: Due to the presence of difficult themes, sexual content and other potentially upsetting scenes, this work isn't intended for readers below the age of eighteen. (A full content warning list can be found at the beginning of the book.)

∽

THE CLASSIC EDITION IS AVAILABLE ON **AMAZON** ONLY.

THE INTERNATIONAL EDITION IS AVAILABLE RIGHT NOW ON **AMAZON, BLACKWELL'S, THE GREAT BRITISH BOOK SHOP** AND MORE (AND ON REQUEST AS YOUR LOCAL BOOK SHOP).

Printed in Great Britain
by Amazon

58751434R00280